# DUAL VISIONS
## Book 1
## The Ancient Alien Series

Jill Smith

MILES STREET PUBLISHING

Coolangatta, Queensland

**MILES STREET PUBLISHING**
**Jill Smith Aussie Author**
**Coolangatta, Queensland 4225**
**www.** authorjillsmith.wordpress.com



Book Layout ©2020 Kate Russell, & Pamela Ueckerman@Spiral Designs

**Book Title/ Author Name**. -- 4th ed.
ISBN 978-0-6481708-2-2
ISBN-13: 978-0-6481708-3-9

For Heather

A wonderful mother who believed in me.

ACKNOWLEDGEMENTS

Thank you to all my family and friends who have supported my writing ambition. This revised edition has been completed with the invaluable assistance of my mentor, Robyn Lee Burrows, herself an accomplished author of many books both fiction and non-fiction. I have added to the original story and enjoyed the process. Many thanks also to my writing friends, members of Gold Coast Writers Association and fellow subgroup members of The Ten Penners for your continued support, particularly Marion Martineer and Kate Russell. The learning process for any writer is ongoing. I have developed from the original e-book version released through Zeus Publications to the first and second editions released through Publicious with Andy McDermott's assistance. The journey continues with this reworked fourth edition and follow up books in 'The Ancient Alien Series' with book 2 'Vashla's World' and a soon to be released third book in the series 'Travellers'.

## *Davidson Family Tree – Link*

https://authorjillsmith.wordpress.com/dual-
visions-davidson-family-tree/
A detailed list of the main characters and their rela-
tionships to relatives in the story.

*Other Characters*

*Cal Bennett* (5/4/1939) Texan (met Orthama returned to Earth)

*Andre Lebeau* (6/8/1942) French (met Orthama)

*Imi* (dual) partnered (Andre on Orthama returned to Earth together)

*Yoshi Hishida* (human) Japanese (met Orthama returned to Earth)

*Anthony Cassurina* (human) met Orthama and stayed there

*Neville Long* (human) met Orthama stayed Orthama initially then returned with dual partner

*Todd Longmire* (human) partners Tris (dual)

*Nick O'Donahue* (Bon's friend - Shea's father)

*Sandy O'Donahue* (Nick's wife) daughters Becky, Claire

*Jake Corman* (human) Gem's close friend and psychiatrist

*Amber Corman* (human - Jake's wife) Gem's close friend also

*Madeline* (human) (nee Trethowan) Sympkins - Richard's former girlfriend

*Alana Derwent* (human) doctor surgeon

# CONTENTS

## CHAPTER ONE

# THE DISAPPEARANCE

## June 1957

The day he disappeared, Richard was cold, wet, and determined to move on with his seventeen-year-old life. Letting himself quietly out the farmhouse door, he looked towards the grey clouds and turned up his collar against the wind. Standing there the gentle drizzle forming droplets on his nose and trickling down his cheeks, he felt a momentary pang of guilt. His dear old aunt would be upset at his unannounced departure and the note, too quickly scribbled, and left on his bedside table, was short and inadequate. He should have said goodbye in person, that was the right and proper farewell. But he couldn't face her to say the words. Couldn't bear the look of disappointment on her face. Couldn't trust himself and his own emotions, either. Instead, he swallowed hard and, ignoring the chill that seeped into his bones through the well-worn duffel coat, he hoisted his bag over his shoulder and started with loping strides northeast towards the sun, on the long road that led to the horizon.

He walked for what seemed like hours. From time to time he blinked the rain from his eyes and stuck out his tongue to catch the drops. The roof of his mouth felt rugged and stale, still flavoured with the taste of his hastily eaten breakfast, baked beans. In the distance, puffs of smoke curled slowly into the sky and he imagined a small, homely cottage nestled into a curve in the landscape, over the next hill. A combustion stove, just like the one his aunt kept lit, was probably the source of the smoke. Suddenly hungry, he thought of bacon and eggs sizzling in the pan, and delicious cakes and pies that were his aunt's favourite treats.

The farm had been a haven of sorts, after his parents' deaths seven years earlier in a car accident. Aunt Nance was a kind-hearted woman, generous with her affection and home-cooked meals, and Richard couldn't deny he had been loved and cared for by the old woman. Yet he had always had a feeling of not quite belonging, that it wasn't really his home. There had been tension and arguments with his cousin Bill, who had retaliated in spiteful ways when his position of only child had been threatened. Sly pokes and punches when no one was looking. Snide remarks. But he had taken it all in his stride and pushed away the cruel words. And stayed out of Bill's way whenever he could, keeping his own counsel. His aunt would have been mortified, had she known. Again, he felt a wash of guilt. What had he thought? Leaving and not saying goodbye after all she had done for him?

The road ahead divided a multitude of green and brown paddocks as far as the eye could see. In them, scattered groups of cattle and sheep continued grazing, disinterested in the lone hiker passing by. Trees stood in random clumps about the slopes, occasionally converging at a dam like schoolboys around a fight.

Richard's bag was heavy on his shoulder. The previous day he'd gone into town and withdrawn his meagre savings, spending it in the local Army Disposals Store on items he hoped would see him through his journey. How useless were most of the things he'd learnt at school now. Nouns and adjectives wouldn't keep hunger from his door. And logarithms and equations couldn't help him light a fire. He smiled involuntarily as he thought of his uncle George, who had patiently taught him that art. How he had loved the robust grey-haired man.

Nineteen fifty-six — the year uncle George had died — had been one of the saddest years of Richard's short life. His death, coming so close to that of his parents', had hit him hard. His uncle had taken him camping and fishing, whenever he could spare time from the farm. Together they had slept out under the Southern Cross on balmy nights, practising survival techniques which he could now put into practice. Bill had rarely joined them on those trips, and Richard had relished the time alone with the old man, temporarily free from the constant arguments with his cousin. But he thought now, those arguments were behind him, left back at the place he had departed from this morning. Today, one year later, with the knowledge his uncle had given him, he was ready to take on the world. And the knowledge that all his worldly possessions were stored in the bag he had slung over his shoulder gave him an exhilarating sense of freedom.

The incline ahead became steeper and Richard strained against the wind. The clouds before him had slunk low, concealing the crest of the next hill. The road disappeared into the mass of it. Puzzled, he blinked, staring ahead. Faint flickering lights came from within. Had there been an accident? Perhaps two trucks had collided in the poor light? Worried, he hurried towards the crest.

Suddenly he was surrounded by the cloud. It was grey and swirling, and immediately he was disorientated. The ground seemed to buckle up below him and he felt unsteady, confused. Where was the road? He stretched his hands before him, feeling his way. Shapes moved around him — formless featureless figures. He heard voices, indistinct muffled sounds. Could no one see him? He began to shout, but the cloud swallowed the sound and it echoed back at him, dull and flat. Hands grabbed him, pulling him forwards. The bag fell from his shoulder and he reached back for it, but the hands pulled him on.

Sometime during the afternoon, the grey cloud rose rapidly upwards, revealing the road and the crest of the hill. Two cows in the nearby paddock blinked large dull eyes at the gentle rain that shrouded the bleak countryside. The wind whistled mournfully through the treetops. Ahead, the road lay empty, except for a bag lying on the verge, open, its contents spilled in random disarray on the damp grass.

No one on Earth knew that Richard had gone.

CHAPTER TWO

# THE EXPERIMENT BEGINS

Richard woke feeling dazed. Surreal. Reality faded into the whiteness around his body. Drifting in and out of awareness he began to realise he was not alone. Blue eyes and featureless faces came in and out of focus. Voices whispered and droned. It took a long comprehension came to him long enough for him to get his bearings. Others were nearby. Like him, young men, naked and suspended. Yet, he appeared to be lying on something. It faded into the white surrounds. Some crisp clear eyes were detached and uncaring, while others were pools of concern. He wasn't cold or uncomfortable. He felt well fed, but he knew he was a prisoner. He was a captive at the mercy of those who had taken him.

Sensations became clearer and he felt probing hands touch his body. The intrusion of mechanical devices left him trembling with fear. The pain, although short lived, was intense.

He began to recognise the figures that faded in and out of view.

Somehow reassured by the voices, he began to speak, hoping for a response. The voices replied in shouts and tortured cries. He couldn't understand what they were saying. One figure with a melodic voice seemed gentle and caring. Even though he couldn't understand the words, the soft rhythmic tones helped ease the sense of violation.

Richard started to become aware of his surroundings. Where was he? His vision cleared. The cubicles and partitioned areas now revealed an antiseptic spartan colourless world. He was beginning to wake up from the nightmare. The voices were more distinct.

'Who's there?' he called. Richard moved to the edge of his platform. He took a tentative push slipping his toes over the edge. He sought the surface below with his feet. His legs were jelly. Gripping the edge for support he stood taking a deep breath. He shivered. Sliding his feet further along to the end of his bed space. He was in some cold and clinical room. 'Feels like a hospital,' he muttered. What were they doing to him? He wanted to know.

This time he listened to see if there was some voice he could remember. He fumbled along and pushed back a curtain. There in the bed beside him was another young man. He had red hair and rugged complexion. When he looked up there was no disguising his surprise.

'Howdy partner, you been here long boy?'

'I don't know,' Richard answered. 'I had to see where I am.'

'Nothin' to see, as far as I can tell,' the other man swung his legs off his bed. In two strides, he was at Richard's side with his hand extended. 'First time I got up, I almost fell flat on my face.' Richard shook the offered hand.

'I'm Cal Bennett. Where you from boy? You got a crazy accent.'

'You should talk. You must be a yank with that drawl,' Richard replied. 'I'm Richard Davidson, from Australia.'

'Next bed is a Frenchie,' the American nodded towards the curtain. One after that a Chinese is my guess.' Cal pushed aside Richard and moved to the next partition pulling it aside to reveal the occupant.

A thin face with smooth skin topped with a mop of thick brown hair, peeked around the next curtain. 'Bonjour, I'm Andre Lebeau.' The Frenchman reached out his hand. Richard didn't hesitate to shake the small soft hand.

'Cal almost crushed my hand,' Richard complained.

'Sorry about that boy,' Cal moved back to his bed. 'Don't know my own strength.'

'Where the heck are we?' Richard looked at both his companions. Neither were that much older than he was, he guessed maybe the Yank might be over twenty. The Frenchman looked younger.

'Beats me. A hospital ward, I reckon,' the tall American shrugged his shoulders in reply.

'So, we were all drugged? I couldn't see or hear anything but shapes and hear muttering.' Richard ran his fingers through his mop of hair.

'I reckon so, boy,' Cal nodded. 'They have been doing things, examinations and the like.'

Richard shivered. 'I'll go back before they return.'

They all nodded and did the same.

The group of young men became bolder.

'Meal over and we're on our own again,' Richard smiled. He walked to the door and tried to force it open. 'No getting out,' he sighed.

'Okay,' Cal clapped. 'So, I reckon we should find out who else is here.'

'They're giving us food and we are warm,' Andre got up and joined Cal and Richard. 'Let's see,' Andre pulled on a coverall that had been left for him.

'Perhaps we should try talking to them?' Richard suggested.

'I swear the one that brought in these clothes for us smiled at me,' Andre held up the coverall at the end of Richard's bed. 'They would never sell this in Paris.'

'Not something my Aunt Nance would see me in either. She'd say I was wearing PJ's,' Richard grinned.

'Well, we can get about now, not hang around na-ked,' Cal pulled up his coveralls and fastened the front. They the three of them walked along the room pulling curtains back as they did.

'Hello,' Richard held out his hand to the Asian man in the next partition. 'We knew you were there ma-te, but the curtain was always drawn.'

The Asian man bowed.

'Here buddy,' Cal handed the Asian a coverall from the pile that had been delivered.

'What's your name mate?' Richard asked.

'Name,' the Asian man looked puzzled.

Richard pointed to himself. 'I'm Richard, from Victoria in Australia.'

'My name Yoshi,' the other man said with a short

bow. 'Yoshi Hishida, from Narita, Japan.'

'I'm Cal Bennett, from Texas in the good ol' USA.'

'Andre Lebeau, I'm from the French Bordeaux region. Bonjour.'

The Asian man nodded and bowed again, then quickly retrieved a coverall before disappearing behind his curtain.

'I'm ready to get out of here. How long do you reckon we've been here?' Richard fidgeted with his collar.

'Can't rightly tell. Maybe a couple of days. It's hard to judge the time,' Cal answered.

'You were awake before me, I think,' Richard nodded. 'I've been trying to work out time too. I'd like to know what that horrible smell is.' Richard held his nose. 'It always arrives with our meals and nearly puts me off putting the sludge in my mouth.'

'You and me both,' Cal agreed.

'You make too much noise!' another young man shouted. He snapped his curtain open and strode over to the pile of clothes. His imposing solid build and height was capped off by his olive complexion and large roman nose, which he sneered down.

'Hi there, partner,' Cal offered his extended hand.

'I've heard all the introductions,' the Mediterranean man replied. He picked up a cover all and strode back the way he'd come. He glared back at them then closed the curtain.

'What's his beef?' Richard shrugged. 'Who knows?'

Andre had returned. 'It fits!' He held out his hands

and did a slow spin to show off.

'Looks just as geeky on you as it does me. Guess we'll just have to get used to them,' Richard did a little turn too. 'Maybe he doesn't like carrot tops,' Richard nudged Cal playfully.

'Well, I reckon he'll have to get used to me,' Cal winked at Richard. 'You got a problem with me boy?' Cal called out.

Silence.

'Look, we don't know where we are, or how long we're going to be here, so we've got to get along,' Richard prompted the Mediterranean man.

Abruptly the partition was pulled aside. The tall man strode back to the pile of clothes and rummaged through pulling out another coverall.

'Anthony Casstallana is my name, I'm a security guard,' he looked at them with disdain then turned on his heels and strode back to his cubicle.

'Don't fit?' Richard asked.

'Not judging by the length of the trousers and his unbuttoned top!' Andre grinned.

'If looks could kill boys, his would have done me in,' Cal grunted.

'He doesn't like Japanese,' Yoshi came out. 'He looked at me with black eyes. Scared me.'

'Only two left,' Cal picked up the remaining clothes. 'Maybe there's more folks here?' Glancing at the other drawn curtains.

'Let's look.' Richard pointed down the room.

Three young men flung back the other partitions around them, except for the Italian's. The first few were empty. The next wasn't. The terrified young man screamed.

'It's okay, we're not going to hurt you,' Richard said as they approached.

'True enough boy, we ain't here to hurt you. We're just like you, not here by choice,' Cal reached out his hand in welcome.

The young man trembled and screamed, 'Allah', then cringed at the head of the bed.

'Here, we have clothes. Put them on and you can get up,' Andre handed the cowering man the clothes.

The man kicked the garments off the bed, waved his arms and yelled again. 'Allah, Allah, infidels.'

'We'd best leave him Andre and Richie boy. It's all too much for him to manage I reckon.'

'Okay,' Richard put the clothes back on the end of the bed and backed away. Running his hand through his hair again he shook his head.

They kept checking the booths and found only one other young man. He was unconscious.

'What happened to him?' Richard asked.

Cal had taken a closer look. Andre reached for his wrist to check his pulse.

'Do you know what you're doing?' Cal asked.

'I've done first aid,' Andre answered. 'He's alive, but he looks badly hurt. His head has been hit with something.'

'I wonder where's he's from. I've never seen someone so white before. Even his hair,' Richard kept his distance.

'My dad had a guy from Denmark come over to check out something to do with our oil rig. I'd say he's from that part of the world,' Cal suggested.

'Something or someone bashed his head,' Cal turned around.

'Let's hope he recovers,' Andre straightened the young man up and put his head in a better position on the pillow. 'I'll see if we can find out what happened when our food arrives.'

They couldn't find anyone else.

'So, that's seven of us,' Richard concluded as he sat back on the end of his bed.

'Time for food if my stomach is anything to go by,' Cal's stomach rumbled loudly.

'I thought we were having an Earthquake,' Richard laughed.

'Here comes our food,' Andre announced as the door opened.

'I could smell it,' Richard held his nose.

Anthony flung back his curtain. 'We need to protect ourselves,' the Italian snapped.

'What more can they do, mate?' Richard asked. 'We're stuck here.'

'I'm a security guard. We should demand to be set free. We have rights,' the Mediterranean man said.

The tall pale creatures bearing trays of foul-smelling sludge in bowls entered and handed them out.

'You're right Andre, that one did smile at you,' Richard nodded.

As the creature came closer Andre spoke.

'I'm Andre. What's your name?' Andre pointed at his chest. 'This is Richard,' he pointed towards his friend. 'This is Cal, and Yoshi. My name is Andre, what's your name?'

'Rimi,' came the reply, and then with a nod to his

companion, 'Davrew.'

Andre smiled, 'Rimi, I like that name.'

The creature smiled back.

'Rimi,' the creature pointed to his chest, then at his friend, 'Davrew.'

'Rimi, can we go for a walk?' Andre asked.

'They don't understand you, you pillock!' A stocky little man from a cubical around the corner put in.

'Where did you spring from?' Cal asked. 'We checked the whole area.'

'Didn't check too hard, did you?' The stout stubble bearded young man continued, 'I've been listening to all of you carry on.'

'So, there's eight of us,' Richard stood up cradling his bowl of food.

'I think I'll sling me hook here,' the cockney man said as he flung back a curtain on one of the empty cubicles. 'Bit short of conversation on the other side of the room.'

'You're welcome,' Cal held out his hand.

'Where're you from, mate?' Richard asked.

'From London, of course. England, the fair and pleasant land, unless like me ya can't find work.' He pulled on his beard and continued. 'Name's Neville Long, but you lot can call me Nev.'

'Bonjour,' Andre stood also and extended a hand.

The Englishman looked at the extended hand for a minute before accepting it. 'Me dad would have a fit if he saw me fraternising with a Frenchie.'

He took a bowl from the creature called Rimi.

'I'm hungry, so, whatever it is, I'm eating it.'

The Italian grabbed a bowl and sat on the end of

his bed keeping a wary eye on everyone.

Davrew opened the curtain with the middle eastern man in it. The tray crashed to the floor. Rimi rushed to join his companion. Richard followed but stumbled back and fell onto the nearest bed.

'You're white as a ghost Richie,' Cal came over to investigate. Then he saw the reason Richard had fallen back. The figure of the Arab man was hanging by a cloth from the partition framework. His face blue, eyes bugged out and his body hanging grotesquely.

'He's dead,' Richard stammered.

Andre took a seat beside his friend. Shivering and dumbstruck.

'Now, why would he top himself?' Nev asked.

'We don't know where we are,' Richard lamented. 'He didn't make a sound.'

'Now there's seven,' the Italian pointed out. 'He did scream 'Infidels' and pushed us away. It's not their way. The Arabs have deep beliefs.'

'If we die here, no one will ever know,' Andre wailed and curled into a foetal on the bed, while Richard slumped to the floor.

'Well, I sure as Hell don't want to stay here. Wherever the Hell we are? I want to go home!' Cal thumped his bowl down.

Rimi and Davrew had raised the alert. Others of their kind arrived and removed the body. Any evidence of the young man's existence was erased.

'Blimey, it had to be bad for the poor bastard!' Nev stood staring at the vacant cubicle.

CHAPTER THREE

# THE EXPERIMENT CONTINUES

Many months later, they all knew where they were.

The white walls and clinical detachment of the space station orbiting above the planet Orthama, were less imposing. Richard smiled as he made his way to the communal living area. His new friend Davrew had shown him most of the facility. They had developed a game - a language game. Often laughing at each other's attempts to mimic the words of each other. The language was strange, for them both, Richard found Davrew's words, were virtually unpronounceable, and it was very much the same for Davrew. The door slid open and Richard saw his friend near the entrance. He stood alone. They both smiled. 'Hi.'

'Hi,' the tall blonde alien mimicked. 'Let's go.'

'Okay,' Richard nodded and followed his friend out the door. 'What's up? I thought we were going to stop and play some games.'

The sentence that followed was beyond Richard's grasp.

'Slow down. Davrew, I'm not that quick! You're saying something about you going to ask Rimi and Andre to join us. So?'

They were walking at a fast trot along the outer passageway. Passing the living quarters with windows on one side of the corridor showing the vast space-scape. Richard caught up. Pulling on his friends sleeve he halted them both. 'What's wrong?'

Davrew pulled away.

Richard stood in front of Davrew blocking his path. He tried to make some sense of the words.

Davrew continued a barrage of unintelligible sentences.

Richard could only catch snippets of what Davrew was saying. 'What is who doing?' Richard tried again.

'Rimi and Andre,' Davrew snapped. They arrived at the entrance of Andre's living quarters. Putting a hand over Richard's mouth to silence him, Davrew dragged him inside. Richard was trying to wriggle out of Davrew's grip, but the hand tightened like a vice. Davrew pointed to the bed on the opposite side of the room letting go of Richard. The occupants looked up briefly. Richard's face began to burn, and he backed out quickly.

'We shouldn't spy on people. That's private.'

Davrew retreated on Richard's heels. The mystified look on Davrew's face said it all.

'Wow!'

'Wow!' Davrew imitated again.

'They were doing it,' Richard whispered.

'Doing it?'

'Man, oh man, don't ask me to explain. I don't know anything about it.'

'Andre and Rimi are doing it?' Davrew asked again.

'Yeah, they were... you know, having sex. Kissing, touching, the whole bit. I've never seen that before.'

'Touching? Kissing?' Davrew repeated.

'This is weird.' Richard shrugged and walked back to the windows on the wall of the corridor. 'I didn't know you, I mean, your kind, touched.'

'Touch,' Davrew at Richard then quickly grabbed his hand. 'Touch.'

'Yes, touch,' Richard was trying to wriggle out of

Davrew's grip, but the hand tightened like a vice. Then Davrew proceeded along the outer walkway. The view of the space scape outside was a dark backdrop contrasting dramatically with the white walls and floors as they marched hand in hand along the corridor.

'What's the rush?'

Davrew didn't reply.

'I thought seeing Andre and Rimi together was enough. You know, I feel kinda silly Dav, like mum is holding my hand to cross the road.'

Davrew ignored Richard's resistance, gripped his hand tighter and sped up until they were moving at a fast trot to the other end of the space station.

'I've never been here before,' Richard still couldn't loosen Davrew's grip.

They came to a wide door which opened into a vast cavernous space. Along the walls there were cubicles, each with a bed and flimsy looking yet solid partition. In the centre of the room there were tables. Lights and mechanical devices on the walls, like a hospital. The smaller cubicles they passed led onto larger cubicles with several beds in each. These were occupied. Some lying on their sides were groaning and clutching their stomachs.

'Are they sick?' Richard asked.

Davrew shook his head. Richard tapped his forehead.

'Pregnant then, about to have babies?'

Davrew nodded.

'All these people are about to have babies. Like a herd of cows on the farm, all at the same time? But that was because, they were all serviced at the same time by some big old bull.'

Davrew shrugged his shoulders.

'Okay, I know I'm not making sense,' Richard finally slipped out of Davrew's grip. 'Where, are, we, going?'

'We are going to see Vini.'

'Oh. Is Vini your friend?'

Davrew simply nodded as they arrived at the entrance to the sixth four-bed cubicle. They entered and walked past the first bed to the second. The occupant was as pale and blonde-haired as Davrew, with a slightly plump face and welcoming grin.

'Vini, meet Richard,' Davrew introduced carefully in English before launching into a long often-incomprehensible conversation with Vini. To Richard's surprise a tiny baby was cocooned in the aliens' arms and suckling at a small, yet rounded, bosom.

'Touching,' Davrew nodded bringing Richard's hand toward the infant and ever so delicately putting flesh to flesh.

'I had a picture of me as a baby with my mum cradling me,' Richard pulled his hand away. 'Only looked at that album with my Aunt once. It made me feel sad. Knowing I'd never see my parents again.'

'Mother? A new word,' Davrew asked.

'Like Vini has a baby, my mother had me.'

'Mother, like Vini?' Davrew nodded. 'We do touch.'

'Yeah, I see that.'


A few days later, Richard and Andre, stood at a large window looking out at the stars. They were not the stars above earth. The planet below looked orange and yellow, not a comforting blue and green.

'It's called Orthama,' Andre nodded towards the planet below them.

'It's a long way from home,' Richard leaned against the window to allow the chill reaching his skin to make him feel it was real. The red-headed American, Cal Bennett, joined them. He was softly whistling the familiar sounds of 'I wish I was in Dixie'. They all laughed as he added in his Southern drawl, 'ain't no place like home, boys.'

'We were just talking about our hosts, Cal,' Richard smiled at his friend. 'What do you think about getting friendly with them?' Richard's Australian accent seemed pronounced. Too fast against the slow slung out drawl of the American.

'If you guys mean really friendly. The way the Frenchman is with Rimi?' Cal shook his head slowly. 'I don't think I want to know.'

'Rimi is very accommodating,' Andre added with a gleam in his eyes. 'Besides, my dear friends. We are a long way from home.'

'They all look the same to me,' Cal remarked. 'They might have tight little asses, but I can't help thinkin' they're not like the girls back home.'

'No, Cal, they're not like the girls at home,' Richard agreed. 'But...'

'But...' Andre prompted.

'Davrew and I find a lot to talk about. I like that.'

'You like Dav's cute dimple and those cool blue eyes too, Richard,' Andre smiled broadly at his friend.

'I just find Davrew shy and sort of innocent.'

'You're still a kid yourself, Richie babe,' Cal nudged Richard. 'Never been with a girl, have yer?'

Richard's face started to burn. 'I'd just like to know more about them, these wardens of ours. We've been here ages. We don't even know if we'll ever see home again.' He voiced the fears they all held.

'Well, they sure can have youngun's. We've seen that right enough,' Cal started to stretch pulling his elbows across his chest to loosen his shoulders. 'I say it doesn't much matter unless they can take us back home, boys.' Cal added, 'well, I'm off. Must stay fit to catch those pretty beauties waitin' back on Earth.' He turned on his heels and started jogging off along the corridor.

Richard and Andre turned again to view the space scape and stood silently watching the stars.

'Perhaps, I can tell you something about us?' A metallic voice spoke behind them. Startled they both turned around to see the alien they had nicknamed 'the old man' hovering nearby. Richard and Andre exchanged glances. He hovered about half a body above them on a disc. His elevation made him very imposing. Together with a mass of white curls that converged around a pale and wrinkled face. The white cover-all he wore fitted like a second skin, on stringy scrawny muscles.

'This planet used to be home to millions of my people. An advanced civilisation with cultural centres and population developments. So much like those on your Earth. We lived in comfort. Some were greedy, fighting over land and wealth. Wars began and raged unchecked. Again, much like your own people.' The old man sighed. He hovered closer to the space-scape window. Intent on taking in the view.

'Something terrible happened?' Andre suggested.

'We had many opportunities to prevent our worst fears becoming reality. We even planned to avert such a disaster and this orbiting space station was to be our shining light to save our people.' The alien looked directly at them. 'You are here as guests. We have been studying your people and you were chosen to assist us.'

'What if we don't want to assist you?' Richard asked. 'I mean. We didn't exactly join you by choice!'

'No, that is true. I shall try to explain. Just as you hear me now speak your language you may see we are capable of adapting. It is not easy to say.' He cleared his throat. 'I was a senior geneticist in charge of the Orthama Satellite Project when the final battle took place. No one won. The planet itself was left a wasteland. Nothing on the surface remained alive for more than a few days.' The platform swung around the old man had his back to them for just a moment while he wiped his eyes. 'There were seven scientists and a shipboard crew, just forty-seven in all.'

'So, you began again with just forty-seven people,' Andre repeated.

'I am the only remaining survivor of the original population.' The old man nodded.

'How can that be?' Richard demanded. 'There are at least sixty-five different workers that I know of.'

'They are the results of our work, our experiments. The only word I can find to explain it in your language is 'cloned'. They are new beings created from our original genetic makeup, reproduced exactly from the framework of our anatomy.'

'But what happened to the other survivors?' Richard turned to glare at the old man.

'Some tried to re-colonize. The planet was still too deadly for success. Others died trying to perfect our experiments. You must understand, we were all men here when the final catastrophe destroyed our planet. To survive as a species, we could clone ourselves. But we would never be able to produce our own offspring.'

'Would that matter?' Andre asked.

'The first and second cloning we believe it would not,' the old man hovered a little lower. 'But later the fabric we need to reproduce would be incomplete. We would certainly perish as a species.'

'Hang on,' Richard shook his head. 'Haven't you already perished as a species?' He turned and stared at the alien. 'I mean. If you're the only one truly left?'

'Yes, in a way,' the old man answered. 'We did find a way of adapting our structure to make semi-suitable dual gender individuals. On them we build our next strategy.'

'So, my Rimi and Richard's Davrew, are clones!' Andre stated as he slumped against the window.

The old man nodded and lowered his platform nearer while turning again to face them. 'We searched our ancient history and found possible descendants of our ancestors. We searched many other planets for them. When we found suitable candidates, we used them to continue our work.'

'Us!' Richard whispered.

'The baby Rimi is going to bear is mine?' Andre asked hopefully.

'Perhaps. We do use artificial insemination. The child could be the result of our sperm collection with another of your group.'

'We've given you our sperm, our time, our everything old man,' Richard spat. 'I think it's time to take us home?' He ran his hand through his hair. 'There's only so much a bloke can take.'

The old man was silent beside them now looking at the view. 'Isn't this beautiful?' The old man pointed at the orange yellow planet.

'Yes,' Richard agreed, 'but it's not home.'

'You could take us back,' Andre butted in. 'But I want to take Rimi with me.'

'Very bold of you to make such a request, human,' the old man raised his hover disc again. 'You could be a branch of our experiment on Earth.' He turned away, then slowly turned back. 'We've never released anyone before. I will consider it. My life is near its end. Perhaps another change may be successful.' He floated away and left the two men wondering.

'I don't know, Andre, if Davrew will even allow me to touch her, him. Crikey. What do we call them?'

Andre grinned broadly. 'Lovable.'


It was several weeks later Richard noticed the way Davrew was being treated by his peers had improved. He had known for some time his friend rarely had conversations with the other workers and the occasional bump and trip was not accidental. Just lately things seemed different. He'd noticed some breaking of the ice. It was time to ask Davrew directly why they treated him this way. After all, Davrew was one of their own. Richard had slept restlessly. He needed to solve this puzzle. He was surprised his friend was nowhere to be found in their usual haunts. Richard continued to look for Davrew but today his search was proving fruitless.

He walked up to the sleeping quarters. Each of their hosts had their own cubicle space in the communal sleeping hall. Richard knew Davrew's place and was surprised to find it empty and unused. Another of the aliens grunted at him when he asked Davrew's whereabouts. He decided to go to the hospital end of the space station. He rarely went there. Maybe something had happened to Davrew. At last Richard succeeded. He found Davrew on a bed in the first part of the chamber area where the single cubicles were.

'Hey Dav, I've been looking for you everywhere.' His friend was lying curled up on the bed and seemed to be sleeping but Richard could see moisture on his face. He sat down beside his friend. 'I don't know what's wrong, Davrew. I hope you'll tell me. I don't like this hospital part of the place. Let's get out of here?'

Davrew didn't move. His breathing was shallow, and he didn't utter a sound. Richard sat there for a long time. There was no reason he could think of why Davrew would be acting like this. No reason for him to be in the hospital.

'Why are you here?' He asked again. Before Davrew uttered another word, Vini walked in.

'You're the one that had a baby, aren't you?' Richard smiled at the alien. 'How's the child?'

'Child?' Vini replied.

'Baby,' Richard linked his arms and rocked them.

'Child,' Vini nodded. 'Growing well.'

'Why is Davrew here?' Richard stood up and stepped towards Vini.

'I speak, a little of your talk. Davrew has taught.'

'So, can you tell me? Davrew has just laid like a

lump since I got here. Not said a word.'

The alien visitor looked puzzled. Richard sighed, threw his hands in the air. He turned to Vini and looked him in the eyes. Being much shorter than Davrew, Richard looked down at him.

'Well?' Richard demanded.

'Davrew, no baby now. Baby gone.' Vini replied.

'What?' Richard screamed. Vini reacted to the flash of anger in Richard's eyes by backing away. Richard went back to the bed.

'Davrew, no baby now,' Vini repeated then retreated.

Richard sighed, 'I've frightened off your mate.' Davrew barely looked up. 'Dav, what is Vini on about?'

Puffy eyelids opened partially showing dull blue eyes racked with pain.

'I was going to have a baby, Richard. Something went wrong though. It's bleeding away from me.'

'What?'

Davrew began to sob, drawing in choked breaths while wailing.

'The others all have been able to have babies, but not me. Every time I think it will work; I lose the child.'

'Shit, Dav. Is this happening right now?' Only then, did Richard notice, Davrew was barely clad. A sticky white liquid covered the bed.

'I can't believe it, Dav!' Instinctively Richard sat his friend up, cradling and rocking her/him gently till the wailing became a soft sobbing. Davrew's tear stained face buried in Richard's neck. They sat there for a long time. 'Shit, Dav,' something shifted in Richard's heart. 'Bloody mean of them to leave you like this, on your own.'

'No good, this Davrew body, no good.'

'Don't be bloody stupid, Dav. It shouldn't make a blind bit of difference if you can have a kid or not. You still work here. You're still part of the plan. The bastards should realise you've got feelings.'

'Feelings,' Davrew mimicked.

Richard stared into crystal blue eyes and began to gently wipe away the tears from Davrew's face, first with gentle fingertips, then with his lips. Soon the embrace was a kiss, a kiss filled with tenderness and passion. Silently they pulled apart. Richard didn't want to move. Davrew looked tired. For a long moment, they sat holding each other. This was a new sensation for them both. The discovery of a deep mutual affection.

The old man shuffled into the cubicle. His frail body looked much smaller when he walked rather than standing on a hover disc.

'You will have your wish, Richard. It has been decided. You and four of your kind are to be returned to your home world. Including Andre with Rimi. Although the child will remain here. If Davrew wishes to go with you, it is permitted.'

Davrew nuzzled closer to Richard. A simple nod to the visitor to acknowledge the impending change.

'I will call for someone to attend you, Davrew. You need to be cleaned up and settled in a comfortable cubicle. It has not escaped my attention you have not been treated well for some time by your own. I apologise for that. I wish you well in your new future on Earth.'


Richard visited Davrew with Andre and Cal the next day.

'So, boys, we are going home!' Cal smiled and thumped Richard on the shoulder.

'The old man said four of us are going,' Richard walked over to the bed. 'Dav's really tired, we better keep this short.'

'So, who else?' Andre asked.

'I saw Yoshi and he's going. He found out that the

Danish guy didn't make it. He'd thumped his head resisting being taken aboard and never woke up.' Cal joined Richard at Davrew's bedside, 'you gotta get better boy, Richie wants you to come with us back to good old Earth.'

Davrew smiled shyly and took hold of Richards hand. 'I will be up soon.'

'So, that's Richard with Davrew, Andrea and Rimi, Yoshi and me,' Cal smiled.

'We have a sleep while travelling, Rimi told me,' Andre made himself comfortable sitting on the end of the bed.

'What about the Italian and Pom?' Richard asked.

'Anthony was talking to the old man when I got my last meal. He said wants to stay. He's been pretty-thick with Nev doing martial arts training. My guess is that they must both be staying,' Cal stood up and stretched.

'Bring on the big sleep and waking up on Earth,' Richard smiled. Leaning down he tenderly kissed Davrew farewell. 'It was June nineteen fifty-seven when I left, I wonder what day it'll be when we get back.'

'It'll be an incredibly good day,' Cal grinned.

'Rimi is waiting for me back at the nursery wing,' Andre stood up. 'Leaving the baby will be hard.'

'Did you give the kid a name?' Cal asked.

Andre nodded. 'Rimi called the baby, French.'

Cal laughed then covered his mouth, he saw Richard tip toeing away from Davrew who had closed his eyes. They all left the cubicle and headed towards their own quarters.

'Look out Earth, here we come!' Cal hollered in the corridor.

## CHAPTER FOUR

# THE RETURN

### March 1960

Nancy Davidson heaved the heavy washing basket off the ground and struggled towards the clothesline. Rheumatism had begun to cruelly invade her hands. She gritted her teeth and began to lift the dripping, sodden garments aloft. She was feeling reflective. Memories of good and bad times came to mind. This was the home George had built her. The home they had shared all their thirty-six years of married life. Nowadays, the old weatherboards needed repair and the path was covered in weeds. It did look a bit tatty and worse for wear, but it was still comfortable in a lived-in way.

Many good times they had shared while raising their son and nephew. She recalled how devastated George had been when his brother Peter and wife Eileen had been killed in a car accident. Nancy was sure he would never get over it, until Richard had come to live with them. He was an appealing child who had many of his father's features and mannerisms. George took to him at once, as did the child to his Uncle.

A smile crossed her lips as she looked to where George had chopped wood nearby while she hung clothes on this same old line. He'd always been strong and robust with a ruddy country complexion. That was until cancer stealthily stole his vigour. Her smile disappeared. The bad times had been horrendous. Crippling droughts, pitifully low prices and depressed demand for the wheat crops, a change in the economic climate had sent many farmers broke. Then there was a devastating storm and a fire caused by lightning. Throughout all these times, the good things would balance out their lives and outweigh the pain.

This day was bright and crisp with white billowing clouds occasionally blocking out the sun. The clothes should dry by the afternoon. Nancy picked up her empty basket and strolled towards the laundry. After stowing away the basket she washed her hands. Moving into the kitchen through the creaking door she sighed aloud. 'It was a day, just like this, when Richard left us.' Three years had passed. She still wondered where he had gone and how he was. A nagging feeling of guilt still clawed at her. 'If only...' she thought. Nancy felt sure she could have done more to prevent ill feeling developing between the two cousins. George had spent many hours with Richard on the weekends. Fishing, camping and generally spoiling him. Bill, on the other hand, was left behind to do the chores and keep the farm running. Their son had resented Richard's presence from the start. The favouritism didn't help. In hindsight, there had been opportunities. Even now though, Nancy could only recall how good it was to see George happy again after being so distraught.

Through the thin terylene curtains at the kitchen window Nancy watched a little battered car approach the house. 'Pat is such a lovely girl,' she said to the cat she scooped up into her arms. The animal squirmed until Nancy put her back on the lino floor. Shortly after, the petite girl backed in through the fly-wire screen door, laden with two large bags of groceries. Her hair was dark and hung shoulder length in a neat bob, which reinforced her common-sense appearance. Her blouse and jeans were both practical and feminine. The cat darted through the back door the instant it opened.

'Thank you for getting these for me dear,' Nancy smiled warmly at her future daughter-in-law. Slowly she began taking the items out and laying them on the table. 'Make a cuppa for us, dear. The kettle is on.'

'The kettle is always on here,' Pat replied with an impish grin as she walked to the familiar black combustion stove. Taking three cups from the nearby shelf she put the tea in the pot to brew.

'Bill saw me as I drove in. He'll be here any minute,' she explained. Bill walked in as Pat was just pouring the hot black tea into the mugs.

'Hi,' Bill smiled and brushed his crumpled Akubra hat across his legs to shift the dust. 'I just checked the back gate. It's off again and the post needs replacing. I guess I'll do that this arvo.' He walked over to Pat and accepted his mug of tea. 'Thanks for the cuppa, Pat.'

Nancy smiled at her son. He was heavy set and robust with a ruddy outdoor complexion. She knew he wouldn't make a show of affection to Pat while she was in the room.

'Its cold out there. This is a lovely drop,' he sat down and threw his hat on the table. Bill wrapped his thick fingers around the cup to soak in the warmth. He made a show of looking around the room and shaking his head. 'Crikey, Mum, this room needs a touch up.'

'You never noticed till now,' Nancy jibed. Pat giggled, sharing the joke. Bill had been noticing a lot of things since Pat had become a regular visitor.

The phone in the hall chirped its cheerful ring. Nancy got up quickly to get it.

'That's another thing we should get changed, mother. It's too far to the phone. By the time you get to the bloody thing, them on the other end think you're not here and give up.' Nancy was on her way out of the room. She didn't hear Pat's remark but saw her cross look. Bill would be put in his place.

Nancy covered the distance quickly enough. She sat heavily on the small telephone table seat. It was as old as the house itself, rickety but held her weight. It decorated the entrance and went well as the pale green walls of the passage. Nancy took a couple of deep breaths before lifting the receiver to her ear. She saw Pat had followed and was watching her from the kitchen doorway.

'Hello,' a deep voice said through a crackling connection.

'Hello,' Nancy replied. 'Who's that?'

'It's Richard. Can you hear me alright? Aunty Nance, can you hear me?' Nancy was dumbfounded and unable to answer.

'Bill, come quick, somethings wrong,' Pat motioned for Bill to join her as she stepped along the hall to her future mother-in-law.

'Aunty Nance?' Richard prompted again.

'Yee...ees,' was the only reply.

'I'm in France and travelling around Europe. Can you hear me, Aunty Nance?' Nancy no longer heard the crackling on the line over the thud of her own heart. Seeing Pat rush towards her with Bill following at her heels brought her back to reality.

'Richard? Is that really you? It's been so long since you were here. We thought something terrible might have happened to you.'

'Aunty Nance, it's so good to hear your voice, can't tell you how good. I can't talk long. How are you? How's Bill?' There was a slight crackle in his voice, or was it the line?

'We're both fine,' she replied. 'Bill is getting married soon to a lovely girl. But where did you say you are? France? How are you? Where have you been?'

'Can't really explain now. Where I've been, I couldn't keep in touch, but now I can. I just wanted to tell you I'm fine. I'm with friends, we'll be in France for a bit, then travel on to America and back through Japan on the way home. Listen, Aunty Nance. This is a pay phone and I'm nearly out of change. I'll write soon and let you know where I am.'

'Richard,' Nancy stammered, 'you sound so grown up.'

'Do I? Well, before I run out of time, I just wanted to say I've missed you...' Beep, beep, beep and the connection broke. Nancy held the receiver to her ear for a few moments as if willing the voice to return. Reluctantly she returned the hand piece and looked up with amazement into her son's eyes.

'Richard is alive,' she said simply.

'Maybe now he is. If he turns up here, I'll knock his bloody block off!' Bill spoke with true venom. Pat's jaw dropped. Bill stormed out and they heard the kitchen door slam behind him. Nancy began to sob. Pat put her arms around the older woman. They walked together back to the kitchen.

## CHAPTER FIVE

# THE HOMECOMING

### June 1961

Bill laughed at his reflection in the cracked dusty window of the machinery shed as he straddled the old farm motorbike like an elephant riding a push bike. He turned the key and pushed the throttle, the little bike putted down the track. Aware that his mother and Pat were preparing for dinner guests, he had to get out of the house, and to ride to the site of the new home he was building for his wife. He would be back in time to see Richard and his lackey arrive.

He looked across the fresh-sown wheat paddock. The early part of the sixty's decade seemed to be bringing problem after problem for the Davidson farm. The clouds above offered a promise of rain and he prayed it would arrive soon to boost the crop growth. While riding along the northern boundary he saw frequent 'For Sale' signs. Many properties had gone that way. Sometimes he thought he might take the easy path to a comfortable life. Not for his sake, but for Pat and the family they hoped to raise. But he couldn't do it and had rejected subdividing the land to make a quick buck. Instead, he had kept his mother's property as it had always been, a working farm. Keeping fewer head of sheep and diversifying back to wheat production had kept them afloat.

The green diagonal 'Sold' on the 'For Sale' signboard opposite made him angry. It was the old McGuire place where his parents met and fallen in love forty years earlier. His mother a slim and agile apple picker, his father a robust roustabout.

Bill recalled his father telling him of happy times in his youth spent at the McGuire place. George had been close to that family and had spent a lot of time there. His father showed him and Richard old sepia photographs and had spoken of days playing cricket and target shooting by the packing shed. And how they cleared a clay court, scraping it clean of grass, to play tennis behind the packers' quarters. The place must have been a beehive of activity in its heyday.

The remnants of the orchard were still there. Large, gnarled apple trees grew in rows, with some petering out only a couple of meters from where they'd begun. Derelict sheds and packing equipment lay about, rusting away, leaving the image of busy time visible to anyone who would care to recollect them. Bill scanned the old gravel drive and overgrown hedges, taking notice of the holes in the roof of the homestead and the brittle trellis on the verandah. It would take a lot of work to renovate the old place.

Bill doubted that Richard and his buddy were up to the task. It had been two years since his cousin had announced his impending homecoming, since then, as good as his word, he'd written and kept in touch. It made Bill feel sick, knowing Richard had returned, arriving just before his twenty first birthday to claim his inheritance, then spend it. Even more annoying, his mother was happy that Richard would be living in the old homestead. Bill smirked as he thought of his cousin. Richard would be well out of his depth and soon would be floundering.

He looked back at his own block. Tomorrow he would come out and peg out the foundation for the house. Pat had made him so happy since their marriage on a balmy November day in 1960. He wanted to give her a modern home to live in. Bill adjusted his hat and wiggled his bottom back into a comfortable position on the bike, starting up the motor, he pushed down the throttle and rode back to his mother's home.

It was late in the day when he returned. Bill parked his bike in the machinery shed and strolled towards his mother's cottage. The days were short and the sky a pink and orange glow shining through the scattered clouds. He admired the sunset with delight.

Wiping his boots before entering. 'Hi,' he called. 'I did wipe me feet.'

'So, you should,' his mother said.

The kitchen was a hive of activity, filled with the welcoming odours of a home-cooked meal. Nancy looked up at her son and smiled. 'Go get cleaned up. They'll be here soon.' Earlier in the day Richard had accepted the dinner invitation. He'd insisted that Davrew would join them.

Bill nodded and walked to Pat's side. He gave her a peck on the cheek and a rough hug.

'I'll peg out the house tomorrow. It'll be there to see then,' Pat smiled and nodded her approval. Nancy smiled too. 'We should have a house by the end of summer.'

'It'll be lovely to have our own place,' Pat put her arms around Bill and gave him a hug.

'It's nice living here and all, Mum, but it sure will be good to have our own place,' Bill agreed.

'Richard will be here for the housewarming,' his mother said in a bright and cheery way. Bill groaned and saw Pat shake her head at him. He shrugged his shoulders in reply. Pat just didn't understand the history behind his contempt for Richard. He sighed. Tonight, for Pat's sake, he would keep his mouth shut. She wouldn't want him to argue with his cousin.

Freshly showered, Bill walked back into the kitchen, just in time to hear a car pull up, followed by the sound of two doors closing. Richard entered with his friend Davrew at his heels. Bill let out a deep breath.

'Hi Aunty Nance,' Richard walked over to the small grey-haired woman and gave her a bear hug. Then he turned to Pat and gave her a brief hug. Davrew, at Richard's prompting, shook hands with both women. He was a full head taller than Richard, with long blonde hair framing a lean long face featuring high cheekbones.

'You are a bit alike,' Pat whispered to Bill.

'He's nothing like me,' Bill replied as he sat down sullenly without greeting the guests.

'He has your smile and impish eyes,' Pat added. 'Say hello.'

Bill looked his cousin over. He had a much slimmer build and was taller than he remembered. Not as tall as his fair-haired offsider, though. Richard still had dark hair that flipped onto his face, with dark tanned skin on a robust frame. Bill was fussy about keeping his own dark brown hair trim and slicked back.

'Don't tell me you like him Pat?' Bill stared into his wife's eyes.

'Say hello,' she insisted.

'Okay,' Bill stood up and thrust his hand out to greet his cousin. They shook hands for a bare second.

'This is my cousin Bill,' Richard introduced Davrew. 'This is my business partner Davrew.'

Bill again offered his hand and was surprised by the firmness of the return grip. The newcomer had broad shoulders, and an athletic upper body. He was wearing a white t-shirt and jacket over blue jeans, concealing a lean physique. Casual but smart, Bill approved of such practical attire. The two friends seemed to be complete opposites physically.

'We don't bite,' Nancy said. Richard nudged Davrew whose pursed thin lips parted to show a bright line of perfect teeth, and an illuminating smile.

Nancy put them all to work setting the table. Large mats were laid out, on top of which Pat placed a sizzling roast leg of lamb, and beside it a dish of piping hot vegetables.

'You're a lucky devil, Bill, to have found such a lovely girl. A good cook and a willing one with it, I'll be bound,' Richard said.

'Hmph,' Bill retorted. 'She's bound to me so keep your wandering hands to yourself.'

'Bill! Don't be so stuffy,' Pat protested. 'I belong to me. I'm not one of your sheep dogs.'

Bill felt his face redden. 'You know what I mean, love. He's been who-knows-where. It is the swinging Sixties, so the radio keeps blaring. We don't know what kind of habits he's picked up along the way.'

'I'm back home now, Bill, and with Davrew. We haven't caught any dangerous diseases!'

'Bill, dear,' Nancy interrupted. 'In this day, and age, it pays to keep in mind lots of people travel all over the world. Look at the Murphy's down the road. They just came back from the U.S. of A. They went to Disneyland. Alice was telling me all about it,' she turned to Davrew. 'There's plenty of meat,' she prompted.

'No, thank you,' Davrew continued to eat the vegetables.

'Aunty, I told you Davrew is a vegetarian,' Richard smiled at her.

'You must need your strength, after all that travelling. Just a slice to keep you strong?'

Davrew shook his head. 'Thank you, but, no thanks.'

'Vegetarian! I've never heard of such a thing,' Nancy muttered.

'Nor have I, mother,' Bill shook his head. 'How did you two come to be mates? And why on Earth would two blokes want to buy an old homestead that needs to be rebuilt? It's gonna' look a bit strange to folks around here, don't you reckon?'

'People will think what they want,' Richard shrugged. 'We've great plans for the McGuire place. We want to bring it back to life, the way George used to describe it. First up we need to clean it up, paint and repair the plumbing, electrics and fix the roof.'

Bill snorted.

'I know I left suddenly without much explanation, and where I was, it was impossible to contact you. I couldn't let you know I was okay. Not till a year of more ago, it was just impossible.'

'Yep, October 1961,' Bill spat.

Richard ignored the barb and carried on. 'In America, we stayed in Texas with our friend Cal. Then we went to France with Andre and Rimi. We spent a bit of time travelling around Europe before we headed for Japan to catch up with our other friend, Yoshi, who had travelled ahead of us.'

'Jeez, Richard. You don't half love the sound of your own voice,' Bill pushed his empty plate aside. 'How did a lay-a-bout bugger like you and a quiet lad like Davrew ever become pals?'

Pat glared at her husband.

Nancy rose and started collecting the plates. 'People do things different overseas, Bill dear. After we've done the dishes, I'll pick out some odd furniture you can take over to the McGuire place. I have too much laying around here.'

'Funny that, mother. We'll have a new house in under twelve months, Pat and I won't have a stick of furniture,' Bill grumbled. 'Will you have anything just taking up room to hand over to us then?'

'Bill, that's enough!' Pat scolded.

Half an hour later Bill stood with his mother and wife watching an old ute rattle down the drive.

'Thank you, son, for helping get the old chairs out

of the spare room. And really that old rug was just taking up room in the corner.' Nancy sighed, 'he was just a boy when he left,' she put her arm through Bill's. 'He's back now.'

'He's very charming, Bill,' Pat hugged his other arm.

'He's never stuck to a single task in all his life!' Bill held them both tight. 'He walked out on us, remember! Hell Mum, he left without warning or explanation. Right as you were planning his eighteenth birthday party. Just a scribbled note saying he had to go.' He pulled his arms free and strode back into the kitchen. The women followed him. 'I know we used to fight. But it was years before he even bothered to let us know he was still alive and kicking!'

'He did explain, Bill,' Nancy replied in a half-hearted way, as if to convince to herself.

'Bull dust he did,' he spluttered angrily. 'But he sure made quick work of getting back here to claim his inheritance! Even quicker at spending it all! Look at those highbrow ideas of restoring the old McGuire place. What drivel he carries on with, getting the old place back the way Dad would have liked it. Crikey Mother, he's no more a farmer than I am Prime Minister.'

'Bill,' Pat spoke softly, choosing her words with care. 'That's all true. But he does seem to have his heart in the right place.'

'Yeah,' Bill grunted, struggling to stay in control of his anger. 'Don't be fooled like that young lap dog of his, Davrew. Mark my words, both of you. He'll no more stay to face up to the task ahead than I'll go dancing tonight!'

With that remark hanging in the air he grabbed the dog's lead and headed outside. Perhaps a brisk walk would help quell his anger.

## CHAPTER SIX

# NANCY

### September 1964

'Thank you for bringing me over, dear.' Nancy gratefully accepted Pat's help with the door, allowing her daughter-in-law to steady her with her arm. I'll just get Carly out of the car. She always falls asleep in the car.' Nancy waited while Pat unbuckled the baby and cuddled the babe to her chest.

'I'm glad you could come over for a while. We've done a bit since you were last here,' Pat smiled as she led Nancy into the lounge. 'Take a seat by the bay window. It's a lovely view.'

'This growing old business isn't much fun,' Nancy complained as she sat in the large recliner. Arthritis racked her joints making even the simplest tasks a nightmare to perform.

'Now Mother, you're only sixty-nine,' Pat scolded. 'I'll just put Carly down and then I'll bring you a cuppa, and, when you're ready I'll show you what we've done.'

Nancy nodded and smiled. Bill and Pat were a wonderful support to her. She glanced around the room. The furnishings were Spartan, comfortable and homely, all so very much Pat's style. She loved the solid wood mantelpiece over the large fireplace, and the rock surround. The carpet was a practical tight weave, and the curtains had been pulled back, allowing the full height of the windows, and the view beyond, to be exposed.

'It's so good to be able to take a good look about. My, the view from here is beautiful. I love what you've done to the garden,' Nancy admired the flower beds outside the window.

'Thanks, Mother,' Pat placed a hot cup of tea and small plate of biscuits on a small coffee table. 'I made those biscuits yesterday when Carly was sleeping.'

Nancy admired the delicate cup and saucer. Her gaze fell on the row of cards on the mantelpiece. 'Can I look at those cards, dear?'

'You can,' Pat nodded and put her cup down. She gathered up the cards and passed them to her one at a time.

'That's from our friends Mick and Kim,' Pat said with the first.

*Sugar and Spice, and all things nice.*
*That's what little girls are made of.*
*Congratulations on the arrival of*
*Carly Meg Davidson.*

'This one is from Dav,' Pat handed over a hand-made card. The words were written with precision. 'Not bad considering Dav couldn't read or write before Richard left.'

As Nancy read the words, a tear crept to the corners of her eye. 'This world is more beautiful because your little one Carly is here. September '64.'

'I always thought you might find Dav a bit too odd for life here,' Pat remarked as she put the rest of the cards on the coffee table.

'I'm not so set in my ways that I can't see a good person when I meet one,' Nancy admired the hand-drawn pictures of stars. 'He's always so excitable. I love that.'

'So does Bill. He never tires of being caught up in Dav's next project. They've worked so hard together to bring the McGuire place back to life. They've done a mighty job of it too. That's not to mention all that they've done here.'

'I do wish Bill weren't always right about his cousin,' Nancy sighed and picked up the next card. It was a gaudy shop bought card with cliché words, just signed Richard. 'It's not even his writing.'

'No. I think he has a secretary do everything for him,' Pat snorted. 'The view of the McGuire place is good from here. Bill and Davrew have done heaps more work since you were last here.'

'Can I see another a new machinery shed being built?' Nancy looked across the highway to the now stately colonial home opposite. Pink blossoms coloured the rows of trees that swayed gently in the rising wind. She grinned at the memory of Davrew's almost naive pleasure in those early days. It was September 1961, twelve months after Pat and Bill's wedding when Richard and Davrew began the task of making the McGuire home habitable. It was all very much an adventure then. The work hadn't seemed too difficult. Together, the pair had focused on the task at hand. Then money had been tight, and Richard had come to tell her the plans they'd made. 'Davrew is such a kind, quiet lad.'

'Yes, he's certainly a big part of our lives now,' Pat agreed.

'Just the other week he arrived with a knapsack he'd carried on the bus from town,' Nancy picked up her cup again. 'Such a dear. He bought new taps and fittings with lever handles. So much better for me than trying to grip knobs. So very thoughtful.'

'And Dav insisted they keep the apple orchard going, ignoring Bill's suggestion of turning it over to crops,' Pat added as she stood up. 'It's turned out to be a good thing. The apples have been crated and sold. It's very profitable. Bill tells me Dav has a keen business head. He doesn't wait for Richard to approve anything now. Richard's not been back enough to see what needs doing.'

'Is Davrew making enough profit for Richard to return from the city?' Nancy stood up to stretch stepping towards the window.

'Perhaps,' Pat answered. 'I'll show you around the house now if you like.'

Pat put her arm through Nancy's, and they did a tour of the house, finishing in the kitchen where Nancy took a seat while Pat took out a breadboard and proceeded to make sandwiches.

'Richard came to tell me he was going, you know,' Nancy shifted her glasses back on the nose.

'Did he?' Pat looked up for moment.

'It was an odd conversation. I remember it like it was yesterday,' Nancy shifted the cushion on the wooden chair to support her back. 'Richard and Davrew had both worked hard for the first six months. Painting and repairing the home, patching up the shedding and generally making the place liveable. By the middle of the following year Richard began to complain about the lack of money, so it was no surprise when he came to have his little chat.'

'What did he say?' Pat continued buttering bread stacking the layers.

'He just said there's still so much work to do on the old place. Not only inside the house, but the orchard, outbuildings, and grounds as well. They'd already sunk everything they had into it so tight they'd decided Richard had to go to the city to earn some money,' Nancy sighed. 'Richard waited for me to speak. I just nodded. I could tell where he was going. Goodbye is never easy to say. Then he said, he'd lined up a sales job and had to go to training the next week.'

'It was supposed to be temporary?' Pat shook her

head.

'What he said next has stuck in my mind.'

'What was that?'

'He was worried about Davrew, with everything being so different here. Different to where they came from. New, exciting, and a challenge. Richard said he didn't want to leave all the work for Dav. Kept saying they were partners. Well, goodness me, Pat, what would he think we think of two blokes doing up an old farm? Of course, they were business partners.'

'Well he certainly did leave most of the work to Dav. If Bill hadn't got stuck in with Dav, the house would still need work. The money Richard sent was only a help at the start,' Pat pursed her lips.

'I know. Richard said they'd talked about him going to the city. It was a short-term plan to bring in funds to do the renovations. He said he'd be back most weekends. Except for when he was in training in the first month,' Nancy smiled at Pat. 'That's a big plate of sandwiches, dear. More than we can eat.'

'Bill will be here soon,' Pat pushed the plate into the center of the table then put some smaller plates beside it.

'Richard insisted I keep an eye on Davrew, keep him in touch by telephone as they didn't have one at the McGuire place at the time.'

'As if you needed to be asked,' Pat scoffed.

'I know, that's what I said. Keeping in touch should be the last of his worries. I told Richard that Davrew was our friend too, that you and Bill would help, as well. I told him then, Davrew is clever. A little odd with his European ways, but up for work. Richard said he'd only be gone for about eighteen months at most.'

'Well, it's been more than that now,' Pat smiled and wiped her hands on the tea towel.

'He said another funny thing,' Nancy got up to

wipe down the bread board and put it back on the bench. 'He said Davrew had a hang-up about being thought of as a bloke.'

'That's a strange thing to say,' Pat put out the tea-bags beside the mugs, she cocked her ear towards the nursery. 'I can hear Carly stir. I'll be right back.'

Nancy wished Richard had been true to his intentions. It had been a fine October morning in 1962 when he left. At first, after his training, he had come home every weekend. Then, as money was tight, he made it fortnightly, then monthly, and eventually two or three months would pass between visits. Richard had written to Davrew often at the beginning of his city days and Davrew was always excited and delighted to hear what was happening. He had to learn to read and write English, much to Nancy's surprise. That had become another adventure and one Davrew had mastered quickly. Davrew was obviously uncomfortable about using the phone at Nancy's and preferred the written word. So, the first money Richard bought home was spent installing a phone. Still, it had rung infrequently from what Nancy gathered.

Pat returned, cradling the baby close to her breast. 'I'll just let her have her fill.'

'She is so lovely,' Nancy smiled at Pat. Sipping her tea Nancy delighted in watching her granddaughter. 'I suppose I should be getting home when you've finished.'

'What for, Mother?' Pat shook her head. 'Bill will be here any minute. There's plenty of lunch. You've no need to rush off.'

The back door opened. Bill wiped his boots on the big mat. He looked up and his face beamed at the sight of his wife and daughter.

'Hello Mother,' Bill walked across the tiled floor and kissed his mother's cheek. 'Been across at the old McGuire place.'

'I wonder how Davrew is getting on with re-upholstering that old wreck of a lounge suite? The one you bought at the auction last month,' Nancy held her son's hand tight.

'Well, I think it's finished,' Pat shifted the baby. 'We'll go over later if you like. Is it alright?' Pat asked her husband. He nodded and winked.

'Yep, Dav is expecting us after lunch.' Nancy looked towards her son and daughter-in-law, at first slightly annoyed at the conspiracy, but she was quickly mollified by Bill's impish grin.

'It's all planned then. An afternoon visit to the McGuire place, is it?' Nancy scolded playfully.

'It'll do you good, Mum. You're stuck in front of the box far too much,' Bill smiled and sat down. He grabbed a plate and piled a couple of sandwiches on it.

'You are a torment to me,' Nancy tutted. 'Making plans for me without my approval.'

'You'll enjoy seeing what Dav's been doing. It really is a masterpiece,' Bill laughed.

'What does Dav think about my darling little granddaughter, Carly?' Nancy protested.

'Dav just loves her to bits, you'll see, Mother. It's no trouble at all for us to visit the McGuire place. In fact, we're all looking forward to it,' Pat assured her.

That afternoon Davrew welcomed Nancy as though she were royalty. Taking her arm, he led her from room to room, describing each addition, ending with the latest achievement in the lounge room. Pat and Bill had taken Carly outside to soak up the sun to leave Nancy to enjoy the tour.

'This is the old lounge suite now completely reno-vated,' Davrew grinned with delight as Nancy eased herself into the high-backed chair.

'It's so comfortable.'

'We had to peel off the old fabric. Repair the bro-ken supports. Replace the damaged springs in some of the cushions and then recover it all with the new fabric.'

'We?'

'Yes, my friend Tod Longmire. He's an artist and has been helping me with specialised decorations on the furniture.'

'So, where you met this clever chap?'

'Just at one of my evening hobbies classes, Nancy dear. Richard hasn't met him yet. He's not been home for ages. I'm managing without the little bit of advice he offers. All I do hear from Richard is about parties, meetings, sales, and nothing really useful to me.'

A chirrup of the telephone in the kitchen interrupted the tour and Davrew excused himself to take the call. Through the lounge window, Nancy could see Pat and Bill with their daughter, all enjoying the warmth of the sun in the wind-sheltered garden. Davrew bounced back into the room with an enormous grin.

'Richard will be here on the weekend.'

'And?'

'He's staying the whole weekend. I'm nervous about the changes I've made. I hope he likes what Bill and I have done.'

When Davrew and Bill went to the outbuildings she said to Pat. 'I was thinking if Richard was more like Davrew, then he and Bill would get on.'

Pat nodded as she settled in the comfy chair.

Nancy hoped the weekend would all go well for Davrew. These days he seemed to need her nephew less. She wondered what Richard was up to. Now Davrew was thrilled and excited, and a little nervous.

Nancy was glad to be there with her family, her new little granddaughter asleep in her arms. She felt content.

CHAPTER SEVEN

# RICHARD AND DAVREW

### Early October 1964

The next weekend Davrew had the house looking spic and span. Freshly showered and wearing blue jeans and white t-shirt he glanced up at the wall clock as he had done many times in the last hour. Nervously running his fingers over the freshly hand cut carvings on the kitchen table he looked up to the window. A car was coming towards the house. Would Richard like what he saw? It was time to find out.

Richard got out of the sleek sedan. His hair fell over his face. Davrew watched him flip it back as he got some things out of the back of the car. Too nervous to go to meet him, he decided to appear calm and stay inside. There was a huge bunch of flowers in Richards arms and too many bags to carry. Davrew went outside.

'Hi lover,' Richard greeted Davrew with a smile, then held out the flowers.

'Hi yourself,' Davrew took the flowers and let Richard follow behind with his luggage. 'You're only here for the weekend?'

'Yes, afraid so, Madeline has a whole heap of work lined up next week.'

Davrew didn't answer right away. Filling a large plain vase with water then putting the flowers in a big vase he turned to place the arrangement on the table.

Richard came close and planted a lingering kiss on his lips.

'You don't have to go,' Davrew said huskily after a few minutes. 'It's Friday night, the weekend is so short.'

'Let's make the most of it,' Richard replied hungrily seizing Davrew's lips again.

'I want to show you the house,' Davrew resisted.

'Later, let's catch up with each other a bit first. God knows Dav I've missed you,' Richard pulled off his shirt and pulled at Davrew's belt. They didn't make it up the stairs to the bedroom till much later.

Richard stretched and got up. He walked to the window. Davrew watched him pick up the letters that were left on the table. He recognised his own uneven scrawl.

'You sent those to me just after you went to the city. Do you remember?' Davrew sat up and watched Richard's reaction. 'I often re-read them. They are all I have to remind me you are coming home.'

'Please don't row with me Dav love. I row too much with Madeline.'

'Go on, read them,' Davrew prodded.

*October 1962*

*It's early days for me in the city, but by the stars I miss you Davrew. The boss has big ideas about getting computers into every business in the big smoke. His niece Madeline Trethowan has been helping me get settled. She said I needed to get smartened up and took me to the shops to get some good business shirts and trousers. I've got a small unit not far from work. Madeline says it's a good position as its close to cafe's and clubs. Not that I want them, I just want to get home to you. Earning money to get things done on the farm is why I'm here.*

*Training is for another three weeks. I'm learning about DOS the computer programming. Its primitive to you my darling, but it's complicated for me. I've got to be able to sell these large machines to customers so they can save time and money.*

*I miss you so much it hurts. I don't know how I can bear being away from you and your loving embrace. My first pay I'll send so you can get the phone put on. I miss hearing your voice. I miss kissing you in the morning. In the evening. I miss talking about our plans.*

*I'm so glad Bill is getting on with you and that you are starting to work out what needs doing with him. I'll be home as soon as this damn training is finished.*

Richard put the letter down, glancing at a few others. 'This one's full of what Madeline had done to the unit. That probably left you cold,' going back to the bed Richard pulled Davrew into his arms.

'I know it's stupid. Madeline is just there. I don't know why I let it get this far.' He paused to run his fingers down Davrew's spine. 'I'm not so strong where women are concerned, I guess. It's only temporary, Dav, this job, the unit in the city, and the party life to seal the deals. It's only till a nice little nest egg builds up in the bank. Just think of what we'll be able to do with the money for the sheds and equipment with all that money for the orchard.

'You can be a real bastard, Richard,' Davrew turned to arch his back to match the curve of Richard's body, flesh against flesh.

'That sounds like Bill, not you.'

'I spend a lot of time with Bill these days. We've done so much to the property. We don't need much money. The orchard is already operating, and we have our first apple crop sold. You could come home now,' Davrew planted another lingering kiss on Richard's willing lips. 'I told you when we first came here that I would never stop you being with your own kind. I could see when we were in Texas and Cal was with one girl one day, and another the next, that you wondered what it would be like to be with a woman.'

'You are too good to me Dav, by the stars I love you,' Richard mumbled while nuzzling Davrew's neck.

'Do you say things like that to her?'

Richard stiffened. 'That's not you either. Have I been away that long?'

'I miss you Richard, that's all.'

'Dav, my love, I don't feel anything for Madeline, it's just sex, nothing more. I don't want to hurt you.'

Davrew had turned away. 'It does hurt, Richard. You know anytime I can go back home, or even to Europe to be with Rimi and Andre and their little brood, if I want to.'

'You don't want to though, do you?' Richard whispered.

'No, I don't want to. But I don't want to be alone. We don't need much money. Come home.'

'Don't be angry with me, love. I'll make it all up to you, I promise.'

Turning the caress into a gentle massage punctuated with light kisses all over his partner's body, Richard smiled when Davrew let out an involuntary sigh. Then pressing harder, he began to slide his hands over sumptuous thighs, hips, and small firm breasts. Davrew allowed moist lips to greet Richard's and they both surrendered to desire.

'I'm not a bloke you know,' Davrew tickled Richard's hairless chest.

'Don't I know it?' Richard smiled.

'I was thinking about that beautiful birthing bath that Rimi and Andre have,' Davrew sighed. 'I'd like to have one here.'

'Why not?' Richard mumbled as he was beginning to doze.

'I'd love to have your children, but here I'm a bloke.'

'Ahem,' Richard muttered.

'So, I'd have to have the children in France then

come home,' Davrew rolled over and watched Richard sleeping.

It had been a wonderful to have Richard back where he belonged.

Next morning Davrew slipped out of bed, pulled on a dressing gown, and crept downstairs. Whistling some silly song, he'd heard on the radio. A simple breakfast would be a great way to start the day. They'd slept in. Beating the eggs and preparing the toast, were simple things he'd never done before coming to Earth. On the Orthama Space Station the food was provided and eaten in the dining area. The variety was limited to what the hydroponic garden grew. It was never appetising or prepared by someone wanting to present it well. Here food was a delight and discovering that was wonderful. Rimi had been so excited with the local markets when they went shopping in France. Andre was happy to show off his culinary skills. The finishing touch to the tray with juice was a little flower. One from the bunch Richard had bought. They had two whole days ahead of them to share.

Then to his horror he heard a car door slam. He looked out through the curtains and there was Madeline Trethowan marching towards the house. She burst into the kitchen.

'It's Davrew isn't it?' Madeline's sculptured eyebrows raised slightly. She looked around the kitchen, saw the flowers and the breakfast tray. 'Is that for Richard?'

Davrew just nodded.

'Good, I'll take it up. Just point the way.'

'Richard was to have the whole weekend here without interference from you or the city folk. Why can't you leave him be?' Davrew spluttered as she ignored him and picked up the tray delicately balancing her high heels stepping on each tread. She was wearing an outfit that looked like it was from a fashion magazine. Her hips wiggled. Davrew just followed her up the stairs.

'Richard, she called, I've got a surprise for you,' Madeline called as she swept into their bedroom. She turned to give Davrew a pointed glare. 'We've a barbeque to go to this afternoon to woo the clients from the west. I've come to get you up and ready for a big day.' She waved Davrew away. 'We've got a dinner to go to this evening as well. No time for you to sleep in.'

'What the hell,' Richard rubbed his bleary eyes. 'I had the whole weekend free.'

'Change of plans lovely,' Madeline fluffed up a couple pillows behind Richard and made him sit up. Her boobs close to his face.

'Oh, come on Maddy, I'm entitled to the weekend off. Dav and I have plans,' Richard glanced at Davrew standing in the doorway.

'We do,' Davrew added.

'Nothing that can't be changed, I'm sure,' she glared at Davrew. 'We want to impress my Uncle, don't we? You want you to still be employed by the company, don't you?'

'For Christ sake Madeline Trethowan, you knew I had this weekend planned. I'm entitled to a break. Dav and I do have plans and they don't include you. I'm sick of you and your controlling ways. I'm not going. You can go back and manage without me,' Richard shouted.

'You can come here any time you like,' Madeline waved Davrew away again. 'Come on, get up! Or do you need some persuasion?' She lent over and kissed Richard fiercely. 'Come on, we have to be back in the city by twelve and it's a two-hour drive.'

'I don't want to go back. I don't want persuasion. I came in the sedan for a weekend away from the city. To be here is important to me, and you should just turn around and go back.'

'I won't do that. And you will come back or risk

losing everything you've done over the last couple of years. My Uncle listens to me and he wants the best for us both. You heard him say so just yesterday. I drove up in the Bentley, it would be better if we arrive in it to show our clients who we are. Style is the key sweetheart,' she slapped Richards face playfully.

Richard swung his legs over the side of the bed. 'You really can't be serious.'

'I am, and you know it. Why would I drive from the city to this god-damned backwater if I weren't?' She scowled with her hands on her hips.

'Oh hell, you are a conniving bitch! You aren't giving me any choice, are you? Give me time to talk to Dav.'

'That's the boy,' Madeline smiled triumphantly and pulled the sheets away. 'You slept au natural, you just need me for company.'

'I don't you know,' Richard stood up. Grabbed his bag off the floor and pulled out his clothes.

'This is shit, I know. Dav, let me explain.'

'Richard, if you must leave, go now,' Davrew stared back. Then backed out the door. Richard followed and grabbed his arm.

'Please don't argue about this Dav, I'm just about sick of fighting. I do too much of that with her,' he nodded towards the bedroom. 'I'll make it back soon, I promise,' Richard pulled Davrew towards him. 'Please try to understand. I have put a lot of time and effort into securing this position and the job is a good one. I'm making good money now,' Richard stared into the pool blue eyes he loved. 'I'll ring tonight, and be back as soon as I can, I promise.'

'Don't make promises you can't keep Richard. It appears you have a whole new life in the city with Madeline.' Davrew couldn't keep the bitterness from his remark.

'You know that's not true,' Richard pleaded.

'Do I?' Running down the stairs Davrew felt tears welling up.

'Please Dav,' Richard pleaded as he followed Davrew down the stairs. 'I bought you a present.' He pulled a parcel the size of a shoe box out of his bag and handed it to Dav.

'Oh Richard,' Davrew accepted the parcel.

'When you two have finished, we have some travelling to do,' Madeline was standing outside the bedroom door. 'We have to go now.'

'Oh shit, you'll argue with me all the way back I'm betting,' Richard sighed.

Davrew watched as Madeline Trethowan descended the stairs clicking her high heels as she did. She was prodding Richard verbally the whole way.

'I'm just a heel,' Richard told Davrew as he walked past.

'You are,' Davrew agreed.

'Dav, I will be back, and I'll make this up to you. I want to tell you about an idea I had about starting a computer shop in our local town. Farms are businesses and need to be run well to survive.' Richard squeezed Davrew's arm, 'that way I could be here all the time and still earning money.'

'Come on,' Madeline clicked her fingers as she walked out the door.

'Please think about a little business in town, we could run the computer shop together,' Richard begged. They walked outside and saw Madeline get in the car.

'Come on,' she yelled from the passenger seat.

Davrew shook his head. Now was not the time to think about the future. Not with Richard leaving again. He and held back the tears until the Bentley pulled away. Today he stayed away from Pat and Bill. Even having little Carly about wouldn't cheer him up.

# CHAPTER EIGHT

# PAT AND BILL

June 1965

Eight months later Nancy lay in her old bed. The early sixties had been difficult, but 1965 was proving to be her hardest yet. The familiar pictures hung around the room were tired looking. Age had robbed them of their sheen. Nancy knew a new coat of paint was needed to revitalise the place inside and out. The curtains, once hung with care, were now mottled and grey.

A faint morning light trickled in through the glass, waking her from a restless slumber. Memories filled her waking hours as much as the pain choked her joints. How silly it was to slip on the front porch steps. Only one month had passed since she'd had the fall. It had been such a cold May day with frost on the ground, and the entrance to the house was like an ice-rink.

Spring had been an unhappy season, as she lay in her bed recuperating from the broken hip. One week out of hospital, and frustration at her immobility had trebled. The grey sky with constant drizzling rain, which continued throughout the month, did nothing to ease her temperament.

Her room, her house, her life had become tedious.

During this early morning contemplation, her thoughts were interrupted. She heard wheels screech to a halt in her driveway, followed by the slam of two car doors.

'I'm not expecting anyone,' she whispered to the walls. 'Only the health care sister later this morning.'

Craning her neck like a turtle, she strained to hear the approaching visitors. The heavy stamp of feet trudging up the gravel path, followed by the lighter footsteps of another person close behind, were easy to recognise. 'Pat and Bill,' she murmured. 'What on earth are they doing here at this hour?' On her bedside clock, shining with a soft green glow, Nancy could see the time, 7.30 am.

'Wipe your feet, Bill,' she called at the top of her voice. Smiling with the realisation she still thought of Bill as her baby boy. Soon afterwards the back door creaked and creaked again before shutting with a resounding bang. Hurried footsteps came along the passage past the kitchen and Bill burst into the bedroom huffing and puffing. Pat hot on his heels.

'Calm down, Bill, there's nothing more we can do about it,' Pat said anxiously.

'About what?' Nancy asked, as she struggled to sit higher in the bed.

Pat came to the bedside. She adjusted the pillow and helped raise her mother-in-law to a comfortable position.

Nancy looked closely at Pat. Her once-glowing face now seemed pale and drawn. Her usually bountiful bowed lips were tightly pursed. Her breath was short. Nancy caught her hand and motioned the young woman to sit.

'Bill, what have you been doing? Pat is pregnant and not well, and you are putting her through some torment,' Nancy snapped.

Gratefully Pat settled on the side of the bed, she had been quite ill in her first trimester, and Nancy knew it.

'It's alright, Mother, it's not Bill, really,' Pat protested.

'Well, what then?' Nancy demanded.

Both women looked at Bill who was restlessly pacing about the room, his brow furrowed in anger. Large leathery hands beat the air as if punching an invisible opponent. They let him continue with his tirade, knowing from experience once it had subsided an explanation would follow. Nancy had only seen Bill this upset twice before, both times involved arguments with or about Richard.

'I'd love a cuppa,' Pat sighed in the vain hope Bill would take the hint.

'Bill,' Nancy spoke sternly to her son. 'Stop this and tell me what's going on. Can't you see this sort of outburst isn't good for Pat or the baby?'

'I could wring his bloody neck,' Bill began loudly.

Pat's pleading glare bought him to a sudden halt. Before his mother could scold again, he took some deep breaths and began to calm his nerves.

'Richard came to our house half an hour ago, we were having breakfast when he stormed in, wanting to know where Dav was and why the house empty?'

Bill stopped his pacing. He sank into the old comfortable chair beside the bed. 'Silly bastard thought he was at our place.'

Pat silenced her husband with a crisp stare and carried on with the explanation. 'Well, we told him Dav had left two months ago to go back to friends in Europe.'

'He didn't believe it!' Bill blurted. 'Kept asking, why didn't Dav write or ring? Why didn't we tell him? What made Davrew leave? Bugger me, Mother, he had the gall to say he hadn't heard a word from Dav for months!' Bill waved his arms impatiently. 'The last few months, before he left, as you know, Dav kept very much to himself. He always wrote though, at least once a week. Crikey, we posted a lot of the letters for him.'

Pat got slowly to her feet and put a finger to her lips to silence her husband again. 'Anyway, we explained what had happened and gave him the last letter and the keys to the house. The letter had bank books with it and a brief goodbye message.' As the younger woman moved towards the door she concluded, 'Richard stormed out of the house and went straight across the road. I'll make us a cuppa now, I'm gasping.'

'You're tired,' Nancy remarked with an icy glare in her son's direction. Pat just smiled and walked out into the passage and down to the kitchen.

'Dav left the house ready to sell, so I guess that'll be next. Damn shame. It's looking a picture, and the orchard is a real goer now,' Bill added with a sigh.

Nancy studied her son for a moment. He was, after all, a good judge of character. She had desperately hoped he wasn't, where Richard was concerned. The McGuire place now looked close to its former splendour, and the thought of it being sold saddened her even more.

Davrew had indeed become something of a recluse in recent months. Nancy was puzzled by this. Still, he had always found a way of keeping in touch with her. The phone had a new extension to her bedside. The old-fashioned black box shaped device with circular dial sat on the table within reach.

He'd phoned nearly every day from Europe since she had fallen, to ask how she was and to let her know he was thinking of her. They'd spoken down a clear line that seemed to come from next door, she'd felt glad her shy friend should be so concerned.

Bill had calmed down a bit. Pat took a few minutes to assist Nancy in reaching a comfortable position.

'Carly, your dearest, where is she?'

'Oh, my mother is staying for a few days. She's looking after her,' Pat replied. She handed her mother-in-law a mug of tea, with a saucer just in case of spills. Nancy thought, she's such a considerate young woman.

'It's a good thing your mother being here. You need a break Pat dear.'

'Mad bugger, he is, Mother,' Bill continued to grumble. 'Doesn't deserve a friend like that.'

'May...be,' said Nancy quite sternly. 'Maybe you should be paying some attention to Pat. What about her condition? She's worn to the bone, Bill my boy, and...' They were interrupted by a noise outside, again a car pulling up in Nancy's drive. The door slammed, and hurried footsteps on the gravel path were soon followed by a knock at the door.

'Aunty Nance, are you there? Can I come in?'

'I don't know why Richard can't stay in the city where the bastard belongs,' Bill grumbled as he jumped to his feet.

This time it was Nancy who silenced her son and motioned for him to sit. 'I'm here, in the bedroom,' she yelled. 'Come in, dear.'

Glowering, Bill slowly sat back in the easy chair. Nancy reached out to touch her son's hand briefly, in the hope of quelling his simmering rage. 'No yelling and carrying on now, Bill. There's two sides to every story.'

'Yes, and you always take his side,' Bill threw his hands in the air. 'It's no use arguing with you.'

Nancy glared at Bill as Richard came in the room, then stopped.

'Aunt, I didn't realise you were ill,' he said feebly and bent to kiss her warmly on the cheek.

In his left hand, he clutched a letter so tightly, his knuckles were white. His legs buckled as he sank heavily onto the foot of the bed. Nancy noticed his well-fitting jacket and blue polo shirt, together with smart trousers and stylish shoes, highlighting her nephew's fondness of the creature comforts. He looked like a city person out of place.

'Can't you bloody well read, you, ignorant city fool?' Bill erupted. Nancy silenced him again, with a warning glare.

'I told you before, Bill, I haven't had any letters for ages from Davrew, not from anyone. I suspect I know why. Only yesterday, when I had a temp in the office did I receive a phone call through to me from Charlie, the mechanic from the garage here. He told me he'd been trying to get on to me for weeks about my old car. I couldn't understand why he or anyone hadn't reached me before. So, I rang my regular girl, who was sick at home. She told me, under sufferance, she was not allowed to put phone calls or mail from this district through to me. She wouldn't tell me who gave her that instruction, but I can sure guess.'

'My goodness, Richard! How could anyone be so rude as to vet your mail and calls! Seems like a strange way to run a business,' Pat said. She sat opposite her husband at the bedside, scrutinising Richard.

'My guess is Madeline, the boss's niece. She's been making all my appointments and scheduling my social events related to work since I started. It was only since she moved in with me, I began to think of her as conniving. She kind of treats me like her little toy.'

'Leave off, you dick! No-one stopped you calling us,' Bill retorted.

'That's true, in a way, but you see, she kept planning events and making sure I was kept busy. I guess I just couldn't see what was happening, always putting off calling because something would interrupt me when I was about to. I was just stupid.'

'Stupid alright, all about a bit of crumpet. You couldn't be dumber than that!'

'I'll have none of that talk in this house, Bill,' Nancy scolded.

'I know it's dumb of me to ask again, but all of this is still sinking in. When and why did Davrew leave?'

Richard asked shakily.

'Takes a bloody lot to sink into that thick skull, doesn't it?' Bill snorted.

'Hush up, Bill, and let Pat explain,' Nancy decided some motherly control was needed. 'She won't work herself up into a knot.'

Pat looked at her briefly, then directly at Richard. She took a deep breath then began. 'Davrew left because his friend died, Rimi I think was the name,' Pat began.

Richard nodded slowly, adding, 'it's in the letter. They grew up together.' His voice quivered and body slumped as though he'd been punched. 'I don't understand. Tell me exactly what happened. The house is done up a treat. I don't want to sell it. What made Dav or anyone else think I do?'

'Well, your total lack of interest in everything here is a fairly good reason, I should think,' Pat snapped. Then seeing Richard's pitifully pleading eyes, she continued. 'If you want to know the circumstances, I'll tell you.'

'Please,' Richard begged.

'It was late in the evening. We were just getting ready for bed when I saw the kitchen light on across the road. Bill told me Dav hadn't met him that morning as arranged. Neither one of us had seen movement at the place all day.'

'Get on with it, Pat, I've got work to do,' Bill urged.

Nancy silenced him and waved for Pat to continue.

'The long and the short of it is we went over to the house. The back door was open, and the house was very cold.' Pat shifted in her seat uncomfortable at being the focus of attention. 'We realised something was very wrong straight away. Davrew was sitting at the table like a statue. The breakfast things were everywhere. It seemed like he hadn't moved all day. Dav hates the cold so...'

'I know,' Richard whined.

'So, Bill set about making a fire, while I cleaned up. All the time we talked and chatted, but Dav said nothing. I remember having to put the receiver back on the phone. Dav had left it dangling on the wall.'

'We didn't get a word out of him until the heat hit the room,' Bill chipped in. 'Dav was dressed in a thick woollen jumper and dry-z-bone coat so the warm air sort of hit him and brought him to his senses. I think he was surprised we were there.'

Richard grimaced as Bill added to Pat's description of events.

'And ashamed he hadn't realised it,' Pat continued. 'Anyhow, Davrew started talking about Rimi and the family in France. We all had a cuppa and let him ramble on. Early that morning Dav had a phone call from their eldest child, as Andre was too distraught to speak. Rimi had died in childbirth. He kept saying they'd come on a long journey and talked about you and how the pair of you had been travelling together. Eventually the conversation came back to Rimi, Andre and the children.'

'I shouldn't wonder the sound of the phone ringing didn't damn near give Dav a heart attack. It sure hadn't rung in a long time,' Bill stuck out his chin and spat these words as if throwing a resounding blow at his cousin.

'Then calm as you like, Dav got up and fetched the bank-book, notepaper and pen,' Pat added. 'He wrote the letter you have there and gave us the spare keys, saying he had to be with them,' Pat added, 'and it will be good for him too.'

'He asked us to look after the place, and that was it,' Bill concluded.

Richard shook his head, then unfolded the crumpled note he'd been holding, studying it to regain his composure. He read it aloud as if to confirm what the words contained.

*'Hello Richard,*

*I'm going to Rimi's. Andre and the children need me. Rimi is dead.*

*If you've not read any of my letters, look around the house and grounds. You'll see I've got everything looking and working well. You can sell if you wish.*

*I may be going home for good.*

*Goodbye, Dav.*

*PS: If you remember the times we travelled together with a smile, then your life and mine will be happy.'*

'By the stars, Lord knows, I've been stupid,' Richard groaned after a long pause.

'I'll agree with that,' Bill smugly added as he got up out of the chair and faced his cousin.

'You always said I was an idiot, Bill. I wish you had clobbered me years ago; it might have knocked some sense into me.'

'I'll be glad to oblige now,' Bill coolly replied.

'The last time I came back to the McGuire place, Dav and I had a great evening and when I woke up Dav went to get breakfast. Next thing I know in walks Madeline with the breakfast tray. Dav looked shattered. I should have stopped it then. She arrived in a slinky number leaving nothing to the imagination.'

'What the hell are you on about?' Bill flustered and red looked at his mother before going on, 'you match your name, Dick!'

'It must have been Madeline. She kept me busy, even planned my weekends. I've never had a break, even though I wanted to. She always controlled my appointments. Even when I did get away, she followed to make sure I'm soon back to do what I was told.' Richard rolled his eyes, 'I can't imagine what Dav felt like when I last came back to the farm. Madeline came to take me back to the city. Like a stupid twit, I left early.' Richard hung his head, burying his face in clean manicured hands and fingers, mumbling, as if to himself, as he continued. 'Weekend luncheons, barbecues and parties with the well to do clients kept me busy in the city. The boss was over the moon with my performance. Goes to show you how thick I am.'

'Madeline did seem attractive in a city kind of way,' Nancy commented. As always, she forgave Richard just for being himself, a fallible young man. 'She called into my place for directions that day, and I'd say, she was a bit overdressed for the weekend.'

'She was the boss's niece, Aunt Nance. I should have seen it from the start, what she was doing. Now it seems so clear.'

'You haven't any proof....' Pat remarked despite her disinterest in Madeline.

'I didn't plan on her moving in. I let her curves and bumps get to me. That sort of happened after a party where I got drunk. Yes, I'll admit not having experience with women made it easier for her. What a fool I've been to let it go on, and to let her use me this way. Damn it all, she's a conniving, manipulating bitch!'

'Now, Richard, you really don't know this for sure,' Pat scoffed.

'No, that's true enough, but I know Madeline Trethowan fairly well. She's very sharp to be around, believe me. The fact I was lonely put me right where she wanted me, trapped!'

Nancy tried to re-position herself and sighed involuntarily at the surge of pain racked her body and limbs. Pat rushed to assist her, and Bill looked on anxiously.

'Aunty, I'm sorry to say I've neglected you, too,' Richard took the frail woman's hand in his and clasping it firmly between long strong fingers. He smiled reassuringly at her. 'I'm going to try and repair the damage I've caused. Can I use the phone, please?'

'Of course, dear, anything,' Nancy whispered.

While settling to dial the number on the old phone set, Richard rubbed his forehead absently with his free hand while waiting for the dialling ring in his ear to cease.

'Hi Ralph!' After a few minutes, the silence seemed eternal to the curious onlookers. 'How are you today? Good. Mate, I won't be using my flat for a while. I'm going overseas for a short time,' he paused briefly. 'Yes, I know it's sudden. Can you do me a favour?' After another short pause, he added, 'don't let anyone except my cousin Bill and his wife Pat in. Change the locks if you must. I don't want Madeline Trethowan in the place. Hmm. No, it might not make sense to you, but that's what I want, Okay? I've paid up to the end of the month so that should give Bill time to get my gear out.' Silence again then the receiver clicked back onto its rest. 'Pat, Bill, is it Okay with you to go and clear out my flat?'

Bill nodded, dumbfounded by the request.

'But what will we do with the furniture? Do you want us to store it somewhere?' Pat asked.

'No, I really don't want all the fancy furniture and junk. You can have it if you want. Call it a belated wedding or birthday present. I paid for all of it, but Madeline wanted it, not me. If you don't want it, sell it and get something you want.' He was dialling again.

'Hello, Mr Trethowan? It's Richard Davidson. I'm ringing to let you know I'm leaving the country for a while. I've important personal business to attend to.' Everyone could hear the reply from the other side of the room. Richard held the receiver away from his ear briefly and smirked. 'I know it's sudden, boss, but I've no choice and neither have you. If you wish, I can keep in touch. I may be of some use scouting out new merchandise while I'm over there. What do you think? Fine, Mr Trethowan, you can give my final paycheque to my cousin. He will be coming down shortly to clear out my flat. What about Madeline?' Richard almost snorted. 'Madeline will be fine without me. She's quite fond of her own company. She's quite sure there's no one like herself or quite as wonderful as herself, in all the world.' The yelling on the other end was quickly followed by a sharp click.

'You've flipped,' Bill announced.

Pat and Nancy looked equally stunned.

'I'm sorry, Aunty Nance. Sorry I have to leave so quickly,' Richard stood again at his aunt's bedside, holding her hand. 'I don't think I've flipped, Bill. I think I've finally come to my senses. Madeline nearly cost me the best thing that ever happened in my life. I must try to make amends with Davrew and start afresh.'

Richard lent over to his Aunt's forehead and gently kissed her brow. 'I'll return soon as I can, Aunty Nance. You get back on your feet again quickly. There'll be another little one to cuddle shortly and Pat will need your help.' Richard stood and looked directly at his cousin. 'Can I ask you to look after the orchard and the house, Bill?'

'You just did, didn't ya?' Richard released his grip from the frail hand and reached out an open hand towards his cousin.

'You've been a great friend to Davrew and helped heaps with the orchard. I don't deserve your help, but, Dav's your mate. I'll bring Dav back, Bill. I've been a heel. Christ, the thought of facing Andre and the children after Rimi passing is just unthinkable.' Shaking his head and clasping Bill's hand firmly he gulped, unable to say any more.

After Richard left the room, Nancy slid her feet off the bed and turned to sit looking out the window. She watched as her nephew climbed into his sleek sedan and sped back along the drive to the main road with dust trailing behind him. She looked at her son, who was, for once too stunned to speak.

CHAPTER NINE

# RICHARD

June 1965

With sheer self-loathing Richard admitted to himself he had allowed Madeline to seduce him in every possible way. Her pristine beauty and crafty feminine wiles had them both surrounded in luxury. The apartment, car, furnishings, and clothes were all her choice, none of which he could truly afford while running the farm nor, he now knew, did he want them.

Recklessly he drove from his Aunt's old farm towards the McGuire property. Pulling up beside the new machinery shed Richard got out and locked the car. Quickly bridging the distance between the car and the house, his heart pounded as he leapt up the steps to the beautifully carved old wooden doors. Turning the key in the lock, he slipped inside to marvel again at Davrew's handiwork, admiring the carved and hand painted finish to cabinets and the large solid colonial table and chairs in the kitchen. Touching one high back chair and caressing the delicate different star patterns that adorned it, he smiled. It was stunningly beautiful and showed the essence of Davrew so much Richard almost cried. The need to see his partner increased. How could he apologise and make up for such foolish behaviour? Richard ran up the stairs taking them two or three at a time. He paused at the bedroom door and peeked in, the thought of the last time he was in that bed was heartbreaking. Remembering the hurt in Davrew's eyes as Madeline dragged him away that weekend left him aching.

The sound of a car stopping outside brought Richard back to the present. The car door slammed as he retraced his steps to the top of the stairs.

'Hello,' a deep voice called from the entrance. A tall wiry young man was peeking around the door he had opened, 'anyone home?'

'Up here,' Richard replied as he started back down the staircase. 'Who are you?' He greeted the visitor with a scowl.

The man looked up in surprise. 'I'm sorry to come barging in,' he muttered in embarrassment. 'I thought, when I saw a car in the drive, that Davrew might be back.'

'I'm Richard Davidson, Davrew's friend and partner in this orchard and home. You're a friend of Dav's?'

'Tod Longmire,' he nodded while holding out a large, callused hand in greeting. Richard scrutinised the stranger. The name fitted the tall lean frame. Tight dark curls covered his head and crowned his angular bearded face. The pronounced Roman nose reminded him of a school friend whom Richard had taunted endlessly. 'Yes, I helped Dav renovate some of the furniture. I mean...' Tod paused, 'Bill across the way helped with the basic sanding back and restoration, I helped with the artistic side.'

'The artistic side?' Richard queried.

'The painting, carving motifs and the like,' the stranger replied.

Richard looked again towards the table in the kitchen and recalled the other delicate and intricate designs throughout the home.

'You've done a wonderful job, Tod.' He paused and studied a spot on the floor for a moment, shuffling uneasily. 'I didn't know you were Davrew's friend, I'm ashamed to say.' Tod dismissed Richard's discomfort quickly.

'Davrew was very particular about the designs.'

'I bet,' Richard nodded. 'I was just about to leave when you pulled up, so, if you don't mind...'

'I saw you pull up because I was in the old shed at the corner of the block. Davrew asked me to stay there and finish some other work. I've been pretty much living there, with Dav's Okay, of course.'

'Of course,' Richard added, feeling surprised and pleased with Davrew for leaving someone to look after the place other than Bill and Pat.

'I've just finished a big job Dav asked me to do. When I saw the car, I thought it would be a good time to bring it round.'

'You want to bring it in now?' Richard ran his hand through his hair. 'Is it big?' Tod nodded. 'Do you want me to help you bring it in?'

'Yep, I've got some other jobs on the go and I need to make room for them. It won't take long, and you can be on your way.' They both walked out through the front door to the battered old ute Tod had driven up in. Richard noticed the load was making the tray ride low. It was a multi-coloured truck, scratched and well worn. A large tarpaulin was draped over something in the back. 'I'll just move these,' Todd moved aside paint tins, a small step ladder, an easel, rope and other assorted artists' needs. Then he flipped the cover away dramatically.

Richard stood, mouth agape. 'It's fantastic!'

'Thank you.' Tod accepted the accolade. 'Dav was very insistent with this one. Not only did I have to create the exact design, but the colours had to be exactly right too. If you feel the stars, you'll see they're raised like Braille.'

'It's perfect! But...' Richard's face went pale. 'When did Davrew ask you to do this?'

'About six or seven months ago, I guess.'

'Did Dav have a special place in mind to put it?'

'Yep, upstairs. Are you feeling strong?' Tod added jocularly.

'This is just beautiful. I bet it surpasses all Dav's expectations.'

'I hope so, Richard,' the tall man tapped the ornately decorated bathtub. 'We'd best make a move. It'll be a job to get it up those stairs, but I think the two of us can manage it.' Tod had the bath loaded onto a caster-wheel trolley, which with some effort they unloaded from the ute. Richard opened the front doors wide and they carried the load into the foyer. They rested at the bottom of the stairs briefly before making the assault. The staircase was the most difficult part, but they managed to reach the top with only a few brief stops on the stairway.

'I finished the bathroom tiling last week, the tile rectangle is its resting place,' Todd nodded the way.

Richard opened the door to the bathroom and noted the pale blue tiles Tod had laid for the purpose. The floor around it was polished wood and the walls painted a very pale lemon, the ceiling was also very pale blue. After they jostled the tub into its resting place, they took a break.

'It really looks at home here, doesn't it?' Tod announced admiring his handiwork.

'Yes, it's brilliant. I can tell you Davrew will be delighted.'

'Davrew belongs here too, if you don't mind me saying so,' Tod added, looking a little apprehensive at Richard. 'Dav always said this place needed to be used, full of people, children and laughter, seemed to me like this place was kind of special for him.' Richard didn't know how to answer. He just nodded stupidly and shook Tod's hand saying his farewells. They walked quickly to the door and Tod was out and in his ute moments later, trundling back down the drive.

With a quick look at the sky Richard was pleased to see thick clouds overhead. Rain threatened, a storm was brewing. Gladly he locked the front door from the inside and bounded up the stairs past the bedrooms to the landing leading to the attic.

'I've got some apologising to do,' he mumbled to himself as he pulled down the attic ladder. 'I think Dav might have some explaining to do too.' Soon Richard sat comfortably in a small bus sized silver craft, checking dials and weather. A panel in the roof of the old home slid aside and his little vehicle swept quickly upwards into the storm. Looking at the rear-view panel he made certain the roof had rearranged itself and that no evidence of his departure could be seen. He was glad they'd made this addition to the house so that friends like Andre and Rimi could come visit. Their own small spaceships fitted into the attic space. Now it was empty.

Hours later Richard was in France. Nervously he watched the shed roof open as he slipped his craft down through the cloud. His small spaceship concealed in the vineyard outbuilding Andre had provided. He jumped out and stretched his shoulders. There was no one there to greet him. Even though he'd let them know he was coming. The breeze was warm, he could smell the jasmine that grew in abundance around Andre's cottage. Summer in the northern hemisphere and late afternoon or early evening Richard thought. With a heavy heart, he walked along the track to the house. It was a small stone-built farmhouse, with pitch roof, shuttered windows, and beautiful surrounding garden. The small Giet not far away from the main home was for guests. He and Davrew had lived there for several months on their return from Orthama.

Andre came out of the house, with his hand outstretched he closed the distance between them. At first, he shook Richard's hand, then pulled him into an embrace. Andre was sobbing.

'Your timing is good,' Andre pulled away as he wiped his eyes. 'Davrew is having your baby now.'

'Jeez,' Richard whistled, 'and you are thinking of Rimi.' Andre nodded and they went inside up the stairs and into large bathroom. A beautiful birthing tub in the middle of the room.

'Richard,' Davrew smiled then grimaced. 'Our Miri is coming into this world.'

'Miri?' Richard knelt beside the tub as Davrew let out a scream. 'Jeez Dav, I didn't even know you were pregnant.'

'You had other things on your mind,' Davrew panted.

'I've been a bloody fool,' Richard knelt beside the tub.

Andre was on the other side of the bath. 'Davrew is doing well, Richard.

'I've so much to talk to you about,' Richard sighed.

'It'll, have to, wait,' Davrew took Richard's hand and squeezed it tight, letting out another scream as the contraction pulsed long and hard. 'Not long now.'

'Davrew has been in labour since the middle of the night,' Andre yawned, 'only got in the birthing tub in the last hour.'

'Miri,' Richard smiled, 'what a lovely name.'

'Giving me hell right now,' Davrew wheezed, tightening his grip on Richard's hand again, as the next contraction hit.

The off world medical team offered advice from the console in the corner of the room. Only an hour later, Andre helped ease the child from Davrew's tired body. They all watched the baby swam in the nutritious fluid in the birthing tub exploring the star pattern inside the tub.

'They learn from the moment they are born,' Richard watched in wonder. 'Miri, you are perfect.'

'Of course,' Davrew smiled, 'Miri is our child. Yours and mine, Richard.'

'I've left the city for good,' Richard still held Davrew's hand. 'I handed in my resignation. I'm coming home for good. If you'll have me.'

Davrew looked up and smiled. 'We'll have to talk about that.'

'Not now,' Andre interrupted. 'Davrew needs sleep, the baby will sleep comfortably, still getting the nutrients from the birthing fluid. It will be a few days before Miri is ready to take a first breath of air.'

Davrew was already nodding off.

'Won't Dav get cold?' Richard slowly disentangled his fingers.

'No, the tub is heated, just warm enough to make it comfortable for them both, your partner has done you proud.'

'Davrew always has,' Richard sighed.

'You'll work it out. Now your baby Miri, born on the twelfth day of June 1965, will keep you both busy,' Andre grinned.

'I didn't even think of the date, it was the thirteenth back home,' Richard stood up slowly. The baby was in the crook of Davrew's arm, still covered and sipping in the fluid. 'It's amazing.'

CHAPTER TEN

---

# BACK TO THE FARM

February 1966

'That's strange,' Pat muttered. 'Bill, both the travel agent and the airport say they have no international flights from Europe today at that time.' Bill walked across the kitchen and put his empty mug in the sink. Pat watched him from her stool, perched beside the wall phone.

'Doesn't matter what they say, love, Richard rang twenty minutes ago saying he and will pick up Dav and they'll be home in an hour. He probably came in from Hong Kong or somewhere after a couple of stops on the way.'

'Guess so,' Pat agreed. 'I'm sure you are right.'

'I'll head off now and pick up mother,' Bill walked to Pat's side and pecked her cheek, 'I won't be long.'

'Ask her to bring her nightie, Bill, she can stop over. I only hope both girls will be sleeping while she's here alone with them. It's really a bit much for her these days, with a seven-teen month old and three-month old babies.'

'Pat, my mother is a tough old bird,' he scolded. 'She gets about pretty well on her stick. She can still cook and clean for herself mostly. You know she loves the girls and minding them is a treat. She adores Carly and is besotted with our little Debbie.'

'I just worry she might have another fall. She was so down after the last one. I had hoped she would keep getting meals on wheels, but I guess it's good the home help come once a fortnight to make sure she's on top of the housework and shopping. There's room here, Bill, and with her sight getting worse, it would be no problem.'

'Now, Pat, don't fret about mother. She likes her own space and until she says she wants to leave the old house, that's where she should stop. I'm off now. I'll ask her to if she will sleep over, but I don't think she'll have a bar of it.' Pat sighed and nodded as he stepped toward the back door.

'You're looking forward to seeing Davrew again, aren't you?'

'Too right,' he grinned back. 'Richard's been hard at work in the garden, getting the packing shed in good shape too with extra benches for sorting. Maybe that lazy bastard has changed his tune and is now ready to work.'

'Richard does keep saying things have changed, and soon we'll see how much,' Pat reminded her husband. He waved quickly and left the house, shutting the door behind him with a thud. Pat had been relieved when Richard returned the month before, after eight months in Europe. Bill had kept things ticking over at the orchard while they were away. Being February now, with the shearing due to be started, and, the new wheat crop to be sown, she was glad Bill could hand the dramas of the picking season, back to his cousin. Last year had been a nightmare she knew he didn't want to repeat.

An hour later, Nancy was happily resting in their lounge recliner chair while both the girls were asleep. They said their good-byes and climbed into the battered old ute. Bill gripped the steering wheel like a vice and sprayed dust across the highway as he spun the vehicle into the McGuire property driveway.

Shortly afterwards they stopped beside the beautiful new central garden circle, Richard had planted, with Bill's help. Filled with lovely English shrubs that would grow to cover the entrance roundabout. The aromas were already evident and even though the plants were young and small it was a delightful display. Pat smiled as she watched Bill bounce up the stairs ahead of her.

'Yoo-hoo, anyone home?' Bill called.

'In the kitchen,' Richard replied. Pat followed her husband across the foyer and past the stairs into the adjoining large country kitchen. 'Hi,' Richard greeted them warmly, shaking Bill's hand firmly then kissing Pat on the cheek. 'Dav's freshening up, it was a long journey. Would you like a cuppa?'

'Love one,' Pat answered. Bill nodded and pulled out a high-backed chair.

'You'll have a lot of work about here soon,' Bill remarked while slipping his solid bulk into the comfortable body-hugging chair.

'Oh, Bill, let them settle a bit, will you? There's plenty of time to talk of work,' Pat scolded. Richard poured the hot dark brown liquid into four mugs. He handed two to his guests, then put the others on the table.

'We've got some surprises for you. They may take some getting used to, but I hope you'll be okay about it all.'

'What do you mean, Richard?' Bill asked.

'Well, a couple of things really,' Richard added while sitting to look directly into the eyes of his guests. 'Firstly, I'm opening a little shop in the town. I did manage to keep in touch with my old boss and I suggested an outlet in the country could be the thing. Farms are business and need organising. The future is in computers for farms and private use. Right now, of course, people don't see it so much, but they will.'

'Computers are big bloody useless machines from what I can see. So, you'll be leaving Dav to run the place again,' Bill huffed.

'Not at all, Bill. I wouldn't have a shop that wasn't local. Not only that, but Davrew will have a hand in it as well.'

'How?' Pat couldn't control her curiosity.

'Dav's a dab hand at computer repairs. We make an unbeatable team. I'm the super salesman and Dav's the best technician. Naturally showing local farmers the benefits of keeping accurate records in running the orchard and this property will help.'

'So,' Bill gulped a mouthful of the still steaming liquid. 'What about this place?'

'We'll be living here and working here all the time,' Richard explained. 'The shop is a diversification. Just like you have wheat and sheep, we'll have the orchard and the computer shop. It's a tough time in the apple market right now, we are thinking that we may have to go into whole new varieties to survive. That takes financing, Bill. You know, it's never easy.'

Pat shifted in her seat. 'Richard,' she spoke slowly, 'you said there were other changes?' He nodded simply and smiled. 'Well, just now, I thought I heard a child cry.'

'Come on, love,' Bill scoffed, 'you're a good mother but you can't hear them from here!'

'Pat's not hearing things, Bill. That's our other big change. We've got an eight-month old babe to rear now, which is great. Dav says our baby Miri gives us a real sense of purpose. We just love being a family.'

'What do you mean? Baby? Are you bloody mad?' Bill spluttered. 'You two blokes can't just start getting' kids to raise and stop the town from gossiping!'

'Bill, you don't understand,' Dav was at the door with a babe in arms. The infant was fair skinned, blond haired with clear blue, alert eyes. 'Hush now, Miri,' Dav jiggled the child and added in soothing tone. 'This is your Aunty Pat and Uncle Bill. They're here to welcome us home. There's no need to cry.'

'What the,' Bill stood up. 'Hells Bells,' Bill continued, 'what the flamin' heck is going on?'

'My God, Dav,' Pat announced, 'you look radiant, and if I didn't know better, I'd say you have a baby bump.'

'I'm only in my first trimester, and I've been unwell with it,' Davrew bought baby Miri over to Pat and handed the child to her.

'Miri,' Pat smiled, 'that's a lovely name.'

'Don't be silly, love, Dav can't be,' Bill spluttered in disbelief. 'It can't be Dav.'

'Miri is our first-born child, and Pat is quite right, I am pregnant. I'm still your friend, and of course it's me, Bill.'

'Oh, shit,' Bill stammered feebly, shaking his head.

'We can explain,' Richard pleaded. 'It's a long story though.'

'I'm not sure I want to hear,' Bill remarked.

'We can hear you out,' Pat agreed, 'but there's nothing to say we'll like it.'

Davrew sat down beside Richard, 'please hear us out Bill, don't go rushing off in a huff.' Bill sat down and shifted in his seat.

'I'm not promising anything,' Bill grumbled.

'Dav, this baby has your eyes,' Pat rocked the child gently.

'You think so. I think she has Richard's hair,' Davrew replied.

'How the heck can that be? You've flipped,' Bill grunted.

Half an hour later Bill was running out of the house. He ran down the stairs like the devil was at his heels. Pat followed close behind. 'Bill wait, give them a chance, perhaps we can still be friends.'

'No bloody way, Pat,' Bill was adamant. 'I'm keeping clear of this place, and it from outer space living here. Cripes, I've never heard such a thing.' He slammed the door of the ute waiting only long enough for Pat to slide into her seat before planting his foot on the accelerator and speeding out of the drive. Pat also realised the brief reconciliation between the cousins was over.

'What will we say to mother?' she whispered.

'Nothing,' Bill replied. 'Let her think we've had a blue and leave it at that.'

CHAPTER ELEVEN

# KNOWLEDGEABLE NANCY

September 1968

Nancy felt the warm spring sunshine seeping into her body, penetrating chilled bones and aching muscles. She was distracted by the sound of heavy footsteps and something being dragged across the wooden floorboards behind her. She heard the door shut and the key turn, closing a part of her life.

Leaves rustled in the trees, and the fragrant smell of flowers blooming nearby was carried to her on a gentle breeze, which caressed her face. Turning her head to the sky, she squinted and smiled imagining an expanse of blue scattered with cotton wool clouds. Her eyes could no longer show her these visions, but her mind brought it vividly to life.

'Just finished, Nancy,' a woman's deep voice grunted as she made the final effort and dragged the cases further onto the verandah. 'The house is all clean and I've packed your clothes and knick-knacks.' Her heavy breathing began to subside a little as the woman stood for a moment to catch her breath. 'It's quite warm today, isn't it? Perhaps I should move you into the shade.' Without taking heed of Nancy's protests the woman moved her wheelchair back against the wall under the overhang.

'Thank you, Susan, I'm alright in the sun.' Her

friend ignored her.

'That's better, isn't it? Well, I must be going soon, my little darling grandson Ned is in a school play today. Remember I told you about it?'

Nancy sighed, 'yes, Susan, you told me last week. Thank you for helping. Pat said she'd be over mid-morning, I'm sure she won't be long.'

'Alright then,' the plump woman concluded. 'It's just on 11 o'clock. If you're okay, I'll go now.'

'Good. Thank you, Susan,' Nancy tried not to sound relieved.

'Oh my,' Susan announced. 'That friend of yours is coming up the drive. I expect he'll wish you well. I doubt Pat will have the likes of him in her house.'

'Davrew, you mean. Why ever not?' Nancy squeaked.

'Now, Nancy, don't go getting upset,' Susan chided. 'I wonder if Pat will mind if I ring tonight to see how you are settling in.'

'Of course, she wouldn't mind,' Nancy scolded. 'I'm going to live with my son and daughter-in-law, I'm not going to prison. I'm not dead yet and I can still do what I please.'

'So, you will, dear,' her friend agreed in a condescending tone. Then with a brief peck on Nancy's cheek, Susan left. Nancy listened as Susan trudged down the porch steps. Shortly after, Davrew's soft foot fall made her grin. He bounced up the wooden planks without causing a creak.

'Hello, Dav, dear,' Nancy called in delight, 'so glad you're here.' Long strong arms wrapped around Nancy's frail body, hugging her warmly.

'I'm always happy to see you, too,' Dav smiled and kissed her gently on the cheek. 'It's such a beautiful day. You feel cold, Nancy. Would you like to sit in the sunshine?'

'Yes, dear, I certainly would,' Nancy sighed.

'I see,' Dav remarked, 'Susan has been bossing you around again.'

'Oh Dav, she means well, and she's been a great help, but she never listens to what I say,' Nancy shook her head. 'Still, I'm not complaining. I'd never have got the house packed up without her.'

'But you want to enjoy your last little while here, doing what you want to do.'

'You always understand.' Nancy nodded.

'I know how you must feel. Back home, before I came here, I tried doing things for myself. It wasn't popular. I think Richard and I became friends because I was a little different.' Davrew perched himself on the old suitcase beside Nancy's wheelchair. They sat together soaking up the sun and holding hands.

'Thank you, Dav, for always being there for me. Helping build the ramps as well as making sure I could always get about.'

'I'm glad to always help you, Nancy. It could be a little harder for me to see you as often from now on. Bill hasn't spoken to me for years, but Pat has asked me to come over as often as I can, when he's not about.'

'What time is it, pet?' Nancy asked.

'Eleven fifteen, Nancy. Why? Is Pat due to come already?

'No, we have an hour or so before she'll arrive,' the old lady paused. 'Time enough for you to tell me why Bill hasn't spoken to you in years. He won't tell me, and Pat is always vague, saying it was a silly disagreement. My friend Alice tells me there's all sorts of gossip in the town about you and Richard. She's kind about it, really. Susan, on the other hand, can be quite cutting. She makes no bones about saying you two are 'boys who like boys' and that kind raising children is a sin against God. She's always making remarks about how strange it is that a nephew of mine should get mixed up in that sort of thing,' Nancy sighed. 'I'm blind, Dav darling, not stupid. I could see how much Richard meant to you the first night you came here. So, tell me the truth. It's time I heard it all.'

'It's a big universe out there, Nancy. I'm always amazed at how narrow-minded some people are here. When we told Pat and Bill, all about how Richard and I met, they couldn't accept the truth.'

'And you haven't told me for fear I'd turn away from you too?'

'Well, I don't want you to hate me. Pat is alright now. She talks to us and even enjoys the children visiting, but Bill,' Davrew blew out a frustrated whistle.

'I'm not Bill, Dav. You've been a good friend to me for many years. So, tell me the truth, I'm not afraid to hear it.'

'I don't think Bill would want you to know,' Dav swallowed then lent forward and nearer to her face, 'alright, I'll tell you.'


Pat pulled up to take Nancy to her new home over an hour later. Davrew had time to explain the whole story. He told her all he could tell about the world he had come from, and how he and Richard had met. Nancy was delighted, not afraid at all, and happy.

'Now I understand, Pat love. I still want to be able to see Dav and Richard and especially the children very often, and I will, won't I dear?'

'Yes, mother, of course.'


The months passed more quickly for Nancy. Pat and Bill led busy lives and their two beautiful daughters Carly and Debbie were a constant delight. Davrew brought their three children, Miri now three, Gem an inquisitive two-year old and the youngest baby Bon. The sound of giggling as the children played together was music to her ears. Although it was hard to get about, even with the wheelchair, she hid the pain she felt as much as possible from her family. Nancy did not want to be remembered as a grumpy old woman.

Davrew went to France in May 1968 and returned late October with another babe in arms.

'Nancy, what have you been up to?' Davrew brought the new baby to Pat and Bill's house as soon as possible after getting back.

'Oh, Dav dear, I've gone and had another fall,' Nancy squeaked her reply

Davrew looked up at Pat and Bill who were hovering in the doorway.

'We did everything we could to make mum comfortable. To take any obstacles away,' Bill snapped.

'I'm certain you did,' Davrew replied. 'No one is blaming you for an accident.' Bill snorted and stormed out of the room.

'He's just upset it happened,' Pat walked over to Nancy's bedside and plumped up her pillows.

'No one is blaming anyone,' Nancy wheezed. 'I just slipped.'

'Dav, it's good to have you back,' Pat nodded towards the baby capsule. 'And who is this little one?'

'Sal,' Davrew lifted the baby out then handed the infant to Pat. 'Born on the 20th September 1968 now just over a month old, feeding well, growing strong. The children are just so wonderful together.'

'May I hold Sal?' Nancy held out her arms. Pat, who was rocking the child in her arms, held back. Davrew nodded. Pat gave Nancy the child, she arranged her to sit comfortably.

'Sal,' Nancy whispered. 'I hope I'll be here to see you turn one.'

Davrew sat beside Nancy and put his hand on hers. 'Of course, you will.'

Nancy hugged the infant on her lap and touched

the child's face with the fingers of her other hand. 'Beautiful,' she smiled. 'Dav, dear, you'll have your hands full with four now.'

'Is Richard coming over soon?' Pat asked.

'Yes, he'll here shortly. He wanted Tod to come to the house while he came over. He's a bit worried about you Aunt,' Davrew squeezed Nancy's hand.

'I'm alright, please don't fret, either you or Richard,' Nancy smiled and nuzzled her nose into the baby's head, savouring the smell. When Richard walked in, he kissed his aunt and smiled at the sleeping child.

'They are so quiet when they are asleep,' Richard grinned at Davrew.

'That's a blessing from the stars,' Dav beamed.


As 1968 ended and the new year began, Nancy found the radio a great comfort. She loved the music but found the news about the Vietnam War disturbing. When she heard reports of battles being won or lost, the sound of gunfire and explosions behind a reporter's commentary, she shivered. Pat's younger brother had been called up in the draft.

'Bill, you could be called up, and so could Richard.'

'Not likely, Mother, there's no fear of that,' Bill reassured her, 'I'm over thirty and Richard is twenty-eight. They only want the younguns. We also provide a good excuse because we run farms.'

Meanwhile, Nancy waged her own war against pain. Gradually, she lost interest in everything, even the radio. Nurses and therapists came in to clean and change her and exercise her deteriorating muscles and joints. Finally, the doctors stopped prescribing tablets and started giving her injections. Family and friends visited, to say hello, coming and going quickly. Only Davrew came and sat for long periods reading, chatting, and rubbing her aching muscles with soothing cream. Bill tolerated these visits for his mother's sake. Even allowing Richard to come and share meals with the family and all the children. The house was full on those visits. But the noise ebbed when Nancy became frailer.

Finally, in late November 1969, Nancy was released from her battle, and the pain ceased forever. At the local church, a short service was held. Afterwards they all gathered around a burial plot, dug under a large oak tree at Nancy's home. She was laid to rest beside George, who had been buried there so many years earlier.

CHAPTER TWELVE

# GROWING FAMILY

### February 1970

Davrew walked into the kindergarten glass-room porch which served as a foyer to the kindergarten. Even before opening the next door, he knew Gem was crying. The old weather-board building was brightly painted and adorned with colourful posters on childcare tips and information.

With a brief polite knock, Davrew opened the door and peeped in. Children were gathered in many small groups about the large, well-lit room. Some sat at the tables and chairs, creating works of art out of cardboard boxes. Others were in the dressing up corner, trying on hats and old clothes. Still others were busy splashing paint on the paper, floor, easels, and children around them.

There was Gem near the kitchen, almost drowning out the general hubbub of sound with an incessant wailing. The teacher had the child on her lap, trying vainly to pacify his distress. She was a large round woman with the type of hair that seemed to still be in rollers. She pursed her lips in a slight smile of relief and gestured Davrew to go to her aid.

'Hello, Mrs. Eldridge, what seems to be the problem?' Davrew tried not to sound too anxious. The kindergarten year had begun two weeks earlier, and

Gem had been settling in well, up to now.

The teacher was a little flushed as she answered, 'oh, it's just children teasing each other, you know,' Davrew nodded and let the woman continue. 'Gem has been working well at all of the activities today. Why, just a little while ago he made a beautiful tower out of the blocks. Didn't you dear?' The blue eyed, fair-haired child looked at the woman briefly, and the wailing momentarily stopped.

'I was just playing. They were being mean,' the child sobbed.

'Now, Gem darling, there's no need to get so upset,' Davrew bent over and plucked the child up from the woman. The teacher looked him up and down momentarily giving Davrew the impression he was being assessed. He hoped the loose-fitting navy tracksuit he was wearing was baggy enough. Or, the woman would mistakenly think Davrew had a slight 'beer gut', as often happened with the local townsfolk.

'It is unusual for a lad of Gem's age to start playing with dolls and say he's going to have babies when he grows up. Naturally, the other children teased. Perhaps we can discuss why this might be? Gem is a charming child in all other respects.'

'Thank you, Mrs. Eldridge, for your interest, perhaps another time,' Davrew quickly headed towards the door with the child clamped around his neck in a bear hug. 'Now if you'll excuse me, I've just dropped our eldest off at school and two others younger are being cared for by their aunt, so I'll head home and take Gem with me. We'll talk about what's happened here today, Mrs. Eldridge. I can assure you this won't happen again.'

'It's just I've heard some strange stories about things that happen in your part of the world,' the dark-haired woman followed him to the door. 'Gem is only four, Mr Davrew, perhaps he just needs another year at home.'

'It's just Davrew, Mrs Eldridge. Gem will be fine for the rest of this year, I'm positive. Bye.' Quickly closing the door in the teacher's face, Davrew blew out relieved breath, then darted across the foyer through the outer exit and to the car.

At the dinner table in the evening the Davidson family sat around the table, eating steamed vegetables. Sal, the youngest sat on booster seat at the end of the table between Richard and Davrew. Bon, the three-year-old was beside Gem the four-year-old, Richard's side of the table, while Miri, the eldest, sat beside Davrew.

'This is the best part of the day for me,' Davrew pushed a fresh plate of food slightly away and rolled his eyes. 'What a day I've had though. Miri never cried at kindy about such things,' Davrew sighed.

'Such things?' Richard prompted. 'Every child is different, Dav darling. I'm sure it'll work out,' Richard smiled and wiped Sal's pea green smeared face.

'By the stars, Richard, that's the 'she'll be right' apathetic attitude I get from most people around here. Our differences won't just go away. We need to discuss how we are dealing with people around us.'

Richard nodded but didn't get the chance to speak when a feisty five-and-a-half-year-old Miri cut into the conversation.

'Please don't argue about this,' Miri pleaded. 'I'm older than Gem, and I like people to think I am a girl. I want to have lots of babies. When I do, I don't want to travel to France, so people won't talk about me.' Richard stifled a chortle. Miri was only fourteen months older than Gem after all.

'This is serious,' Davrew glared at Richard. 'It would be better, Gem, if you just let people treat you as a boy. Please try not to get upset about it.'

Gem pouted and pushed the remaining food around his plate with a spoon. 'They are just silly kids.

They can't even read or write. They don't even do homework! I just hate it when they say I can't do something I know I can.'

Richard nodded, 'it isn't easy, little one, but you have to try to get along with your kindy friends.'

'Yes, Gem,' Davrew agreed. 'And we must be extremely careful not to let anyone outside those who know us, find out how different we are.'

Silence descended as they ate, only the clang of spoons against bowls being heard. Davrew got up and brought over large Lemon Meringue pie, putting it in the middle of the table. Knife in hand Davrew began to serve everyone generous portions. 'This was one of Nancy's favourite desserts,' Dav stated simply.

'Can I ask a question?' the three-year-old between the adults queried.

'Of course, Bon love,' Richard touched the child's shoulder, briefly, tenderly.

'Why can't we tell people about why we aren't the same? I think they should all know.' Richard nearly choked on his next mouthful while Davrew's jaw dropped. Miri giggled and nudged Gem, who promptly sprayed lemon meringue in all directions.

'We can't do that Bon,' Davrew began. 'You know just how different we are. You are starting to learn how to be our medic from our kin in space. You have chosen to be our healer and one day you will be able to care for us if we get sick.'

'And when we have babies,' Miri added.

'Bon, it's because it's so strange people can't understand it. Just like when we go to visit your cousins across the road,' Richard struggled to make his fears clear. 'We can only go when Bill isn't there.'

'That's Uncle Bill's prejudice, isn't it?' Miri chipped in.

'No, darl', it's just complicated. Bill is a good man. He just finds new and strange things hard to get used to. Sometimes he just won't try to get used to things, he'd rather stay the way he is.'

'Simply sums up most of the townsfolk here,' Davrew sighed. 'Mostly, they accepted me. It was when they realised that Richard and I were raising children and living together as a family that rejection began.'

'Dav, it's a small country town, naturally there's talk,' Richard reached across the table and squeezed his partner's hand.

'As naturally as, I have to go to Europe shortly, to assume my feminine identity, and have our new baby,' Davrew sighed.

'But' Bon persisted, 'if they know we're different, why not tell them, why?'

'Bon, dear,' Davrew answered, 'we are so different and strange they may want to hurt us or even send us away.'

'That's it,' Richard declared, 'I need a hug from my four wonderful children.' Miri, Gem and Bon left their seats and jumped up onto his lap.

'Me too,' Sal was standing in the highchair. Davrew lifted Sal out and dumped him on top of the other giggling children. Richard hugged them all.

'Okay, you lot, enough. Time for studies and bed,' Davrew ushered the children away.

'And another hug for me,' Davrew smiled while sliding into Richard's now empty lap. Richard patted Dav's stomach that had been expanding more noticeably in recent weeks. They kissed passionately before Richard looked in to Dav's eyes.

'I've got to admit, Dav, I'm feeling out of my depth already with our young family. How can I hope to help them with homework in the future? They already learn things I was doing in upper primary school. It scares me a bit.'

'Don't worry, the computers will help them. Bon will be a wonderful physician and Miri will have many babies.'

'And Gem and Sal?' Richard wondered. 'And Ren,' Davrew pointed toward the unborn child, 'will all contribute to the family.'

'Yeah,' Richard nodded, 'I guess we'll all learn along the way.'

'I've got so much to do today,' Davrew sighed as Richard finished helping put the last of the breakfast dishes away.

'I need to check the orchard. The apples are ready for harvest. Then I can get stuck into the packing shed. There are crates to be pre-stacked for the pickers and sorters,' Richard turned around to give Davrew a hug, patting the large baby bump. 'Are you alright?'

'Yes, it was just a twinge last night,' Davrew planted a lingering kiss on Richards lips. 'I'll run Miri to school and Gem to kindy. Pat said she'd look after Bon and Sal for a while. I do feel a bit tired.'

'You mustn't overdo it,' Richard grinned and started for the door. 'Don't bother doing anything today. Just have a rest.'

'I wish,' Davrew shook his head. 'The pickers will be here next week, and I need to make sure their cabin is ready.'

'You leave for France soon. I can do the packing shed. Half a day and it'll be ready. Bill helped you get it set up well. I do wish he'd get used to us being a family,' Richard wiggled into his work boots. 'Do you need any help in the cabin?'

'No,' Davrew laughed, 'I just need to make sure the beds are made, the plumbing is connected, the shower works, the little wood burner is usable, and the kitchenette stocked with plenty of crockery and utensils. Bill does the same for his shearers, only a little more basic. We've got five gal's and three guys coming. I'll set up a curtain petition, apparently, that's a must,' Davrew shook his head. 'Unbelievable.'

Richard grinned and walked out the door. Davrew followed to see him leave. 'I'll have lunch ready for twelve.'

'I'll be back.' Richard loped off towards the orchard.

Davrew mustered the children into action to prepare for the day. Once all four were clean, dressed, with lunches in their bags. Davrew did the school run. When the battered old sedan sprayed dust up the drive to Pat and Bills house opposite, Bon and Sal squealed with delight.

'You be good for Aunt Pat, won't you?' Davrew looked at the children in the rear vision mirror. 'With both Carly and Debbie in school, like Miri. Aunt Pat gets a bit lonely.'

'We'll be good,' Bon and Sal nodded. 'Can we ask about our homework?'

Davrew shook his head. 'No, I don't think logarithm's and equations are something that she'll expect you to be doing. Just stick to reading and writing but do it playing, remember, you are babies to her.' They all got out of the car.

'Hello, how are you all?' Pat smiled. 'Run into the house, there is a surprise for you in the kitchen.' The children dashed inside. 'We've some new chickens hatching. I bought them in and put them in a box. With the combustion stove on all hours, the kitchen is like an oven. Ideal for the chickens, they've just started hatching.'

'They'll love that,' Davrew moved slowly back to the car clutching his stomach.

'Are you alright?' Pat asked.

'Yes, it's just a twinge,' Davrew replied, 'you go on. I'll come for a cuppa later and pick up the children just after lunch.'

'Ring me if you need me,' Pat smiled.

'I will,' Davrew waved as Pat turned to go into the kitchen.

Back at the McGuire place Davrew collected the egg basket and headed towards the chicken coop. Richard was in the opposite direction. The basket was light and the sun warm in the sheltered chicken hutch that smelled of hay and manure. Davrew started collecting speckled eggs, large and small. The last at the back of the hutch was in the corner. Davrew lent in.

Struck with a spasm of pain Davrew stopped moving and took a few deep breaths. 'Oh, my little Ren, don't leave me,' Davrew cried. The pain intensified, bending over in agony, dropping the egg basket, he limped back to the house. Slow uncomfortable steps across the kitchen to the wall mounted phone. Davrew struggled to see the dial as the pain increased. With a great effort, swirling the old dial around, he called Pat.

'Hi Davrew, missing your two already?' Pat giggled.

'I'm not well,' Davrew answered. 'I think I might be losing the baby.'

Not long after those words were uttered Davrew collapsed on the floor.

Pat made quick work of getting Bon and Sal into her little sedan and skidding out along the drive, crossing the main road, then tearing into the McGuire entrance. Spraying dust as she tramped along then pulled up sharp. She jumped out of the car with the children in tow. Letting out a loud 'Cooee', she prayed Richard had seen her arrive.

Rushing into the house behind the children she found Davrew struggling to sit up.

'We need to get help,' Bon looked up at his aunt.

'I've called out to your father,' Pat answered.

Seconds later they heard the gate creak and Richard ran into the kitchen.

'Dav, oh no, my Dav. Are you alright?' Richard

rushed across the room and knelt beside his partner.

'You do ask silly questions Richard,' Pat snapped.

'I'll make a call,' Bon squeezed Davrew's shoulder. Getting up on a stool the three-year-old dialled. 'Andre, we need your help. Davrew has collapsed and may have lost the baby.'

'France is such a long way away,' Pat shook her head, 'what use is it calling your friends there?'

'It's not so far for us Pat, they have a trainee medic, young Zena has been studying for a few years. With the help of off world tutors, Bon has just begun training in the same field.' Davrew winced as he sat up between Pat and Richard.

'Surely, they are children,' Pat stammered.

'Yes, Zena is nine, with off world help, we'll get Davrew right in no time, at least I hope so,' Richard muttered. 'It sounds crazy I know.'

Within an hour Davrew was upstairs in bed, resting. Richard keeping a bedside vigil. Andre and his three children had arrived. Zena ensured that Davrew was comfortable, vital signs checked, the aborted foetus and other excrement were cleaned up.

'I don't understand how you got here so quickly,' Pat looked at Andre and his children. They were sitting at the kitchen table hot tea in hand. Pat felt like she needed to have a cuppa to quell her own shock.

'We visit often,' Andre looked at her sadly. 'Usually, we have happy visits, this is not so happy. I lost my Rimi in childbirth. Davrew is fortunate you were close by.'

'Pat, we keep our visiting spacecraft in the roof. It slides open and shuts when all are safe inside,' Miri explained.

'What if this had happened if no one was around?' Pat sighed.

'Our loves are from a long way away. We knew the risks when we came back to Earth. Leaving Orthama was hard for both Rimi and Davrew,' Andre sighed. 'Richard has asked us to stay for a while, until Davrew is well again. Losing a child is hard, losing a partner harder.'

CHAPTER THIRTEEN

# MIRI

August 1977

Peter Van Den Gill couldn't shake off the image of one of his English Literature students. He sat at his desk in the crowded teachers' room with eyes closed, and her image filled his mind. She was only twelve, yet quick witted and polite, and answered all questions intelligently without being precocious.

Perhaps his European background was why he found the girl's very pale skin and fair hair enchanting. She always sat erect and attentive in his classes with her neat hair swept back from her face, tied in its perfect ponytail curling just below the collar. This highlighted her high cheekbones and crystal blue eyes. Everything seemed slightly amusing to young Miri Davidson. The smile that so easily sprang to her lips was slightly crooked. He had passed comment on her to his fiancée, once too often, and she'd retorted angrily, 'you're becoming obsessed with that child. Anyone would think you were looking at her with more than academic interest. We're in the seventies now, Peter, but as far as I'm aware Carnal Knowledge is still a crime.'

Since then he'd kept his thoughts to himself. Peter totally rejected the thought he might have any physical interest in any of his students. Every teacher in the college was aware of the furore which had developed over 'sexual influences' of girls who were extremely susceptible to their mixed emotions during puberty. He knew many of the girls had enormous infatuations for the more attractive male teachers. He counted himself, rather immodestly, as one who had a large following.

Peter sat at his desk, pencil in hand, in front of a pile of papers still to be marked. The afternoon was growing short, long shadows falling across the desks from the high windows on the opposite side of the room.

Now he pushed the papers aside to concentrate on the proposal for excursions to be approved for the following semester. He'd put forward the proposal of a visit to a working orchard. This had been met with official interest, pending final details being arranged, and Peter's follow up on the idea. An essay on the day's excursion would fill the English department requirements and satisfy the Principal. This would go towards the annual assessment for students attending, so Peter was happy to do the legwork.

He had approached Miri with the idea, and she had insisted there would be no problem. After speaking with Miri's father Richard on the telephone, it was arranged. The following Saturday he would visit the farm and discuss the details of possible dates and ideas for the excursions.

The orchard was only a twenty-minute drive from the school. A day trip would be inexpensive for parents and students alike. The Economics Department and Business Studies Departments had agreed the visit would be well worthwhile. Peter didn't mind being left with organising the details.

Saturday Peter found the drive to Davidson's orchard relaxing, with the sun streaming in warmly through the car window on the brilliant late August day. Slowly he drove up the impressive tree lined drive that ended in a circular round about. A neat old English garden was planted in the centre piece adding charm to the setting. As he got out of the car, the biting chill and fresh smelling air assaulted his senses. The chill of winter still lingered, he plunged his hands deep in his pockets, and turned his collar up to protect his neck. A tall fair-haired man was walking down the front steps with an outstretched hand. He wore jeans and a roll neck jumper. Peter received the warm welcome eagerly, dissolving the last of the initial fears he had about asking permission for these excursions to take place. It was, after all, not an easy thing to allow large groups of adolescents to come tramping through their property.

'Hello, I'm Peter Van Den Gill, Miri's English Literature teacher.'

'Hi, I'm Davrew,' which was accompanied by a strong handshake. 'Let's go through to the kitchen for refreshments and a chat. Miri has given us the general idea of what we might expect.' They walked quickly through the foyer and off through a short passage past a sweeping staircase into the warm kitchen. Peter gratefully accepted a cup of hot tea and began to discuss details of the excursions. A woollen rug lay on the floor between the table and an old combustion stove. On it sat a youngster happily playing with blocks. Beside the busy child a baby was attempting to roll about while chewing on the end of a plastic toy. 'This is Tam, who is three and making terrific towers,' Davrew beamed at the children, 'and Ash is our new baby.' Other older children peeped into the kitchen full of curiosity.

Davrew instructed one of the wide-eyed children who stood at the door, to fetch Miri.

'Please call me Peter,' the teacher insisted.

They discussed the number of students who would attend in each bus load, together with possible arrival and departure times.

'I thought on arrival the students could assemble

in the machinery shed. We could explain some of the history of the property and add a little about our natural farming methods and economics,' Davrew smiled while explaining the possible schedule. 'Perhaps some hands-on work in the vegetable garden would help work up an appetite for lunch.'

'Sounds great,' Peter nodded enthusiastically.

'We could explain more about our organic farming methods too.'

'One way of getting the message to sink in, some of these students need a little help there,' Peter quipped.

Davrew laughed, 'and ... some are so quick it's frightening.'

'With your family, I'm sure it is. Miri is a first-class student.'

'Naturally,' Davrew accepted the compliment. 'After lunch, perhaps a walk through the orchard would be a pleasant way of relaxing those curious minds.'

'Wonderful!'

'Then to the packing shed where we'll show the students how we process the fruit. My children are all looking forward to taking part in the whole day, explaining what happens on a child to child level, if it is acceptable?'

'Sounds Okay to me, there would be teachers and yourself or someone present?'

'Of course, Richard or I would be able to assist. The children are extremely capable and often more adept at explaining in everyday terms to their peers, don't you think?'

At that moment Miri walked into the room with an armful of carrots. She quickly crossed the room to the sink and dropped the load, smiling.

'You'll be happy to host these excursions then, Davrew?' Peter confirmed.

'Certainly.'

'Miri, if you will show Mr Van Den Gill around the

property? If you'll excuse me, I'll get on with my other duties.'

'Of course, Davrew, I've taken up a good deal of your time already.'

'Happy to help, Peter.'

'If the first excursion is a success, I'll ask you to do more. Is that alright?'

'I'm sure there will be no problems,' Davrew sealed the agreement with a strong handshake. Peter noticed a knowing smile and wink Davrew directed at Miri. He felt it would be impolite to do more than wonder what it was about. Perhaps it was just admiration for a clever and witty child.

Miri led him through the back door down a path, which was partially overgrown with shrubs on the side, encroaching on its neat clean lines. It was a planned effect, which added to the country charm of the home.

Peter felt relaxed and at ease with the place right from the start. The garden afforded them some shelter from the biting breeze. He felt warm from the sun and the hospitality. They walked through a rickety old gate, which creaked as Miri pulled it open. This brought them in to the farm proper. The gate sealed an isolated garden, beside a large vegetable patch. He was surprised not only by its size, but also by the great variety of vegetables they grew.

Peter realised he was only half listening to what Miri was telling him, so he tried to focus his attention. Something about the Davidson family being highly allergic and having an intolerance of pesticides and chemicals did sink in. 'I didn't quite catch all that, Miri, would you mind repeating what you said?'

'I wondered if you were paying attention.' The quip was an obvious slant on the kind of remark Peter used with students in his classes. They both laughed. Miri's curling lips were thoroughly enchanting.

'I'll try to be more attentive, Miss Davidson.'

'Very well,' Miri assumed a prim posture of reprimand, 'don't let it happen again.' She wagged her finger sternly then allowed herself to be overcome with an attack of the giggles.

Miri spent the rest of the time chatting happily about how they had developed alternative organic and Permaculture methods for their fruit and vegetable farming. The vegetable patch was the main source of nutrition for the family, who were for the most part vegans.

They walked a discreet distance apart while strolling past the vegetable garden through to the orchard. A few of the younger children Peter had seen earlier trailed along behind them. 'Miri loves teacher, Miri loves teacher,' they chanted relentlessly.

'Get back to your chores or I'll see you're set twice as much study tonight!' Miri glared at the youngsters who quickly vanished into the trees. 'I'm the eldest,' Miri explained with a shy smile. 'They are all quite knowledgeable about the property, though. It looks like being a great day for everyone involved with the excursion.'

Peter smiled warmly. 'Well, I must be heading home, it's getting late.'

They walked side by side in silence back to his car. Peter wondered why he felt so sad to be leaving. Briefly they bumped arms as they stepped in unison. It was like an electric shock sped through him, and he was careful to make certain it didn't happen again. Very soon he was fumbling with his keys to open his car door.

'Well, Miri, you have a beautiful home and a lovely family from what I've seen. I do believe the group excursions here will be extremely successful,' he held out his hand to say goodbye. Miri clasped it, then put her other hand on top of his.

'We are a different kind of family, Peter. Unique, in many respects. I hope you see how much soon.' Miri looked intensely into his pool blue eyes. Her own eyes shone in mirror image. Before he realised it, she moved forward and kissed him passionately on the lips.

'Miri – don't!' Peter pulled back, dropping his keys as he did. 'I'm engaged to be married! You know that. You're a student of mine so don't even imagine there can be anything more…'

'Hush,' Miri silenced him with a touch of her fingers on his lips. 'I mean to make you mine Peter Van Den Gill. I am letting you know now so you may choose. It will be a completely different life for you. You may be disgraced in your life outside this farm. But…'

'No buts, Miri. This has gone far enough.' He retrieved the keys from the dirt at his feet and sat quickly behind the wheel of his car.  He slammed the door and tried to start the car, only to flood the motor in his vain attempt at escaping quickly. The car window was open, and Miri touched her hand gently to his arm.

'The choice is yours, Peter, but I'll help you decide,' Miri was amused, he could see it in her crooked smile. The smile had distracted him during classes and left him feeling lost.

'This is preposterous. I'm about to marry Carolyn. Next year I'm in line for a promotion to Deputy Principal. My mother is delighted about both prospects and life couldn't be better!' He yelled as the car finally started and he swung the wheel taking off at speed down the driveway.

Wiping the perspiration from his brow. 'No one else knows what just happened. It is just a juvenile infatuation after all,' he spoke softly to himself.

Suddenly the thought of the excursions being held at the Davidson orchard seemed very daunting. How would he be able to avoid those beautiful eyes and her impish attractive smile?

## CHAPTER FOURTEEN

# PETER

### September 1977

After the first excursion, he had enjoyed time at the Davidson property. Peter's mind was troubled, but Miri made him feel welcome and he had begun to want her company.

'You would be welcome to move in here,' Richard suggested. 'As a lodger there would be no threat of criminal action from us. In fact, if you decide to join our family, we'd offer some protection from recrimination.'

'Thanks for saying so, really there is no reason for me to change my life,' Peter shook Richard's hand and walked away.

The next day at school his class had finished, and he was packing away his books. Miri had joined him at his desk getting too close for comfort. He had chosen this time during recess to speak to her because most of the other students were having sports day. Only a few who did not participate stayed behind.

'Miri Davidson, this charade has got to stop.'

'There's no need to shout.'

'This is all very embarrassing,' he lowered his voice. 'As a student of mine the ramifications, even if nothing happens, rumours and innuendo can kill my career.'

'Why?'

'Why? Why, you ask? Miri, my whole future hangs in the balance. Your behaviour jeopardies everything.'

'How?'

'How? You know how! You are a child, underage in every legal and moral sense. Just the suggestion we're having a relationship is damning.'

'I'm not a child, Peter Van Den Gill. I could prove that to you,' she put her arms around him.

'There you go again!' He pushed her away.

Peter noticed Miri's chin wobbling, although, her hard-set expression proved the battle had only just begun. She walked to the classroom window.

'My father told you we would welcome you into our family,' she added.

'Yes, he did. It's just not that simple.'

'What if I told you something quite unique about me and my family? What if I left this school to complete my studies overseas? And' she turned, hand on her hips staring intently into his eyes. 'What if I asked you to join me?'

'Miri, you really never give up, do you?'

'Well, wouldn't you like to know our family secret?'

He did want to know. In fact, he knew he needed to know.

'We are not the same as you, genetically we are totally different,' Miri returned to Peter's side. She put her hands either side of his face and gazed into his eyes. 'We are not human. Our origin is on the other side of the galaxy.' They heard a noise at the door. Another student had come back to the classroom. Peter realised that the gossip would soon spread. He had to do something. A knot in his stomach began to churn.

As the days passed, Peter realised he was in a foul mood. His thoughts swimming. He found himself seeing his fiancée Carolyn in a different light. They often bickered over the silliest little things. Today he didn't want to battle so he stormed out as an argument began. A walk would settle his nerves, he decided.

Three blocks later he was at his mother's home.

'Hello,' he called while marching through the rose arch along the path to the Victorian style terrace cottage.

'Darling,' a large straw hat bobbed up from the garden bed, her eyes concealed from the visitor. 'Please help me up, dear.'

He took her hand in his and placed his other hand on her elbow to steady her.

'I'm glad you came around. Peter dear, I've a bone to pick with you.' Clear blue eyes fixed her son with a penetrating glare while they walked quickly to the rear entrance. There she took off her gloves and gardening shoes. Her silence sent a shiver down his spine. His mother opened the door and allowed her son to follow her inside.

'I must be in real trouble,' Peter stated the obvious. 'I'll warn you now Mother, I'm in no mood for an argument.'

'You've had another tiff with Carolyn, have you?' Mrs Van Den Gill's eyes became as sharp as piercing arrows aiming at their intended target.

'Son, I'll get right to the heart of the matter. Carolyn says there's nothing she can do to please you right now. You've bought a lovely little unit together. She's getting it ready for when you're married. Decorating, cleaning, working, and tolerating your strange whims. I believe you have a good catch in her, and you'd be foolish to let all that go for some little floozy of a student. Carolyn says you talk about her all the time!'

'Oh, come off it, Mother. There's nothing happening for either of you to be concerned about.'

'Nothing? She's only a child, and, as I understand

it, she is throwing herself at your feet. Can you imagine what the teachers are saying? How much damage has already been done to your career prospects, I can't guess? Why, even when I went shopping yesterday, I overheard some people whispering about me as the mother of the teacher who's having a fling with a child. You can't afford to let this get out of hand, Peter. Your future and reputation are at stake. I shan't stand by and let you behave so ridiculously.'

'Mother, this child has a name, Miri Davidson. She is an intelligent, attractive young adult, strong willed and enchanting. That doesn't mean I'm going to throw this life away for a completely new one. Honestly, I don't think you have the right to judge her without having met her.'

The silence that followed was condemning.

'So, Carolyn is right,' she shook her head and ran a wrinkled manicured hand through her hair so recently released from the confines of the hat.

'Nothing has happened, Mother,' Peter answered the accusation softly.

'You'd better make sure it never does, son. Carnal knowledge is still a crime and I really don't want to visit you behind bars.'

'It won't come to that,' Peter turned on his heels. He'd decided it was time to get away from his mother's barbed tongue and icy glare. 'There's nothing more I can say to you now, Mother. I'll see you later.'

Miri was on his mind a lot. He yearned to taste the lips of the feisty young woman. She was turning his world upside down. Could he change his life? The invitation was there and tempting.

Near the end of the school year in late November, with sweaty palms and a huge lump in his throat, Peter stood outside the Principal's Office. The folded letter held tightly in his hand was neat and practical. It held so much within a few short sentences. He knocked firmly on the door. Some of his teaching colleagues walked past whispering and pointing as he entered the chamber.

'Ah, Peter,' the plump man replied in a slightly squeaky voice. 'Good of you to come at such short notice.'

Peter stood silently as the Principal made some fuss of rearranging papers on his desk. It was a small dingy office crammed with bookcases and filing cabinets. Mr Bob Drinkwater was desperately trying not to look flustered. Yet, the constant repetition of his neatening the folders and papers, together with the slight trickle of perspiration on his brow, displayed his nervousness.

'I believe I can save you any embarrassment, Bob. Here's my resignation,' he lent forward and put the buff envelope in the seated man's hand. The recipient released a deep breath. It was obvious that a weight had been lifted from his shoulders.

'You know you'll never teach again.'

'The resignation is from this position and the Teachers Union. I have a totally new life ahead of me.'

'She's just a child, Peter. You know you are throwing away a very promising career?'

'I know the consequences of my actions. I've already lost a fiancée and my mother has disowned me. Either of these things would have destroyed me last year. I believed this job would be my life.'

'So why give it up? You could take a position in a small country school for a couple of years, let all this gossip fade away, then come back ready to carry on where you left off. You could regret this decision for the rest of your life.'

'I have no regrets. Miri is remarkable in every way. Her family is wonderfully supportive, and I have a new home at their orchard and a new job, too.'

'Perhaps that's what you think now, remember though, Peter, she's so young. She could leave you high and dry in the future.'

'I doubt it,' with that remark hanging in the air, he turned and marched out of the office and away from his former life.

## CHAPTER FIFTEEN

# GEM

### November 1979

It was early morning on a late spring day. The air was crisp, and a heavy dew covered the ground as a tall, lean youth strode purposefully through the orchard across the paddocks into a timber forest. As he walked a pre-determined path, his senses alert to everything around him. The rich smell of eucalyptus filled scent added to the beauty of the surrounding native flora and fauna. Twigs breaking underfoot added to the melody of bird calls greeting the day.

Gem had thick flaxen hair tied back in a ponytail. The thick woollen jumper and moleskin trousers did little to keep the morning chill at bay. A broad content-ed smile covered a face illuminated with joy. Watchful eyes like the deep blue pools of crystal-clear lakes scanned the foliage. Gem loved nature, and this daily ritual set the mood for a wonderful day ahead. He was looking forward to the school camp beginning today. There were opportunities to socialise, learn, and just maybe, to show Terry Ayres just how close their friend-ship could be.

It had been nearly two years since Gem had achieved sexual maturity as a twelve-year-old, he was now fourteen. He felt the differences between fellow students and the Davidson's very keenly. Terry had been the object of true adoration for some time, but it was obvious he didn't take Gem's attention seriously.

Being good at sport helped a great deal in becoming accepted as part of the class group, the main downfall was needing to be very careful not to get injured, as the Davidson anatomy meant that it was important to avoid hospitals and doctors. Even school medicals were curtailed with notes excusing each Davidson child because of religious convictions. Their main differences were their white blood, intolerance of cold or extreme temperatures, which was constantly monitored by Bon, the family medic. This was always done under the direction of the off-Earth base tutors. These same tutors also set each family member an educational study program to offset the primitive human school system. With his unique physical needs in mind, he took great care, and because of this, he was able to participate in most sports.

Gem reflected on how frequently Terry would ask his group of friends to his home to practise basketball. He had a great set up in the drive and usually four or five mates would be 'dribbling' and trying to out 'slam dunk' each other. Terry's mother would call out for them to come and have a drink and biscuit. Gem was glad to be one of the gang members. Today he came home refreshed from his morning walk to collect a pre-packed backpack, and to catch the school bus. He was ready for the school camp to begin.

One week later and Gem had to admit the camp was a bit of a disappointment. The cooking and cleaning rosters were so like those of the Davidson family routine Gem felt cheated of a holiday. Each morning a clanging gong would be sounded at seven am to call the students to breakfast. Every day a rostered group would get up at six thirty to prepare breakfast. The meals were basic and easy to prepare. 'Nittingbool Camp' was hardly roughing it in Gem's eyes. There were four dormitories with fifteen beds in each. All were wooden bunk huts with corrugated iron roofs and built on brick stumps off the ground to protect from flooding. Two teachers or parents slept at either end of the bunkhouse to control the midnight chatter. Each night one hardy parent slept in the nearby recreation hall adjacent to the kitchen to tend the fire in the combustion stove.

On the first day, it rained, but they still managed to get in a short nature walk. Gem soon discovered the well-meaning volunteer parent knew little about the local flora and fauna. The parents and teachers alike welcomed Gem's sound knowledge. The students were divided into three groups, which rotated so everyone had an opportunity to do all the activities. The nearby river provided a canoeing course, a small cliff nearby the abseiling climb and a walking track ran through the forest.

On the fifth and final night, it was planned, the students would camp out under the stars, weather permitting. The Camp provided two, four- and six-man tents for this purpose. After a hike to the campsite five kilometres from the bunk huts they would set up the tents. The plan was to have a roaring campfire with songs and laughter cap off a jolly week in the bush. Many of the students felt less than jolly when the day finally arrived. By now, with the basic washing facilities, and exhaustion setting in, the whole group looked and felt bedraggled.

Gem felt slighted by Terry, who was either deliberately avoiding any contact or just acting dumb. In every case where Gem made flirtatious remarks or subtle suggestions, he had completely ignored them. Tonight, Gem realised, would be his last-ditch attempt to reveal his true feelings.

Early morning saw a mass clean-up of the 'Nittingbool Camp' buildings, outhouses, and kitchen. Then after a tiring hike, the whole group, teachers, parents, and students spent a frustrating two hours assembling tents. A campfire area was cleared, and the packed lunches quickly devoured. Gem was ecstatic to be able to share a two-man tent with Terry. The afternoon was a final sports fling with most people either watching or playing cricket on a makeshift pitch near the evening campfire site. A large barbeque had been brought over in someone's four-wheel drive. Food for a feast was being prepared, as the afternoon shadows grew longer. One teacher yelled instructions for firewood to be collected and four volunteers were needed to help gather kindling.

Naturally, when Terry and his other two friends offered to do the job, Gem did too. The energetic youths all followed in the teacher's footsteps.

Mr Blackmore, the tall, dark-eyed teacher with olive skin and greased back hair, was known to the students as 'Black Adder.' Several students had been expelled after being caught out by the 'Adder.' He was well known for his ability to sneak up on unsuspecting students who were up to no good. He'd catch them either picking a fight or sneaking a smoke behind the shelter sheds. His booming voice and stealth made him a teacher to be treated with care.

They quickly gathered odd sticks and kindling. Mr Blackmore had an armful and piled them into a chubby pair of arms.

'Take these back, Jerkovic, the twigs you've been picking up won't toast marshmallows.' He soon followed suit with the other taller youth called, Cliff Robert's, who spent a lot of time at Terry's as well. 'Ayres take these as well and go back. I'll follow with Davidson shortly.' Terry obliged. Leaving Gem behind with the teacher. He decided to follow quickly. 'Davidson, watch your step!'

The warning came too late. It was getting dark

quickly, and in the half-light, Gem didn't see a large tree root under his armload of kindling. The fall was awkward and heavy. 'Black Adder' loomed above Gem who expected to be helped up.

'You're the one coming on strong to Terry Ayres, aren't you?' The teacher sneered.

'I don't know what you mean,' Gem shook momentarily, feeling a little disoriented.

'I'll show you what you can get for your trouble, child!' The teacher lashed out and Gem felt the blows as they slammed into his doubled-up torso. Each time he struggled to stand; another blow would make Gem crash again into the thick tree trunk.

'No, Sir, Stop!' Gem pleaded.

'You bugger, you little bugger. I'll show you what it's like.' Gem felt clothes being torn while fighting nausea and dizziness. He squirmed and writhed to prevent suffocation. Soon he was completely pinned underneath the heavy sweating body of the crazed teacher, all resistance thwarted.

'No, Sir, please no,' Gem sobbed. 'This is crazy.'

'You, vile scum, this is what I used to do to your kind in Adelaide. You deserve it, slime-bag.'

'No!' Gem yelled defiantly, still wriggling, while large hands closed tighter around his throat. The penetration was excruciating, and Gem's scream was silenced by a huge hand tightening around his neck, almost suffocating and seeing stars. Gem was a helpless victim. Adrenaline seemed to drive the attacker on. Veins stood out on his forehead; Gem could see them pulsating as the man glared through searing eyes.

Back at the camp everyone was sitting quietly listening to the sausages and hamburgers cooking with a gentle sizzle and splutter. The students and adults were all generally winding down after a hectic week. Talk of what they would do when they got back home filled the air. Stephen Raine noticed Gerard Blackmore had been out gathering wood for some time.

'Alex, you went gathering wood, didn't you?' The boy nodded his positive reply. 'Would you take a torch then, and a friend if you like, and see where Mr Blackmore has got to?'

'Yes, Mr Raine,' the boy agreed grudgingly.

'But keep the camp in sight. Listen to where we are. We don't want anyone getting lost now, do we?'

'No, Sir,' the boys called back. The Deputy Principal watched as they disappeared into the trees, waving their flashlights ahead, believing they would all be back soon eating a hearty meal.

Several minutes later the boys came back yelling and wailing. 'He's killing him, it's murder! It's bloody murder!' Stephen Raine rushed to find out what they meant.

'Calm down, boys,' the Deputy Principal spoke reassuringly.

'Mr Raine, you've got to stop him. He'll kill him for sure the way he's going!' Alex exclaimed and grabbed the teachers' arm, pulling him towards the trees.

'Stay here the rest of you, I'll investigate. I won't be long.' He followed the boy with the flashlight for a few minutes before he heard a terrible sound. A muffled struggle was taking place not far away.

'No, stop, please stop.'

Stephen Raine heard a strangled cry, his heartbeat faster. Then he heard the frenzied reply.

'I'll stop you, you little bastard. How does it feel, you little creep?'

'Over there, Mr Raine, I don't want to see it again,' Alex handed the flashlight over and bolted back to the camp.

The Deputy Principal felt his palms become clammy as he walked closer to the fight. 'Gerry, stop it!'

he shouted while trying to pull the crazed teacher off the adolescent. He picked up a large branch to act as a club, hoping at the same moment there would be no need to use it. He saw quickly enough he had no choice, use it he must. With as much force as his sinewy arms could muster, he raised the club and set it crashing down on Gerard Blackmore's back and shoulders.

Gem heard a sound, almost as though he were at the end of a long tunnel. He had no fight left; it was a struggle to breathe. Suddenly it was over. The teacher was struck from behind and fell limply across Gem's torso.

They carried him back to the campsite. He could see the Deputy Principal Stephen Raine looking at him anxiously. Then he saw his friend Terry Ayres speaking to the teacher.

'He'll need these, sir,' Terry Ayres had pulled the thick thermal sleeping bag and blanket out of the two-man tent and brought them with him. 'Gem's family can't take the cold, so he came prepared.'

'We'll have to get him to the hospital,' the teacher said.

'No, Mr Raine,' Terry looked up at the man with pleading eyes, 'Gem's family live near here, we should take him there. They have a kind of clinic at the house because the Davidson's have a rare blood problem.'

'Now, Terry, I know you are good friends with Gem but I'm sure professional care is in order here. We were not informed of any special needs,' the teacher added.

'What about us, are they safe? Black Adder won't come here, will he?' Terry was busy helping put the blanket around Gems shoulders.

'He's almost unconscious,' the teacher replied.

'Please, Mr Raine, we could take Gem in the four-wheel drive we brought the gear here in. The other teachers could take everyone else on a hike to Davidson's orchard. It's only about fifteen walk due north of this camp,' Terry begged.

Gem grunted and tried to nod but began seeing stars.

'Please, Mr Raine, Gem could get worse or even die if he's not treated right, and soon. They know what to do at his place.' They sat Gem down by the campfire. Terry tugged at the teacher's sleeve. 'All the other kids would be better off getting away from here too. The hike will take their minds off what's happened.'

'Thanks for the suggestion Terry. I hope that, other than young Alex and yourself, no one really knows what's happened,' Stephen Raine sighed. He looked around him at the anxious faces and made his decision. 'Very well, Terry, we'll take Gem to the Davidson orchard. I've passed it many times on my way out of town, so I know where it is. I'll go tell the others to prepare for a hike.'

'Okay, everyone, listen up! We've a change of plans. Everyone is going on a short march to an orchard just up the road. Take what you can carry, put on as much clothing as you can. Torches are a must.' Stephen Reine organised the other teachers to start the march. 'This is where it is,' the teacher pointed to a spot on the map. 'Leave the tents. We need to go now.'

Gem looked through half closed eyes as they loaded him into the four-wheel drive. He was struggling to stay conscious. The door slid shut. Terry had Gem's head on his lap on the back seat. Alex was in the passenger seat, the Deputy Principal jumped into the driving seat.

'Before you go,' Gem heard the teacher issue his final instructions, 'bring Gerard Blackmore back to camp. I hope he'll be unconscious for a while. Then get everyone on the move.'

'There's going to be Hell to pay for this little lot,'

the other teacher mumbled, voicing the fears of everyone there. 'What a way to end 1979.'

The head teacher crunched the gears and sped off down the dirt track that led to the highway just as Gem blacked out.

## CHAPTER SIXTEEN

# BON – The Aftermath

### November 1979

Peter had been taking his usual evening stroll to the gates to lock up for the night. He regularly checked the boundary to make sure everything was secure. The gates were large and decorative forming a wrought iron arch across the double width drive entrance. The antique gas lamps, standing on their pillars on either side of the gates, shone softly. Just as he was certain everything was in order, the bright lights of a car shone through into his eyes. It was a four-wheel drive Peter thought may have been using the entrance to turn around on the road.

'Hello,' a voice yelled from the vehicle. 'Is this the Davidson's orchard?'

'Yes, but this is private property. What do you want?' Peter spoke with all the authority his former school-teaching role had afforded him.

'We're from the Camp. Gem is here. There's been some trouble and young Terry Ayres says it's best we get him to you for help.' Peter opened the gates then shone his torch through the window. Seeing Gem was there, he waved them on up the driveway and ran along beside the vehicle until they reached the house. The stiff sliding door of the four-wheel drive creaked open to reveal Gem lying across the back seat, his head cradled by his friend Terry. It was clear he was in distress, with the thermal blankets pulled up to the chin, not preventing teeth chattering and body shivering.

'Wait here, I'll get help,' Peter instructed. Soon a small crowd gathered on the steps.

'What the hell happened,' Richard asked the driver. 'I'm Gem's father.'

'I'll explain, but can we get inside first,' the teacher answered. His red hair shone in the light that hit the vehicle from the well-lit verandah. 'These boys may be in shock, Gem obviously, but Alex and Terry as well,' the teacher nodded towards the boys in turn. 'They should receive medical attention immediately. I can call the hospital and arrange an ambulance.'

'That won't be necessary,' Richard stated and motioned to the lean fair-haired boy at his side. The youth jumped into the vehicle and began a first cursory inspection.

'What the devil?' the teacher asked.

'It's alright, Mister, I'm sorry I don't know your name,' Richard continued.

'Steven Raine, Vice Principal of the school. I'm in charge of the camp. I take full responsibility for the action of our delinquent teacher.'

'Never mind that now, Mr Raine. Bon is competent where our medical needs are concerned. We have a fully equipped clinic upstairs and I'm sure the best place for all of us is there, right now.'

'Really?' the teacher started to get out of the car.

'You can explain the details after we've gone upstairs,' Richard nodded, then helped Terry move Gem towards the door. 'Peter, will you help Mr Raine and I carry Gem?'

Davrew ran down the stairs and added to the group carrying Gem up the stairs. The other children on the verandah stood aside to let them through. Peter and Richard took Gem's arms, while Davrew and Mr Raine his legs. Soon they were moving quickly up the stairs with the unconscious youth between them. At the top of the landing Richard allowed one of the other children who'd followed, to open the door. They lay him on one of the beds at the side of the room.

Bon quickly and thoroughly attended Gem's visible injuries. 'I'm just going to give Gem a mild sedative, Mr Raine. Terry, did you put the thermal blankets around Gem?'

'Yes, Bon. I know your family members don't take the cold well.'

'Thank you, Terry, you probably saved Gem's life,' Bon gave the boys and teacher a quick examination. 'Mild shock, Mr Raine. Did you both see what happened?'

'Just these two, Alex and Terry. They would have an idea of what happened,' the teacher nodded towards the boys. 'Alex discovered the attack and returned to the camp to raise the alarm. I went out and had to stop it.'

'What did happen?' Davrew asked. Richard at his side.

'A vicious attack,' Bon replied simply looking up into his parent's concerned faces. 'These boys need a warm bed tonight. Can we fix up the room next door? I can check on them from here.'

Davrew nodded. Richard put a comforting hand on his shoulder.

'The rest of the camp will be arriving soon. They have hiked here. We couldn't leave them there in case Blackmore revives,' the teacher explained to his hosts.

'We could all do with a night cap and sleep,' Richard ran his fingers through his unruly hair. 'Peter, will you make the machinery shed comfortable for the students?'

'Of course,' Peter started towards the door.

'I'll get the room next door ready,' Davrew moved

mechanically.

'We're all in shock,' Richard squeezed Davrew's arm. 'I'll have a drink for you downstairs when you're finished.'

'I'll help get the shed ready with you if that's okay?' Terry looked at Peter, who nodded.

'Can I stay inside,' Alex whispered.

'Yes, you could join us for a drink first, if you like,' Richard looked at the pale faced lad, who. nodded acknowledgement. Terry shook his head from side to side and followed Peter out the door.

'Are you Okay, Bon?' Davrew whispered.

Bon nodded.

'I'm going downstairs,' he squeezed Bon's shoulder briefly.

They all left the clinic to allow him to do his job.

At the tender age of twelve, and the family medic, the burden of responsibility was heavy on his two slight shoulders. Even as a toddler he knew what being the family doctor really meant. Once Gem was asleep, Bon sat and thought about what to next. It was nearly an hour later he decided to downstairs. Having done as many tests as he dared with his sleeping sibling. The impact of the event suddenly hit home. Sitting at the top of the stairs Bon buried his head in his hands. He'd been surprised at how calm he'd been delivering that first inspection. It was something he'd had to get used to.

The older Davidson children, Sal, and Tam stayed in the dormitory upstairs talking for a time with Alex till his eyelids grew too heavy to keep open. Bon checked on Alex after leaving Gem and was glad to find him drifting off to sleep. He looked exhausted so Bon ushered Sal and Tam away.

'Okay, Bon, we were just leaving,' Sal said defiantly in a hoarse whisper.

'Sal, we almost forgot, Peter wants us to help in

the machinery shed,' Tam's eyes bulged with dismay. 'We promised ages ago and we've been talking.'

'Cripes, Tam, we'd better get goin',' Sal replied taking off quickly down the stairs with Tam rushing behind.

Bon smiled and enjoyed the silence Sal and Tam left in their wake. It was good to be alone. Slowly moving towards the bottom of the stairs, he listened to the muted voices filter up to engulf him. Sitting for a while to gather his thoughts. Although having recently become sexually mature, he felt inept. Would this kind of demand on him increase? It was likely to.

The front door opened. Peter had returned from the machinery shed with Sal and Tam. The older man smiled up at him. Sal and Tam passed Bon as they headed upstairs again.

'We have to go and sleep with Ash and Mica,' Tam told him as they passed.

'I hate being in with the babies,' he heard Sal complain. Bon smiled and continued down the stairs.

'Those two are scallywags, Bon,' Peter watched the youngsters go up the stairs. He drew a deep breath before asking, 'how are you coping with all this?'

'I'm okay, Peter. I just feel kind of washed out.'

'You'll soon feel better down here. The lounge is really the most welcoming room in the house. When I first came here to be with Miri I was struck by its warmth and charm. Here you can really relax.'

Bon nodded. It was time to move on. Reality might wake up deadened senses. He suddenly felt anger and disgust. How could this happen? He got up to speak to the teacher in charge to get an explanation.

He followed Peter across the foyer into the comfortable living room. A large fire burned with a gentle crackle and a flickering glow illuminated every corner with a flickering glow. In the recliner chair, at the fireside, Miri held their baby Fee. Peter reached Miri and kissed her tenderly. Then he stood up and acknowledged their guest.

Bon realised everyone had rallied around in the Davidson family way. Miri handed the baby to Peter and stood up to hand out drinks. The babe slept. Miri plied the visitor with warm drinks and idle chatter. They spoke of the world outside the property. Astronauts and assassinations, movie queens, marriages of the Royal and famous, anything and everything to keep reality temporarily at bay. Now more relaxed their guest let his shoulders slump and stretched out his legs.

Miri sat on the arm of the lounge chair beside Peter after handing Bon a drink. 'Eggnog for you Bon,' Miri grinned.

'Thanks,' Bon felt his face burning. He turned to Peter. 'You've no regrets about changing your life so completely?'

'None what-so-ever, I'm glad to leave that dull and drab former life behind,' Peter smiled and played with the tiny hands of the infant in his lap. Then turned his attention back to the visitor sitting on the couch. The red headed man sitting had arrived as the head teacher at the camp. Bon tapped Peter on the shoulder and nodded towards Richard.

'Sorry, Richard. What did you say?'

'I just wanted to know if they are all settled, Peter, that's all,' Richard said while accepting a glass of port from Miri.

'Yes, hay bales and kerosene heaters, sleeping bags and idle chatter. Just what a school camp is all about really.'

'Good,' Richard agreed. 'I was waiting for you both to arrive before asking Mr Raine here to give us a full account of events.'

'I can tell you all I know, Mr Davidson. But are you sure the child should hear this?' the teacher looked pointedly at Bon.

'Are you Okay, Bon?' Richard asked before going on.

'Yes, Father,' Bon nodded and sipped the eggnog, allowing the warmth to revive him.

'Bon, darling, you don't have to stay if you don't want to,' Davrew spoke softly.

'I would like to know. I am the family medic,' Bon put down his glass and sat down on the floor in front of Davrew. 'Perhaps you should all know Gem has concussion, a fractured nose, ribs, and lower right arm, along with severe scratches and cuts. There'll be a lot more bruising surfacing in the next few days. It looks like Gem had an argument with a truck and lost!'

'And' Peter added, 'child is hardly a word I'd use to describe Bon who is twelve, or my Miri who is fourteen. The Davidson's are mature beyond their years.'

The teacher swallowed hard. 'I don't really know how it began, but I know how it ended. The teacher's name is Gerard Blackmore and till now, I'd have taken him as an ordinary chap. He had a fiancée until recently. It was called off. I know him to be a top rate teacher. I can't imagine what came over him.'

'Gerard Blackmore, you said,' Peter interrupted, 'I've heard of him.'

'And I've heard of you. I only came to this school at the beginning of the year but the gossip about Peter Van Den Gill leaving the school and a promotion to take off with a child is still doing the rounds.'

'Ha, as you can see,' Peter smiled as Miri draped her arm over his shoulder. Their baby now asleep.

'I'll take Fee upstairs to be with Ash and Mica in the nursery,' Miri stood slowly and lent over to take the infant, giving Peter a delicate kiss before moving off. 'Peter will tell me all about this later.'

Peter watched Miri leave. 'I remember sitting in the teacher's office surrounded by papers when Blackmore and two other teachers walked past. They were talking about or listening to that man bragging about his exploits in Adelaide when he was an adolescent. He was with a gang that went 'poofter bashing' I think he said. The other teachers warned him to be quiet that sort of talk could get him in big trouble.'

Steven Raine went white. 'I had no idea.'

'He kept it hush hush after that warning. I never thought about it from that day to this. I was just eaves-dropping,' Peter got up and scooped more eggnog in his cup.

'That's no excuse for this happening to Gem,' Richard snapped.

'No, of course not, well we needed firewood and Gerry, I mean Mr Blackmore, took a group of boys out to fetch it. A couple of the boys returned with arms full and I really didn't notice the others hadn't returned for a while. When I did, I sent Alex, that's the chubby lad upstairs, to investigate. He came back yelling fit to burst, so I went to investigate.'

'That person, he can't get into the property can he, Peter? The gates are secure?' Davrew asked.

'No chance, Dav, I close the gates every night, but tonight, I locked them after the other students arrived. I doubt that's happened in years,' Peter assured.

'Well?' Richard stared at the teacher.

'Well,' Stephen Raine stuttered. 'We got within earshot and Alex wouldn't go any further. He took off back to the camp. I saw what was happening and tried to get Blackmore off Gem who was pinned down and helpless against the onslaught.'

'So, what happened?' Davrew pressed.

'Like I said, I couldn't get Blackmore off, he didn't hear me shouting. I ended up getting a tree branch and thumping him on the back. I was petrified. Thankfully, it knocked him out.'

'How could this happen?' Bon shouted. 'What kind of monster would do this? He was a teacher, by the stars! He should be strung up!'

'Not a monster,' Peter suggested firmly, 'just a prejudiced bully who never really got a handle on his emotions. Somehow, he got away with it, till now.'

'You've had a shock too, Bon. You must rest,' Davrew put a hand on his shoulder.

Steven Raine swallowed the last half of his drink in one go, 'I don't know how his views were never put in check. I can only say it will have some lasting effects on us all, and I'm sorry.'

'We're all sorry but it doesn't help much,' Peter stretched his arms up and stood up. 'I'll go out and check on our campers.'

'We all need to rest now,' Davrew commented. 'Tonight, we've lost something of Gem.'

'You must rest too,' Richard added resting his hand tenderly on Dav's shoulder.

'There are comfortable beds upstairs, Mr Raine,' Peter coaxed, 'or would you prefer to join the other students outside?'

'The warm bed sounds appealing,' the red headed man replied. 'If you don't mind, I'd prefer to be outside with the other teachers and students. They all need to know a responsible person is in charge.'

Miri had returned and met Peter at the door.

'I'm going outside to check on everyone,' Peter hugged Miri briefly. 'Mr Raine is going to go out with the others.'

'My you are tall Miri,' the teacher blurted. 'Sorry, just thinking out loud.' Miri laughed. They all retired for the night.

Bon was glad it was the end of the day but somehow doubted he would sleep well. He'd forgo his own bed for one in the clinic to be near Gem. It could be a long night.

The following week brought to light the realisation of

Bon's worst fears. He knew these were tests far harder than any external exam, they were his own character-building stumbling blocks, as well as Davidson family dilemmas. Humour, and a genial bedside manner were essential and hard won. The first blow after the attack passed almost unnoticed. Terry Ayres did not come back into the house to see Gem. Whether by accident or design, several other children and all the teaching and support staff for the camp, returned to see Gem and say awkward farewells. He was glad they had come but became depressed when Terry hadn't joined them. Bon felt extended to the limit, tending both Gem's physical and mental scars.

The second blow was a result of the attack, and simply meant Gem's formal education had to be postponed temporarily or continued in an alternative way. Gem chose the latter option and decided to go to France and recover. Gem had become pregnant as the result of the rape. Despite pleas to abort the foetus, Gem insisted on allowing the unborn child to grow.

'I want to go to France with Gem.' Bon announced at the breakfast table, the day before Gem was due to leave. It was nearly a month after the attack.

'What will happen if we get sick?' Sal got right to the heart of the matter.

'Don't be silly, Sal, we managed before Bon started training, we can manage again,' Tam chided the younger sibling.

'No buts. We shall discuss this as we always do. Every family member has the right to choose a path in life. Bon has chosen to be our physician. That doesn't mean our child should exclude everything else from daily living, now does it?' Davrew insisted.

'I'll follow later if you wish.' Bon added.

Davrew shook his head. 'You wish to see Imi?' Bon grew suddenly embarrassed and refused to look directly at anyone seated around the large ornately carved table. Mica giggled and nudged Sal who was smiling broadly. They would be going to Andre's property, a small provincial farm in the French vine-growing belt. The families remained close and visits in both hemispheres were common.

It wasn't just an excuse to get away from the pressure that would be appealing. Imi was the second born child of Andre and Rimi. Beautiful rolling fields surrounded the quaint French cottage they lived in. The peace and quiet together with Imi's self-assured companionship would help to revitalise Bon's flagging spirits. Bon and Imi were promised as toddlers. Now after tending to the needs of the family it was time to do some self-healing. Bon hoped Imi would agree to return to the southern continent after Gem had recovered enough to remain with Andre. They would be partnered as soon as practically possible. Bon's heart soared with anticipation.

Bon was annoyed that Gem had refused to press charges. Of course, the family anonymity was at stake and they had to be careful, but knowing Gerard Blackmore had escaped legal retribution, made Bon feel frustrated. Fortunately, the school and the Education Department had taken the matter very seriously. The man had been dismissed and would never teach again. Last news of him was he'd had to leave town. The local gossip mongers had done a hatchet job. Bon fervently hoped he would never hear of Gerard Blackmore again. Tomorrow they would go together to a new future.

'I'm going over the road for a swim,' Gem interrupted Bon's musing.

'You'll be okay, Gem,' Bon thumped Gem on the back. Gem flinched.

'It is real, isn't it?'

'Yes, it's real,' Bon nudged Gems shoulder. 'Tell me how you feel.'

'I'm, confused,' he admitted. 'I'm a bit scared.'

'Of course, you are,' Bon let the smile slide from his face. 'Whatever happens we'll work though it together.'

'Hi, Aunt Pat,' Gem called, entering through the back door of her home.

'Hi, Gem darling,' Pat smiled as she hugged the youth warmly. 'It's a beautiful day for this time of year. Did you enjoy the walk here?'

'Aha,' Gem nodded enthusiastically, 'is it alright if I take another swim? I know I've been over here a lot lately.'

'Your Uncle is in the south paddock mending some fencing, the girls are at school, and' Pat picked up her basket of wet washing and sat it on her hip, 'naturally you're welcome.'

Gem smiled and walked out through the breezeway to the heated in ground pool, unashamedly undressing along the way, throwing towel and clothes into the sun lounge at the water's edge before immediately diving in. A short while later Pat appeared with cordial and biscuits for Gem.

'Here you are,' she called while placing the tray on the small white plastic table.

'Good, thanks,' came a gurgled and delighted reply. Pat noticed the bruising more with each visit. Gem had come over for a swim nearly every day since the terrible night of the attack. Bon had explained how the injuries would show themselves on such pale skin while explaining what had happened. Bill, as usual, didn't want to know. It was as though everything his cousin and family did no longer existed. Pat had done her best to patch up the rift, but a chasm had widened over the years, and she feared it would never close-up.

'When are you leaving for France?' she asked while sitting, sipping her tea, at the poolside table.

'We go tomorrow. Bon has decided to come with me to see I settle in.'

'Oh, that's good. Bon needs a rest from everything too,' Pat said.

'Bon has another reason for going,' Gem smiled widely while stepping out of the water. 'Imi. My guess is Bon wants a partner.' Pat lifted her eyebrows and tried hard to control her facial expression. This family had often surprised her, and this was no exception. Gem chose to ignore her discomfort and drank the cordial quickly.

'I look a sight, don't I?'

'Not really, Gem,' Pat managed to say unconvincingly, noticing the large bruises and water protected cover of the plaster arm bandages. Pat cleared her throat, 'I hope you don't mind, but can you leave by two o'clock? Bill will be back for afternoon tea then.' She sighed and added, 'I only wish your Uncle would try to understand.'

'It's Okay, Aunt, I'll be away. It'll be a while before I see you again. I'll be finishing my studies in Europe. Well, my regular schooling that is. We've always got other things to learn, of course.'

'Are you going to be alright Gem? I mean health wise?' Pat took hold of Gem's hand. 'I know, I mean Bon did tell me, about the baby...' She liked all Richard's children, and was concerned for their welfare. It was difficult to keep her distance for Bill's sake yet remain friendly for Richard.

'I'll be fine. Aunt, really. I don't believe I'm pregnant. I know that sounds silly. If I don't think about it maybe this will just go away.' Gem finished the biscuits. He towelled down and dressed, giving her a hug and peck on the cheek before leaving.

## CHAPTER SEVENTEEN

# TAM

### Early November 1985

Tam Davidson was tall for his age, a head higher than most of his classmates. He was known as the class smart Alec, yet others often turned to him for friendship and advice. They were older, but not wiser in his eyes at least, so he tolerated their whims.

He was a born leader as far as his teachers were concerned, clever enough though to fit into the daily activities of his school peers. Unruly light brown locks hung limply about his often dead-pan face. School was boring, and the restrictions of the middle-class secondary education barely tolerable. He regularly passed his examinations with flying colours, at a level, three years above students in his own age group. Now he was faced with a daunting decision. The academic levels passed meant he would be able to leave for Tertiary education the next school semester. Possible positions in the local country region were not as challenging as the opportunities in the city. The best option would be to board in the City University, which meant leaving home for long periods.

Tam knew being clever didn't stop him from being scared or lonely. His biggest fear was simply that he didn't want to leave his family. His second biggest fear was he didn't know what he would do with all his education once he'd gained it. What sort of future lay ahead? Everyone who knew Tam either loved or hated him. Such polarisation was extended to most of the Davidson family, so it was a familiar experience. Mostly fellow classmates teased him and were jealous of his knowledge and prowess with the pawing, playful girls who found him so appealing.

He would retaliate with, 'you're only interested in getting your license so you can cruise the main street to pick up chicks.' As a twelve-year-old the prospect of driving a car was in the distance, but for his fifteen-year old companions it was an eagerly awaited achievement close at hand.

Tam didn't mind however, because girls virtually lined up to see if what they'd heard about him was true. He was very flattering and capable at 'chatting up' these prospective romantic entanglements. Often, much to the girls' surprise, they found he was ready, willing, and able to take the chat one step or even two steps further. His classmates were still looking forward to delights he already regularly enjoyed.

Most of Tam's siblings were fair haired and pale, his skin tones were more like his father's. He was glad of that, as well as the way people remarked about their other similarities. Many of the mannerisms and way-ward ideas came as easily to Tam as they had done his father. No point in beating about the bush as his second eldest sibling Gem was fond of doing. He was prepared to be accepted as a male, for convenience and practical daily living.

What would he do with all this knowledge gained at university? How could history, archaeology, and inti-mate details of rare cultures from other parts of the globe be beneficial to himself or the Davidson family? These were the thoughts flowing through his mind, while he looked about the huge hall filled with students bent over their examination papers. The neat rows of desks stretched from the back of the hall to the front in exact metre spacing. Teachers were walking steadily and silently about the room on the lookout for would be cheats. The atmosphere was tense, and Tam felt sure for some fellow students it was very intimidating. The odd tapping of a pen on the desk rang in echo around the room as the composition of an answer was being formed in a strained hopeful mind. Shadows hung long across the room from the sunlight streaming in through high small windows, which ran along both side walls of the auditorium. Tam was starting to feel bored as he had completed his paper and re-checked his answers twice. A teacher at the front of the room was staring at him, so he decided to re-read his answers for a third time. They were all correct, but perhaps he could add a little more.

Suddenly, every head in the room jerked upright. A strange whirring noise above them was followed by a huge crashing explosion, which rocked the building. It had come across from the eastern sky and ended after a thunderous pass directly overhead and to the left. Smaller rumbles followed moments later from the same direction.

Students started getting out of their seats and crowding around the windows on the left to see what it might be. A teacher at the front of the room was hammering a mallet into a wood block to silence the curious crowd.

'Be seated everyone,' he yelled, 'I'll have silence in this examination room now!' With each word, he pounded heavily on the wood block. 'Those who do not return to their seats NOW will forfeit this examination and be failed. Do you hear me? Everyone, SIT DOWN.' The message finally got through and students began reluctantly making their way back to their desks. Two of the more curious teachers, who had been standing at the door, approached the mallet wielding man.

The head teacher looked annoyed but nodded agreement.

'Every-one-be-seated!' He stood and looked around the room menacingly. The last stragglers were just reaching their desks. The hall resembled most of its former order, enough for the booming voice to break the silence again. 'This examination will re-commence now. We will allow a ten-minute extension due to this disruption, however...' The three teachers briefly whispered together looking down the hall in Tam's direction. 'Tam Davidson, I believe it is?' the head teacher asked while looking directly at Tam.

'Yes, sir,' Tam answered and stood bolt upright beside his desk.

'I believe you have completed your paper?'

'Yes, sir.'

'Then hand it in and go with Mr Peel to find out what caused such a terrible commotion.'

Tam couldn't believe his luck. He rushed to drop the papers on the front desk and quickly headed for the door with the Mr Peel. The head teacher sent a comment at his heels as they bolted through the door. 'You had better have completed every question, Mr Davidson, or there WILL be trouble.'

'It is unusual for anyone to finish a History exam more than an hour ahead of time,' Mr. Peel remarked, as they rushed through the door. Tam smiled and began to run. The unfit and slightly overweight teacher struggled to keep pace at his side, across the bitumen quadrangle which served as school assembly area in the summer. They passed the last block of low-slung grey buildings, which housed the 'Trade Wing', and catered for woodwork and sheet metal on a basic level.

On the far side of the oval they could see smouldering black smoke billowing up. A crowd had gathered, and more students were flowing out from the buildings, excitedly running towards the smoke.

'Might be one of those new jet planes that are falling out of the sky like flies,' Tam suggested while the teacher nodded breathlessly. They were running across the oval now. Some teachers were trying to turn the tide of students ordering them back to their classrooms with little success.

'Go back to your classrooms, NOW!' Mr Peel added his voice but quickly realised it was a futile effort. They pushed their way to the front of the crowd.

A deep soil furrow was gouged from the edge of the oval right through the running track and into the adjacent golf course. None of the students had crossed the boundary fence, knowing the wrath of the green keeper who was notoriously severe with interlopers. Mr Peel decided to remind the crowd of the consequences.

'Quiet everyone,' he yelled. 'We mustn't cross the school boundary. You all know what would happen if Mr Sands catches you?' He beckoned to another teacher, 'Brian, I think we should have this area restricted and notify the authorities, don't you?'

'Certainly, Alex, I'll go tell the Head and get the word out. Looks a right mess over there, Sands will be beside himself,' he waved quickly and ran off towards the school.

'You - Bumpstead, Cullins,' Mr Peel shouted. 'Go stand at the boundary and don't let anyone past. Davidson and I will investigate. Everyone else stay back!' With that command hanging in the air, some of the students in the crowd took off.

Tam laughed as they set off following the disrupted turf trail. They climbed over soil and debris. Fallen trees and bushes were squashed flat as pancakes closer to the point of impact. The ground was soft from recent heavy rain, so mud clotted and clung to their feet as they continued plodding doggedly towards the huge mound they could now see. Rain still threatened so they hurried as best they could. Something large was half embedded in the dark brown soil. It looked very odd with trees teetering at various angles around the mound.

'It sure isn't one of those F1 11's, you know, fighter planes,' Tam announced assuredly. 'They have jets.'

'We'd better be careful. It might even be space junk.'

'The Yanks would pay a pretty penny for that, if it is,' Tam replied excitedly.

'Probably,' Mr Peel agreed. The two curious companions edged closer to the half-buried object. Tam noticed they were becoming caked in the chocolate loam soil as they scrambled side by side up the embankment towards a silver-grey object. Suddenly they heard a noise, so they stopped and listened. Where was it coming from?

'Hey, what's that sound,' one of the students perched in a tree on the school side of the property shouted. Tam noticed movement behind the human barricade.

'Shut up, you lot, we can't hear,' Mr Peel called back. The sounds were loud enough to discern. Someone or something was shouting. Sweat beads began appearing on Mr Peel's forehead.

'This doesn't sound good, Davidson. I'm going to get some help.' The teacher scrambled back the way they'd come, shouting as he did to the students nearby. 'Stay away from this area, all of you.'

Tam was too curious to move and was glad when some more intrepid students decided to join him. They all watched and listened, after some time an orifice slowly opened halfway up the submerged silver object. The shouting became clearer. 'Not a happy chappie,' Tam stated the obvious. Whatever the owner of the voice was saying, in whatever language, it sounded like a tirade of abusive adjectives.

There was a gasp from the onlookers behind them. Tam heard a crash a one lad fell from his vantage point as the creature emerged. It was a heavy-set man-like being, very hairy and barely clad in trousers and a singlet like vest. Oblivious to the crowd it began surveying the damage and removing debris from around the vehicle.

Sirens rang out in the background, coming closer to the school, and closer still as they careered across the oval. Doors slammed and shouts drifted to Tam's ears from the school ground. 'The cavalry has arrived,' Tam quipped.

'They want us to go back,' a thin boy with broad-rim spectacles whispered.

'I've got a good view here,' Tam replied. Some of the others moved away. Another teacher called Mr Smalley appeared on the ridge of the mound. Tam thought at least he had some brains. In fact, he quite liked the teacher, so he tried hard not to be obnoxious around him.

'Hi, enjoying the view?' Mr Smalley asked conversationally while getting into a squat position beside Tam to watch the alien. He let out a long slow whistle. 'Wow, our crash site has turned up something pretty surprising, hasn't it?'

'Sure has,' Tam muttered. 'This critter is as strong as at least ten elephants I would say.' Rocks, shrubs, and soil were being thrown away from the vehicle at a rapid rate. The creature appeared to be unperturbed about where the remnants of the crash site fell. With complete disregard for anything other than clearing debris off the vehicle he continued his work. The edge of the school ground and golf course now resembled a war zone. The police had arrived, and the area was being cordoned off. The students were being pushed back. The school principal arrived too and began ranting about the damage and who would have to clean it up.

'They want you back behind the barriers,' Mr Smalley nodded towards some policemen who were motioning frantically at them. Tam instantly took a dislike to the Police Chief, who was stout, and had an enormous bushy moustache. His voice bellowed endlessly from the moment he arrived. The uniformed men in blue were gathering in numbers and the students sent back behind their yellow tape.

'Do you think our unwelcome guest might like a helping hand?' Tam nodded in the alien's direction.

Mr Smalley chuckled. 'Maybe so.'

'These guys look like they might try something stupid on their own,' Tam pointed towards the police. 'The Police chief sure looks like he's about to have a heart attack. So, why don't we do something stupid? Why wait for them to declare war? Why not go ask this strongman if we can help? It'll probably think it's a joke, but there's no harm in asking. What do you say, Mr Smalley?'

'We could try,' the teacher agreed. The pair began to slide, rather clumsily in the wet mud, towards the creature down the embankment. Tam smothered a smile and snicker behind his hand as Mr Smalley began attempting to communicate with the being.

The teacher looked ridiculously small and frail beside the creature. Tam thought this was strange. He'd always felt this tall heavyset man with receding hairline combed into a standing wave as intimidating. Perhaps, Tam thought that is true of students in relation to a teacher, but not in this case. The alien regarded the man with crystal green eyes that shone vividly from a leathery wrinkled face. It appeared that this was the first time he'd noticed he was being watched. The Police Chief was yelling for them to get back and not to interfere. Mr Smalley pretended he couldn't hear them. Valiantly he continued trying to get a greeting and some response. The alien began grunting at them in some incomprehensible language. Mr Smalley repeated his feeble greeting. The creature grunted again and crawled back into the silver vehicle which was now mostly uncovered.

'That doesn't look like his usual door,' Tam remarked.

'Maybe he's been crawling through an escape hatch. But Davidson, what makes you so sure it's male or female or anything like us?'

'Nothing much except it's got two arms and legs and an obvious appendage in the lower regions under those tight pants. Didn't you notice the huge...?' They both laughed. A Policeman joined them, cursing the mud and recent soft shower of rain.

'What in the blazes do you two think you're doing?'

'We're offering to help,' Tam replied simply.

'And who the Hell said you could do that? The Boss up there is going spare. He thinks we should blast the beast away. The Principal just wants the damned mess cleaned up, and you're offering to help?'

'My guess is, Officer, if we offer him somewhere to do his repairs and leave him to it, he may just leave us alone.'

'Can't hurt to try and talk to the beastie, Officer, before we try and blow its brains out?' Mr Smalley added dryly.

'My family live on a property nearby, with a few vacant pastures beside the orchard, we could take him there. He could be left to himself and we could watch,' Tam suggested.

'We've got to get him to understand us first,' the teacher countered.

Just then the orifice widened again and out crawled the creature. He held a small box with a loop around his wrist. The Policeman started to pull out his gun. On the mound top the Police Chief ordered guns to be trained on the creature.

'Don't be stupid,' Tam stopped the Officer from

moving any further.

'This guy is strong, although a little outnumbered,' Mr Smalley reassured the policeman.

'I am Rakal,' the alien's voice chanted through the box.

'Wow, I mean, hello. I'm Mr Smalley, this is Tam Davidson and Officer...?'

'I am Rakal. You are Earth people. I have heard your noise before.'

'In space?' Mr. Smalley couldn't contain his excitement. The creature nodded then looked each of them over closely.

'I will fix this '@' and go,' The alien announced. 'You are weak.'

'Perhaps we can help fix your vehicle?' Mr Smalley added nervously.

The creature stood for a moment and his expression was clear. 'Are you crazy?' it said. He began to laugh, slowly at first, then more deeply and with a touch of menace.

'I will fix. I will do it where this little one said I can be alone. You will not follow me. Your people will not come near me. I will leave and you all may live,' Rakal grabbed the policeman's weapon and squashed it like a ripe tomato.

'Hang on,' Tam looked at the creature, 'You were inside that thing when I told the Officer and Mr Smalley what we might suggest. How did you know?' The creature grunted, took a step closer to Tam, and looked directly into his sapphire blue eyes before answering.

'I hear,' then he crawled back into the vehicle.

'You also talk like a moron through that little box,' Tam murmured. They all heard the alien roar with laughter again.

'Tam, the authorities are never going to allow this ape a safe-haven at your parent's property! They won't want to let this out of their sight. They'll probably want to take it to some military institution and pull it apart.'

'I'd like to see them try.'

'Aha, I know what you mean. It sure has made on hell of mess around here. You think it'll do what it wants to do.'

'Yep,' Tam nodded. 'At least this way we can have a ringside seat. How about we tell the boys up there and see what happens?'

'Either way, it's out of our hands,' the teacher sighed. They began to clamber up towards the crowd.

## CHAPTER EIGHTEEN

# SAL

Early November 1985

Sal had a lean and strong physique, fair hair, and crystal-clear pool blue eyes, all of which marked him a Davidson. Early in life Sal had decided what career path lay ahead, even then his love of nature, and all manner of flora and fauna was a true passion. Caring for plants, tending the orchard, and growing seedlings throughout the property, would be his vocation.

At seventeen the joy of living and learning about the bounties of nature came first and foremost. This meant juggling studies, chores, and nature trips into a well-planned diary of activities. No time was wasted, with every minute precious as a learning space. Even digging the vegetable garden over was a pleasure because Sal could feel the sun and wind on flexing muscles.

Gem was two years older and fond of backpacking through mountains on precipitous walking tracks. Sal sometimes tagged along for company, which was often silent but fulfilling. They walked today and chatted endlessly about the differences of the track since last treading down it. The two siblings were both well-versed in botany, the many local varieties of birds, flora, and fauna, gaining more knowledge with every trip. Sal was always careful not to mention the latest heated family argument Gem had stormed away from. Their temperaments were two extremes Sal was patient and reliable, Gem was easily excited and often volatile.

Sal smiled as they hiked purposefully through tall ferns surrounded by towering gums, while crackling undergrowth snapped beneath their feet. Gem always took the lead with Sal marching a few paces behind. It was a respite from regular schoolwork, as he attended the Agricultural College nearby. His exams were over for the year. Gem had finished his school days and ran the Computer shop in town with their father.

'Tam is cooped up in an exam while we are out enjoying this brisk walk, lucky for us.'

'Yep, and lucky for me father is at the store and I can get a day off,' Gem thumped Sal on the back urging him to move faster.

That evening they made camp at the foot of a small mountain range. This was a regular and often used spot, popular with hikers and campers who travelled the mountain ranges.

'Looks like we've got the place to ourselves,' Gem wriggled out of his backpack.

'Yep, it's great,' Sal chirped as he started collecting kindling. 'Still a bit chill for tourists I'd say.'

'Good size clearing, the rock wall will protect us from the wind a bit,' Gem nodded towards the northern overhang. Then he started raising the tents.

'Could be a strong wind tonight, so the forecast says. It'll be a biting wind. I like the semi-circle of trees, we don't have to go far for firewood,' Sal added. A short distance away a stream trickled melodiously on its journey down from the mountain peaks to the lake catchments below.

'I can't wait to see when Sim will be here, sometime tomorrow, is the plan,' Sal beamed.

After eating, they both checked for messages on their personal computer 'mail', and of course, set about to do their homework. Getting away from it all really meant taking it with you in the Davidson family. Education and constant renewal of information was such an important, integral part of their lives, no one questioned the need to work hard to gain it.

Five years had passed since Sal had been promised in Partnership to Sim. One thing or another had kept them apart. The latest was Andre's health and Sim wanting to stay with her father till he was stronger. It was time to get the formalities over with and start a new life together. With anticipation Sal opened his communications console. The need to return and meet Sim uppermost in his thoughts.

The unexpected message was unwelcome. It read simply: *'Out-worlder named 'RAKAL' arrived. Staying with us. Causing some disruptions. Return when ready with care. Sim's arrival delayed till more suitable time.'*

Sal reread the message to Gem. 'Shit Gem. Causing some disruptions is right!' Gem didn't intrude on Sal's disappointment and busily went about clearing away the dirty dishes.

They were good companions. Unlike most of the family Sal chose not to moralise or judge Gem about parental obligations. The fact that, with a young child, Gem still took periodic sabbaticals into the bush alone did not seem wrong. A brief 'time out' seemed a good idea really.

Nor did Sal feel concerned about Gem's sexual preferences. Being an adult and sexually mature in the Davidson home usually meant being a partner and producing many heirs. This attitude was expressed often and sometimes felt suffocating. The hikes and camping trips were a good escape they both enjoyed.

After clearing up, the stars began to appear overhead as brightly shining lights illuminating the dark sky. The slightly cooler evening breeze started the leaves in the trees rustling soothingly. The sounds of frogs croaking and the water running gently down river added to the bush lullaby. Sal prodded the fire with a stick as Gem added more logs.

'It's a beautiful spot,' Sal's sharp eyes were dull with disappointment, but there was no point in expressing it.

'I'll bring Maya here, someday soon, I guess,' Gem spoke wistfully. Sal understood Gem completely. Maya was one of the most demanding children ever to enter the household. Since they'd returned from France, when the child was barely one year old, everyone's lives had been disrupted. Now Maya was six and still a hand full.

'Hmm, I'll bring Sim, when we're partnered.' There was a long silence which was swallowed up the tangible longing in Sal's voice.

'Tomorrow, first thing, we'll break camp and head home. I want to see this Rakal,' Gem stared into the fire while sitting close to it to keep warm. Sal nodded agreement.

'Gem, do you mind if I ask you a question?' Sal asked softly.

'No, ask away. Everyone else does.'

'I'm not prying about your personal life Gem, that's your business,' Sal paused to look at his older sibling. 'I just wondered why you spend so much time in the city when you love the country?' Gem laughed softly; this wasn't the kind of question other members of the family would ask. This was very much a concerned Sal question. His reply was honest and direct.

'I work in the city. I enjoy the work, and, naturally put a lot of effort into it. The small computer shop in our local town is now part of a wider franchise. Setting all this up has been a buzz I don't find anywhere else. The social life is a different kind of buzz, it's not real, you see, it just happens for fun.'

'You don't fall in love then, with these young

boys? It's just sex then for the sake of it?' Gem nodded in non-committed way. 'You be careful, Gem, don't get hurt. You're my best friend as well as sibling. I just kind of...' Sal stopped, fearing the boundary of limitation had been reached. Gem didn't seem concerned, Sal was genuine and caring so without a hint of annoyance, or getting worked up, as had happened with other members of the family, Gem simply mussed up Sal's hair and smiled while saying goodnight.

'Poor Sim, making the long journey here, only to be told to go back, and wait some more,' Gem voiced Sal's thoughts.

'Yeah, it's a pain.'

## CHAPTER NINETEEN

# RICHARD

### Early November 1985

'Here Richard, take this with you. Pat wants some more fruit trees in her garden,' Davrew handed him a large tub with a well-established apple plant in it. 'I wish I could come too, but you're probably right, I'd best stay here.'

'Don't worry Dav, I'll be back soon,' Richard heaved the tub into the tray of the ute. Davrew quickly closed the gap between them and they embraced briefly. Richard got in the ute and drove off. The multi-coloured rust and yellow truck kicked up a trail of dust as it screeched around the top of the drive towards the gates. It had been many years since Ricard had visited his cousin. The steering wheel slipped in his clammy hands as he reached the exit. The highway was clear of traffic. Richard sent a silent prayer to the stars that it would stay that way. The ute engine roared as he crossed to the opposite side of the road and sped down Bill's driveway.

Soon he pulled up in front of the elegant home with beautifully maintained gardens and surrounds. The windows shone and the lawn edges were precisely trimmed. That was testimony to Pat's meticulous care of her home.

'Hi,' Pat called from the verandah as he got out of

the ute. 'Bill's inside, Richard, but he won't stay long. There's lots of work to be done today.' It sounded like a lame excuse but there was no point in taking it at anything but face value.

'Hi, Pat,' Richard smiled and hugged his sister-in-law warmly before unloading the plant. 'This is for you. Davrew is sure you'd like a beautiful apple tree in your backyard. I hope you like 'Red Delicious', you know they're a very tasty variety. Call it, the ice breaking tree!' They both laughed. Pat kissed Richard easily on the cheek.

'I remember you hugging me like that when we first me, thank you, Richard. Thank Davrew as well, won't you? I've missed your company. If only you and Bill could make amends.' Richard allowed Pat to put her arm in his and wheel him into the living room. Bill was sitting in his comfortable recliner looking out through the large bay windows. He got up and led them all to the kitchen table, pulling out a chair, he gestured for Richard to do the same.

'Don't start with small talk, Richard. What's so important you had to ring us? Can't you leave us out of it and let us alone?'

'Cousin, if it were possible, I would,' Richard began. 'It's your children, I mean, your family I was wanting to protect.'

'*Protect?*' Bill's eyes flashed angrily as he started to rise from his chair. Pat put a hand gently on his shoulder and tried to quell his temper.

'Well, maybe, protect is a little strong?'

'Maybe you can get on with it so we can all get back to work,' Bill retorted.

'I've come to tell you news I know you won't like much,' Richard began. 'Tam, our fifth born, rang about an hour ago, and...' Bill fidgeted in his seat while Richard's throat went dry. 'Apparently we're to have a house guest for a short time. At least, I hope it will be a short time.'

'So, Richard, what's that got to do with us?'

'Well, I hope little, Bill. It's just that he's not from around here, in fact, he's not of this world. He crash-landed in the school grounds. So, there could be police, and maybe the press too, at our place while this visitor is here. Although, I've insisted any news people be kept in the dark. It's really too dangerous for us!' Richard paused and swallowed. 'I was, well, we were, worried about your girls. Naturally, we want it all kept hush hush. A spacecraft being unloaded by the police in our drive is a bit strange, they could get curious and come over to investigate.'

'Shouldn't worry you to have out of space creatures in your midst, I would have thought it was normal!' Bill spluttered.

'Now Bill, don't be rude,' Pat walked over to the window and studied the view. 'How long will this visitor be with you?'

'We don't know really, Pat. Not long I hope.'

'We can see your home and gardens quite clearly from here. Police and a spacecraft will stand out like a sore thumb. Our curious girls could want to check it out. I certainly don't think that's a good idea. So, Richard, what do you suggest?'

'A short holiday,' Richard shrugged his shoulders at the audacity of his proposal, but he could see no other choice.

'Don't be dumb, cousin. The girls aren't stupid, they'd smell a rat immediately if we sprang a stunt like that,' Bill laughed softly at Richard's growing discomfort. There was silence for a few moments, the air thick with tension.

'Bill, I've just the solution,' Pat announced. 'You know you've been promising to take the girls to your mother's place to stay. This would be the perfect chance to fix up those urgent repairs and take the children for a camp away from home. Carly could use the short cut behind mother's when they drive to Uni. They wouldn't even pass your place on the way.'

'Bloody trouble for nothin' if you ask me,' Bill added with surly displeasure.

'Now don't you two argue. I don't want it,' Pat snapped. 'I'm laying down the law. You've let this fester too long. I'm going to say my piece, and I don't want either of you butting in before I've finished.' Pat put a hand on Bill's shoulder to keep him seated and motioned for Richard to sit.

'Over the years, it's been hard for me to keep a lid on the gossip that goes on in the town. You know it, you must have heard the whispers. Richard, when you came back from Europe that second time with Davrew bulging pregnant and little Miri in tow, what did you expect to happen? Naturally, Bill blew his cool. A best mate became a nursing mother! We had little Carly only a little younger than Miri ourselves. Did you think we'd settle into happy families with such a massive change?'

'But Pat...' Richard stammered.

'Stay quiet, and listen,' Pat urged. Bill sat back in his seat to let her vent. 'It hasn't gotten any easier Richard, not with the girls going through school and now going to Uni. Carly is now twenty-one and Debbie twenty. They're not children.'

'Oh, Pat, the girls have always been on good terms with our kids,' Richard interjected. 'They've come to birthday parties and special occasions.'

'Yes, they have. Recently though it's easier for them not to tell anyone how many children are running around your place. What with Miri already the mother of six children. Miri was only fourteen when she took up with Peter and not long after started a family. The town gossip was already running wild with two blokes having a family. Then Peter happily turning his back on his career and family. It's no wonder his mother ostracised him.' Pat took a breath as she sat on the bay window seat. 'Then Gem bought young Maya into the world, he's a six-year-old hand-full, you'll agree. Bon and Imi have four children now. Your place has been babysitting heaven for our girls as they grew up. Right now, though, they just want to study and go out with friends. I think both Carly and Debbie are afraid to mention their cousins to anyone.'

There was an awkward silence.

'Well, you know what I bloody well think!' Bill blurted before his wife cut him down with an icy glare.

'I've given up trying to fend off the gossip. I just let people say what they will. I'm proud to say Bill never bad mouths your family,' Pat let out a long sigh as she picked up her glass of water and sipped it.

'Carly has just had her twenty-first party, as you know. I was glad she invited her older cousins. Everyone had a great time, but there's always the elephant in the room,' Pat paused to cough before continuing. 'Bill, to his credit, was a perfect host. I think twenty odd years of not speaking is long enough. I'd like you two to try and get on.'

'Can't see that happening!' Bill glared.

'I think going to your mothers for a month or so is a great idea. It probably needs a huge clean out too. Carly is doing interior decorating and could help refurbish the place. I certainly believe we could all do with steering clear of any more gossip, don't you?' Pat put her glass down with a thud.

'I was hoping you'd see it that way,' Richard sighed and stood up.

'Bill?' Pat prompted.

'Mum would like to see the old place done up I reckon, and Carly has been onto me to take her over there,' Bill agreed.

'Aunty Nance has been gone a long time,' Richard added.

'Sixteen years,' Pat reminded them both.

'There's a lot to do,' Bill admitted. 'I did let it slip. The rental tenants we had a couple of times didn't last. Kept complaining something needed fixing,' Bill stood up grabbed his hat off the table and brushed his legs with it. 'Best get to it, you'll tell the girls Pat.'

'Yes, of course,' she replied. 'Richard, this house guest of yours won't cause any trouble, will he?'

'We'll see to it that he doesn't,' Richard rose and gave Pat a peck on the cheek. 'I'll see myself out. Thanks, you know, for trying.'

'Don't think for a minute this'll change anything. You're still not flavour of the month in my eyes,' Bill stated as he briskly walked out through the back door.

Pat rolled her eyes heavenward.

Richard walked back out to the ute with Pat following.

'Davrew misses you both, you know,' he said. Pat nodded and gave him a quick hug.

'The girls are both going through difficult times right now, what with boyfriends changing like the wind and studies being so intense. Uni is a real headache for them both, especially our Carly. Debbie seems to be holding her own. I'm glad you warned us.'

'Least we could do,' Richard said as he jumped into the ute.

## CHAPTER TWENTY

# RAKAL

### Early December 1985

Tam's houseguest was hardly a welcome one, intolerably irritable, constantly rude, lacking any subtlety whatsoever. Most people were glad to keep their distance.

The Davidson household tried to ignore the imposition as much as possible. Rakal himself proved to be extremely good at being detached. The main proviso of the Davidson family accepting the creature's presence was that no reporters would be permitted on the property.

The police had taken over security of the Davidson property and they were all housed outside the family residence, and as far as possible from the house and away from the main road. They kept a constant eye on the alien's activities. Two policemen always stayed near the spaceship.

The youngest of the Davidson children, Mica, found Rakal's language fascinating. With a small hand recorder, and the ease of a child capable of seeming to be invisible, Mica was Rakal's constant shadow. The only place Mica didn't go was into the semi-repaired spacecraft.

Tam brought out trays of food for the guest,

which he devoured almost instantly.

'You have disgusting manners, Rakal. Did you never learn how to thank someone for taking the effort to bring you food?' The alien simply grunted his reply and thrust the empty plate into Tam's arms.

'You'll blow yourself up messing about with all that,' Tam pointed at wires and lights underneath a huge side panel Rakal was working on. 'This thing looks too small to have come any distance. I bet you haven't got half what you need to fix it here either.'

Rakal looked surly and snapped. 'I learn fast, little one. You need to learn to keep your mouth shut.'

The police guards snickered at the youth's remarks but kept their distance. Rakal had made it clear how strongly he disliked their presence. The policemen obviously took his threats seriously and made no attempt to intervene.

Mica tugged Tam's arm and pleaded, 'Tam, cut it out. I'm trying to learn what he's saying. I don't want your voice to spoil my tape.'

'I work. You go!' Rakal shouted without the aid of the translator box.

'It won't be long, and he'll be rabbiting on at us, Mica. You'll have lots to hear from your recordings,' Tam didn't wait to see the rebuttal in the creature's eyes. Turning towards the house he added, 'it's too small and a load of junk.'

The whole vehicle was only four meters long by three wide and it reminded Tam of a snub-nosed aeroplane front with no wings or tail.

At the school, and now at the Davidson's farm, the Police operation was kept very secretive the night after the crash. The area was cordoned off and cleared of spectators. The school oval and golf course were declared out of bounds to all but police personnel. Late that first night rumours of an elaborate hoax filtered through to the local community as cranes and a large flatbed truck arrived at the site. With some mammoth teamwork the space vehicle was finally loaded onto the truck and driven to the orchard. It was deposited in a paddock on the extreme end of the property, as far as possible from the family home. The alien had stayed inside the vehicle during this transfer. As the new day dawned the police continued to work on the golf course land, filling soil, replacing uprooted trees, and clearing away the debris. By the next afternoon, no trace of the crash could be seen other than upturned soil.

Many weeks had passed since then and the repairs seemed to progress slowly. It was easy to see Rakal didn't have all he needed to repair the craft. The three doughnut shaped propulsion units at the rear of the machine seemed intact, but clearly something else was very wrong. Tam had begun to enjoy annoying Rakal. He didn't really know why, and the fact it seemed to upset everyone else in the family didn't appear to concern him either.

The police now watched from their campsite, a safe distance from the spacecraft. They retreated after several incidents when Rakal had become abusive and started throwing smashed weapons across the paddock. Then he threw one policeman in a similar manner almost as far as a football field away into a haystack. Both parties were relieved when the police decided to move back, avoiding further confrontation. Yet Rakal tolerated the Davidson children. Mica and Tam would often be seen watching his every move. The creature even began to talk to them occasionally, asking questions.

Tam became more and more tormenting. Rakal seemed to rise to it with equal enjoyment. At times Tam pushed a little too hard and the alien would shout. Once he grabbed Tam and flung him in the air. Mica gasped and then clapped when Rakal caught Tam and spun him like a top. One day when the alien was both curious and talkative, he asked, 'why is that one big?'

Rakal continued to fasten a panel while listening to the reply.

'That one,' Tam nodded at Miri the eldest of the Davidson children. 'That one is pregnant,' he paused, 'Peter and Miri are expecting a child. You must know what I mean...'

Rakal shook his head. Tam tried to make it as clear as possible. 'Miri has a new little person inside. That is why the stomach is so big. Inside is a baby.'

'They do this by choice?' Rakal asked, alarmed.

'Of course, we all do some time, because we want to have little ones to teach what we know,' Tam hoped this was a good enough explanation. Mica sat happily taping the conversation.

'Two policemen now?' Rakal grunted and pointed at the uniformed men.

'Yeah, they're just there to make sure no busy bodies come into the place.'

'Buzzy boddies?' Rakal mispronounced the words and Tam and Mica children laughed. Rakal growled like a lion and Mica ran. Tam, who was as determined as ever to be a thorn in Rakal's side.

'I test now,' Rakal walked upright through the correct side entrance to the craft. The rear orifice was obviously an emergency exit. 'You join me?'

Tam was surprised. He hadn't expected Rakal to be ready to test the craft. He certainly hadn't expected to be asked to join him. Both fear and excitement filled his senses. How could he refuse?

'Mica just tell everyone we're going to see if this old buggy works,' Tam called to the child who was edging back toward the craft.

Bug-eyed, Mica looked up at Tam. 'They won't like this, Tam.'

'I know, but I'm going anyway.'

Rakal had already disappeared inside the vehicle minutes before. Tam thought it was time to follow. The youngster Mica ran off towards the house. Tam was surprised to find two compartments in the tiny spacecraft. The first one he walked through had a bunk and seat arrangement. He guessed that was where Rakal would sleep and eat during a journey. The front was like an aeroplane cockpit with two seats and control panels in front and all around. It was bigger than he imagined it would be. The decision had been made and Tam swallowed the nerves that threatened to show as he sat in the chair beside the pilot. Rakal had tied his hair back in a ponytail and changed into a coverall, which made him look authoritative and efficient. Tam was unnerved by his clean appearance, as his usual line of ridicule was to do with the alien's sloppiness.

'We see now if this 'old buggy' can fly,' Rakal mimicked Tam. With fluid motions his fingers fluttered over the controls. The large ungainly creature that had lumbered around the paddock disappeared as if by magic. Tam didn't say a word for fear it would choke him. The view screen directly before them curved in a semi-circle almost enclosing their seats. It unfolded a panoramic view of the pasture and trees ahead. With breathtaking ease, the small craft's propulsion system sprang to life. The scene changed from pastures flitting away below them to white cotton-ball clouds.

'Well, it works,' Tam uttered with bravado hoping to disguise his surprise. The clouds were now behind them and the upper stratosphere quickly traversed. 'We've given it a spin. Can't we go back now?' Rakal gave Tam a mischievous grin and shook his head. They continued through space and seemed in next to no time to be approaching the Moon.

'This is my little surprise, I need parts,' Rakal announced. Tam looked out and saw a much larger spaceship in stationary orbit around the Earth's only satellite. It looked like a large fat cigar with four smaller cigar shaped cylinders directly attached to the main core.

'I was right! This is just a run-about, that's your main inter-planetary hopper!' Tam exclaimed. Skillfully Rakal manoeuvred the small craft into the docking station. The sound of metal to metal was somehow reassuring.

'Let me show you around,' Rakal pulled Tam up out of the seat. 'This is my usual gravity level. You will feel heavy,' the alien explained with the aid of the translator box. Tam just nodded while clumsily getting out of his chair.

They walked through the small craft's door into a huge room. Tam immediately noticed two more craft almost identical to the one they'd arrived in. Rakal gave a brief guided tour beginning with a cargo hold, engine room, medical facility, meals room and ending in a control room.

'This is where I live as I travel,' Rakal slowly turned around the room with his arm outstretched theatrically. 'And, in here,' he almost dragged Tam to another compartment beside the control room, 'is where I rest.'

'On your own.'

'Yes.'

'Isn't that kinda lonely?'

'Could be, but I take what I want when it suits me.' Tam was just trying to think of a suitably cryptic remark when Rakal grabbed him. 'Like now.'

Tam was too shocked to react. Rakal threw him easily down backwards on his bed. The large alien pinned the smaller body neatly beneath him. Past numbness, Tam felt clothes being torn off his body as Rakal's mouth firmly stifled any sound of resistance. Surprised by the delicate exploration of Rakal's tongue Tam began responding to the sensual touch. All senses were heightened, and a tingling feeling made the initial cold of the spacecraft disappear in euphoric warmth.

The mutual embrace became more passionate, each exploring the other. Rakal quickly dispensed with his own clothing and Tam felt the joy of skin touching skin. Only fleetingly did the pain of physical virginity being stripped away interfere. Soon the pleasure of the moment replaced the pain. Tam did not want to stop and allowed Rakal further into a body aching for the climax. Too quickly it seemed the rocking and simultaneous moans ceased. They lay together spent. Rakal slept.

A short while later Tam got up, pulling a blanket about cool naked limbs. Slowly walking into the control room, a delicious contentment filled his happy mind. Now Tam realised the benefits Miri had gained by simply living as a female. Perhaps choosing the male outlook was a poor choice? At that moment, something flitted across the control room view-screen. It was a good distance away but instinctively Tam felt a danger.

'Rakal, come here. I think something is out there.'

The large lumbering creature temporarily returned walking through the door unsteadily. The image on the screen showed something approaching now more directly. Rakal growled his low guttural throaty growl. Quickly he pulled Tam into a small booth beside the entrance to the sleeping chamber. Tam gladly relinquished the blanket after Rakal gave it a small tug. He snapped a single word command to a machine and instantly they both stood clothed.

Rakal planted a fierce kiss on Tam's willing lips. 'You do get under my skin, Tam Davidson. Is that how you say it?' Tam nodded. Rakal grabbed Tam's hand and started toward the exit. 'Now, we must fight for our lives.'

## CHAPTER TWENTY-ONE

# RAKAL'S REVELATIONS

'Quickly, Tam we must leave here now,' Rakal grabbed some supplies from the storage area on the way, then they jumped in an undamaged landing craft.

'That was the longest sentence I've heard you string together since you crashed in the golf course,' Tam couldn't resist the chance to dig in another needle. The whole element of danger seemed unreal.

'I speak well in my own language. You should try to learn it. It's like your own.'

'You mean OUR language not what we're speaking now?'

Rakal nodded and pointed at the screen. Tam felt uneasy, having the illusion of normality shattered by this outworlder's keen perceptions. 'How much do you know about my family?'

'Enough,' Rakal replied. They hurriedly repositioned themselves at the controls of the smaller craft. 'My enemy, Shakralaz. He caused the damage to my planet hopper. I needed to hide it, so I brought it here. We must leave before it is too late.' The deep throaty sinister laughter began to roll like thunder from him again. 'I will tempt and trap.' Tam felt goose bumps on his arms.

'Will we be quick enough?'

'Watch,' with a deft hand Rakal guided them away

from the main spacecraft. Tam watched the screen image of the huge vehicle shimmer and change.

'Where's it gone?'

'It's hidden,' Rakal smiled, then nodded towards to the opposing vehicle. He began a guttural laugh which sent shivers down Tam's spine. The atmosphere changed with the sound. A foreboding silence took over. 'He's seen us.' They swiftly covered the distance originally travelled. Earth loomed large as they began to descend through the upper atmosphere.

'What will happen if he follows us?'

Rakal's green eyes glowered menacingly. 'We'll fight.'

Tam became scared. What sort of battle could two powerful aliens exact on one another? Then another thought struck like a sledgehammer.

'Where?'

'Does it matter?'

'Yes, Rakal, in the name of the stars, don't do it in our back-yard.'

'Your family's back-yard you mean?' Tam just nodded. The other vehicle had indeed followed them. Its image was clear on a rear-view screen beside the large main screen. A totally different colour and shape to Rakal's silver snub-nosed craft, it was dark, possibly blue, or black, with a flat arrowhead shape.

'Who is this Shakralaz, and why are you enemies?'

'Silence. It begins,' Rakal's fingers fluttered over the controls again and a loud burst of energy exploded underneath them. Tam saw the laser light weapons trained on the enemy's underbelly. Which easily out manoeuvred them by simply turning side on to the blasts. Shortly after similar weapons were heading in their direction. Both vehicles were now skimming over the sea at a low altitude. Land was looming nearby and Tam's heartbeat heavily. This was their island home, the largest island continent.

Rakal looked steadily at the view-screen as the school ground came in sight. The oval once again would accommodate his vehicle. 'Shakralaz is my brother. Today, he dies, or die I here. Your world will live or die as a result. I win - you live, he wins - you die.'

Why? The question rang out in Tam's mind, but his body refused to allow him to speak. He was too afraid of what was about to happen.

# CHAPTER TWENTY-TWO

## RAKAL'S BATTLE

Eight-year-old Ash was helping his parents in the vegetable patch when his seven-year-old sibling Mica came running towards them.

'Father, it's Tam, Rakal has taken him in the spacecraft. Just a test run, he said,' Mica panted bending over to catch his breath.

'Wow! Did it work then?' Ash asked.

They could hear the roar of the propulsion system ignite, and in the distance, they saw the small craft rise quickly into the sky. Swiftly it was out of eye contact.

'Course,' Mica replied.

'Ash, Mica, go inside and tell everyone. We'll come in shortly,' Richard put a hand on Mica's shoulder and gently prompted him to go up the path.

'Oh Richard! Tam could be in danger,' Davrew turned to Richard who nodded.

'There's not much we can do now but wait. I'm sure he'll be okay,' Richard hugged his partner, then they followed their children inside.

'I wish I'd been there to see it take off. I didn't think Rakal had it all together,' Ash raced into the kitchen with Mica.

'Oh, you and your mechanical wizardry Ash,' Mica wailed, 'Rakal's language is much more interesting.'

Two hours later Ash and Mica were in the machinery shed.

'I always feel better if I'm fixing something,' Ash explained as he concentrated on some wiring on a motorised toy truck. Mica was watching him and chewing his fingernails.

'I did try to stop Tam from going with Rakal,' Mica sighed. They could hear their parents in the garden nearby.

'You've already turned the soil there, my love. Let's go for a walk and relax.'

'Relax!' Davrew snapped, but then reluctantly agreed. 'Where are they? They should be back by now, Richard.'

As they passed Mica and Ash saw them.

'Tam isn't back yet,' Mica looked up sorrowfully. 'Am I in trouble for not stopping them going?'

Davrew patted the six-year-old child fondly on the head. 'No one could have stopped them, darling. Don't worry. Tam will be home soon.'

As Richard and Davrew walked away, the children looked at each other.

'Everyone is worried,' Ash said.

'Everyone is scared,' Mica nodded, 'might as well go inside and get something to eat.'

'I guess,' Ash agreed, 'but, check this out!' Ash pressed the 'ON' button on the toy truck and smiled when it roared into action, then handed the remote control to his sibling. 'Why don't you drive that inside?'

'Okay,' Mica agreed, taking the little joystick, and setting the toy truck in motion. 'The little ones will be glad to see it going.'

'This is five-year-old Pip's and Mia's favourite truck. It'll keep everyone occupied for a while,' Ash grinned and followed Mica along the path. Just as their parents returned from their short walk.

All four looked up at the distinctive sound interplanetary propulsion systems roared overhead. They followed the sound and guessed ended not too far from where they stood. A commotion promptly erupted as a group of excited children ran out through the back door.

'We heard them land!' A group of young children chorused.

'Sounds like nearby,' Ash added.

'More than one,' Mica looked bug eyed at his cousins.

'Hush, hush now, all of you. We heard them too. It did sound like two vehicles, but we'll have to wait and see what this means,' Davrew ushered them all back inside taking control of the situation.

'Sounded like they landed back near the secondary school,' Richard followed the children inside. 'I'll give the school a ring and see what's happening. If there's anyone there.'

'Miri, will you look after the children while we go over to the school?' Davrew asked.

'Peter will be back from the markets soon. I'm sure with the help of the older children, we'll cope. I am used to handling these eleven children on the weekend,' Miri reminded her parents.

'We only just returned from town with the babies,' Imi smiled. 'Just as well we did.'

'Aw, can't we come too?' Ash pleaded. 'I'm dying to know what it was like in Rakal's little spaceship. He didn't really tell me much about the workings. I'd love to have got my hands on the engines and wiring.'

Richard shook his head from side to side. 'Ash, you must stay with your siblings and cousins. We are all curious. I know you are a fine mechanic in the making and that's what you're interested in.'

'Just like I'm interested in the way Rakal speaks, I'm making Linguistics my speciality,' Mica nudged his sibling.

'This is a difficult situation, Ash dear. We don't want people finding out too much about us while they see what this Rakal is up to,' Davrew continued sympathetically.

'We don't know what's happening over at the school, love. Two spaceships, two outworlder's, and Rakal who knows where we live. Is it safe for our children here?' Richard asked. Davrew had a pained look on his face and drew a deep breath before answering.

'I can hear something, Richard. Listen.'

Following Davrew's lead they all went back outside. It was only about twenty minutes since they had heard the spaceships return.

'It's Peter returning from town,' Miri said.

'It's Tam, he's jumped out of the car and is running,' Richard said.

Ash ran towards his twelve-year-old sibling, Mica tried to keep up. The other children were stopped by Miri. Tam was crashing through the orchard and howling. Horror written on his pale face.

Peter pulled up in the ute and got out.

'I saw Tam running away from the secondary school yard. He was hysterical and I managed to get him inside the cabin and most of the way home before he jumped out at the start of the orchard,' Peter explained. 'I couldn't make sense of what he was saying.'

Back in the orchard Ash and Mica were running towards Tam.

'Stop Tam, we can all go back together,' Ash called. Tam didn't stop and continued his frenzied running.

'He's mad, a monster!' Tam yelled as he careered into Ash and Mica. He continued to run.

'He's a mad monster!' Tam continued to wail, while Ash and Mica followed.

When he reached his parents, he allowed them to hold him, stopping his tortured run. Shock set in. Shivering, Tam started to sob uncontrollably.

An hour later more of Richard and Davrew's older children returned home. Sal and Bon had been away at weekend tutorials. Sal from botany lecture at the local museum, and Bon from a day medical seminar.

'You missed all the commotion,' Ash greeted them.

'Why? What happened?' Bon asked.

'Bon you'll need to tend to Tam,' Davrew joined them. 'He's had a terrible shock. We don't know the full story yet, but he came home hysterical after Rakal took him on his spaceship to test it out. He came back with another spacecraft at his heels. The school janitor I spoke to said there was a terrible mess to clean up. The Policemen from here went over to investigate. I gave Tam a sleeping draught and tucked him in bed.'

'It seems that when Rakal returned he was being chased and they both landed on the school oval and took to hand to hand combat. That's what he told us when he came back.'

'He also said he's leaving,' Ash chipped in. 'Tam won't go near him.'

'Rakal won't say anything else,' Mica grumbled.

'Rakal said he'd killed and eaten his enemy,' Ash added. 'Too gross!'

'Sal, Tam's school is going to be closed till all the damaged is fixed up.'

The next day, the Davidson family watched Rakal leave Earth forever. They were all relieved to see him go. The authorities were equally delighted with the police busily setting out to erase any trace of the aliens' presence.

A week later Ash and Mica were reading the local newspaper.

'It says here the parents and teachers of East Ridge Secondary School had been distressed by damage to the grounds and school facilities caused by vandals,' Ash read aloud.

'No mention of alien visitors, or a battle to the death, in the grounds?' Mica peered over Ash's shoulder.

'The local government representative, Mr Standthorpe, spoke to a gathering in the local community room hall. In his speech, he announced the whole incident at the school had been an elaborate hoax. No evidence of anything other rogue vandals and or a random act of terrorism by a lone madman. Teachers and students would be counselled and the whole matter was now closed for public record.'

'That's good news for us all,' Davrew smiled at the children. 'Time for you to do your studies.'

Ash folded the paper and put it back on the shelf.

'We can all get on with our lives,' Richard added with a grin. 'We've managed to dodge some unwanted attention there.'

'What about Tam?' Ash asked. Tam had been quiet since Rakal left.

'Tam has decided to go to Uni next year,' Richard replied.

'In the City, away from this quiet country life,' Davrew added with a sigh.

## CHAPTER TWENTY-THREE

# Bon – Further Education

### May 1990

Nick O'Donahue closed the blinds on a bleak grey day. It was late autumn. The wind still held a premature winter chill. His recent haircut let the cold reach unprotected ears. With mouse, brown hair crowning a closely shaved scalp underneath, in the latest style, he was glad to be inside. A small heater warmed the cramped unit. Although the rent for the two-bedroom flat was steep, its proximity to the hospital made it impossible to pass up.

Bon Davidson was a friend and co-worker there. Nick walked across the untidy lounge which was cluttered with papers, books, mugs, and a general mess until he reached the door to the kitchen. Bon was fussing over an assortment of saucepans on the stove. Steam rose as his friend lifted each lid to check the contents.

'Jeez mate, you're going to a bit of trouble, aren't you?' This barely used and ill-equipped room was warmer from the cooking range than the lounge was from the heater. 'Our students and interns won't expect all this. Just some nibbles and beer will do,' he said as he began moving past his friend with a slab of beer.

'You know what I told you, Nick, about my family and these little examinations we all take,' Bon remarked as his friend squeezed past.

'You study too hard, mate, with med school then the hospital. How you have time to sit these family generated tests I don't know!' Ripping the cardboard box and taking the beer cans out Nick quickly loaded the fridge. 'I bought some wine coolers and light beers too. How many are coming?'

'Six plus Jake and Gem, so there'll be ten in all.'

'You mean Jake the psychiatrist?' Nick queried.

'Yep, I bumped into him at the hospital. Hope you don't mind me asking him along. I thought maybe he could talk to Gem a bit.'

'I don't mind. He's a great guy. You know I've been seeing him about this 'dream lover' thing?' Bon nodded while briskly stirring the contents of the largest pan.

'How are you going with all that? I mean is Jake helping or have you had more nocturnal dreams of the deeply intimate kind? It doesn't seem such a bad thing, really.'

'Yeah, well, the dreams aren't bad. They are just too damn realistic. I wake up wanting more, you know. It's always the same, so good, so real! I think Jake is helping, but the dreams only happen every so often. It's easy to get indifferent about it.'

'Wouldn't that be the best way to be? Just accept the dreams and go on with life?'

'Perhaps, but they really get to me. Same as you get bothered about Gem. You hope Jake will talk Gem out of chasing those pretty boys?' Bon nodded again.

'I'm worried about Gem. I've let him know; health wise it's a ticking time bomb. Gem doesn't seem to listen to me, so I hope Jake might be able to do some good.'

'I can't see it happening,' Nick concluded. 'I'm going in for a shower now.'

Half an hour later Nick returned dressed and towelling dry his hair. 'Water is hot if you want it.'

'Thanks, Nick, I will. The gang should start arriving soon.'

'Not setting the table, then?' Nick teased.

'Gee no, it's mostly fingers foods and hot soup. There's no room for a formal meal in your little chicken coop.'

'Chicken coop!' Nick blustered then grinned. 'Better take the pinny off or people might start talkin'.'

Bon laughed and headed for the bathroom removing the offending garment along the way. 'I've tidied up a bit, Nick,' Bon called back over his shoulder, 'let the gang in, will you?'

'You better hurry or I'll be calling the fire brigade to the kitchen.'

'I won't be long,' the voice came from the bedroom. Bon emerged carrying a change of clothes and fresh towels. 'You can bet Gem will be last to arrive,' he remarked while disappearing into the bathroom.

A short while later Nick had let in most of their guests. Bon joined them with his blond hair, still damp, tied back in a neat ponytail. Quickly he rounded up assistance from his co-workers to put the food out. Serving mugs of hot soup and setting a fondue and sauces, along with assorted nibbles to dip on the coffee table, was easy.

Everyone present was sampling some of the delicious tidbits when the doorbell rang. Gem was indeed the last of the guests to arrive. As always Nick was surprised at the close resemblance of the two siblings. Their mannerisms, even dress, were remarkably alike. Both Bon and Gem wore thick roll neck jumpers with neat stylish trousers and comfortable pull on boots. They shook hands warmly at the door and hugged briefly. Gem even had his hair tied back in a ponytail with similar shining golden tousle going halfway down his back.

'Now guys, we're here to do some serious study. We've seen the progress of various patients and we need to study different treatment procedures,' Nick began once everyone was settled and appetites appeased.

'Wait, wait,' Gem interrupted, 'if you are going to talk shop all night I'm going to eat and run.'

'Come on, Gem, don't get squeamish,' Bon taunted.

'I'm only here to enjoy your gastronomical delights and send back a report on your efforts, Bon. Would anyone be prepared to collaborate and state whether these little treats are irresistible?'

A general murmur of agreement went up with toasts being made and compliments to the chef cited. A chubby brunette with round face and tightly pursed lips raised her half-filled glass. Nick always got the impression her clever medical skills were overridden by a surly nature and a constant pout.

'This is a test, is it?' Alana asked bluntly.

'Certainly is, Alana,' Bon nodded. Nick knew from comments Bon had made that he'd found it difficult working with this young woman. Her prickly nature and quick temper often made the rest of the group uncomfortable. Bon explained quickly. 'My family set each other little tests so we all have some knowledge of each other's interests. Gem will report on my small culinary compositions and I'll get points for being good.'

'With med school and internship don't you think it's a bit much?' she retorted with a snort.

'It's not that much really and we don't have to do them if we don't want to,' Bon assured the sour faced woman.

'We certainly don't! I hardly do any,' Gem added with a charming smile.

'You still do a fair bit from what Bon's told me,' Nick interjected. 'These guys never stop. Bon had a doozey of an exam on computers from you last week!

As soon as we get in the door of this flat Bon rushes to the computer to do his homework. Mind you, he only stays here when we're on those late and early shifts. We've barely got time to eat and sleep, much less do extra study.'

'Alright, so we all think Bon's cooking passes the test?' Gem asked while rubbing his hands together.

'Very tasty indeed,' Jake remarked.

'Good,' Gem stood up from the armrest of the chair he was sitting on. 'You're not one of the regulars here, are you?'

'No, I'm Jake Corman, an analyst from the hospital. I came along for a good meal and to see how these guys prepare for their stressful work.'

'And maybe you're interested in Nick's strange dreams of a fantasy lover?' Gem jibed. Nick's face flushed red with embarrassment. Gem knew too much, and, unlike Bon, he couldn't keep his mouth shut about it. 'And maybe Bon asked you to have a talk with me about my going to clubs to meet young male cherubs who attend to my every need?'

'Come on, Gem, let's not be unpleasant,' Bon tried to change the subject. 'We can have a meal and chat without getting serious about our problems.'

'Problems,' Gem blustered. 'My problems are for me to sort out. I'm off! I've got a date. You've got problems of your own, Bon Davidson. You should be worried out of your mind about Imi being pregnant again. You're the doctor, for cryin' out loud. You should know the dangers; you've put your own partner's life at risk, and you want to meddle in my private life! Well, I've told you before - *BUTT OUT!*

Bon's eyes bulged and he remained silent. His shoulder was bruised from Gem's prodding finger, which he'd jabbed while driving home each accusation.

Jake stood beside the two siblings. 'Hang on, both of you,' he interrupted the stormy outburst. 'I'm here for a good meal and pleasant conversation. I leave work at work, and naturally, it's confidential. If you want, I can make an appointment for you both. I only charge sixty-five dollars per half hour.' His infectious impish grin took the chill off the air. This was rewarded by a sly grin from Gem. Bon relaxed a little and walked Gem to the door.

'I think we should get back to discussing *our* patients,' Nick remarked coolly. He was still annoyed at Gem for his indiscretion. 'Perhaps Jake can give us some lessons in bedside manners.'

'I'll call in at the shop and write up your report, Bon,' Gem said softly, while reaching for the doorknob to make a quick escape. 'I have got a date.'

Jake had walked to the door with them and couldn't let his questions go unanswered. 'Wait up, Gem,' Jake held the clear blue eyes with his, 'I'd like to meet you for a coffee sometime.'

'You won't charge sixty-five dollars per half hour for that, will you?' Gem replied flashing a brilliant smile.

'No,' Jake replied with a grin. 'Just a chat and a cuppa. You could join us too, Bon.'

'I don't think so,' Bon replied.

'Is your wife's life really at risk?' Jake asked, full of concern.

'I'm afraid so. The last pregnancy was difficult. We were told not to risk Imi's health with further conceptions.'

'Then why go ahead?' Gem prodded.

'It's complicated. I really don't want to talk about it now,' Bon replied evasively.

'Do you have a computer at home, Jake Corman?' Gem asked hopefully.

'No, I don't Gem.'

'Then I'll meet you for coffee, just you and me. Bon and I always set sparks flying when we're together. We can chat and maybe you'll buy yourself the latest in-home computing from the best darn computer sales-person in this little town.' With a quick farewell wave to the other guests and a nudge of Bon's shoulder, Gem disappeared through the door.

Nick clapped his hands together as Bon and Jake returned to their seats. 'Now, let's get these things cleared away, so we can do some serious medical work.'

The evening went smoothly after that.

## CHAPTER TWENTY-FOUR

# Bon – Secrets Revealed

### May 1990

The next morning Bon rushed to the bathroom and emptied the contents of his stomach into the toilet pan.

'You OK, mate?' Nick asked as he walked past the door, still bleary eyed. 'I hope you didn't give us all food poisoning!'

Bon smiled but couldn't reply as his stomach contracted and he vomited again. The phone rang in the next room as he was splashing water on his face. Nick answered it and Bon heard him speak briefly then return the receiver.

'That was Jake,' Nick called out. 'He's coming around to see you on his way to work.'

'Why?' Bon mumbled through the towel he was patting his face with.

'Something about asking you background questions about Gem. I can tell him to leave it if you're not feeling up to it.'

'No, I'm Okay. It's just a tummy bug.'

'Please, Bon, you're the trainee doctor - a tummy bug, or plain food or alcohol poisoning?' They both laughed.

'It was a good night and we ended up getting a lot of work done,' Bon smiled.

'Yep, your fussing was worth it,' Nick agreed.

Shortly after, the doorbell rang. Bon, having showered and dressed, was feeling much better. He opened the door to Jake with a smile. They shook hands and Bon noticed the blood shot eyes and careful movements of a man suffering the aftereffects of one beer too many.

'You look a little worse for wear, Jake,' Bon stated the obvious. 'Why bother coming around this morning when you could see me at the hospital later in the day?'

'I could have done, Bon, but you know how it is. I'm booked up with appointments and you're in surgery. Chances of catching one another and being able to talk are fairly remote.' Bon had to admit conversations with his colleagues at the hospital usually revolved around a patient's welfare. Jake continued, 'not often, can I stop and chat to doctors from other departments.'

'Well, you're here now. Nick's in the shower. I've a fresh pot of coffee made so let's get to it. Neither of us have a lot of time before we have to go to work.' To sit down they had to clear away a space between empty beer cans and papers filled with sketches of various parts of the human anatomy. The place was a mess.

'Firstly,' Jake began while easing into the soft cushions of the lounge chair, 'how many children do have you now?'

'This is background for Gem, right?'

'It may seem irrelevant, but it will help me put some pieces together,' Jake nodded which Bon realised he immediately regretted. His eyes reflected the pounding in his head. Being familiar with the need to build a patient's family history to treat them, he knew as an analyst, where Jake was coming from. As a Davidson, however, Bon was also determined to be cautious.

'Imi and I have four children. The last pregnancy our little seven-year-old Fin was born, after a difficult pregnancy. We were told not to have any more.'

'So, you've only just found out she's pregnant?'

'Yes. We have been taking precautions, not good enough obviously. We know the dangers, but Imi is determined to go ahead.'

'You live in the same house with your parents and family, is that right?'

'Yep,' Bon nodded and handed a hot mug of coffee to his guest. 'Very much an extended family, it's a huge house. Imi and I have an annex at the northern end of the house. Miri and Peter live in the extension at the southern end. Most of the children sleep in the dormitory in the upper level, that runs the length of the house. Our parents have what we refer to as 'the Grand Room' central to all this.'

'And you can study in all this?' Jake shook his head. Bon laughed and nodded.

'Why do you live all together?'

'It suits us. That's all,' Bon replied quickly.

Nick walked into the room running a comb through his hair before sitting down opposite Jake. Bon had poured an extra cup of coffee for Nick and now handed it to him. 'They've got rare blood, so they stick together,' Nick added by way of explanation.

'You're not old to have so many children,' Jake remarked.

'He's nearly twenty-three, Jake, and these Davidson's start young you know,' Nick grinned, nudging his friend.

'We did start young, and we have four healthy children, as I've already mentioned.'

'Thanks, now I know, that's fine,' Jake smiled, deciding to be tactful and change the subject. 'So why are you worried about Gem? He's an adult who seems very capable.'

'It's just that Gem is a bit of a loner, Jake,' Bon tried to sum up his feelings. 'Mainly, of course, I'm worried about Gem's health. What he is doing is very risky.'

'We have to head off soon, mate,' Nick pointed at his watch.

'Time is getting on,' Bon agreed. 'I really think it's up to Gem to go into the gory details of his personal life. I think it has a lot to do with the assault he suffered, at a school camp years ago, you know, the teacher.'

'Terrible business,' Nick nodded, 'Gem doesn't say much about it and Bon had to help him recover.'

'What exactly happened?' Jake asked while standing ready to leave. 'What kind of assault?'

Bon was collecting the mugs and taking them into the kitchen. 'Gem was physically abused by a teacher. Broken bones, bruising concussion and apart from the savage beating, Gem was sexually abused.'

'I see,' Jake moved slowly toward the door. 'Perhaps I can help.'

'I wouldn't bet on it,' Nick replied. 'Gem is a stubborn and sometimes obnoxious bugger.'

'He's not, Nick,' Bon retaliated in Gem's defence. 'He can be sharp, he's a great salesman. Being tactless isn't a crime. Anyway, Jake can judge for himself about Gem's actions.'

'I won't judge,' Jake assured them. Having retrieved his keys from his pocket he jangled them absently. 'Maybe I can be a friend, just someone to talk to who won't judge or condemn.'

'That's probably just what Gem needs,' Bon admitted, as he shook Jake's hand in farewell.

As the door closed behind Jake, Nick collected his own keys and jacket. 'Are you ready to go?'

'Yes, I'll just grab my bag,' Bon rushed back into the bedroom and collected what he needed, tossing them into the carry bag. As he walked back across the lounge, he decided to voice his fears. 'Nick, you know with the way Imi is, I could be looking at spending Christmas in France.'

'Sounds like a song title,' Nick replied jovially. 'Christmas in France. A ballad or love song, do you think?'

'Christmas 1990,' Bon spoke sorrowfully. 'I only hope that Imi will be with me to see next Christmas.'

'Oh, come on Bon, don't go getting morbid,' Nick grabbed his friend's arm and dragged him through the door. 'We'll be late if we don't get a move on.'

Two months later Bon felt he was living in a nightmare.

'You can't be serious, Bon!' Nick yelled so loud the small apartment almost shook.

'I had to tell you before I left to go overseas. Please try and understand Nick.'

'Understand! Bloody Hell, Bon! You've just told me you have been creeping into my bed at night and letting me think you're the angel of my dreams, so I'd screw you? I can't believe you'd be so dumb. Worse, I can't believe you're telling me this. You know my 'dream lover' thing has been a real bugbear for ages. I tell you what I understand. I bloody well understand you're leaving a very promising career to flit off to try and save Imi's life! By all accounts, you should not have allowed to be at bloody risk in the first place! You've lost it, mate. You're bloody crazy!'

'Nick, please calm down. It was not meant to happen more than once. You just made it so good I had to keep going. I didn't mean to upset you.'

'Calm down! You didn't mean to upset me! Jeez that's a bloody joke. I'll show you bloody calm down. You can get the hell out of here right now! Go on,' Nick pushed Bon toward the door. Then seeing his reluctance to go stormed into the spare room where Bon often stayed. He threw open the window and began throwing Bon's clothes and books out into the night air. 'Bloody, calm down! I'll calm down when you're gone for bloody good, you mongrel. Get out! Get out now!'

Bon felt numb and stood stupidly watching his friend continue his rampage. They were three stories up and the clothes and books were dropping like missiles to the pavement below.

'Nick, I may not see you again for ages. Please try to forgive me.'

'You can take this bloody thing too!' Nick screamed throwing his computer and keyboard out the window.

Bon grabbed his car keys and rushed out of the room and ran to the elevator.

Downstairs Bon felt dizzy and was almost ill. He tried to collect his possessions while looking up to his friend who was still calling abuse from the open window. The old PC was badly smashed after it's short flight.

There was so much happening with Imi being so much in need of support during a dangerous pregnancy. His own condition left him a bag of nerves. The peace and tranquillity of Andre's home in France sounded so good, while at the same moment he didn't want to leave. An idyllic life enjoying work, friendships and love had begun to fragment and crumble about him. Bon realised he was crying and tried vainly to wipe away the tears.

'Bon. Bon Davidson, can I help you?'

He looked up to see a nurse who must have been walking home from work. She was plump, neat, and caring. He knew her name but couldn't remember it.

'Doctor Davidson, you know me, I'm Angela Crosby. I can see you need some help,' the young woman began picking up his clothes.

'Thank you,' Bon mumbled. 'I'm sorry you've seen this. My car is just over there. I'll take what I can and leave.'

With arm's full of belongings Bon and the nurse walked across the small garden divide of the car park.

'I've never seen Doctor O'Donahue so angry,' the nurse muttered.

'No, neither have I,' Bon replied hoarsely. 'I'll be okay now. Thank you, Angela.' Shoving the few belongings, they'd collected in the boot of his car. He nodded to the nurse cursory thanks, then rushed to the driving seat and putting his foot down hard, he sped away. Although he'd told his friend what he needed to know, there was one other secret, the most important one he couldn't tell Nick.

## CHAPTER TWENTY-FIVE

# ASH

### December 1991

It was the last day of term. Miss Olivia Gray gathered her bag and books, and quickly walked out of the school for the summer holidays. On the corner, diagonally opposite the school, was a small service station run by her grandfather, Toby, a qualified mechanic.

Over the years, a student named Ash Davidson had spent a lot of time at the garage, watching Toby working and teaching his apprentice. He could be found there on his way to and from school, and when, she suspected, he felt bored during the day. There was always a shadowed corner for Ash to sit in at the garage. Often the old man would throw an oily rag in Ash's face to send him away, although he tolerated the youth's interest and curiosity. Being a conscientious teacher, she scolded her grandfather for allowing the boy to be there so often, particularly during school hours.

It had been six years earlier that she had first discovered the truant in her grandfather's workshop. Ash was a stocky plain-faced child with square chin and turquoise eyes. A slight eye disorder resulted in the need to wear square thin-framed spectacles. These often slid down the bridge of his nose much to the Ash's obvious annoyance.

Today she met him as she left the school.

'Hello, Ash, are you going to Grandpa Gray's now?' the tall slight woman asked as she as she walked down the stairs towards the car park.

'Ah, I thought I would, Miss Gray,' Ash replied with a cheeky grin. Their eyes now met at the same level. The last few years had given height and self-assured stance to his once ungainly child's stature.

'Then we can walk together.'

Ash nodded agreement. 'Can I carry your books?'

Olivia handed them to Ash. 'Grandpa tells me you're thinking of becoming his apprentice?'

'Yes, Miss Gray. I'll be fifteen next month and there's no legal reason why I can't join the workforce,' he replied cheerily, with a broad grin. 'I'm planning on being the family mechanic. I already do most repairs around home, farm machinery and the like. I also make things, Miss Gray.'

'What kind of things?' she asked.

'Helpful gadgets. We're a large family and need lots of transport and communication. I'm a bit of an inventor if truth be known.'

'I'm glad to hear it. Like the little project's you've made at school to entertain your classmates?'

Ash nodded.

'Do you remember when you came to my home to discuss my concentration, or lack of it, at school?' prompted Ash.

Miss Gray nodded as she recalled the scene vividly. Davrew had been trying to ease her mind and taken her to the boy's room. The bed was in the corner of a room littered with wires, car parts, partially assembled computer terminals, half-dismantled hi-fi system, and general junk. Ash was happily working on a toaster as they entered.

'There's no cause for concern, Miss Gray,' Davrew explained, 'Ash simply finds school boring. I can assure you there's nothing lacking in concentration levels at home or with our home studies program.'

She had walked cautiously towards Ash, smiling, 'what are you doing, Ash?'

'Just repairing this toaster, Miss Gray,' the child had replied candidly.

'You do have a lot of things to fix in here, don't you?'

'Yes,' was the only reply. Ash rolled the turquoise eyes despairingly and glanced at Davrew.

'This one is at least all together,' Olivia had stood beside the only whole piece of equipment in the room.

'That's my home-work computer,' Ash remarked. 'Right now, we're doing astronomy, physics, classical music history and ancient Egyptian history. It's heaps more interesting than school.'

'Now, Ash darling, there's no need to be unkind,' Davrew scolded. 'The school system offers what most students require for daily living. You see, Miss Gray, we have our own home studies program, and as I've already mentioned, there are no problems for Ash with concentration here.'

'I see Mister…I mean Davrew,' she corrected as her host had already asked her to use his first name. 'You have quite a talented child with special higher educational needs.'

'Not really, Miss Gray, all our children do the home program courses. The school system does augment their education. After all, they all need to socialise and develop communication skills. Some of the children quite enjoy school. Ash is the only one to date who has kept to the year level matching age. The other children have gone into higher grades. This does cause other problems, so we don't push any of our children. They do what they feel they can cope with when they wish to. Ash simply finds school–'

'Something I can put up with until I'm old enough

to leave,' Ash had finished the sentence.

Now, stopping at the base of the stairs to adjust the bag on her shoulders, Olivia looked fondly at the young man. 'You didn't care much for school then, did you?' She smiled, recollecting how helpless she had felt after the visit.

'Not much,' Ash agreed.

'Don't you think it would be a good idea to keep on until you have your HSC?'

'Not really. I know a lot more than school can ever teach me. Besides, I won't ever stop learning. Mr Gray won't let me,' he grinned.

'One day, when you have responsibilities of a growing family,' she warned, 'you may wish you had opted for a certificate to advance your career.'

Ash just smiled and didn't comment further. Kind as Miss Olivia Gray's intentions were, she was not a Davidson, and struggled to understand. Responsibilities were already heaped upon Ash's youthful shoulders. His joy of life was being able to create useful inventions for his ever-growing family.

CHAPTER TWENTY-SIX

# FAMILY DEBATE – SAL AND SIM

December 1991

It had been a balmy day and a light breeze had come with the evening shadows. The windows and doors were open throughout the Davidson home. Evening in the kitchen was always hectic yet orderly. The long ornate wooden table was being laid for the last meal of the day. Sal joined the group of siblings and cousins as they set an assortment of salads and vegetables along the centre. Davrew put two trays of sliced bread at either end. Richard added two large jugs of fruit juices stacked with ice cubes.

'Looks like a full house,' Richard grinned.

Only two members were missing. Gem, the second eldest sibling, was in town, as was often the case. Tam, the next born after Sal, was absent also. Off yet again on some obscure overseas archaeological dig.

His younger cousins, Miri's children, Fee, Lar, Mia, Den and Gel were loading plates and juggling glasses filled with the refreshing juice.

'We'll eat outside on the verandah,' Mia was their spokesperson 'Mother said we had permission, if it's alright with you.'

'Of course,' Davrew agreed.

Miri put a large terrine of clear consommé on the table. 'I'm sure your grandparents won't mind a bit of peace. Children you can all go outside too. Don't make a mess out there. I don't want crumbs all over the place.'

'Will you come too, Tris?' Mia asked his cousin who at thirteen was a year younger.

'No thanks,' the child replied while slipping into a chair. 'I'll be able to spread my wings with you lot out of the way.'

Cass, Ash's partner, having fed two-year-old Ness, and having put the baby Rill down for a nap, could eat and join the conversation, without distractions.

Sal picked up the thread of conversation clearly begun during meal preparation time.

'I just think we could do a lot with what we have to relieve the plight of those poor beggars in Africa. It seems a cryin' shame when we could help get food to them, with the technology we have. They are starving to death,' Richard pulled his chair away from the table and sat down.

'Now, Richard,' Davrew replied, we've been over this before. The risk to our family is far too great. We could lose our anonymity altogether,' Davrew replied.

'I thoroughly agree, Father,' Bon entered the debate.

'We could set up some relief charity like the celebrities are always doing. No one need know we're behind it,' Sal put in.

'They only do that as a tax dodge, don't they?' Bon asked.

'Besides, if we did, the whole thing would have to be set up for normal welfare channels to distribute and deliver the goods. Which would defeat the purpose, wouldn't it?' Davrew asked.

'I guess,' Richard nodded.

'We'd be hard pressed to explain how we could get fresh food from one side of the globe to the other in one hour,' Bon concluded.

'It seems such a waste of resources,' Richard continued. 'There must be a way.'

'Not without compromising our safety, Richard,' Davrew argued. 'Have your meal now, Richard, please. Let's leave the 'non-intervention debate' at rest tonight.'

Richard nodded and looked up at Sal. 'You're not eating with us again tonight?'

'No, I'll just take these upstairs to eat with Sim, she's still not well enough to join us,' he replied. Then turning towards his twin offspring added, 'Saz and Sam, I'll be back soon to tuck you in bed. Behave now, won't you?' The two children looked up as though they were two angelic cherubs. Sal sighed while lifting the food-laden tray. 'Let me know if they cause any trouble, won't you?' The twins were imps and his plea to his parents, their grandparents, was genuine.

'We will,' Davrew grinned.

The twins were now four-year-old tearaways. They'd been born in 1989, their first children, a year after Sim's arrival. That birth had been without trouble or torment. The fact no more children had been conceived until now didn't seem important.

Sal was fit, having been active all through life with gardening, hiking, planting, and tending the market garden and orchard for the family. Now his body was weary. While making his way up the stairs he recalled the very first time he met Sim. They spent hours together at Sim's family home in France, the third born to Andre and Rimi. They'd immediately taken to each other. Even the tenderness of their first kiss flooded his frayed senses. Concern for his partner weighed him down.

Sim sat motionless on a chair on the balcony as Sal placed the tray on the table nearby. 'Here you are my love, a delicious bowl of soup with your favourite herb bread,' Sal knew his jovial manner sounded false. How to change his demeanour was a real problem.

Sim turned slowly towards the tray and smiled briefly, acknowledging the offering.

'I'm not very hungry, darling, but I'll try.' Sal removed the lid of the bowl as Sim began to fumble with the spoon. 'Tell me what's happening downstairs while I eat. Are the twins alright?'

'Yes love, they'll come into see you in the morning,' Sal spoke softly.

'So, the debate goes on with no tangible result,' Sim concluded as she put the spoon down.

'Darling, please eat up. You haven't had a sip and it'll be going cold,' Sal chided gently. Sim did manage to swallow a few mouthfuls of soup before asking for the tray to be removed.

After a while Sal headed downstairs with the almost untouched tray.

Bon passed him at the bottom of the stairs. 'Sim hasn't had much of that,' the doctor remarked dryly. 'I'll check on her now before going to bed. Don't be long about getting some sleep yourself, Sal. You look beat.'

'Yes, Doctor Bon,' Sal chanted impishly at Bon's pointed finger. The younger children often did this in torment of their family members. Bon smiled broadly and bounded up the stairs. Sal helped clear the dishes away, then checked on the twins, who were sleeping soundly, before re-joining Sim. Bon was still there when he walked into the room.

Sim lay comfortably in bed while Bon checked vital signs and made sure the unborn child was in no distress. 'The baby will be here very soon. I think Sim will need some time to recover. This has certainly been a troublesome pregnancy.'

'You're telling me?' Sal smiled gratefully at Bon. 'Thanks for dropping in. I'm sure everything will be fine when the baby is born.'

'Maybe,' Bon murmured, 'all the vital signs check out okay. Stop worrying, it'll all be fine.'

'Maybe nothing,' Sal retorted cheekily. 'You are the third born pessimist and I'm the fourth born optimist, remember!' The two siblings hugged and said goodnight.

The night was bright, and the ground bathed in the full moonlight. Trees outside the wide wooden windows swayed gently, rustling in the wind. Sal dozed contentedly under the covers with Sim close, so surrounded by love. Hours later Sal woke faintly aware of the stillness of the night.

Too still.

Suddenly completely alert, he had an overwhelming sense of something being wrong. The air had become cold and reaching over to touch Sim sent ice into Sal's heart.

There was a silence that thundered and roared.

No heartbeat, no breath, no sound.

Immediately the silence was shattered with a piercing scream. Sal shook Sim's body trying to shake the fear away. Everything spun. People ran into the room surrounding him. The screaming continued until a needle pierced Sal's upper arm.

Bon's voice. 'We must save the baby.'

Words drifted around him as his consciousness clouded and numbness descended, pulling him down into a place of darkness.

Later, Bon told him the words he didn't want to hear. Sim had died the moment Sal had woken. Bon had performed an emergency caesarean and saved the life of Sim's and Sal's third baby, pre-named Raz. Sedation barely helped over the next few days. The empty feeling that drowned all senses filled Sal's world. How to go on without Sim? The very thought was impossible.

CHAPTER TWENTY-SEVEN

# The Old Homestead

## March 1997

Bill hitched up his baggy jeans with one hand while turning the dial on the ancient telephone with the other. He was angry and frustrated with himself. It was so stupid to trust those real estate people; they were supposed to regularly inspect the property.

Looking around the old cottage kitchen brought him nearly to tears. Apart from the general filth and grime, empty bottles, newspapers, and cardboard boxes were scattered about. The benches and furniture were scratched, with notches carved in the sturdy woodwork. Broken drawers hung from their cavities, and Bill felt sick knowing the rest of the house was in a similar state.

'Hello, Davidson Residence,' a voice sounded in his ear.

Bill had nearly forgotten having dialled. He felt strange and uncomfortable with the unfamiliar voice at the other end. 'Ah, hello,' he replied clumsily. 'It's Bill, Bill from across the road. Can I speak to Richard if he's home?'

'Sure, Bill, I'll go get him,' the cheery young voice replied.

Bill thought he sounded silly explaining who he was, but not knowing to whom he was talking made it seem necessary. It had been years since he'd spoken to Richard or taken interest in the goings on of his family.

'Thanks,' he acknowledged curtly.

Several minutes passed and Bill thought he had been left dangling too long when his cousin's voice squeaked down the line. 'Bill, is that you?'

'Yes, 'course,' Bill blurted. 'I need to talk to you. I'm at Mum's old place. Can you get your bum over here now?'

'It's Sunday. What's up?'

'Just come over here and you'll see,' Bill growled.

'Okay, I'm on my way. No need to get your knickers in a twist. See you soon.'

Bill slammed down the phone. 'He's so bloody cheerful, makes me sick,' he muttered. How he wished his mother had not made her last 'Will and Testament' out the way she did. Bill had inherited two-thirds ownership of the old home and grounds and Richard had been left the other third. Nancy was a good woman, kind-hearted and loving. She must have hoped joint ownership would bring about some reconciliation between the two cousins.

In Nancy's last few years, Davrew had been there for her, and their friendship had grown a loving and caring companionship. His mother was a wonderful woman. Bill shook his head and started sorting out rubbish. He accepted that it was her way of showing some appreciation of Davrew and Richard. Bill couldn't share his mother's feelings. After she passed, he had distanced himself from them. It was hard to remember when they last spoke. He rubbed some grime off his face. It must have been when they had that out-of-space visitor, back in '85, twelve years earlier.

Bill continued stacking the rubbish into piles. It was going to be a huge task to make the old cottage liveable again. Shortly after, he heard the back-door slam. He drew a deep breath and looked his cousin in the eye when he entered the room.

'Hells bells, Bill. What's happened to the house?'

'It's not what happened, it's what's not been happening. Damn it all, those real estate people said these tenants had to abide by the 'Conditions of Lease' agreement. The last couple were so good, I didn't think to check up on this mob.'

Richard walked around the room, replacing drawers, and looking in cupboards. Nothing rested on the unwashed surfaces except the grey cover of ground-in dirt. 'Cripes, it's unbelievable! They've even nailed this cupboard up.' He yanked hard at the door handle until it came away from the door.

'The worst is,' Bill sighed as he thumped his thigh with his hand. 'They scarpered without paying the last two month's rent. We've got the Bond, but it won't be enough to cover the repairs to this lot.'

'Jeez, Bill, I didn't even know the McCauley's had left. They were lovely people who kept everything in its place. I know because we came and helped them when their house cow calved.'

'Yeah, well, it hasn't been all that long, mate. As you can see, these mongrels were the dead opposite.'

'So, what do we do now, apart from clean this place up?'

Bill felt his mouth go dry. He'd made up his mind; it was a decision he'd hoped he'd never to make.

'It's like this,' he began, 'this is gonna cost a packet to get right. I'll be straight with you, Richard, I can't do it now. The bank is breathing down my neck! What with the wool prices hitting rock bottom and the glut in wheat supplies because of the bloody European Common Market! I'm caught between a rock and a hard place. Renting out this place was supposed to help bring in some cash, not throw it out of the bloody window!' Bill felt exhausted from the outburst and even dared to sit on one of the filthy chairs.

'Bill,' Richard sat down too. 'Why didn't you tell me how bad things are. You know I can help!'

'I don't want charity from anyone, least of all from you,' Bill spluttered. 'Just 'cause those bankers who were so quick to lend me money have changed their tune now doesn't mean I'll come crawlin' to you for help!'

'I wasn't offering you charity. I'm not that stupid,' Richard stared at his cousin then got up again. He silently began collecting newspapers to add to Bill's mounting pile.

'We'll have to sell her,' Bill mumbled solemnly, 'I can't see any way around it.'

'Let's not be too hasty. Perhaps there are some alternatives.'

'What bloody alternatives?'

'Well, for a start, I'll call home for help to clean up this rubbish. Being the weekend, there's lots of helpers available.'

'Clean up's one thing but look at all the damage. I won't have you paying for it unless we share expenses. But it's like I just said, Pat and I are broke.'

'Come on! Neither of us want to sell the house we grew up in, to strangers. Do we? Now, I'm just going to phone home. We can't do this by ourselves.'

Not long after Richard's phone call, several vehicles arrived with able-bodied helpers. The work began in earnest and, within an hour, two trailer loads of rubbish were driven to the local rubbish tip. Floors were swept, cobwebs dusted away, furniture moved, and buckets of sudsy water prepared for the wall washers who lined up ready to begin.

Richard tapped Bill's arm and motioned for him to follow through the back door to the verandah, where it was quieter, and they could talk unhindered.

'I've been thinking,' Richard began, 'our home is getting a bit overcrowded.'

'Hmph, your 'rebuilding the population' rubbish,' Bill grunted.

'Hear me out Bill,' Richard continued. 'We've got lots of room for more, Bill. We have extended the house twice. It's not that so much,' Richard lent on the verandah pillar. 'No, it's like this. Gem sleeps most nights in the room behind the shop in town. Maya, Gem's child, likes to sleep in the bookbinding room we built at the end of the machinery shed. Sal often takes the twins and little Raz, for camping trips, to get them away from the rest of the household. Those twins are lovable imps. So, you see, some of my family don't always like living in a beehive.'

'So?' Bill couldn't see what Richard was driving at.

'Dav's out of town right now so I can't ask him, but I'm sure this idea would suit us all.'

'What idea?' Bill replied, frustrated.

'Well, maybe some of our children and their families could come and live here. They could clean up the place and repair the damage. It's going to take more than an afternoon.'

'Speaking of strange people with strange ideas, where exactly is Davrew?' Bill grunted.

'Just out of town! He went to a Biodiversity seminar in the city. If not, you could bet every nook and cranny would be scrubbed clean by now. Besides, there's nothing strange about Davrew.'

Richard sighed and threw his hands in the air. 'This is a big task, to repair the old home. I had thought you might be glad to keep the home in the family, and my solution seems a good one.'

'Could be,' Bill mumbled while regarding his cousin for a moment. The neat blue jeans and cotton print shirt all screamed successful businessman. Richard was far from being a farmer, but clearly his heart was in the right place. 'I'd have to be paid rent still, at a fair rate.'

'Of course,' Richard nodded. 'That would take some pressure off the bank, wouldn't it?'

'Rent agreement all legal like,' Bill added.

Richard held out his hand and Bill shook it. 'Jeez Bill, you look more like your father every day! George wore blue checked flannelette shirt and baggy jeans. You've even rounded out to have his barrel chest and a bit of a paunch.'

'Ha,' Bill laughed, 'and me hair's a bit thin on top these days too, just like dad.'

Just then Sal's blond head and lean frame walked through the back door. 'Hi, Bill, Father. Have you seen the twins?'

'Yes, over by the woodshed,' Richard replied, pointing to the half dismantled shed.

Sal groaned and jogged down the steps to look for them.

'Sal is our fourth child, a botanist and gardener. He tends the orchard and organises our market garden as well. The vegetables are not only our food supply, but also a handy extra source of income.'

'Pat has a small veggie patch. She's always saying she'd like to do more, but I never get around to digging it over for her,' Bill remarked.

'Perhaps with Sal close at hand, Pat could extend her veggie garden?'

Sal returned, dragging two dirt-covered explorers with him by the ears. He shook his head in bewilderment. 'These two rascals are always getting into mischief somewhere or other. Last week I had to rescue them from a cliff ledge.'

'Are they a lot of trouble?' Bill asked, hoping now Richard hadn't decided this was the family moving into his mother's former home.

'Not really,' Sal admitted. 'We were camped near Johnson's Bluff. I didn't pay much attention to their calls for help at first. The day before they'd doused the fire of the camper next door, so I thought he was simply scolding them again. There's a stream below a small ridge, which leads to a rocky outcrop. You might know it, the one that drops away on the other side to a sheer cliff?'

Bill nodded.

'It falls away to a gully below, and that's where I found them on a very narrow ledge. They were terrified and, believe me, I had to take a few deep breaths to stay calm.' He paused long enough to release the two children and send them back into the house. 'After I pulled them up, I nearly killed them. By the stars, I don't know what would have happened if other campers had found them. They might have been taken to hospital, with our white blood and anatomy, they could have died from their attempts to help,' Sal rolled his eyes and concluded, 'from now on, we'll stay closer to home, in flat forest country.'

Richard looked sheepishly at his offspring. 'Well, Sal, with thoughts of keeping your active family at safe quarters, I've got a proposition for you. It might benefit your family and Bill's.'

'My family,' Sal quizzed, raising an eyebrow.

'Yes, the four of you. You, Sam, Saz and little Raz,' Richard explained. 'You need to keep those children busy and there's heaps to be done here, cleaning and repairing the damage to the house is only part of it. The gardens need work too. So...' Richard cocked his head toward his cousin, 'if Bill agrees, perhaps you could move in here.'

'I'm not sure,' Bill began.

'Neither am I,' Sal interjected. 'Frankly, I have trouble keeping up with the twins with everyone looking out for them. I don't know how I would manage on my own.'

'Not necessarily on your own, Sal. Maybe Miri's oldest Fee, Mia or Lar could join you? Or Bon's teenagers Kar and Pip? We are all still close enough to help and you could have a little bit of independence. The twins might behave differently if there were fewer people to tease. They could be happier here. Having new chores and responsibilities would keep them occupied.'

'Perhaps,' Sal shrugged. 'This place certainly needs a lot of work.'

'Look,' Bill gritted his teeth trying to stay calm. 'You don't have to change anything for me. I'll manage the bank and look after Mum's house. We still might have to sell it after the repairs are done.'

'No way!' Richard was adamant. 'This is Aunty's place and it's staying in the family!'

'In the family; that's a joke,' Bill grunted.

'It will always be your girls' home should they want to come home and live here. Sal and the children could make it a home again. They need to be a family too, Bill.'

'Father,' Sal interrupted, his features reflecting his concern, 'I'll talk this over with my brood. They need love and support, and so do I. Moving out of our secure extended family home could be a disaster.'

'It could be a blessing from the stars,' Richard grinned.

'I'll think about it,' Sal nodded, 'it might be a good idea.' He walked back into the old home. The door creaked and banged shut behind him.

'Sal was so devoted to Sim. Losing such a close and loving partner has been devastating for them all,' Richard explained.

Within a week, legal documents were drawn up. Sal and his small family moved into the cottage with two older children from the household. The major restoration projects were begun immediately. Soon the cottage would resemble its former homely country appearance inside and out. Once again, Nancy's home was filled with laughter and love.

## CHAPTER TWENTY-EIGHT

# The Accident

### December 1997

Bill was working on the boundary fence between his property and his mother's former home, finishing repairs on several gaps in the barbed wire as he heard the twins' approach. It was warm in the early afternoon sun, and perspiration trickled down his face under wide-brimmed straw hat.

'Well now, how are you two on this fine day?' He asked this question with head bent to his task, only glancing to see the youngsters' surprised reaction. They had tried to approach quietly, which was virtually impossible for them.

'Hi, Uncle Bill,' the fair-haired children chorused together.

'Look what we've got!' Sam exclaimed excitedly.

Saz danced, dangling a two-foot snake at arm's length from his body. 'Is it terribly dangerous? Would our arms drop off if we were bitten by it?'

Bill stood upright and grinned at them both. 'It's a beauty, lads, a bit of a baby yet though. They can grow to be over three meters long and give you a nasty bite, but it's not a baddie. No poison or venom in this little one. It's just a carpet snake and they make great pets.'

'It's already dead, Uncle Bill. We found it that way,'

Sam mumbled, barely disguising his disappointment.

Saz nudged his sibling and tossed the snake over the fence wire to let it hang limply in the breeze. He pointed at the yellow tractor parked nearby.

'You came in the tractor! Can we have a ride?' Saz asked excitedly.

'Yes, please, can we have a ride?' Sam added pleadingly.

'Well, I guess so, just to the next paddock, mind. I'm about done here,' Bill picked up his tools and they were soon all aboard the old vehicle.

'Can we help, Uncle Bill?' Sam asked hopefully.

'Not with the ploughing of this patch, lads. It's too steep a block. I've left it three years since its last crop, so it'll not be much fun for you or me either.'

'Oh, please! It's Saturday and such a lovely day. We'll only have to do our homework if we go back,' Saz persisted.

'Not today, but hang on now, it'll be a rocky ride to the next fence,' Bill grinned and started the motor, watching the delighted expressions on the faces of the eight-year-olds. They all began to sing a song Bill's father had taught him and now he, in turn, taught the twins.

> *'There was gravy, gravy,*
> *enough to sink the navy,*
> *in the store, in the store.*
> *There was gravy, gravy,*
> *enough to sink the navy,*
> *in the Quarter Master's store.*
>
> *My eyes are dim,*
> *I cannot see,*
> *I have not bought my specs with me,*
> *I have not bought my specs*
> *With me...'*

Soon they reached the gate to the next paddock and Bill swatted his hat at them to shoo them away, laughing at their antics and glad of their company.

'You kids! I do believe you moving in next door is a blessing.'

'Is Aunt Pat at home today?'

'Yep,' Bill replied.

'Does she work in town every day now?' Saz and Sam ran to the fence and hung over it.

'Well, our girls are all grown up and away most of the time. Pat works during the week now,' Bill adjusted his seat and reached for the starter.

'Just as well we're here to keep you company,' Sam grinned.

'Yep, just as well,' Bill beamed. The tractor was old but never missed a beat. This paddock was difficult to plough because of the slope and the soil. A downpour two nights before meant the going would be slow, and the tractor could be easily bogged.

'Some day kids, I'll get a new tractor, with roll bars and the like,' he called as the engine roared to life and set the levers to drop the blades. For the first two rows the gradient would not be too much of a problem. After that, there would be less traction.

'This is boring.' Saz nudged his twin.

'Yeah,' Sam replied.

'Race you home!' Saz was already down from the fence and away, with Sam running behind him.

At the top of the next rise, Saz stopped and bent over to catch his breath. 'Did you hear a shout?'

'Dunno,' Sam panted.

'Listen.' Saz cupped his hand to his ear.

'Sounds like the tractor droning,' Sam stood stock still to listen.

'Sam, we better go and see if Uncle Bill needs help!' Saz tugged his brother's sleeve then ran back.

'Perhaps Uncle Bill has found a treasure?' Sam squealed excitedly.

Together they dashed back to the gate Bill had sent them through earlier. Quickly they rushed towards the tractor, which lay at a curious angle upside down.

'Uncle Bill, where are you? Sam cried anxiously.

'Sam. He's here!' Saz was on the other side of the tractor. Sam rushed around to where Saz stood.

'Oh no, Saz, he looks like a purple grape ready to burst.'

'So, don't just stand there! Go and get help!'

Sam ran home screaming all the way.

Sal was sitting in the lounge with Raz on a rug building a Lego castle. The four-year-old looked out the window towards the sound and then up at Sal, who smiled.

'The twins are coming home,' Raz said and continued to piece together his creation.

'Yes, they are a noisy pair, aren't they,' Sal replied. The smile on his lips soon faded when he heard what Sam was yelling.

'Help, Father, please help,' Sam was breathless by the time he bounded up the steps where Sal greeted him. After gulping air, the child spat out. 'It's Uncle Bill! The tractor, it's on top of him.'

'What? Where?' Sal blurted.

Sam pulled his father's sleeve and headed back towards the boundary fence. 'Hurry!'

Sal called out 'Raz, come quick, we have to go. Sam, we'll take the ute. Get in,' When they got to the tractor Sal found a distraught and grubby child.

'He won't wake up, father. I tried to pull him out, but he's stuck!' Saz wiped a grimy mud-smeared hand over his tear-streaked cheeks.

'He did say something when we first got here, Saz. Remember?' Sam urged.

'Yeah, he told us to get help,' Saz agreed with his

twin.

'You've done very well, Saz!' Sal said then tried to lift the tractor. It wouldn't budge. 'I'll use the winch. Saz and Sam, if you can, pull out a couple of those fence posts and lay them on the ground.'

The boys set about rocking the old posts to and fro, to loosen them from the soil. Sal pulled out his mobile phone and called for help.

'Raz, darling, stay near the fence. Sam, can you go up to the road fence and direct people here? I've called for help from home, Pat, and an ambulance. When they arrive, you'll need to direct them to this spot.'

'Is this what you need father?' Saz laid a fence post down near the tractor.

'Yes, good work. Can you get a couple more? We'll have to be quick.'

Saz nodded.

Sal took a fence post and tried to force it in near Bill's head to levy the machine. It was too heavy. With a few more fence posts he decided to try a different strategy.

'Uncle Bill, we'll get you out!' Saz lay as close as he could to the old man.

Sal turned the ute towards the tractor.

'Now boys, we'll have to work quickly. Raz, this is the winch button, press it when I say. Okay?'

Raz nodded.

'Saz, you and I need to push some posts in when the tractor lifts enough to get them in.'

Saz nodded and crouched ready to help. Sal attached the winch to the bottom of the tractor. The soft, muddy soil made it hard to get good purchase as he hooked the wire through. He slipped while trying to attach the rope. Saz gasped.

'It's okay,' Sal looked up. He yelled once he'd secured the winch hook. 'Now, Raz, press the green button.'

The winch motor revved, and the cable grew taught. Raz, keep away from the cable. If it breaks, I don't want you getting the backlash.'

'Now, Saz!' Sal shouted. The tractor lifted slowly upwards. Bill groaned and Sal slid two fence posts in beside the trapped man.

'Stop! Raz, push the red button!' Sal tried to sound in control of his wavering voice. 'I can't risk doing more without some help. I think we've taken the weight off his chest and legs a bit.'

'Is he going to be okay?' Saz whimpered.

'He's breathing, he's got an erratic pulse. The fence posts have sunk in, so let's hope. He's being cushioned by the muddy soil. There's no way of knowing what injuries he has till we get him out.'

Peter and Miri arrived first with four of their adolescent children, while Fee and Lar, had driven their own cars. Three of Bon's older children, Kar, Pip and Tris, arrived in another ute. They'd all come across the paddock as directed by Sam, who now returned to witness the rescue.

Saz and Sam watched from the fence. Raz climbed up beside them.

Fee now manned the winch. 'Turn it on now!' Sal called from the other side of the tractor that still rested upside down. The winch motor revved again they tractor lifted enough for the three adults to drag Bill clear.

'He's out,' Saz whispered.

'He doesn't look flat,' Raz stared puzzled.

'His legs do,' Sam added.

The trio continued to watch as their adolescent cousins righted the vehicle.

Sal took off his shirt and make a pillow of it to put under Bill's head. Peter and Miri helped Sal make Bill as comfortable as they could. Pat arrived as the ambulance bumped in through the rough terrain of the next block.

'Oh, my God, Bill,' Pat wailed, and she began to

tremble. Miri put a comforting arm around her.

'Paramedics,' Saz nudged his twin.

'What are they doing?' Raz asked.

'Putting a drip in Bill's arm,' Sam explained.

'And a neck brace to keep him still,' Saz finished for his twin.

Miri and Pat got into the back of the ambulance.

Sal got up and walked over to the fence. Peter followed with the crumpled shirt in his hands. 'Tomorrow is your birthday isn't Raz?' he asked as he lent against the fence. They all watched the ambulance make its way out on to the highway, with its sirens roaring as it disappeared into the distance.

Sal slumped down beside the fence. 'Your fourth birthday Raz.'

'This is the eve of your special day Raz,' Peter handed Sal his shirt.

'We still need to make it a celebration,' Sal stood up. 'Come on you lot, we best go home.'

'Will Uncle Bill be okay?' Sam asked.

'We hope so,' Sal put his hand on the child's shoulder.

'I'll be in touch when I find out what's happening at the hospital,' Peter said as he waved goodbye.

'He will get better, won't he?' Saz asked.

'I'm sure he will. We've all grown very fond of Uncle Bill, haven't we? I think he may need us to help him for a while till he gets well.'

Sal wound the winch in, and they all jumped in the ute for the short drive home.

'Guess who's coming back from Europe tonight?' Sal smiled at his children.

'Grandie's and Bon!' the three boys chorused.

'Yes,' Sal smiled, 'I'm looking forward to seeing my parents, and Bon. He's been travelling backwards and forwards to Europe for far too long.'

## CHAPTER TWENTY-NINE

# BON AND SHEA

### January 1998

Bon returned on the night of Uncle Bill's accident. He had been living in France since Imi's death during childbirth, returning only for brief visits. Gal was the last child they had borne together, and he was now eight years old. His children scarcely knew their Australian cousins, so it was time to put his sorrow behind him, for his family's sake, and come home. Bon was glad to be able to give birth to Shea, Nick's child, only a month after Gal was born. The seven-year-old was his constant shadow.

That night, the Davidson family sang to the stars, asking that Bill, the formerly fit and robust man, would heal quickly from this cruel tragedy. He would be in intensive care for some time. Afterwards, he would need a great deal of prolonged care. It was more than Pat could handle by herself, Bon knew, so the family discussed how they could help.

Less than a month later Bon drove his sleek blue car into the Eastlake Hospital car park. He was not prepared to use a doctor's allotment for the moment, so he circled the visitors' lot while butterflies were doing somersaults in his stomach. The child in the rear seat looked eagerly forward with crystal blue eyes at the large hospital complex. Bon's heart was beating wildly as the car stopped. With a smile for the youngster and a comforting hand, they got out of the car.

'You could have stayed home with Gal and your cousins. I'm glad you came, but you must be good while I'm being interviewed, Shea. I know I've told you before but...' Bon was silenced by the comical pained expression on the child's face. They both laughed and walked hand in hand towards the impressive main entrance. The buildings had been freshly painted, with manicured gardens and an extended car park. So many things had changed in the years since he'd been there. How strange and yet familiar the surroundings were.

'Shea, this is where I worked for many years,' Bon pointed to an upper level, 'up there. The Operating Theatres are in that wing.'

'Is that where we're going?'

'No, we'll be on the ground floor Administration Block today. If I'm accepted, I won't be working there again. I should be in the Emergency or Gynaecological Departments.'

'Why wouldn't you be accepted?' Shea asked directly. Bon smiled broadly and shrugged, hoping desperately the child's faith would be confirmed. 'Why aren't you going to work at the other hospital where you went to help Uncle Bill?'

'That's a rehabilitation hospital, Shea. I was only helping Bill with his physiotherapy as a family member. It was voluntary work and my medical qualifications weren't really needed there. Besides...' Bon paused and pointed to the 'Enquiries' sign above the desk before them. He announced his arrival to a petite receptionist who nodded and continued to stare into her computer screen. She pointed to the waiting area chairs. They quickly moved toward them and took up position beside a magazine strewn table.

'Besides,' the child prompted.

'Oh Shea, I just want to get back to working in a hospital, preferably this one. Just so I can resume the normal daily routine I used to have.'

'You mean since Imi died things haven't been the same?'

'Exactly.'

'Mr Davidson?' A prim, plump young woman appeared nearby.

'Yes,' Bon replied.

'You can follow me? Mr Bandon will see you now.' They walked along a length of passage before turning into another. The woman had her long hair pulled back severely in a bun. She gave Shea a cold stare. 'The child can wait in our reception room while you are being interviewed.'

It was some thirty minutes later the Chief Hospital Administrator came out ushering Bon ahead. The middle-aged man was much shorter than Bon and wore shirt and tie. He rubbed his bald spot absently while looking around from the doorway. 'We've renovated much of the hospital and upgraded machinery and equipment. I'm sure you'll be impressed with facilities in the maternity Birthing Rooms.'

The man motioned for an officious, thin woman with dull steel eyes to come towards them, which she did reluctantly. She straightened the ripples in her skirt and turned towards them.

'Ah, Miss Derbyshire, would you be good enough to show Mr Davidson about the hospital, especially the Maternity Wing and Birthing Units. Perhaps even the surgery facilities, in case of emergencies, of course.'

'Of course,' Miss Derbyshire replied curtly, 'although I do have a lot on right now...'

'I'm sure you can spare a few moments of your valuable time,' the Administrator coerced. 'Welcome back, Doctor Davidson,' he added shaking Bon's hand enthusiastically. 'I'm sure you'll be a valued member of our team again. If you'll excuse me now however, I have a Directors' Meeting to attend.'

'Thank you, Mister Bandon, I will,' Bon replied. The man released his grip and disappeared down the corridor.

'Please don't leave your desk, Miss Derbyshire. I have been an employee here before. If you direct me to the Maternity Wing, I can manage from here. I do have an appointment with Doctor Paterson shortly and I don't wish to be late.'

Miss Derbyshire attempted a courteous smile. 'I am rather busy, I'm sure you understand, Mr Davids. The Maternity wing is on the left side of the hospital. Follow the signs and the arrows as marked.'

'Thank you so much,' Bon accepted her indifference.

'My pleasure,' she replied while waving her arm in the general direction. 'I can ring ahead and let Doctor Paterson know you're on your way?'

'That would be a great help, thank you, Miss Derby,' Bon replied with a grin.

'It's Miss Derbyshire, Mr. Davids...'

'Mr Davidson,' Bon corrected.

'Oh,' the woman started back towards her desk. 'Your child is a well-behaved little boy.' The child rolled crystal blue eyes heavenward.

'Shea is,' he agreed as they passed through the Surgical Department and Bon's heart raced harder than ever. The child's hand began to slip around in the sweaty palms, which strongly held a grip.

'Is this where you used to work with Nick?' Bon nodded briefly and swept the child quickly along the corridor, hoping not to be recognised. Just as they turned a corner and came upon a nurses' station, they collided with Nick O'Donahue.

'Bon, is that you?' The surprised man stepped back to give them both a space, 'goodness, it is you.'

Bon groaned inwardly and tried to sound jovial in reply.

'Nick O'Donahue, I believe.'

They stood face to face with the youngster in between. The conversation was short, even though Bon felt it went on forever. Somehow, Bon introduced Shea and explained he had an interview with Doctor Paterson. Nick immediately suggested Shea stay with him at the nurses' station while he was with the senior surgeon.

'I've got some figures to check on, times and dates to sort out. I don't mind keeping an eye on the lad while you're going through the grill.'

Mercifully, Bon realised, Nick had carefully avoided asking the question likely to have been on the tip of his tongue. Not the, 'why come back now?' he had expected.

'Thanks,' was all he could muster in reply. Meanwhile Shea smiled happily at the change of plans.

'Well, Shea, if you come with me now, I can show you a bit about what I do,' Nick winked at the child as Bon quickly retreated along the corridor. He did catch part of their conversation as he walked away.

'Shea, I like that name. Did you know that Shea is a special name? It has to be, it's the name of my Grandpa Shea O'Donahue!'

Bon glimpsed back to see Shea beaming with delight.

# CHAPTER THIRTY

## Shea's Eighth Birthday

### 10th January 1999

Bon smiled, reflecting on how swiftly the many months that had passed since his return to work at Eastlake Hospital. Shea had been nearly seven then. The enchanting child could always weave a web around Bon's heart. Today they celebrated be the child's tenth birthday. Sal had generously offered to hold the party at the old home. Bon lounged on a tubular plastic chair beneath trees swaying gently in the warm late summer breeze. Tables laden with finger foods, tasty treats and drinks surrounded the scattered seats. The old farm cottage garden provided lush green lawns and flowers that added to the aroma of the party's festivities.

Children ran in between chatting adults who chided their misbehaviour in good humour. Shea was the youngest of the six children Bon now reared alone. Nearly all his family would be at this party.

Bon reflected on how his initial awkwardness around Nick on his return had soon disappeared. They'd rekindled a firm friendship which helped ease his return to work at the Hospital. Neither of them mentioned the terrible fight they'd had the last night before Bon left for Europe. It was as though they both had selective memory. Today he greeted Nick and his wife, Sandy warmly. As their two little daughters joined the festivities taking gifts to Shea. Sandy was now a true friend. She was kind, loving and understanding towards Nick, extending the same kindness to Bon, which was a real bonus.

The pain of Imi's death always struck home hardest on these occasions. The month before celebrating Gal's birthday had been a small family afternoon tea. Bon tried to keep the sorrow at bay, refusing to let it interfere with the day's entertainment. Sandy and Nick had a new baby girl to love who was duly tolerated by her toddling sister, Becky.

'Gee, Bon, this was a great idea. Just a little spread at your old farm home, you said. What a spread!' Nick let out a slow whistle of appreciation.

'Just a small country show, friend,' Bon smiled as he replied in an imitation slow Texan drawl. A commotion amongst the children caught their eye just then. 'Look out, there's trouble.'

'No trouble, Bon,' Sandy said with a broad, warm smile. She was an attractive brunette and gladly linked her arms with both Nick and Bon. 'Shea being overly protective of Becky again.'

Nick smiled at his wife and hugged her arm. 'You'd think they were brother and sister; the way Shea stands up for our little girl.'

'Now, now, Nick O'Donahue, can I hear some terrible sexist language around here? This is a Davidson stronghold. I hope you realise, there's to be no gender calling here!' Gem called out jovially.

'Oh, Gem,' Bon defended, 'cut it out. You're the only sensitive one.'

'Not really,' Gem added. 'We all have children here who find it at odds with the way they've been brought up.'

'Oh, you lot,' Sal chided. 'This is my home. Richard's Aunty Nance would be glad to see us all having a good time, so let's not bicker. After all, we are all mostly sole parents here, so what does it matter?'

'It matters to me,' Gem added with a grin.

'You're just stirring, Gem. You do that so well,' Sal replied.

'What do you mean, mostly sole parents?' Sandy asked with a shake of her head.

'Oh, Sandy, I should explain,' Bon replied, hoping to sound casual. 'Gem has Maya with no partner. I have my brood to rear, since Imi's death. Sal has three including the twins to rear alone now, since Sim died. And, I do believe, yes, Tam is just arriving with Kat.'

'Sandy, I told you they were a big family,' Nick smiled at his wife's dismay.

'Are there more?' Sandy squawked. 'I mean, it's so sad. You're all so young.'

'It is sad, Sandy. Still we all cope. The rest of the Davidson clan is at our main property in the grand home opposite. And...' Bon paused to beckon Tam to join them.

'And' Sandy prompted.

'And, oh, Sandy, our parents are travelling far and wide right now. Our Aunt and Uncle live in the farm next door. We all help to run the orchard and keep everyone fed and educated.'

'We also help Bill and Pat run their farm since his accident,' Sal explained.

'Accident?' Sandy queried.

'Yes. Bill, our father's cousin, had a tractor roll on top of him a while back, just about when I came back from France permanently. It left him paralysed from the waist down,' Bon paused to pick up a biscuit before going on. 'It was touch and go for a while, but he pulled through. Pat was a brick through the rehabilitation, which I helped by doing physiotherapy. It was Sal's twins who really set Bill on the road to recovery, emotionally I mean.'

'They wouldn't let depression get the better of him,' Sal added with a grin. 'Now we do the work, he supervises like a general directing his troops. He just loves it.'

'And that's all?' Sandy shook her head.

'We're not all widowed, Sandy,' Ash added lightly. 'Cass and I have two beautiful children and we're both still about.'

'With a thriving business, too!' Nick nodded. 'Ash is the best mechanic in town. I told you that before, Sandy.'

'Yes, I know,' Sandy smiled. The adolescents near-by interrupted the conversation by nearly overturning a table.

'Maya,' Gem called out to his cavorting youth. 'Leave the child alone.'

'That girl, you mean, Gem. A friend from school, is it?' Sal goaded.

'That girl indeed,' Gem retorted. 'Girls could be a problem with our Maya.'

'More sexist language,' Sal teased. Gem huffed and went off to pick tidbits off the table. Everyone laughed and the party continued happily.

# CHAPTER THIRTY-ONE

## Rakal Returns

### June 1999

Tam listened to the dial tone. Kat was born nine months after Rakal left in 1985. He was now thirteen and very much a masculine persona.

'Hi, Kat,' Tam began cheerfully. 'You like the new mobile phone?'

'Sure, it's cool. Miri won't let me take it to school though.'

'Well, we don't want it smashed like the last one, now do we?' Tam knew Miri would admonish her sibling's child as she would her own.

'Guess not. It was just an accident.'

'How are you today, my number one boy?' Tam grinned imagining youths fresh face.

'Great. It's cold, so I broke the ice on the puddles on the way to school this morning.'

'Sounds freezing,' Tam shivered involuntarily.

'Yeah, it's a laugh when everyone here feels so cold and I don't.'

'Kat, you know you have a higher tolerance level, that's all.'

'Today was dumb at school as usual,' Kat let out an exaggerated sigh.

'Why? What happened?' Tam smiled broadly.

'We had our normal morning presentations, you know, some doing talks, some reading from the newspapers and others cooking.'

'Yep.'

'Well, one girl did a talk on Japan. It was okay but I wish I could tell them about how to fly a spaceship. Space is so much better.'

'There are a lot of interesting things on Earth, Kat. Son, we rarely travel to Orthama. You know it's too dangerous. You've lots to learn yet.'

'Anyway,' the youth continued, ignoring Tam's remark. 'It was my turn to cook and I made little pizzas. You know, the ones with real pastry and all the proper toppings. The oven was small, but it took both trays.'

'I hope it went down well.'

'Sure did,' the child replied. Tam imagined the grey green-eyed youth holding the handset to his ear. 'I met Fin and Izzy after school, and we went ten pin bowling.'

'What about Gal? Fin and Izzy are sixteen. Gal is nine, and he looks up to you. I was hoping you might get along with him.'

'Oh, you know Gal doesn't like it when I can beat him 'cause I'm thirteen and he's still a kid.'

'You tease Gal a lot, don't you?' the youth was full of mischief, there was no doubt.

'Not much,' Kat replied vaguely.

'You're big and strong for your age, Kat. You know, my son, it's not normal for a thirteen-year-old to pick up two cousins and throw them several metres. You'll have to be careful.'

'I know. I know. Miri keeps telling me.'

'Are you sticking to the rules?'

'Yep, Tam,' Kat replied. There was a long silence before the child asked, 'when are you coming home?'

'This weekend, son, I'm sorry we've not been together much lately. I've got another dig planned for early in 2000, so that gives us the next seven months straight. I'll be here to study and lecture and be able to get home each weekend.'

'Good, 'cause I want to talk to you about what's been happening in the news. I've been a bit scared.'

Tam took a deep breath. He'd been getting frightened too. At twenty-six, his orderly life was good. As resident student and assistant lecturer at a university campus just a three-hour drive from the orchard, he was well established and respected. The courses he was taking would add variety to an already impressive array of degrees. He was well travelled with first-hand experience assisting at many archaeological digs, and his position was secure. Tam was well thought of by academics, lecturers, professors, and fellow students alike. The only wild card in his sober life was his son Kat, whom he adored.

'There's no need to be frightened,' Tam lied.

'But, Tam, what if he doesn't come and see us, he'll never know about me, will he?' the youth asked.

'You want to meet your father?' Tam felt his breath shorten. 'I was hoping he would stay far away, Kat. I had no idea you might want to meet him,' Tam squirmed. If Rakal came to the Davidson family home now, there would be no protection. They would be exposed.

'He's my father but he doesn't even know me, Tam,' Kat countered.

'How could he know about you? He left Earth the night after you were conceived,' Tam sighed. 'We'll all have to be careful, Kat. Promise me you'll be kind to your cousins and do what Miri asks you to do, please?'

'Okay, I will.'

'I've got to go now. I'll speak to you tomorrow.'

'Wait, I wanted to talk to you about doing an Army cadet-ship the school is offering next year. It sounds way cool.'

'Army cadet-ship? We'll talk about that on the

weekend. Bye, darling. Love you.'

'Bye.'

Tam looked out at the familiar view from his window. The student lodge was a brick box building along the far end of the university grounds. The lawns separating the university proper were manicured and dotted with statues of all shapes and sizes, with all sorts of obscure shapes and titles. Pebble paths wound their way between the buildings leading to one another. This area had become home during the last four years.

The thought of Kat becoming an Army cadet, was a scary one. The Davidson's were all pacifists. Perhaps the lad took after his parents a little too much, one the explorer and historian, the other an interplanetary warrior. The boy was also not sexually mature, which was unusual for a Davidson at thirteen.

Tam still reflected on a brief and terrible event that had taken place years earlier. He only just discovered that a video through the security cameras at the school replayed the whole disastrous event. Mica his youngest sibling had asked to take it with him overseas. The vision of the two aliens attacking one another, intent on destroying each other as brutally as possible, was as abhorrent to Tam now as it had been then. The screams of fellow students, who were at the school for weekend sport, running hysterically about as buildings were damaged, and windows shattered. Supporting pillars were knocked down as easily as a child would scatter building blocks. Tam remembered shouting warnings, which fell on deaf ears. Terror reigned. Even now, fourteen years later, the memories of the day still made him feel sick. The victor yelled the Earth was safe because he'd won. Thoughts of Rakal smiling happily while disembowelling the body of the vanquished, then biting into the freshly torn flesh were truly nauseating.

No one was more relieved, than Tam, when Rakal announced to his hosts he would leave. The alien had stripped parts from his opponent's spacecraft to replace the damage in his own. Tam did not speak another word to the former house guest after the hideous battle.

Putting those memories firmly in the past, his life returned to normal. Each new step Tam had taken since then was designed to obliterate that terror-filled nightmare. Now, the fear returned, Tam became increasingly anxious that this peace would be shattered again.

Mica had gone to North America to the University Rakal had arrived at, weeks earlier. The international media had been given the announcement that an alien had arrived on Earth. Only the Davidson's knew Rakal had been on Earth before.

Rakal had returned, but the question burning in Tam's mind was, 'why?'

## CHAPTER THIRTY-TWO

# Translating for Rakal

### June 1999

Two men and one woman, all accomplished scholars, were quickly making their way along the maze of corridors. The main university building had the best of modern scientific and research facilities available in the western world. This was the centrepiece of the university town in North America.

At the outset of their speedy march through the campus an intense debate began. It was a brisk ten-minute walk from the Linguistics Department in the southern wing to the cafeteria on the eastern side of the campus. The tall balding man pushed aside the swinging glass doors with his large hands. The shorter red-haired man followed in his wake, all the while tugging at his short beard.

The common courtesy of allowing their female companion to enter first was disregarded. The feminist views obviously pushed aside these former gentlemanly graces. She shrugged her shoulders and slipped in quickly behind the two men. The debate continued unabated.

'I can't believe we're doing this. We have the unique opportunity to study an alien with a complex language and we're going to let a child in on this?' the shorter man squeaked, lifting his glasses off his nose, and wiping them with exasperation.

'This young man is hardly a child, and...' The taller man slapped his fingers into the palm of his opposite hand to accentuate the point. 'He does come highly recommended.'

The woman held a clipboard in her hands and cast her knowledgeable eyes over its surface. Her hair was greying and tied back from her face. She looked self-assured and sophisticated with neat small earrings in her ear lobes and slim matching necklace. 'We are only interviewing him to see if he and his recommendations can be helpful to us.'

'Well, let's get on with it. We're wasting time, but you're in charge, Professor,' the red headed man remarked gruffly as the taller man scowled.

It was after the lunch hour and the cafeteria held only small and scattered groups of students. Some young, some mature aged, sitting in small groups randomly about the clean white room, plain plastic chairs scraping the linoleum floor with an unnerving screech when anyone stood.

The taller man nodded towards a couple sitting at a table by the window. Clearly, as they approached, they could tell this was a 'couple'. They seemed engrossed in conversation, holding hands across the table and apparently oblivious to their surroundings.

'Hello, Michael Davidson, is it?' The youth nodded to the tall man. 'I'm Professor Rubens, this is Laura Bandeau, and Don Cameron. Laura specialises in hieroglyphics and deciphering codes and languages in the written form. Don's field is Linguistics with a Masters' at Harvard and subsequent teaching position at Cambridge University in England.'

The young couple stood politely. 'I prefer Mica, spelt m-i-c-a, not Michael,' the young man corrected while offering a hand in greeting. 'This is Charlotte. She came with me from France.'

'Bonjour', she added in a rich voice, with a captivating smile to match.

Professor Rubens was a little disconcerted by their lack of respect for the occasion. 7They both seemed confident and at ease with the world.

'I've seen your face before,' Don Cameron remarked bluntly. Charlotte's long mouse brown hair, clear pale skin, ripe red lips on a beautifully proportioned petite hour-glass body left the red-haired man a little breathless. She was simply stunning.

'Perhaps,' she nodded. 'If you saw 'Vogue' last month, I was on the cover.'

'Charlotte the model,' Cameron spluttered, as she nodded. 'But you're only nineteen, aren't you? I have a daughter your age, and she's always complaining about her looks saying she would like to look like you.'

'Thank you for the compliment, Don Cameron. I'm sure your daughter is beautiful, I hope she can see that in herself,' Charlotte replied with a teasing grin.

The blonde youth rolled blue eyes heavenward and interrupted. 'I'll be twenty-one next month and we've known each other all our lives. My family and hers are close friends as we have relatives living next door. We visit them in France as often as we can. It's only been this last holiday though, we've become close.'

There was a short awkward silence as they all stood surveying each other. Professor Rubens took control of the situation. 'Shall we go to the office?'

Mica surprised his hosts immediately by greeting Laura Bandeau in perfect Spanish, then carrying on a short polite conversation with her as they walked out of the cafeteria.

'Mica is always doing that,' Charlotte explained to Don Cameron who walked beside her, 'first to test the knowledge of the other person, and secondly to test his own knowledge of the language.'

'We are all accomplished linguists in this team, with considerable skills in our chosen specialties,' Professor Rubens heard himself saying while tapping the end of his nose.

The handsome blonde youth blandly replied, 'I really didn't volunteer for this, Professor. You were sent a copy of my Thesis study of Rakal's vocalisations. My tutor has perhaps exaggerated my abilities. I am, however, willing to offer what knowledge I have of Rakal's interesting and complex speech pattern. Maybe I'll be of some assistance, maybe not,' he concluded. The small group reached the Linguistics Department of the building and Professor Rubens pushed the door aside. 'To tell you the truth Professor, I'm not at all keen on meeting Rakal again,' Mica added.

'Why?' the Professor asked, surprised by the comment.

'He frightens me to death, that's why.'

A short while later Professor Rubens had introduced Mica to the rest of the Linguistics team as they sat around a large oval table.

'Colleagues, each of you have before you a copy of Mica Davidson's Thesis. It's a detailed study of the alien Rakal's language as based on taped recordings taken during his earlier visit to Earth.' The murmuring and general astonishment that greeted this remark needed to be addressed immediately. 'I'm aware the fact Rakal has been on Earth before may surprise you. I certainly didn't know about it until I received this Thesis and a testimonial letter from Mica's tutor.' He paused again to regain the full attention of his colleagues. 'You will see the depth and insight into this complex speech pattern is quite comprehensive. Personally, I would like to hear the original tapes to corroborate some of the findings. Mr Davidson, if you would kindly address our little gathering, perhaps you can enlighten us as to how you originally collected this information, and how you came to study the results?'

Mica coughed nervously to clear his throat. 'I'm

reluctant to go into all the details, Professor, as I was so young at the time.'

'You're still so young,' Don Cameron stabbed the air with his finger to accentuate the remark. A scowl covered his face demonstrating his total discontent with events.

'That's true, Mr Cameron, I am only twenty now, and I was only seven when Rakal last visited our world.' Mica returned the older man's stern gaze. 'I did not, however, do a study of the tapes until my fifteenth year. The in-depth analysis took over a year to complete. Not having the subject on hand to clarify any anomalies was a shortcoming. Perhaps, if you agree to allow me to join your team, together we'll be able to solve these mysteries.'

'I, for one, think this is an excellent idea,' Professor Rubens added with a smile. 'I believe everyone should have the opportunity to read this Thesis and decide upon its merits. We will meet here tomorrow to establish if the whole team would benefit from this young man's appointment.'

The door to the conference room opened. Rakal strolled in and looked about the room. An unmistakable glow of recognition covered the alien's face when he saw Mica.

'Okay,' Mica whispered with a quiver. 'Here goes.'

The alien lunged at speed across the room and picked up the youth with a crushing hug as he repeated the same phrase. The joyous greeting was clear.

'Stop it, Rakal, put me down!' Mica squirmed like a wriggling worm in the alien's vice like grip. 'It's good to see you too. Hey guys, would you like to tape what he's saying so we can study it?'

The youth had introduced his girlfriend, Charlotte, whom Rakal favoured with an appraising inspection. Then Professor Rubens had followed with a formal introduction to each member of the team. The basic protocol the alien had asked for now complete, Rakal smiled and said directly imitating their team leader, 'now things will move smoothly.'

An hour later Rakal had been speaking at length, and for the most part, Mica interpreted and offered a reply. By the time the alien walked out of the room Mica looked exhausted. They had a brief exchange about Rakal's last visit. Much of this conversation was indecipherable to the other parties sitting around the table. As soon as the alien left, the vote was taken on Mica's eligibility. Everyone agreed he would be an invaluable member of the team.

'In that single exchange, we've already gained more knowledge about Rakal's common speech than we've heard in the last month. We will be delighted to study the dialect and inflections you've already mastered, Mica, if you will consider our offer a firm appointment?'

'Well, I guess that's what I came to do. I appreciate your confidence in me,' the youth replied. Mica took Charlotte's hand and squeezed it gently. Their eyes met and they lent towards one another and kissed.

'I must leave now, Monsieur. I have a modelling assignment in New York in two days, then I fly back to Europe,' Charlotte rose with exquisite poise.

'Here is my business card, Mademoiselle. It has this Department's phone and fax numbers on it. Feel free to contact Mica early mornings or in the evenings. I don't doubt we'll be working hard during the days,' Professor Rubens smiled broadly at the charming young woman as he handed her the card.

'Thank you, Monsieur. May I dine with Mica before I leave?'

'Of course, you should go somewhere special. There are several good restaurants in the town.'

Later the same evening, after Mica had said farewell to Charlotte over an expensive meal at an up-market restaurant, he returned to the campus in a sombre mood. There was more about the alien Rakal that Professor Rubens needed to know.

The dial tone rang in an unfamiliar way while Mica pressed the digits on the touch phone. The deep monotone voice replied.

'Professor Rubens, speaking. Who's calling?'

'It's Mica Davidson Professor. I wanted to show you something else left behind from Rakal's last visit.'

'The tapes you mean?'

'No, other than the voice tapes, although I have those as well, I'm really thinking about a video tape taken just before Rakal left.'

'Oh, that will be interesting. I've been reading your Thesis again. It's very thorough. I'd like to hear the tapes to pick up the inflections you used. They sound quite difficult.'

'Professor, I'm not sure you'll want to show this video to the rest of the team. Do you have security people who might be able to advise you?'

'Naturally, we have security people. I'm curious now. When would you like me to arrange this viewing?'

'I'd like you to see it this evening if it's not too inconvenient.'

'I can probably arrange one of our security people to meet us in my office. I'll call them now. Just wait for me to ring you back, Okay?'

CHAPTER THIRTY-THREE

# REVELATIONS ABOUT RAKAL

June 1999

Next day Professor Rubens was uncomfortable around Rakal. Captain Smiggins, University Security Chief had also been available to view Mica's video. The images of screaming children running frantically from the fierce battle between two aliens, which preceded Rakal's last departure from Earth, was still vivid in his mind. The stomach-churning ferociousness of the battle, the jubilant Rakal in victory munching vigorously on his dismembered opponent. This sickening image was mixed with the immediate hysteria of the students while they fled the grounds of the small secondary school. Rakal had calmly plundered the vanquished opponent's vehicle amid the chaos, oblivious to the distress he had caused.

Professor Rubens felt compelled to ask the Security Chief to discreetly increase the guards and more carefully follow the alien's movements. He feared the other members of the Linguistics Team might not want to work with their subject if they saw what he was capable of, so he chose to keep it a secret. Reflecting on that, he watched Mica the blonde anxiously.

'Mr Davidson, please don't exhaust yourself,' the kindly senior Professor urged. 'We've all been dissecting yesterday's conversation and reviewing your original audio tapes all morning. It's time we all took a break.

Ms Bandeau, gentlemen, we shall return to this task in one hour.'

Rakal had spent the early part of the day as a silent observer. He seemed amused as they all attempted to repeat his words correctly. A thunderous laughter rolled out of him and reverberated around the room. Rubens wished they could study without his presence. At the same time, however, he admitted privately, it would be beneficial if the alien would help. Apparently, because Mica Davidson had joined the team, Rakal had agreed to cooperate.

The rest of the team seemed filled with excitement. Facing this challenge, with the new insight of Rakal's former visit, all the linguists' expectations ran high. Mica also seemed very enthusiastic, like a child decoding a secret message. The group left the room discussing the new possibilities uncovered in the thesis and tapes. The atmosphere was electric.

The Professor motioned with his index finger for Mica to join him when no one else could hear.

'What I can't understand is how on Earth did they cover that battle up? The media coverage should have been massive.'

'That's what Captain Smiggins asked me last night,' the youth replied with intense blue eyes gazing directly at the older man.

'Perhaps he did, Mica. I'm afraid I wasn't really able to focus on much after seeing the video tape.'

'It was simple really. They didn't allow the tape to be released. The police talked to the school administrators and they covered it up by telling the students it was all acting for a movie, although some of them had to undergo treatment for shock. They soon recovered when they thought it was all an elaborate hoax. The authorities were in on it too. It was election time and they didn't want the town to become a sideshow.'

'I see. Well, we must keep it as our secret for the

time being. Do you think other members of the team will be able to develop enough rapport with Rakal to ask and answer questions the way you do?'

'I can't see why not,' Mica looked quizzically at the older man. 'Professor Rubens, I'm sorry the video upset you. I did think it was important for you to see it though. We should all know of Rakal's capabilities.'

'Yes, indeed,' Professor Rubens tapped his nose. 'We don't want the others to be afraid to work with him though, now do we?'

'No sir. It does make me uneasy when Rakal's around. It's not much fun having Captain Smiggins mooching around while we work either. I don't know if Rakal wants to do any of us any harm.'

He put his hand on Mica's shoulder. 'Have you contacted your charming girlfriend yet?' He smiled while looking at the expression of concern changed into one of delight.

'Yes, Charlotte rang this morning, Professor. She arrived in New York at last night. It was lovely to hear her voice. I already miss her so much.'

'I dare say you'll find many ways to catch up with her. Now go along with you and have a hearty meal.'

It was clear from the first everyone liked Mica. Everyone except Smiggins, but Rubens had decided long ago the Security Chief didn't really like anyone. His suspicious nature was grating and, although necessary, not good for the group.

Over the next few weeks Mica's relationship with Charlotte continued to be a talking point. The famous French model's association with their co-worker caused jokes and snickers amongst the team. These remarks were all accepted with the good nature by which they were given.

Each day Mica would ring Charlotte, or she would call him. They would speak tenderly in fluent French.

The day of Mica's birthday, on the seventh of July, Charlotte sent a stylish modern leather jacket and broad-striped shirt. An enormous bouquet of flowers also arrived with an equally large card. Many other parcels arrived from several parts of the world, mainly from immediate family and friends. Excitedly Mica unwrapped and displayed all the gifts to his new friends in the Linguistics team. Even Rakal was curious to see what each parcel contained. It was the end of a hard day's work and everyone enjoyed the escape from the regular routine.

'This is from my parents,' Mica smiled while holding up a pure wool hand-knitted jumper. Putting it aside with glowing appreciative eyes and excitement he opened what looked like a briefcase. It was a laptop personal computer. 'This has a telephone connection so that I can get in touch with home or any of my friends on the move.'

'Well, son, that should save us from having an enormous telephone bill,' Professor Rubens jibed.

'I'll pay for the phone calls, my family aren't short of a quid,' came the quick reply. Everyone laughed and admired the gifts. Mica continued to unwrap little presents that had been sent from the younger members of the family. Small fragile figures made from plasticine and clay, a hand-painted badge, a first-edition book which looked well read, socks, underwear and some music videos, CDs, and DVDs. The whole Linguistics team including Professor Rubens and Rakal sat down to take away pizzas for dinner to celebrate.

The end July marked two months since Rakal had arrived on Earth and Mica had now been with the team six weeks. Everyone watched as the alien became more agitated with each passing day. The University had been the base for their studies, and Rakal had made it perfectly clear he was tired of his surroundings and restless to move.

That day, Rakal paid a visit to Mica. He scrutinised the small knick knacks the youth had placed about the room. Some of the tiny figures sent as birthday presents were carefully arranged on the bed head. On the desk below the window a small globe sat beside a CD player and discs. Rakal grabbed the globe in excitement then pulled Mica by the arm along the corridor to Professor Rubens' office.

'Call others to meeting,' the alien urged the Department Head. Rubens looked quizzically at him. His deep guttural tones were insistent and demanding. 'Call others now.'

'You'd better, Professor, or I'll end up with a broken arm,' Mica added motioning to the alien's strong grip on his upper arm. Shortly after the whole group of Linguistics researchers were with them in the cramped office.

'We go here!' Rakal demanded while spinning the globe slowly on its axis. The alien pointed large, fat fingers at the other continents.

'All over the world?' Doctor Cameron asked bewildered.

Rakal grunted and nodded. 'We are here, yes?'

Mica replied carefully. 'Yes, we're in North America, but it's this part right here, the central eastern side of the continent. Where would you like to go from there?'

Rakal studied the small globe carefully. He then traced a line right around the northern part of the globe. Mica followed and announced the countries and continents the alien's finger, touched, 'America, Mexico, South America, England, Europe, Africa, India, Russia, China, then down to Indonesia and Australia, every populated place on Earth basically!'

'Hmph,' the alien grunted.

'We'll have to discuss this,' Professor Rubens said sourly.

Rakal left the room leaving the globe in Mica's hands. After some discussion, it was agreed the whole Linguistics team, security team, and medical and catering support would be needed to make such a journey. The logistics involved would be monumental. The next day security was alerted to Rakal's request. Captain Smiggins was totally against any move away from the University.

Over the next few days, the Department Head of Linguistics and Security tried to persuade Rakal staying at the University was best for everyone.

It became clear to everyone; however, the alien had his mind set on leaving the confined University arena. The cooperation formally granted to the Linguistics team was no longer given. Rakal refused to sit in on decoding sessions. The effect was frustrating their efforts.

A week later it was agreed plans would have to be made.

'How are we going to travel all this way without spending a fortune paying for our own private aeroplane?' Professor Rubens explained the difficulties to the group. 'While this project has some great financial backing from the Government and many large business groups...' The pause that followed was dramatic. 'I seriously doubt, however, they'll extend their generosity because of Rakal's whim to travel the globe.'

Rakal walked in as the last statement was being made. 'A problem travelling?'

'Yes, Rakal. We simply can't afford to make such a journey. The team we need to take is simply too large to manage. The problems are too many to contemplate.'

'No problem, no money, come in my transport. We leave tomorrow!' Rakal announced bluntly before turning on his heels and marching out the door.

## CHAPTER THIRTY-FOUR

# A WORLD TOUR BEGINS

August 1999 to early 2000

The journey began with hurried last-minute preparations. Half of each team originally working on the project was eliminated from the travelling party. Rakal gathered his entourage and ushered them into the spacecraft. Professor Rubens was stunned at the size. The interior control and storage areas were large and arranged economically. However, the living quarters were tiny little boxes, apart from one main suite, which was their pilot's. Rakal's choice had obviously been made long before this trip was thought of.

The alien strolled about with an authoritative air while the team prepared to depart, his head held high and shoulders back, barking instructions during the arrangement of supplies.

One storage area became a makeshift dormitory for the security, catering, and medical teams. The original sleeping compartments just managed to house the Linguists and the security chief, Captain Smiggins. Everyone agreed the Galley would be a central meeting place as no other area on the vehicle was large enough, or had table space, for the guests.

The next evening the team members said farewell to their families and friends. Finally, Rakal sat at the main control panel. Professor Rubens and Captain Smiggins sat on his right and Mica and Laura Bandeau on his left.

'We've been discussing with Rakal the best route for our journey, Professor, Captain,' Laura Bandeau nodded towards the Department Chiefs who'd just joined them.

'This is how we will go,' Rakal stated flatly. He pushed some buttons on the panel and the view screen showed a rotating globe on its axis. The view was a much more intricate version of the globe he had originally used to state his plans. He pointed to the highlighted European continent. 'We will be here next.'

'England first, then France, Germany, Sweden, Denmark, Poland, Russia and the rest of the former Eastern Bloc countries,' Laura Bandeau recited the carefully prepared list.

'How long is all this going to take?' Captain Smiggins interrupted with a snarl. His thick grey hair was combed high into a turban-like crown, over sharp features, and squinting steel grey eyes.

Rakal smiled menacingly, then answered. 'We will travel quickly. Tonight, we will be here.' The domineering alien pranced triumphantly towards the view screen. His solid frame silhouetted the image as he pointed to the huge display of England. 'You may leave now if you do not wish to join us. Or, I may ask you to go later.'

'I can tell you're happy to have me here,' Smiggins snorted.

The journey commenced, as it was to continue, in epic proportions of grand exploration. Rakal wanted to see as many countries as possible and the people of the world all wanted to see him. Reporters and camera people from all forms of the media swamped them at every turn. Crowds of curious people greeted them when they landed, so the spaceship soon became a welcome retreat.

Rakal was delighted to be the centre of attention and quickly a pattern developed at each landing site with the Linguistics team interpreting the questions and answers both ways. At first the alien gave short responses to the questions asked, which became longer within a short time, proving to everyone how much he'd already learnt. The shortcomings of the Linguists seemed very pronounced then and the work continued as they travelled.

Usually, after one week or so, Rakal would announce the next destination and they would move on. The alien was certainly calling the tune. After visiting London, then Wales and Edinburgh and Dublin they flitted across to France, travelling through from the cities and provinces then moving on into the rest of Europe, through Sweden, Germany, Lithuania, Georgia, Russia, and Siberia in a similar manner.

Professor Rubens, Mica Davidson and Laura Bandeau were referred to in the newspapers as 'The Translators.' It was exhausting work for several months on end. Everywhere they went Rakal's comments were recorded. The Linguistics team spent long hours dissecting the new information.

Six months into the tour, the team was struggling to keep up. Professor Rubens approached Rakal. 'It's been a while since we had a break, we're all exhausted and need some time out.'

Rakal looked at the Professor and nodded. 'If you must!' he replied. Rakal was clearly advancing his speech and comprehension of humanity.

The break was used to digest as much of the information as possible and the extended stay in one location let them all learn from the country they visited.

The first year of the trek passed swiftly into the second with a Christmas break with their families. In the new year, Professor Rubens re-assembled Rakal's entourage with a reduced team.

All this while, Mica and Charlotte kept in touch by phone, fax, and email. Whenever they could arrange a brief secluded rendezvous they did so. They had met in London, France and Sweden and now planned another meeting in Italy. Charlotte would travel incognito by train from Paris through the Southern Alps. Mica would also be disguised, as his blonde hair and blue eyes had become very recognisable. Those travelling with Rakal did not begrudge the love-struck couple these sojourns, as they were respite from the hectic schedules and public scrutiny. Only Captain Smiggins made blunt remarks in bad taste.

'Where do you plan to go next time, Davidson?' Smiggins asked slyly after several disarming small-talk questions.

'Why, Captain Smiggins, do you think I'm going to give away some important secret information?' Mica was tired from the hard day and the humour he normally rallied to cope with Smiggins had almost evaporated.

'Just asking so we can make sure you are protected,' Smiggins replied smugly, twitching his rat-like nose. Mica knew the one proviso of the interludes was that a security person would accompany them to ensure their safety.

'Oh, for cryin' out loud! There's the trip plan,' Mica slammed a sheet of paper in front of the older man. 'There's where I'll be going, there's even what I'll be wearing. Do you want to know what we'll be up to in the hotel room? Perhaps you can join us and be a complete sleaze-bag voyeur?'

The day before Mica was due to leave, with security person in tow, the Linguistics team took a well-earned meal break. The airport conference room was spacious and tastefully decorated with dramatic portraits adorning the walls, lush carpets and a huge oval mahogany table, surrounded by comfortable high-backed chairs, which now served as a dining table.

They were preparing for another Press Conference at another International Airport in another country. The repetition was becoming tiresome for them all, yet public interest was still high. A television was on in the corner of the room as background noise. Mica sat quietly longing for the hours to pass quickly until he could escape and meet Charlotte. Only a few people were watching the news as it rambled on with uninteresting snippets of information.

'There is a world out there, you guys,' Don Cameron reminded his colleagues, pointing towards the television. Mica just grunted while chewing his last mouthful of tasteless vegetarian pie.

'That man is always trying to stand center stage,' Mica heard someone in the room grumble. 'I do wish he'd shut up.'

'Do you want to know what's going on in the real non-alien whirlwind world tour, out there?' Don Cameron continued without paying attention to the groans and complaints of his companions.

'There's only been another man-made disaster,' he announced. 'A substantial loss of life. Derailed fast train accident in southern France. Hundreds of people still trapped and crushed in the wreckage. Wake up you lot. There's more to life than the inept rambling of our alien's overgrown ego.'

'Where in Southern France?' Mica dropped his food and stood up.

A colleague next to him tugged his sleeve. 'For Gods' sake, don't ask questions, we'll never shut him up!'

'Turn it up! Tell me where in France? What train was it? How many are injured? How many are trapped?' Mica charged towards the television on the opposite wall.

'Mica just shut up and listen! It's on now,' Don demanded. The female reporter on the screen was fresh-faced with a pale complexion. She spoke in English with a French accent through full vivid red lips.

'The cause of the derailment is still a mystery. However, the Police are not ruling out foul play. The 'New Caledonia Train Disaster' will be known as the most devastating in French history. Emergency Rescue Teams are likely to work for several more days to free those trapped.' She turned crisply in her tailor-made suit, pointing towards the wreckage.

'As you see, the first half of the train splintered off the tracks and into the hills. Three carriages were completely overturned and crushed in the pile up. The remainder of the train is still in the tunnel on its side. The survivors are being treated.'

Mica felt sick, his mind was racing with horrible scenarios. Where was Charlotte? Was she still in the wreckage?

Professor Rubens was just entering the room when Mica intercepted his path. 'I must speak to you, Professor.'

'Mica, we are just about to go into the auditorium for the press conference.'

'I know, but this is urgent.'

They spoke quietly for a moment. Professor Rubens face drained of colour. Mica left the room.


'Ladies and gentlemen, the Press Conference is about to commence in the auditorium next door,' his large palm pointed to the right-side exit of the Conference Room. 'Mica will not be joining the translation team. Mr Cameron, would you care to assist Ms Bandeau and I on the platform?'

'Thank you, Professor,' Don Cameron remarked pointedly so everyone present was aware he felt it was his rightful place.

'Professor Rubens,' Laura Bandeau whispered. 'What's wrong with Mica?'

'I'll explain after the conference. I'm not sure if

Rakal will be pleased with these last-minute arrangements.'

Rakal seemed unhappy with the change in translators sitting on the platform beside him. Professor Rubens called a hurried end to proceedings after Rakal answered questions belligerently with terse one-word replies.

They all retired cheerlessly into the conference room. Rakal began to stomp and rant around the room. 'What is laryngitis? Why is Mica not here?'

'Laryngitis means he can't talk, bozo, which is exactly what you just did in there. The Italians will be demanding another show 'cause you just grunted at their questions,' Don Cameron replied huffily.

The door opened and Mica strode in with a backpack slung over one shoulder and laptop computer in hand. He nodded his anxious, unsmiling face and announced, 'the first flight to France is in thirty minutes. I don't know how long I'll be there, but I must try and find Charlotte.'

'Hang on, laddie,' Don Cameron pounced. 'Have we missed something? You're going to meet Charlotte tomorrow, aren't you?'

Captain Smiggins paced quickly to Mica's side. 'You were to travel incognito and as specified in the security arrangements, and now you want to fly off, without so much as a bye your leave.'

'You can talk!' Rakal blurted accusingly. 'Why did you not translate?'

'Now, ladies and gentlemen, this whole situation is somewhat difficult,' Professor Rubens felt like a referee in a sparring match. 'There is an explanation for everything. The problem is, you can't just head off publicly on a rescue mission, Mica. You're too well known.'

'There's no problem at all, Professor,' Mica said flatly, 'as you know Charlotte was on the New Caledonia train this morning. I must find her. If you don't like it, you can lump it.'

'I understand how you feel, Mica, but rushing off drawing attention to yourself may not be the best solution. Have you contacted the emergency information service in France?'

'You can't understand how I feel! I'm helpless here! The information service is useless. They really won't tell me anything more than has been on the news,' Mica flailed his arms in the air in frustration as teardrops welled in his eyes. 'I spoke to Charlotte's mother and she started crying and hung up on me. I have to go there to see if I can help.'

'Imagine what the press will make of this,' Smiggins sneered. 'French Super Model Charlotte mangled en route to meet Translator Extraordinaire', or perhaps, 'French Kiss! Lost for Words!'

Professor Rubens felt suddenly old and burdened. The silencing glare he gave the Security Chief was just short of murderous.

'I don't care what happens. I just want to get there. Charlotte could be crushed under twisted metal and trapped.'

Rakal stepped towards Mica scrutinising his distress. Mica reacted to this inspection by venting his frustrations and pounding the alien's chest. 'You, you vicious,' an ineffectual punch landed on the alien's chest, 'vindictive bastard Rakal, why did you come here? Why the hell did you come back to this 'worthless ball of soil' you called it? You said you couldn't get away fast enough. Did you come back just to mess up my life? I hate the sight of you, you muscle-bound, fat-faced, green-eyed slime bag.'

The pounding and verbal abuse Mica inflicted was as powerful as a feather hitting a rock. The alien picked the youth up by the collar and thrust him in the air. The snarl he issued was enough to give goose bumps to everyone in the room.

'It's a disaster, is it?' The alien roared. 'Droughts, bushfires, wars, floods, earthquakes, volcanic eruptions and epidemics are all disasters, are they not? The list goes on. What kind of fool do you think I am?' Rakal whirled around the room with Mica's legs trailing in the air like a whip being flicked around a cowboy's head.

'What do humans do about these disasters? They talk, send peacekeepers, use rescue machines that can kill as well as release. They talk some more. Your Governments talk, while others make nerve gasses and giant bombs, which can destroy the world! They all talk some more, while others test the weapons of destruction to see if they work! You are talkers, not doers!'

Rakal growled again while throwing Mica in the air and catching him more tightly around the neck. 'You call me a violent murderer, rapist, space pirate, destroyer of worlds, scavenger of space. That is what I have been in the past,' Rakal snarled again as Mica wriggled helplessly. 'What is this compared to what your people do to themselves? All you can do is talk!' The alien stared threateningly at each person in the room in turn. 'Well I know what to do, everyone back to my vehicle. We *all* go to France! Follow me now.'

Rakal didn't release Mica until the spacecraft's doors were closed behind the Linguistics team. Only then did Professor Rubens' notice a glisten in Rakal's green eyes which betrayed amusement at the unease of his passengers.

Soon afterwards they were all in France and their mission was known within the hour. Mica's love interest became worldwide gossip. Rakal was acclaimed as being instrumental in the release of hundreds of trapped train passengers. He and his spaceship cleared debris and lifted the mangled wreck off others trapped below.

The whole world applauded.

After consulting with Professor Rubens, Mica excused himself from committing to the rest of the world tour. The days merged on into another as Mica sat holding Charlotte's hand. Like all huge hospitals, it smelled of antiseptic and the white walls were stark and unwelcoming. She was in a medically induced coma.

On the third night, he left to shower and put on clean clothes. But as he was dressing, the phone rang. It was her doctor. 'Come quickly,' he said. Charlotte is awake.

As Mica walked down the corridor to Charlotte's room, he could hear shouting, followed by a loud crash. He rushed in to find Charlotte's mother standing in shock by the door, teary eyed and almost hysterical. Charlotte had thrown a tray at her and told her to leave.

Mica rushed to Charlotte's bedside.

'Get away from me!' Charlotte screamed. 'I hate you. You made me get that train! You! You, bloody selfish prat! Get out! Leave me alone!'

Mica couldn't believe what he was hearing, his girlfriend was normally so placid and charming. Two burly male nurses ran into the room and a third petite nursing sister administered a sedative.

'What does she mean?' Mica asked her incredulous mother.

'She doesn't want us here. She told me to go. And for you,' Charlotte's mother shook her head, 'she is blaming you for her injuries. She never wants to see you again.'

'Please,' the nurse said, 'can you both come with me to the visitor's lounge? The doctor will come and speak to you shortly.'

Mica and Charlotte's mother waited in the minimally furnished room, the high back wooden chairs were not comfortable, the coffee table had a few magazines on it. There was a plastic box of children's toys beside a blackboard in the corner. It was a temporary place.

'I don't understand,' Mica swallowed the lump in his throat then offered a box of tissues to the distraught woman who sobbed uncontrollably.

Long minutes later a rotund gentleman in a silver-grey suit walked in. He greeted them by name and then pulled up a chair facing them.

He cleared his throat.

'I'm Doctor Phillips, a specialist neurosurgeon at this hospital,' he took the woman's hand in his.

'What just happened doctor?' Mica begged.

'It is complicated to explain, but brain trauma injuries have different effects on different people.' The man shifted in his seat. 'I take it Mademoiselle that this behaviour is not typical of Charlotte?'

'She is a quiet kind girl. I've never heard her utter obscenities before. We've always been so close.'

'We can hope that the change will be short lived, however, as I have seen in many cases, brain trauma can change a persons' personality irreversibly. Time alone will tell.'

'How can I help?' Mica whispered.

'I am sorry to be the bearer of bad news, but, for now, it would be better if you kept away. She blames you for being in the wrong place at the wrong time. It is an irrational response and she may regret her actions today. Again, only time will tell.'

Charlotte's mother crumpled and sobbed and drew several tissues out of the box and blew her nose noisily. 'Mica, perhaps you should go back to what you were doing. I will keep you up to date with the news,' she mumbled.

'But I want to stay with her,' Mica pleaded.

The neurosurgeon stood up helping the woman to her feet. Then he turned to Mica and shook his hand.

'It is best if you both leave for now. We'll keep in contact. Charlotte has a long rehabilitation ahead of her.

She needs to recover in her own time.'

Mica stumbled out of the hospital into the cab the ward nurse had called. He sat unable to focus.

'You going to the airport?' the driver asked.

Mica nodded. An hour later he was back on board the spaceship with the remainder of Rakal's team. He hoped work would keep him occupied and ease the heartache.

## CHAPTER THIRTY-FIVE

# RICHARD AND DAVREW

### March 2000

The day was bright and clear. The morning sun shone while there was still a crisp chill in the autumn air. Richard rubbed his hands together unconsciously while standing on the bedroom balcony surveying his life's work. He heard the balcony door open and soft footsteps close the gap between them.

'Penny for your thoughts,' Davrew smiled at Richard and draped an arm over his partner's shoulders.

'I was just thinking about how lucky we are.'

'We are, indeed, my love,' Davrew replied while running long fingers down Richard's back in a gentle massage.

'We've only been away for a few months, yet it's so good to be home.'

'Ah, but how we love those hot summer nights and the freedom to travel at whim,' Davrew grinned.

Over the last few years Richard and Davrew had spent much of their time travelling to warmer climates, suiting their fancy, and living comfortably. Still, through all those years, this property was home. They both looked contentedly out over the large, well-kept vegetable garden nestled behind the beautiful old English-style garden. The now flourishing and profitable orchard spread over two thirds of the original property, along with two more additional blocks adjoining.

'The garden and orchard are looking good,' Richard sighed.

'Those first few years were so hard. I truly wondered if we'd ever make it a profitable concern.'

'You were the mainstay and got it going, Dav. I know I let you down then.'

'You let yourself down for a short time. The orchard itself was a problem right from the start because of the crop we chose.'

'Apples?'

'The early Sixties was a disaster period for the apple growing industry. The original plantation of Granny Smiths, Jonathan's and Golden Delicious were aimed at the European Market.'

'Yeah, bloody European Common bloody Market,' Richard spat.

'Still, we got through.'

'We did have to sink or swim.'

'We were adaptable. Going for Red Fuji and Red Delicious for the Asian market saved our skins.'

'Your idea. I was a bloody idiot then.'

'What makes you think you've changed?'

Richard chortled, 'you, cheeky minx! Come closer, I need to hug you.' Davrew obliged snuggling close while Richard encircled his arms around his lover.

'I grew up a bit then.'

'You had to. You know I think the Seventies was the best decade.'

'Best? If I hadn't gone to the city and taken a job with Mister 'I'm the greatest' Trethowan, I guess we'd never have started up the computer store.'

'I still can't believe how primitive computers were then, or, for that matter how much and quickly they changed over the next few years. Now everybody has mobile phone, and computers have slimmed down too.'

Richard recalled how most of the finance for those earlier non-profitable years had come from his willingness to work in the city. When they returned from France, after the original fiasco with Trethowan's niece behind them, they'd opened a small shop in the local town. His former boss Trethowan, had kept in touch, and assisted in the establishing an outlet for his own computer division which had led to success for them both.

'I couldn't have done it without your technical wizardry in maintenance and repairs,' Richard winked. He'd used his charm and local knowledge to build clientele, he reflected. Only five years after opening the first store they severed the partnership with Trethowan and began trading as an independent business. The advances in software and hardware packages available had led to further expansions over the following years.

A breeze picked up and gently ruffled Richard's hair. Davrew's long blonde locks were neatly tied back.

'Thankfully, the children have taken on the reins of running of the business.'

'It's a blessing we have seven healthy children of our own, not to mention so many grand-children and great grand-children. The twenty-seven chain stores throughout the country have given them all employment opportunities.'

'Not all the Davidson's have been so fortunate,' Richard reflected. 'Bill and Pat managed, well enough, I guess, with crop and sheep farming, but their two wonderful girls have left the country for fast-living city life.'

'You mean up until Bill had a tractor accident?'

'Yep, funny thing really, the disaster alone did little to close the gap between us. Dav darling, that little miracle was the children's doing, mainly Sal and the tormenting trio of his,' Richard smiled. Recalling how Sal's impish twins, and younger sibling Raz, who loved the rugged ageing farmer unreservedly, had helped heal Bill's broken spirit.

'Just as well, our Bon as family medic, and Sal, being Bill's neighbour and gardener, developed a close friendship with him during his recuperation. What a blessing from the stars!' Davrew grinned. 'Bill has even spoken to me a few times lately.'

'Our children and grandchildren are doing a wonderful job,' Richard agreed and pulled Davrew closer. 'God, I love your blue eyes.'

'I'd never have known,' he teased. 'To think, I was permitted to come to Earth, in the first place, because the originators thought I was infertile. It's a joke, isn't it?'

'Yes, lover,' Richard replied turning to embrace his partner and settle a long lingering kiss on supple accommodating lips. 'Let's go in,' he added huskily with a wry grin. 'Unless you think I'm getting too old for you.'

They both laughed as they walked inside to the bed. The sensual touch of Davrew's body always aroused Richard with such an intensity that warmed him to the core. The joy of that touch was just as thrilling now as it had been when they first embraced. Richard ran his hands gently over the pale soft skin he delighted in knowing so well. Squeezing and kissing pert nipples on small solid breasts, they made love, completely entwined in every level of their lives.

'I still feel as though we are one person, Richard. Time stands still when we're together.'

'We have seven children to prove it doesn't, my love,' Richard taunted. 'We've grown older together. I'll be sixty next month. Bill would bet I'd be lucky to make it to that landmark.' Both sated, he planted one final kiss on Davrew's lips. 'I'll just have a shower.'

He got up and walked into the bathroom, looking back as he did. Davrew hadn't changed very much over the years. The straight nose and pale skin and remarkable clear blue eyes still looked radiantly healthy. No greying hair, wrinkled eyes or expanding abdomen to announce the passing of time. That was all in Richard's department.

Stepping under the warm stream of water, he began to scrub all the sagging muscles and baggy waist. He whistled, then, softly, he began to sing. Davrew was special, different, and the reason he had come to know true happiness.

Several minutes later Davrew walked into the bathroom and splashed water on his face.

'You've still got a special somethin', Dav,' Richard beamed through the steam.

'You do too, lover,' Davrew towel dried his face, then sent a quick flick with the towel at the glass shower door. 'The children are all so special in their own ways too.'

Richard knew what his partner meant as he watched Davrew leave. Miri had always been a tower of strength on the home front, helping arrange rosters for cooking, cleaning, and chores, while developing a strong interest organising homework for all the family. Miri had grown even more mature with Peter, the partner she had taken at fourteen, who had been a great influence on all their lives also.

Gem, however, had always been a worry. Richard couldn't fault his second-born offspring's abilities at work. He'd been delighted when Gem had wanted to work in the computer shop with him upon returning from Europe. He'd recovered from the incident at the school camp, and the child that he bore as the result Maya - was an added blessing. Gem's work in the shop was where he'd found his niche. From the start, he'd shown a true sales flair and management skills. The stores were all now run effectively and efficiently with his controlling hand as General Manager. The advances from lumbering great laborious machines to slim-line effective smaller devices was smoothly done, as was the expansion of franchise stores.

No, the bugbear was, in Richard's eyes, the fact

Gem's personal and social life, playing the 'gay' about town and bedding every young male that showed even the slightest interest. Thankfully, however, at Bon's insistence, Gem had settled a little, due to the help of analysis.

Bon, on the other hand, had been born to be the family physician. The heavy load was carried well with humour and a caring bedside manner, together with a competent gathering of knowledge. Imi had been Bon's much-loved partner and constant support with matching wit and charm. Bon's smile and jovial attitude to life waned the day Imi had died in childbirth. Their children seemed to be his only source of joy after the heartbreak. Richard could see things improving over time, much brighter when Bon returned to Eastlake hospital and became re-acquainted with former colleagues.

Wrapping a towel around his torso and stepping out of the shower, Richard smiled at his reflection in the large bathroom mirror. He began to lather his chin to remove the dark stubble with the blade shaver Davrew had given him. It was a joke between them. Richard was so hairy, while his lover never needed to shave.

His thoughts turned again to his family.

Sal, the fourth born child, had lost his partner Sim earlier the same year that Bon had lost Imi. Although distraught at the time, he now is coping well. They had been such a devoted couple. It was hard to believe one could live without the other. Richard thanked the stars Sal's first-born twins were such a handful. It had kept his mind occupied. The younger child, born from Imi's death, had always followed in the older children's footsteps. Everyone in the household had breathed a sigh of relief when Sal finally took the children to live at the old farmhouse. Richard was sure his Aunty Nancy would have been happy with the arrangement.

While dressing, Richard looked out the bathroom

window at the flower box and inhaled deeply the fragrant odour of the many coloured blooms. His children were as varied and talented as the flowers were vibrant in as many different hues.

Tam was next in line and the one offspring that made him especially proud, although he was careful to make sure favouritism was not an issue. There were times though, he felt, it wasn't quite that simple. Education had been the one area Tam had more than excelled in, going through the whole school system in record time, much as Bon had done. Only Tam chose to remain within the system and become a teacher while continuing to study. History, archaeology, and geography, on the face of it, seemed useless requirements for the family needs, but Tam had made everyone think hard about where they were in place and time.

Tam's child, Kat, was a joy to Richard. What would the boy think, knowing his father Rakal, had returned to Earth? He was clever, strong, athletic and had a way of always saying what was brutally truthful. They were a winning combination. Richard felt a little sad about Tam being away so often. Kat missed being with his bearer and that close companionship. Dressed now, he chuckled to himself. They were away a lot of the time these days, so who was he to judge? Davrew and Richard were still head of the family and top of the pyramid when they were home, although life ran smoothly at the orchard without them.

On reflection Richard realised that for Ash, the sixth born, school was too boring to be bothered with. This disinterest caused problems, just as much as having extremely gifted children who learnt the school system too fast. Something altered the child's perspective around the time the alien, Rakal, had his brief first visit. Ash had become even more enthusiastic about repairing anything and everything mechanical or computerised in the home. He had started to pay attention to passing exams, just to get through to become apprenticed to the mechanic who had a small garage opposite the school. Richard remembered with pride how delighted they had been to have their own unique mode of transport tailor-made by Ash for each family member.

Thoughts of what was happening in the world presently brought Mica to mind. Being the youngest, and probably the most spoilt of their offspring, the study of linguistics had seemed unlikely to become a career. How wrong could one man be? Mica had stood directing journalists from many countries during Rakal's world tour. What the future held there was unclear and unsettling.

Richard walked back into the bedroom, Davrew had gone downstairs. A hearty breakfast was just what his rumbling stomach was asking for. The need for everyone in the family to be cautious was critical. The family anonymity was at risk. Who knew what Rakal was planning?

Besides, plans were well under way for his sixtieth birthday celebration, a party to rival the huge bash for the turn of the century that had recently taken place world-wide. What good would it do to worry about what might happen? The aroma of freshly cooked toast and brewed coffee dispelled fears that could wait until he'd satisfied his ample appetite.

## CHAPTER THIRTY-SIX

# TAM FACING FEARS

### Late April 2000

April was nearly over and on a grey autumn day at Tam's university home, he reflected that he'd allowed his emotions to get in the way of common sense that morning.

'You're the historian, Tam,' his friend Rob had asked innocently, 'do you think this is history in the making? An honest-to-God alien doing the rounds of the planet like Royalty on Earth?'

'I'm bloody sick of hearing about this Rakal, and the media circus parading him. Why the Hell is he going all around Europe making such a song and dance? We don't know what this creep is up to, do we? Why did he land in America first up, for crying out loud? By the stars, it's history alright and we could all be in shit.'

Tam felt his face redden; he was ashamed at how worked up he'd become. His friends we're taken back by it. Since Rakal's arrival Tam's temperament had degenerated further whenever the alien was mentioned.

He didn't applaud when hearing the news about Rakal making a daring rescue of hundreds of people trapped in a train disaster in southern France. The international media went wild with tributes and accolades, and Rakal was glowingly portrayed in the newspapers. The local top media brass sent their best reporters to get firsthand word on the rescue. An elegantly dressed woman who spoke with rounded diction began her report.

'Hello, this is Madeline Sympkins-Trethowan reporting from the site of the horrific rail accident. This disaster would certainly have claimed the lives of hundreds of people, but for the intervention of Rakal, the alien ambassador, who single-handedly saved the day. I'm speaking now to the Chief of the Southern Mountain Rescue Service, Albeair Rosser. Monsieur Rosser can you describe what happened?'

'Mademoiselle, clearly we were working against time. The rescue operation had released many of the people trapped in the carriages that were unattached to the main train, but the position of the linked carriages made access exceedingly difficult. These carriages were jammed into the mountainside and the rest of the train whiplashed into the other side of the mountain pass. The only way we could get to some trapped occupants was to remove each section. It was time consuming and many people, no doubt, would have died while we were working to reach them.'

'How then did Rakal assist?'

'It was fantastic, Mademoiselle. He used his spacecraft to lift each carriage gently away and into an upright position. The people were released, and ambulances attended their injuries immediately. What would have taken us days to accomplish with cranes and our most advanced rescue machinery took only an hour or so. It was a marvel.'

'Thank you, Monsieur Rosser, for your account. I will have a full detailed report this evening on 'Newsmakers' program. So be watching then. This is Madeline Sympkins-Trethowan reporting.'

Tam was embarrassed by his last hysterical outburst and didn't want to repeat it. Sitting with his friend Rob eating, he'd almost choked when the report came on the television, which hung at the end of the cafeteria.

'Rakal will be a hero now,' Rob remarked.

'Guess so,' Tam had pushed his plate away having lost what little appetite he'd had when he arrived at the cafeteria. 'I just can't help wondering what he's really up to.'

'Don't you trust the alien?' Rob quipped.

'Not that one,' Tam replied honestly. 'I'll tell you a funny story, though,' he paused to make sure he had Rob's full attention. 'The reporter Madeline Sympkins-Trethowan is the only woman I've ever seen my parents throw off our property.' Rob raised his eyebrows. 'She came snooping around our place trying to make an instant name for herself.'

'So? They all do that,' Rob suggested.

'Well, she got wind of us having a strange visitor from another world staying with us at the time.'

'A visitor,' Rob's eyes bulged.

'Yes, well, they didn't want her around and they actually threw her out. My folks are usually calm, placid people.'

'What strange visitor?' Rob enquired.

'Oh, just some muscle-bound alien with green eyes and no manners. You might as well know but keep it to yourself. That was the last time Rakal was here,' Tam's friend almost fell off his chair. 'The Police kept a lid on the fact we were hosts to an alien presence. He left quickly enough, thankfully. Rakal was hardly your ideal house-guest.'

'So, that's why you're so upset about him being here,' Rob exclaimed. 'But why didn't you say this before?'

'Oh, come on Rob, who would believe me? We had to try and get on with life after he left. We were told to say nothing and that's what we did.'

'Didn't anyone investigate? I mean like the X File or N.A.S.A.?' Rob couldn't hide his excitement.

'Not really. Back then, there wasn't much talk

about such things. The authorities just wanted to forget it ever happened, and we were happy to oblige.'

Later, in the chill of the early evening, Tam walked across the campus towards his room. The last of the day's tutorials just completed, there was time now to mull over the day's events. He looked out at the expansive manicured lawns and gardens that divided each faculty building. The grandeur of the original buildings with their Gothic pillars and sweeping curves was a total contrast to straight lines and glass facades of the more modern additions. It was cold and his jumper and jacket didn't stop the chill wind getting into his bones. Not many other people were heading to the dormitory. Most were on their way to the cafeteria or driving out of the campus to their homes nearby.

'Tam! Tam Davidson!' A voice in the distance was calling and he stopped to see where it was coming from. Rob was running towards him at a galloping lope. 'Tam, wait up. Have you heard the latest?'

'Slow down, Rob,' Tam put his hand on his friend's shoulders and allowed him to catch his breath. 'I've just come from a late tutorial, so, I haven't heard the latest.'

'It's on the telly and the radio. Everyone is going mad about it. It is history Tam! This Rakal has just let off a bomb, and everyone is clamouring to know more about it.' They hurried towards the dormitory. 'Tam, Rakal has announced he's not the only creature of alien origins on Earth. He's going to tell us, no, show us in fact, some of these alien inhabitants. Can you believe it?'

Tam froze, before struggling to stammer his reply. 'When? How? I've got to see this.'

They both ran inside the dormitory games room where a large television graced one wall. There was a crowd gathered, watching the reports. The atmosphere was electric.

'I'm going upstairs to watch this, Rob, I can't hear it well enough here,' Tam excused himself. Rob nodded and joined his friend.

'Do you know what Rakal means? Having met him and all, maybe he let something slip,' Rob asked. Tam groaned as he heard his friend ask the obvious question.

'I don't know anything, Rob, except I should keep my big mouth shut. Don't dare breathe a word of what I told you before. All Hell could break loose,' Tam pleaded uselessly.

*I let something slip, my big foot in my mouth*, he thought as they watched the television reports. *At least it's not here. So long as they stay away, perhaps we can carry on as normal*, Tam hoped in vain.

One hour later, his peace was shattered. The blast of an interstellar propulsion system intruded, as Rakal expertly landed his vehicle in the University sports grounds. The media circus that had swamped his entourage overseas soon converged in the expansive foyer.

Rob was still sitting with Tam when the spacecraft arrived. 'I'm going to get a better look. Are you coming?'

'No, I'll watch on the box. I'm already sick of this show,' Tam replied with a grunt.

A short while later in his room, Tam sat at the window looking out. Rain fell continuously against the pane. The room was a cosy sanctuary from the thick morning frosts and penetrating chill. The suite he sat in was certainly not spartan. As a student lecturer, and the beneficiary to some extra home comforts, a small en-suite and personal cooking facilities, usually shared by groups of four, had been added for his personal use only.

In the mirror, a few feet away, Tam could see his own reflection, mounting tension drawn in the furrowed brow. His mousy brown-blond hair was cut in the latest under-cut style, a mass of hair crowning a shaved scalp beneath. The bright casual shirt and denim jeans smacked at normality that was so far from the truth. He sat watching the events unfolding with growing trepidation. *What was Rakal up to?*

Rakal looked calm and in control, asking to meet the school administration and requesting a tour of the facility. A crowd had quickly gathered and buzzed excitedly as the broadcasts went out worldwide.

The interview began.

'Why have you come to Australia?'

'Are the other aliens here?'

'How many creatures like you are there?'

A woman pushed herself amongst them and asked, 'are these aliens living amongst humans? Have they bred a mongrel race?'

Rakal did not answer these questions directly. Instead he made a statement.

'I have come to this continent after seeing and learning much about your people in the Northern Hemisphere. I now wish to learn about people from the southern part of your planet.'

'What about the other aliens? When will we meet them?' The woman pressed on persistently.

'Soon,' was Rakal's only reply. He then turned and muttered something to a young man at his side. Rakal moved behind the young man who raised his arms to quell the crowd.

'Please, ladies and gentlemen,' the young man shouted. 'Rakal is wanting to see this University, he has nothing more to say. Thank you.' Tam knew the young face and admired the calm control he exuded with authority over the press contingent. *Mica, way to go!*

The spaceship was exactly like the image of such a craft from a science fiction book or film, the ideal UFO, the saucer shaped circle with central dome and impressive lights around the base of its perimeter. Tam hated the sight of it, but there it was, visible from almost every vantage-point in the accommodation wing. The building was designed to give easy access to recreational facilities as well as direct paths to the lecture halls. This had the added advantage of giving the students a great view of the whole facility.

Later in the evening, Jarred, the tall ungainly lad from the next room, peeped in to see Tam sitting at the window. 'Are you going down to the oval? There's a party on beside the spaceship. It could end up being an all-night rage!' The youth swung a bottle of whisky to tempt acceptance of the invitation.

'No thanks,' Tam replied stiffly. 'The star of the show has retired with his entourage, and I'm going to do the same.'

'Okay, if you want to miss out on...' Jarred took in Tam's stern expression and realised it was a good time to leave, so he pulled the door quietly behind him.

Just a few steps along the corridor Jarred remembered he wanted to ask Tam about what Rob had told him earlier that day. Immediately retracing his steps, the young man tapped softly on the door he'd just closed. When no one answered, he opened it and stepped inside. Tam was not on the ledge as before. 'That's funny,' he muttered and went in to check inside. The occupant of the room was nowhere to be found.

'He couldn't have come past me I was just outside. There's no other way out either. Very strange.'

He left the room feeling puzzled.

Tam had pressed the transport button on his watch computer pad and instantly disappeared in a white light. This had been another great invention Ash had created for the family. Although the range was limited. He rematerialised inside the spaceship in the secured private room Rakal now sat in.

'Tam,' the alien squealed in delight.

'Don't 'Tam' me you great lug. Don't you come near me either! If you think you can just waltz into my life again, you've got another thing coming!'

'I have learnt much about your world since we last met.'

'So,' Tam pushed the barrel chest away from his immediate body space. 'Do you think I should be impressed? You green-eyed lump of lard. Do you have any idea what you've done?'

'I've come to speak to you.'

'You've come to put my family and myself at risk. What do you think most human people will do when they find out we're here? Do you really think they'll walk up to us and say, 'gee, you're not human, but, that's okay, we can still be mates! That's crazy, and so are you.'

'Tam, I came to speak to you because I need to.'

'You need to. That's rich.'

'Yes, I need to,' Rakal grabbed Tam by the upper arms and dragged him to his chest smothering his lips with his own. Once his passion abated, he stopped and set Tam down. The coolness of the reaction was dampening.

'You need to, do you?' Tam swatted Rakal's arm. 'You took your time getting here. Don't think for a minute I'll make anything you want to do easy. I'm not easy. I'm ashamed I let my libido get the better of me back then. I'm damn sure I won't let it happen again.'

The alien sat down on his bed. He looked confused.

'I took time to understand how much I needed you. I took time to travel your world so that you might learn that I mean no harm to humans,' Rakal scratched his head and looked up sheepishly. 'I came for you. I thought you might want me. There has been no other thought for me since I left.' Rakal slumped.

'That just sums it up then, doesn't it? No other thought! Could even some ounce of concern for the people of this planet creep into your brain?'

Stunned, Rakal sat silent.

Tam looked him up and down. He'd barely changed since they last met. The kiss still lingered on his lips. Slowly Tam walked over to the bed and sat beside the lumbering giant.

'I won't make anything easy for you Rakal. You should know it's not in my nature.'

Rakal looked despairingly at Tam. 'I wanted, I mean, I needed...'

'You hoped,' Tam finished the sentence. Then taking pity on his companion, he reached out and took Rakal's hand. 'You hoped I would want you; is that right?'

The alien nodded.

'I can't just forgive your manic behaviour, Rakal. I can't understand how you could do that. Fighting is one thing, wrecking a school another, but the big bad thing was eating your foe. That was really sickening.'

'It was all I knew.'

Tam understood. He'd often thought about how Rakal had acted that day over a decade ago. The realisation Rakal had defeated his enemy the only way he knew how. He reached up to the large forehead and ran long fair fingers across the wrinkled brow.

'I can't change what I am, any more than you can, Rakal. But I have something important to tell you.'

Rakal began to breathe again, 'you do?'

'Yes,' Tam nodded. 'I'll be honest, I didn't want to tell you this, but I know I have no choice.'

'Choice, none?'

'Yes, Rakal, we have a child, his name is Kat. He is a boy child only,' the alien listened and nodded. 'Can you see why I'm angry with you? You left me pregnant. Today we are no longer safe because you came back. Worse still, Kat wants to meet you. Can you do that?'

'I came to ask you to be with me. Can you do that?'

They sat silently holding hands. Neither looked directly at the other.

'Tomorrow I will introduce your family to the world. Will you accept my pledge to protect them all with my life?'

'I'll accept that you'll try.'

Tam stood up and took a step away. 'We've both got some thinking to do. I guess I'll see you tomorrow.'

Touching his wristwatch side panel, a white light enveloped him. Tam was back in his room.

Less than an hour later Jarred was bored. The only revellers were fellow students were getting blind drunk and the alien hadn't made an appearance. A row of guards blocked the entrance to the spacecraft. These barrel-chested men were as imposing as a brick wall and made sure none of the party goers could get inside the craft. Jarred decided to leave and go back towards his room. On impulse, when passing Tam's door, he knocked. Hearing a reply, he opened it. Jarred was surprised to see the occupant at his desk, typing happily on his computer.

'Where did you go before?'

'Just out for some fresh air,' Tam replied.

Jarred nodded, still wondering how. Perhaps he opened the window and slipped outside that way? Tam turned back to the computer and Jarred knew he was too busy to bother so left him to work.

Tam worked well into the night, sending messages. Tomorrow was going to be a big day, and everyone needed to be prepared.

The words of a song he knew lingered in mind. Tam liked the group and slotted the *Eurythmics* CD into the player nearby. It was an old song and a real favourite. He listened while bending to the task, smiling as he sang.

> *'And you know that I'm gonna be the one*
> *who'll be there,*
> *when you need someone to depend upon.*
> *When tomorrow comes, yeah, yeah,*
> *when tomorrow comes.*
> *Can't wait, till tomorrow comes.*

## CHAPTER THIRTY-SEVEN

# THE COMMITMENT

### Late April 2000

Professor Rubens felt the antipodean University cafeteria was familiar. The smell of slowly cooking steamed foods and human body odour was reassuring.

The room was filled to overflowing with curious onlookers, even at this pre-dawn hour. Rakal enjoyed the attention, savouring each mouthful to prolong the moment. After his last bite was masticated, he rose with dramatic flair. Pushing away from the table he surveyed the people in the crowd then pointed to the gathering. At random he selected and motioned for several students and lecturers to come to the front. Once they were all at close quarters beside his table, Rakal made a booming announcement, which carried to every corner of the room.

'Professor Rubens, you and your team will join this small group of representatives of this institution. Follow me!' It was a demand not a request, and no one bothered to question it. The group of Linguists headed by the professor trailed along behind Rakal. They spent the next two hours walking around the University grounds and buildings. Rakal seemed pleased with his actions as he took great interest in the activities of the campus. He was the center of attention and the crowd followed behind, lectures were cancelled, and the usual university routine was totally disrupted.

Just as the Linguistics chief was beginning to feel the discomfort of a headache, which promised to become a migraine if the noise and constant pressure of the crowd continued, Rakal led them back to his spacecraft. As they walked up the ramp into their travelling home Laura Bandeau was at his side.

'Did you notice he picked a lanky spotty lad with a 'Student Press' badge and notebook?' she whispered.

'I did indeed, Laura. The lad has been scribbling notes since we left the cafeteria,' the Professor nodded.

'Captain Smiggins is seething,' Laura glanced towards the Security Chief. Then she mimicked the dour man in a low gruff voice she said, 'we must keep up the tight security.' They both laughed. 'Do you think Rakal chose him deliberately to annoy the Captain?'

The professor nodded but had no time to reply. The doors of the vehicle slid closed behind Rakal's guests and shut out the sound of the throng outside.

'Before we go any further, my guests, ladies and gentlemen, I wish to make a statement,' Rakal spoke slowly, enunciating each word with care. He raised his arms and his rough bass voice reverberated around the control room. The silence of his rapt audience as he gazes around the room encouraged him to continue. 'Listen with care, I have prepared this statement with the help of my translators,' he nodded towards Professor Rubens who replied in kind. 'This is being recorded and is to be given to the nearest world media outlet for immediate release.'

With his green eyes twinkling, Rakal paused to add to the drama of his announcement.

'During my last visit, I took to me one amongst you now, who is here today. We parted in silence. I left this world wondering about my own reasons for living. I have recently discovered, the one who had been with me had a child, due to our brief union.' He nodded briefly towards the professor again, 'Professor, play the tape now.'

The Linguistics team chief starred at Rakal with bug eyes.

'Now Professor,' Rakal repeated.

Slowly taking a disc from his pocket the professor placed it in the tray he'd been shown earlier, then he pressed the button and watched the view screen light up. Soon it was filled with horrific images.

'This is what happened just before I departed from your world the last time I was here,' Rakal provided the commentary. 'The enemy I fought with had caused my unwanted landing on your planet. He also provided me with the necessary parts from his vehicle for me to re-pair my craft. He was tasty too.'

Rakal allowed the full impact of the vicious battle and subsequent disembowelling of his adversary to register with the people gathered. He smiled at their discomfort. Some turned away with ashen faces, others held hands over their mouths, others groaned in disgust loathing what they were seeing.

'The one I touched did not speak to me after this. That special person had watched and then ran away from me refusing my touch.' He paused again and titled his head as the tape ended and the view screen turned to blackness. 'This was strange to me. I could only see that I had beaten my enemy. I had taken my rightful reward. In defeating him I gained revenge, recovered parts to repair my craft and left this planet after enjoy-ing the taste of his flesh.' Rakal sighed dramatically, 'I decided not to be concerned about the rejection of the one person. I was free to return to the life I had left and forget this worthless episode in my life.'

The stunned silence was now replaced with whis-pers of disbelief and concerned glances, mixed with shoulder hugging and support for those becoming weak at the knees.

'Silence!' Rakal demanded with a roar. 'I began my return journey. I told myself to ignore the strange things that had been happening to me.' The audience now stood in silent stupor as he continued. 'The life I had led before, destroying lone ships after pillaging their cargo, raping the occupants, and the like, no longer appealed to me. When I did have the opportunity to take another ship for my vehicle collection, or, to wipe a race from some other worthless planet, I did not.'

He paused and crossed his arms over his rotund chest.

'Then I began to ask myself why? I began to question my past. I started wondering how those who had tolerated me on this planet could change my thinking? Then one day, after much travel alone, I realised I missed speaking to others. I missed the honest criticism of the one I touched. No one had ever told me I could NOT do something before. No one had ever tried or dared.'

'I have come to ask the one I touched to join with me, to be my Partner. Of course, you will need to consider this carefully. I will allow time for this.' Rakal then walked swiftly to Professor Rubens and nodded at the computer. The computer spat out the disc while Rakal retrieved another recording from a different aperture.

'You, spotty one, take these now and immediately have them released to the International media. This must be shown all over the planet within ten Earth hours. Do not fail to do this, or the events that follow will not be welcomed.'

The ship's entrance was opened long enough for the spotty youth with the 'Student Press' badge to make an ungainly exit. Everyone inside could see the relief on the youth's face as he escaped the confines of the control room.

'That's a heavy responsibility you've given that young man,' Professor Rubens said to Rakal.

'He'll do it and survive. Some may not,' Rakal turned on Captain Smiggins. 'What are you hiding?' Rakal growled a deep guttural growl. This became a resonant rolling wave of laughter which vibrated though the room. 'How easily I could take your life, but for now, I'll only take your weapon.'

Rakal walked steadily towards the Security Chief who stared back. Captain Smiggins neatly combed grey hair almost stood on end as he attempted to out-stare the green-eyed alien. The professor couldn't believe how cocky the foolish Security Chief had become, however it was all undone when Rakal swiftly lifted him by the collar, removed the gun from his jacket, and threw the weapon into the computer aperture, where it disappeared.

'You should never have been allowed to play your silly games, Rakal,' Smiggins snapped. 'You're evil and the tape proves it. Why we've been wasting time showing you all over the world and letting people question you is beyond me. We should have killed you as soon as you landed.'

'Silence,' Rakal roared again. 'If I allow you to live, you may see how I can be of use to your people!' Rakal then stabbed buttons on the control panel. 'We are leaving Earth now.' Those who'd not seen the image of the planet below spread majestically across the view screen, stood spellbound. After a short while Rakal threw Captain Smiggins roughly to the floor.

'You will stay silent and not disrupt,' the shaken man sat cowered and panting to regain his breath. Embarrassment and faltering pride kept him from looking directly at anyone in the room. Rakal walked to the control panel again, like a conductor to his podium. With a great flourish his hands sped over the panel. 'I am setting an educational course for you all,' he paused long enough to give the Security Chief one last glare before summoning him to his feet.

'Smiggins, you may rise and join your companions and enjoy the view. You will see your orbiting sphere you call the moon, then the latest of your own technological developments in the space station now being constructed by your joint association of northern countries. You call them 'Superpowers'.

'Ahem,' Rakal cleared his throat to suppress the laughter that lurked menacingly close to his tongue. 'Your space shuttles and supposed space station will make an excellent diversion during the trip. We will take ten of your Earth's hours to complete this journey to the moon and back.'

Don Cameron let out a long slow whistle, 'that's some quick trip.'

Rakal laughed, a short happy bark, not the threatening resonant laughter they'd heard earlier. 'It is a slow trip. I am allowing my special one to prepare for the coming events. The decision is an important one and must be considered with care. There are rest areas, meals can be taken, and necessary needs met throughout the journey. The Linguists will show those not familiar with this vehicle where everything is,' he waved his arms in the general direction of the exits.

'When we near our return to Earth, you may prepare for the festivities. I suggest you all change into some other appropriate clothes. I have a large collection from all parts of the universe in there,' Rakal's large hand waved towards a side door. 'Many of these clothes were worn by rich and important people and are special in their design. I will leave you all now to prepare myself for the new life I hope to lead. Your people have made many advances since my last visit. They could make many more, and I could assist.' The alien turned and strode towards his quarters.

'Wait, Rakal,' Mica Davidson called after their host. 'You mean to tell us you came back to Earth, travelled the globe to learn more about us, planned your reunion and hopeful partnership, all of this after you decided where and how you could fit in here?

'Yes,' Rakal replied, simply giving the youth a sideways glance.

'You came back to Earth for LOVE?' Mica pressed.

'Yes.'

Rakal slid quickly through the door without further comment.

Professor Eli Rubens shared his colleagues' sense of disbelief.

## CHAPTER THIRTY-EIGHT

# THE ARRIVAL

### Late April 2000

Professor Rubens mingled with the group who had been brought aboard. He was enjoying meeting new people and seeing different reactions to the unusual situation they all found themselves in.

Annette was one of the students chosen in the cafeteria. She was tall, slim and wore outrageous clothes to suit her personality. Her brunette hair was cut in an equally eye-catching style. The shaved layers, from the nape of her neck to her mid ear lobes, crowned with a thick mop of bright red dyed hair.

'I've just got to check out this crazy gear,' she said.

'The invitation to put on something literally 'out of this world' is tempting,' he said as the girl walked past him.

'You bet!'

Rubens was glad his headache had started to wane and enjoying meeting fresh faces and bubbly personalities that diverted his thoughts, helped.

Other members of the linguistics team showed the new visitors about. Nearly everyone spent some time in the clothes area, which became known as the wardrobe room. During the flight, every guest was thrilled to glimpse the sights few human eyes had ever seen. The moon at close quarters was quite remarkable. Both space shuttle and space station held the small crowd transfixed during their brief encounters.

Annette had already tried on and showed off several outfits when Captain Smiggins approached her. He had by now decided she must be Rakal's love interest and followed the vivacious young woman devotedly, all the while making probing remarks and questioning her past.

'You, old geek,' Annette retaliated, 'I'm not the one the alien dude is on about. Where do you get off thinkin' that anyway? I've sure never met the guy before; I can tell you. So, leave off.'

Captain Smiggins looked smarted as Professor Eli Rubens intercepted him before he could chase the girl into the wardrobe room again. 'Smiggins, we'll find out soon enough what and who this is about. There are some other women on this trip, you know.'

'Only a few likely prospects, wouldn't you agree, Professor Rubens?' Smiggins insisted.

'Now, Security Chief, I wish to speak to everyone before we arrive at our destination,' Smiggins took the hint and rounded everyone up in the control room.

'Ladies and gentlemen, we have little time left, it's over nine hours now since we departed Earth. We've all seen the lovely Annette displaying the remarkable variety of styles in the wardrobe room. We've all, in fact, looked in for ourselves. I think it would be a good idea if we could do as our host suggests and choose some interesting item to wear.' He cleared his throat with a short cough to draw complete attention from his audience.

'Ladies and gentlemen, I believe this day will become an important historical event. I understand our young linguist, Mica Davidson, has been working during our journey on an extensive communications array. Naturally, Mica is following Rakal's stringent guidelines.'

'Finally, ladies and gentlemen,' Professor Rubens added with a huge smile, 'we may have concluded our whirlwind tour of Earth. I cannot judge what Rakal is planning. I can, however, thank all the members of my team for their hard work and perseverance.'

Annette didn't stay to hear all the speech. She headed back into the wardrobe room. Rubens could see she was more interested in all the fabulous clothes and what she was going to wear. A few others joined her. And he followed their lead when he'd finished addressing his companions.

'Are you going to choose something, Don? Or are you just browsing?' Mica asked his red headed co-worker with a cheeky grin.

'I was just looking,' Don Cameron replied, while absently stoking his short red beard. 'But, since it's going to be a party, maybe I should join in the fancy dress.' Swiftly he whisked a green coverall from the rack of clothes and disappeared into the change room.

'Now, that's a choice!' Annette laughed shaking her head. 'A green grow suit dude.'

People had been coming and going. The room became crowded.

'This would suit you, Laura,' Mica suggested as he held out a shimmering multi-coloured garment for the olive skinned aristocratic looking woman to view.

'You think so?' she replied with a distinctive accent. It fitted her well and flattered her trim and elegant small frame with its simple lines.

'You are taller than you look on the box dude,' Annette nudged Mica as she retrieved her outfit. 'That Don guy picked something that makes him look like a leprechaun.'

Those in the room laughed as they were caught up in the frivolity.

'This would suit you,' the blonde Linguist held out a body suit with cape and flounce attached. It was stunning and Annette gladly accepted Mica's choice.

'I'll try it,' she took the offered garment and returned after changing. She blushed while modelling the flattering contour hugging outfit. Now she had no excuse to linger.

'Excellent choice, Mica, for both myself, and our young student friend,' Laura commented, doing a pirouette herself before going out of the room.

'What are you going to wear?' Annette asked twirling her finger in her hair flirting with him.

'I thought maybe this,' Mica held up a clear sky-blue suit with tight leggings, padded shoulders and deep 'V' neck cut to the waist.

'I can't wait to see it on you. It looks outrageous.'

Mica laughed and walked close by her to the change room, all the while training pool blue eyes in her direction. Squeezing past, them both in his original clothes, Rubens left the room as others walked in.

Tam waited until no one else remained in the wardrobe room so that no straggler could disrupt his selection. It was almost ten hours since the spacecraft had taken off. After changing Tam slipped back into the control room unnoticed, then took up a position at a handhold on the sidewall. He waited for the countdown to be completed.

Professor Rubens now stood at the front of the control room before the view screen, mesmerised by the view of Earth growing larger.

'We arrive at our destination in five minutes Earth time,' Rakal's disembodied voice boomed from the walls. 'There will be a brief time for final adjustments to the communications linkages. I will join you then.'

The view-screen image changed, now the planet below grew ever larger and closer until it filled the screen. A mechanical voice now issued from the walls.

'Entry imminent, secure positions, co-ordinates locked in. Landing in twenty marks and counting, nineteen, eighteen, seventeen…' the voice droned on.

They were back on Earth so quickly Professor Rubens barely believed they'd landed. Everyone in the control room had watched spellbound. The wide view had altered from space to racing land vistas after dashing through the stratosphere. The ground sped past, as if on fast forward film, came to a halt just as abruptly as the ending of a mini film would do. There was little detectable thrust and the landing was so gentle he hadn't bothered to brace for impact.

Upon landing the view-screen showed quite a different scene. Outside the craft was a hive of activity. People were making final preparations for a party. Long tables laden with a huge variety of foods were being covered with flimsy cloth to protect the feast from insects. Beside these tables, a bandstand, complete with drum-set, organ, and guitars, stood awaiting musicians. Torchlights around the platform flickered red and orange as their flames danced in the breeze.

Behind this clearing area was a large colonial homestead with beautiful flowerbeds set around a circular driveway. A large crowd was milling around in the foreground. All heads turned to the right of the screen and jaws dropped in the control room as they watched another delicate looking crescent moon shaped silver disc shaped vehicle settle in the dust. Moments later, a tall distinguished looking person followed by several smaller ones alighted from the craft. A gaggle of youngsters ran to greet them.

The smaller ones from the other vehicle ran off and mingled with the crowd. The taller guest was greeted warmly by some adults from within the crowd and quickly disappeared into the sea of faces. Apparently, this was not an unusual event for these people.

'Looks like some folk have come a long way to be

at this party,' Don Cameron remarked, accentuating the 'long' for the benefit of those who might be impressed. Stating the obvious was his forte.

The linguistics team leader surveyed the scene outside and noted the reaction of the people within the control room. The blonde youth beside him was as wide-eyed as the rest, although for a different reason. He had spent most of the trip working on the control panel following Rakal's instructions. Now he was looking in a different direction to the rest of the audience. Following his gaze, Rubens realised he was looking at the mousy brown-haired student or teacher who had also been picked out randomly from the crowd in the cafeteria. He was wearing striking apparel.

With barely time enough to draw breath, Rakal strode purposefully into the room. His appearance was at once formidable and dramatic, every ounce the consummate warrior. His tight and black vest barely covered the mountain of muscles on both forearms and rotund chest. His leather shining black trousers hugged the equally muscle-bound thighs and calves which bulged ominously and was complemented by high black boots. A large red sash, which held an arsenal of unusual weaponry, hung across his torso. The group gathered fell silent, watching Rakal stride to the control panel where he adjusted dials, while snapping commands at the computer.

'I am making the final link complete. We shall have an extensive audience.' He turned and waved Mica towards the controls and spoke as though he was the only person in earshot. 'This will reach not only every person on your own world, but...' Rakal paused then pressed another dial as though it was the final stoke of a masterpiece. 'This will also reach out to those we know will listen in the galaxies beyond.'

'You - Mica Davidson. You're the one!' Smiggins spat with searing disgust.

'Silence, you fool. This is not my special one,' Rakal sneered at the Security Chief who froze on the spot. 'Mica, you will press this button on my command.'

'Sure, Rakal, just say the word.'

Now the alien, without casting a glance at the people gathered, marched to the entrance door of the spacecraft. Rubens wondered if he was imagining the creature was nervous, a casual wipe of the brow, opening and closing his hands, gave the Linguistics Chief the impression he was. Rakal turned slowly and looked each of his captive audience in the eye. Each one getting a cold stare until he set upon the one intended. A broad smile filled his face and his eyes welled briefly while he fought for self-control.

'Press the button NOW, Mica.'

## CHAPTER THIRTY-NINE

# THE GATHERING

### Late April 2000

Everyone in the room turned in the direction Rakal looked.

Mica mouthed silently 'Are you sure?'

Tam nodded. He was wearing an emerald green body suit that glittered with golden translucent fabric that hung in triangles from the waist. At the collar, a shimmering green and gold fan splayed behind mousy brown fair hair which fanned in matching peaks.

Rakal held his hand out and watched as Tam walked slowly across the room. 'This is my special one. Let the Universe behold my Tam,' the rugged aliens eyes showed a light no one had witnessed before. 'If you will leave with me this day my life will be complete.'

Having crossed the room, Tam held back from taking Rakal's hand. 'If I leave with you this day what can you offer my life?' Tam deliberately stood two paces away from Rakal and asked the question coolly. 'Will you present a danger to my family? Will you learn to love and care for our child, Kat? Will you be willing to give more than you've ever given before?' Tam looked around the room as though deciding to step away.

Rakal's face clouded with concern.

'I need to know that you will protect my family, and my extended family and Earth. I need to be sure you will guard us all.'

With a swift fluid movement Rakal unsheathed the blade he carried in his sash. The blade glistened as he swung it with precision in the air, each graceful slice demonstrating his expertise. Finally, he held the blade as an offering, in his large flat palms.

'I give you now my life. I will protect you and your own kind with it. I will protect humanity too if they wish it. I will gladly assume the role of father,' Rakal swallowed hard and stared at the shining treasure.

'I'm an historian, Rakal,' Tam replied. 'Last night I told you I would not be short of demands.'

'Last night!' the security chief yelled. 'No one came aboard this spaceship, certainly not you!'

'Silence, imbecile,' Rakal ordered sharply.

Tam continued, 'I know much of the history of this world. I'm aware of true bigotry and hatred for people and things of different backgrounds and origins. We, by that I mean my family, could be forced, due to your candour about our presence, to leave our home. I'm also sure that in Partnership I need to be myself, Tam Davidson, Kat's bearer, your friend, and ally. I need to be sure you'll agree to all this before we leave the vehicle.'

Tam paused while scrutinising the rugged alien features. Rakal appeared to be fighting for self-control as he struggled to reply. 'Right now,' Tam added in a gentler tone while stepping towards the muscle-bound guardian of the exit. 'I want to walk from here to embrace each other in mind and body, to grow together in understanding of each other's mind and soul.' Tam ran a finger slowly up Rakal's arm to his cheek, gently caressing the exotic flesh.

'As you wish,' Rakal replied hoarsely. The silence that followed as they stood face to face was like a thunderclap announcing a coming storm.

'We should present this to my parents,' Tam's finger moved to the glistening blade, briefly touching the gilded metal, 'as a symbol of our union.' Rakal nodded as a large smile spread across his face, opening his features like a riverbed in a canyon.

'Tam,' Mica stood, and Tam allowed the emotional Mica to embrace him. Then Mica hugged Rakal.

'May the stars bless you both in happy union,' Mica added, wiping the moisture from his eyes. He looked at Professor Rubens whose mouth had dropped open.

Tam and Rakal linked arms and entwined hands tightly while turning towards the exit. They walked in unison slowly down the ramp to the ground.

Bewildered the audience on board the craft looked about and peered at the exit.

'We must still translate,' Professor Rubens prompted, his broad hand motioning for everyone to follow like a traffic policeman at the lights.

'Yes, we must,' Mica replied with a radiant smile. 'Come on, Smiggins, it's party time!' With an impish grin, he tugged the sour faced security guards' arm, dragging him through the exit.

As they alighted the cool breeze met them with a chill reminder of the autumn season in the southern continent. The sunlight that did reach them, however, when the clouds parted briefly, was warm and took the edge off the cold air.

The view was impressive from the top of the ramp. Apart from the trestle tables laden with food that sent out fragrant aromas to arouse unsatisfied appetites, the bandstand seen on the view screen inside was larger and some of the instruments were unfamiliar. Even more remarkable was the conglomeration of spacecraft parked along the other side of Rakal's vehicle. The imposing backdrop of an old colonial style homestead, lush green grass, abundant flowering blooms, all capped off with bright lights. Delicate star shaped decorations hung on tinsel along the bull nose verandah at the front of the home.

Rows of neatly trimmed trees fanned out from behind the spaceship parking lot. The fruit laden crop was testimony to a well-run orchard. In the distance a mountain range loomed with various shades of lilac and blue. It was a breath-taking scene.

As the descending party of Rakal's guests stepped off the ramp, they noticed another group of people lining up in some order, ahead of them queued in front of the bandstand. There was a crowd gathered behind them watching proceedings.

'Professor, if you don't mind,' Mica whispered in the older man's ear. 'I'll do the first bit, then, hand over to you.' The still gleaming expression on the youth's face, together with his impish grin, left the older man little room for compromise. Simply nodding his agreement, they moved to stand behind Rakal and Tam.

If the spacecraft were a strange sight in such a setting, the huge screen that appeared suspended in the air above the ground was even more incongruous. It was at least three meters square and showed a reporter obviously doing his introduction to proceedings for television. The presenter was below the screen with a cameraman taping the event.

All eyes were now glued to the immense image of Rakal and Tam, which now replaced the reporter's square jawline. Mica stepped forward and spoke briefly to the assemble gathering.

'People of the Universe, I present Rakal and Tam, now Partnered for life, love and productivity, as they wish to be. May the stars bless this union!'

The small crowd opposite them answered in unison. 'Star union as agreed.'

Mica nodded to the Professor then disappeared into the crowd. All eyes were drawn, as if by magnets, to the huge screen.

The screen now filled with the newly partnered pair in front of a distinguished middle-aged man with silver suit and red polo-neck shirt. His hair was very dark and ragged apart from the grey streaks at the temples which were neatly combed back. At this man's side stood an elegant tall blond figure wearing a similar outfit to Tam. Hair similarly styled to match the fan of the fabric collar, this over a sleek fitting golden yellow body suit that hugged a slim shapely outline. Rakal made some show of presenting the blade to the opposite pair who accepted graciously and with similar demeanour.

'You are the center of attention, Rakal. Others may notice it and follow your lead to this planet,' Tam whispered in his ear. The smile faded from Rakal's lips. He answered loudly for everyone to hear.

'I give you this and my pledge to your people. Others may come after me, knowing I am here. I will protect you all from any harm. The greatest jewel on this planet is its people. I will protect my home from my own kind.'

'I, Davrew, descendant of the dead world Orthama, thank you for your pledge. It is accepted, Rakal. I welcome you to my home and into my family,' Davrew then carefully handed the blade, on flat palms, to the silver suited man.

'I, Richard, partner of Davrew, also accept your new position in our lives.' The sword glinted in his hands, 'you may sheath this now so no one can come to harm from it again.'

Both Richard and Davrew smiled and embraced Tam and Rakal in turn.

'Now we will formally introduce our family to our neighbours, friends, and naturally the rest of this country and world and the wider universe,' Richard announced.

'They are all watching, through your courtesy,' Davrew nodded to Rakal, 'and will know us now and always, descendants of a dead world who now multiply here.' He turned towards the stupefied Professor.

'Professor Rubens, would you be willing to interpret where necessary?' Davrew extended a large pale hand to the broad-shouldered man.

Rubens accepted the strong grip while moving toward the imposing figure. His rotund frame also stepped into the picture on the large view screen.

'This is my wholly human partner, Richard Davidson,' Davrew relinquished the linguist's hand and Richard took a firm, if slightly sweaty, hold.

'I'm pleased to be of assistance.'

'Thank you, Professor,' Richard acknowledged, and led the older man slowly along the row of people lined up in queues. That's when he realised there were others lined up behind those in the front.

'This is our first-born Miri, who is partnered to Peter Van Den Gill. They have six children, Fee, Lar, Mia, Den, Gel and Izzy.' Each child introduced in turn politely shook the Professor's hand.

'This is our second-born Gem, who has no partner and one child named Maya.' The image on the screen became an intimate introduction to each person.

'This is our third-born Bon, who was partnered to Imi, also descendant of our origins, who died in childbirth. Bon has six offspring to rear, five of Imi's body and one from Bon's own. These are Kar, Pip, Tris, Fin, Gal and Bon's own is Shea.'

All three paused briefly before each of Davrew and Richard's children. Behind each stood their children, wide eyed and excited. Professor Rubens was intrigued and delighted with events. So, it went on, until they reached the seventh-born child who was single.

'Naturally, you know our youngest child, Mica,' The Professor tried not to let his jaw hang for long, desperately schooling the all too open expression of shock. Davrew continued, 'Mica, as you know, is a linguist, as you and the whole planet have witnessed over the past months.'

'Don't look so surprised, Professor,' Mica grinned back happily into the face of the older man. 'It's really great! Now, I'll be able to give you some background on other inter-planetary dialects and languages to study. We'll have heaps to do, and everyone will be able to grasp the basics of Rakal's unusual derivative language. By everyone, I mean the team, of course.' Suddenly the youth seemed unsure and carefully watched the sceptical expression of the man opposite. 'That's if you still want me on the team.'

'Of course,' the Professor mumbled in reply.

Finally, other relatives and off-world guests were introduced. The whole event had been broadcast worldwide, and into space, as was seen on the huge screen. Professor Rubens was glad to hear the last of the formal introductions had been made. It was already growing dark when his part of the ceremony was complete. Rumbling in his ample stomach was a reaction to the delicious smelling food coming from the trestle tables. Time to relax and enjoy the party, and chew over the remarkable events of the day.

# CHAPTER FORTY

## REACTIONS

Late April 2000

Eastlake Hospital

'Paging Doctor O'Donahue, Doctor O'Donahue, please report to your nearest nurse's station.'

'What the Hell?' Nick thought, 'I've just finished a complex operation. Can't I even scrub up afterwards without being badgered?'

'Paging Doctor O'Donahue, Doctor O'Donahue...'

Nick groaned and headed through the nearest exit to the operating theatre scrub room still drying his hands. As he approached the nurses' station, he could tell something was wrong. The usual quiet serenity, which surrounded the efficient dispatch of lifesaving care, was missing. Several nurses and interns were in a flap and talking loudly.

'What's going on?' he asked briskly, trying not to snap at the young nurse behind the desk.

'Look at the computer monitor, Doctor,' the fair headed young woman motioned towards the screen. It seemed to be a picture like a television program, not the regular bright flashing digital display usually issued from these units.

'Doctor, all the monitors are showing this, even the ones in intensive care. We could lose patients because of this alien business,' his white, starch coated colleague squawked in frustration.

'What the Hell are you talking about, Adrian?' Nick tried to assess the situation calmly.

'Look,' his colleague pointed at the screen. 'Isn't that Doctor Davidson in that line? You know his family, don't you? You tell me what it means.'

Nick pushed aside the two nurses obscuring his view. It was the Davidson family at their home. The view overlooked the property where food and entertainment were laid out before several spaceships. It was incredible to see Rakal stepping down the spacecraft rampart towards the crowd gathered below.

'My God,' Nick muttered, 'my wife Sandy and the girls went out there for a party. Bon invited us all and I was going out after my work was done here.' Silence fell around Nick as the astonished audience listened and watched. Nausea touched his stomach as the impact of the words swept through every fibre of his being.

'Look, it is Bon,' the young pale-faced nurse exclaimed, 'they are introducing themselves.'

'This is our third-born Bon who was partnered to Imi, also descendant of our origins, who died in childbirth. Bon has six offspring to rear, five of Imi's body and one from Bon's own. These are Kar, Pip, Tris, Fin, Gal, and Shea.' The man in the silver suit, tenderly touched the cheek of the youngest child.

An explosion went off in Nick's brain. 'I've got to get out there.' As the introductions continued, Nick left the nurses station and rushed to his office. He hurriedly dialled the number he knew only too well. The whole Davidson family had become firm friends over the years. Bon was close to his own small family. How could it be his best friend was an alien? It was too unreal to believe.

The phone rang for what seemed like an age. Finally, a click and a voice answered. 'Hello, you've called four two three four three two. Pat speaking.'

'Pat,' Nick squeaked, 'Bill's Pat?'

'Of course, who's speaking?'

'Pat, it's Nick O'Donahue. Sandy and my girls are out there. Can I talk to Bon?'

'Well, it's a bit hard right now. Have you seen any of the show? It's on all our TVs and even our computer monitors.'

'That's why I'm calling. It's playing havoc with our emergency care screens. But I must talk to Bon. I'm coming out now.'

'Don't drive, Doctor Nick, the roads are blocked. People have come out to ogle at their alien neighbours in person. There's quite a crowd gathered, and the police are guarding the gate.'

'I've got to get out!' Even Nick realised his voice sounded desperate.

'I know, don't panic,' Pat reassured him gently, 'I'll get Lar to come and get you in a skip. Can you get to the rooftop? You are at the hospital, aren't you?'

'Yes, but I don't get it. What do you mean get to the roof?'

'I know it sounds odd, just go to the roof. Lar will be there shortly. Bye,' Pat replied without further explanation.

Nick quickly cancelled the rest of his appointments scheduled for the day and raced upstairs. He was out of breath when he barged through the roof access door. He stood looking up at the sky, what now? While trying to calm his racing heart and slow his breathing, he walked across to the edge of the building.

What could he say to Sandy about all this? She was the best thing in his life, apart from the girls. How would she react to this news? The knot in his stomach had tightened; he began to feel sick. Shea, little Shea, he was like a brother to his own girls. Crikey, Shea was their half-brother! The child was his! No, it couldn't be. Then the question nagged him. Why had Bon named the child after Nick's grandfather? Nick shook his head and screamed into the chill breeze.

'I must be bloody mad!'

Bon and his family had become such an important part of the O'Donahue clan life. This couldn't be happening! A strange whirring noise interrupted his musing. It was a drone that was coming closer. There were only a few clouds and the late afternoon breeze had picked up, buffeting his ears. Turning towards the sound he could see a shape in the distance, growing larger as it approached. It was a car with glide-wings running the length of either side of the vehicle. It landed easily on the roof beside him. A door slid open.

'Hi Nick,' Lar called, 'hop in.'

In stunned silence Nick followed the voice and peered inside. 'Hurry up, everyone is there. Bon and Sandy are waiting for you.'

'I don't know about all this,' Nick answered as he slipped into the seat beside the driver.

'Guess you don't, Nick, but I'm betting you'll find out very soon. Buckle up. We'll be there in ten minutes.'

'I just can't believe it. You've all been such good friends. I just can't understand how I could not have known.'

'It's not such a drama, Nick.'

The door slid easily to a close behind him. Effortlessly they ascended from the rooftop. The roads below became thin ribbons and the houses looked like matchbox toys.

'Just like flying.'

'It is flying.'

Flying, like Bon's computer had done when he threw it out the window all those years before. He'd never mentioned to Sandy about his 'Dream Lover' phase. The fight he'd had with Bon the night he admitted to the lustful nocturnal wanderings had been forgotten too. Very quickly he'd distanced himself from

Jake Corman, the analyst, and his prying questions after Bon left for Europe.

He'd closed that door and hoped it would never be reopened. Nick felt Bon was running away from his responsibilities at that time by going to Europe. That's when Bon had told him what had really been happening. The revelation was too much to bear and the unceremonious ousting of Bon and his possessions was an act of cleansing.

He later regretted his impromptu behaviour. Although never apologising for his actions, he'd allowed Bon to re-enter his life as a friend. Sandy had accepted his friendship warmly and the two little girls they raised treated Bon like an uncle.

Now Nick felt betrayed. It couldn't be possible. After so many years, he'd discovered Bon had conceived during those late-night embraces. A feeling of revulsion swept through his body, making him shiver. His immediate reaction was to get out to Sandy and the girls and to take them as far away from the Davidson stronghold as he could, away from their differences and their alien history.

Nick O'Donahue wanted nothing more to do with them.

## CHAPTER FORTY-ONE

# MICA

### Late April 2000

Professor Eli Rubens sat at the far end of the trestle tables away from the bandstand. He'd been given a seat, fine food and palatable wine. Laura Bandeau sat beside him and they both shared the pleasure of listening to interesting snippets of conversation. Now he watched as their youthful colleague, he'd thought of until recently as his protégé, manoeuvred through the crowd towards them.

'Hi Professor, Laura,' Mica greeted cheerily with a broad smile, 'I see you have something to eat and drink. Are you enjoying the party?'

'Yes,' Rubens answered simply.

'Very much, Mica,' Laura Bandeau added. 'We've been all ears.'

'Aha, Laura,' Mica teased. 'Eat, drink and be merry for tomorrow we put it all under the linguistics team microscope?'

'Mica,' Professor Rubens began, 'are we going to find out a little more about your background?'

'You mean the Davidson family background?' Mica qualified.

The older man tapped his nose and nodded.

'That's all about to happen. It'll be a bit boring, I'm afraid. Long-winded sort of stuff,' the blonde youth replied. He then turned and lit three large gas lamp torches nearby with a long-handled flint. 'There you are, Laura, this may help you to stop shivering.'

'Thank you, Mica,' Laura smiled, 'I was starting to feel the chill wind in my bones.'

'I can't see how any of this could be called boring, Mica,' the professor commented.

'I guess it's a question of where you sit and how you see it. I mean, of course, kitchen duty is over and chair duty has begun. We run a tight ship because there are so many of us.' They all laughed at Mica's feigned agitation.

'Your family are well organised, Mica,' Laura pointed out. 'There are so many people here.'

'There are a lot of us, more than there used to be,' Mica agreed. He pulled a chair off a stack he'd been carrying and put it beside his two colleagues. Sitting astride the chair backwards, resting his chin on folded arms across the back support, the youth began to explain.

'Next up, in a nutshell, we'll sing a bit to the stars. My parents will explain how they got together, which they'll probably drag on. We'll do some debating about what will happen next. Please add your comments then. They would be very welcome.'

Mica's blonde hair shone in the flickering lights. He glanced quickly towards the crowd. Smiling a mischievous grin, he turned back. 'Just checking to see if anyone's noticed I'm resting on the job.'

'Briefly, our immediate ancestors destroyed their world. They left some clones of themselves to carry on. Davrew is a second-generation clone, who couldn't regenerate with his own kind. The clones were overseen by the last survivors of the native species.'

'Those survivors implemented a series of experimental reproduction programs with similar physiological species, from other words, including humans. We are the results. We came here because it's

Richard's home-world and he wanted to be here. We weren't born when they came here, of course. The others, back at Orthama, didn't think Davrew could bear children. So, they agreed living here wouldn't upset their plans. Although, they did allow some others, including Davrew's friend, Rimi, and partner Andre, to return to Earth when they they'd been successfully reproductive. Being artificially conceived though, they must have believed Rimi and Davrew could not conceive naturally.'

'I see,' the Professor reflected. 'Mica, I've been meaning to ask you how Charlotte is?' The wince in the young man's face left no doubt he'd hit a raw nerve.

'She's a different person, Professor. I had no idea the accident would have such a dramatic effect on her personality. She won't have anything to do with me. It's my fault, the way she sees it, that she was on the train. Even her parents have noticed a dramatic change. She drops things, forgets things she's just done. I know the specialist neurosurgeon said it could take a long time for her to get back to normal, but I just never expected such a change.'

'Mica,' Laura spoke slowly. 'Can you tell me who that person is? The one coming this way, who's has been hanging around you, all night? I think he's the one who arrived and landed the spacecraft parked beside Rakal's.'

'Oh, that's just Vel,' Mica replied with exaggerated frustration. 'We were promised to each other when we were infants.'

'Promised?' Laura prompted. 'Watch out! Vel is heading our way.'

Mica paused and leaned closer to speak more intensely. 'Yes, promised! But it's not binding. You don't have to partner them if you don't want to. Vel did partner another and they have three children. That partner died in childbirth along with their fourth child. I think Vel is looking at me as a replacement,' Mica stood up.

'I'm not at all sure I want to be partner and parent all in one hit. So, we'll have to see what develops.'

Out of the crowd another mousy haired Davidson youth appeared. 'You've been a long time, Mica,' he remarked while nodding acknowledgement of Mica's seated companions.

'I know, Kar,' Mica replied, 'and you're just in time to save me from Vel.' Both youths smiled at each other and in unison said, 'chair duty!'

They waved farewell and disappeared into the throng. Vel appeared briefly, then followed Mica as quickly as the milling crowd would allow.

A roar went up from the increasingly large crowd gathered at the gates and periphery of the property. All heads turned to watch a small vehicle hover briefly overhead then land in a spot near the home. It was the same as a conventional car when it landed. Two people got out to be quickly greeted by a woman with two young girls. They all hugged, and Professor Rubens noticed the family member introduced earlier as Bon was with them, draping an arm casually over the shoulder of the vehicle's driver.

'Don't be concerned. The fences are electrified, and the police are out in force. Peter is keeping a close watch on the situation,' another tall Davidson youth stood before the two guests. 'Hi, I'm Maya, Gem's child. I didn't mean to startle you, Professor Rubens,' a winning smile captivated the attention of both the seated friends. 'You did look surprised by the crowd noise.'

'I was, Maya,' Rubens admitted. 'I must also say I'm surprised how quickly people came to this property. It's in the middle of...'

'The middle of a small rural farming community, everyone and every property is known, and our home is very distinctive. It's been a landmark in the district for generations, long before we came here. You know how word gets around?' Maya smiled while taking the seat

Mica had recently vacated. 'Would you mind if I join you? This is my favourite part of the day.'

'Mica said it would be a bit boring,' Laura remarked while pulling the flimsy fabric of her out-world costume around her arms to ward off the cold.

'I doubt you'll be bored,' Maya smiled. 'Too much going on I suspect. Here comes Mica now with a blanket and coat to keep you warm, with Vel in tow, of course. And here's young Tris with a hot drink to warm your bones.'

They watched as the adults, all having donned coats and blankets, were now arranged in a semi-circle in the large open-aired shed beside the immense screen, surrounded by a long row of flickering gas lamps.

The many children now stopped running randomly about and took comfortable seats on blankets in front of the adults. Two chairs were placed in front of the crowd. The rumbling noise of the onlookers outside reminded them all the view screen was still operating.

'This is a lovely drink, Maya,' Professor Rubens raised his third cup to the youth before draining it quickly. 'Whatever it is, it's warmed me inside for certain.'

'It's like a hot port, Professor. We drink it at evensong as we are very susceptible to the cold.'

'The children seem to be getting impatient for things to begin,' a large man with ruddy face wearing only a short sleeve shirt and vest, announced as he pulled his wheelchair up beside the professor.

'Bill Davidson's the name, I'm Richard's cousin,' he held out a large weather-beaten hand to the professor. 'This is all new to me too. My good-lady-wife Pat has been helping with the food and things all day. She sent me out here, saying she'll be along shortly.'

'Here they come,' Maya nodded towards the pathway from the home, 'Aunt Pat is just ahead of them.' Maya waved frantically at the petite, middle-aged woman, beckoning her to join them as he got out of his chair and rearranged the seating beside Bill's wheelchair. Quickly the dark-haired lady joined them and sat down, after draping a warm blanket around her husband's shoulders.

'Thank you, Maya. It's cold out here,' she smiled warmly at the professor and Laura while rubbing her hands together.

'I was just sayin' to these good people, Pat, this is all new ground to me too. See, I've always kept myself to myself, a bit of a stick in the mud so Pat says.'

'I just had time to finish in the kitchen as Dav came back to change. That formal out world dress is a bit impractical he said,' she smiled. 'It all just takes a bit of getting used to,' Pat added, while adjusting another blanket around her legs, and placing it over her husband's legs also. 'Bill adores the kids.'

'You're just in time, Aunt Pat, they're ready to start,' Maya remarked, while sitting cross legged before them.

'Welcome friends,' Richard began as he stood beside the two chairs in front of the gathering. Davrew stood at his side. 'We are here with our large immediate family, many of our extended family and many more of our friends. My partner, Davrew, has a story to tell you all. Children, listen well, as your knowledge of what is said will be tested,' he smiled while pointing a finger around the younger crowd seated on the blankets before him.

Torches flamed brightly either side of the chairs. Richard sat down beside Davrew. His dark hair glinted in the flames; the silver streaks highlighted in the amber glow. The warmth of the port and surrounds relaxed every person in the audience. 'This is for your eyes and ears, and, also for the people of our world and others who are still listening,' Richard nodded at the reporter and camera man who were still recording images which appeared simultaneously on the view screen.

Davrew began almost in a whisper. All eyes turned towards the hypnotic, melodic voice. 'An age ago, on a planet of similar size and composition, there lived a contented people. Contented, because each morning their sun would rise in their pastel pink skies, over the tangerine landscape of mountains and valleys, and turquoise rivers and streams to spill into great lakes and oceans. The land was bountiful, and every necessity grew in profusion. They had developed from mere hunters and gatherers to become an ingenious people. Food production was perfected, the arts and sciences developed, together with many forms of transport. They even dared to touch the stars. With the travel, they discovered friends and enemies on other worlds.'

'Greed grew with the knowledge, and contentment was no longer all they sought. They began to fight terrible wars amongst themselves. In bygone days, wars began with a simple need, and ended when the need was fulfilled,' Davrew paused to lift a little child onto his lap.

'An age passed, and contentment had become a memory. The people sought jewels and treasures on other worlds as well as their own. Many millions of people died in the name of prosperity. As I mentioned before children,' Davrew's golden hair blew gently about the pale intense face, 'they were an ingenious people.'

'A small group of concerned scientists developed a hybrid race, based on their own genetic structure, combining strength and intelligence, with flexibility of mind and body. These creatures were set high above the planet in orbiting life-supporting modules. They watched and waited in the hope sanity amongst their host family would prevail. They discovered also, during the long years of constant war, a remarkable shared ancestry with many other people of diverse and distant planets. The Ancient Ones had left many archaeological clues on their own world, just as they left them on Earth. The likes of Stonehenge, the etchings in Peru only clearly seen from a great height, and even the lost city of Troy, all these are clues of our shared heritage.'

The roars and abusive language coming from the fence was hard to ignore. Car horns tooted and lights flashed incessantly. Police dogs barked at the crowd and the distant hum of helicopter blades grew ever closer.

'They found the key to survival in their own past. The original inhabitants of the beautiful world did not listen to the scientists and their findings. They destroyed all beauty and hope on the planet in a terrible cataclysmic battle. The hybrids had become the legacy of a corrupt greed-ridden society. The scientists remaining in orbit decided to re-populate the world, once it was inhabitable again, and to make sure no such catastrophe occurred again.'

'One disaster after another occurred, hindering them from achieving their goal. The first attempts at reproduction failed. An illness, caused by bacteria brought up from the planet's surface, killed half of the remaining scientists. Those left embarked on a reproduction program involving the Ancient Ones' descendants. That's why we came to Earth, as we did with many other worlds.'

'This program was moderately successful with our first wave of birth-children being incubators for future generations. We milked the sperm of our genetically compatible subjects and were inseminated ourselves. Many offspring resulted and have grown. It was believed I was unable to reproduce,' Davrew smiled broadly and took Richard's hand. 'Our scientific overseers, all dead with one exception, did not expect us to find our subjects people we could become attached to. However, this is what happened.'

'Richard and several of his companions insisted

once a good success rate had been achieved, they should all be permitted to return home. Three years after his original abduction this is what happened. I returned with Richard, believing I could not contribute to our re-population program.'

'No one realised love could create such an abundance of procreation, quite the opposite of what was expected. Many of my former attempts at artificial insemination had been unsuccessful. As you can see, however, natural conception has resulted in our seven healthy offspring, and their continuing productivity,' Davrew lifted the child off his lap before concluding.

'So, ladies and gentlemen of Earth, children of our bodies and your offspring, people of the universe, this is who we are. That is why we are here. We will sing to the glory of The Grid which the Ancient Ones provided as a link between galaxies.'

Maya laughed, 'sounds like some old-fashioned preacher announcing a hymn, doesn't it?'

## CHAPTER FORTY-TWO

# GEM IN LOVE

### Late April 2000

Gem was barely listening to Davrew's words. The story was too familiar. All the details had been passed on to each family member hundreds of times since birth.

Instead, the memories of the previous evening were happily being replayed in his mind. When did Bon introduce him to Jake Corman? The analyst his sibling had suggested might help to curb Gem's tendencies of chasing young pretty boys around the local nightspots. It was a good try, but to no avail, of course, at least not until last night.

Years earlier, when Bon was working with Nick in the operating theatre of the local hospital, the two co-workers had been doing one of those dreadful shifts, starting early and finishing late, that interns and trainee surgeons endure. Bon had asked Gem to join them at Nick's apartment for a meal with a group of fellow students.

Jake, the psychologist, who had been there to try and clear up Nick's obsessive 'Dream-lover' problem although neither of them really knew what had been happening. Gem was well and truly in control of the situation. That's when Bon introduced Jake and the long, close friendship began.

Gem never tried to be cured or to be less promiscuous and Jake never made demands. He merely offered to listen. How many times at ridiculous hours of the night did Gem knock on Jake's door and crash on his couch? It must have been hundreds since they had met. He never complained, even if it interfered with Jake's love life. Many beautiful women had fallen in and out of Jake's bed over the years. Gem had been there to see their arrival and often caused their departure. None of them had seemed right until Amber came along.

She was something special, in every way. Apart from the fact she was stunningly beautiful with rich red hair and lips, her personality was vivacious. Amber never objected to Jake's tolerance of Gem, the patient-come-couch-dweller, however unbelievably arrogant the interruptions to their lives became. They were a threesome where shopping and dining were concerned. Gem still went afterwards to seek physical release in the arms of the effeminate young boys in town. Jake had told him several times he wouldn't do anything to stop him.

'I am not a sexual being therefore, I am not homosexual. I am who I am, and I sleep with whom I wish,' Gem often stressed.

Jake and Amber both listened patiently to Gem's most explicit accounts of rendezvous and exploits. They seemed not to mind and turned a blind eye and ear unless it affected Gem's health. That was where their concerns lay.

Then, last night the most wonderful thing had happened. Gem recalled knocking on the door of Jake's prestigious, expansive home, commencing yet another impromptu late-night call. Amber answered the door in a satin nightgown and robe. She looked radiant and alive. Gem sensed she was in an aroused state. Her full bosoms were scantily hidden under the flimsy fabric. Her nipples protruded in a provocative way.

'Hi Amber, have I come at a bad time?'

'Not at all Gem, we were just talking about you,' she stood aside to allow him to enter. Jake rushed towards him from the next room.

'Gem, how wonderful. Just when I wanted to ask you a pertinent question, here you are,' Jake greeted his friend warmly then held out a small photo. 'Do you remember this classmate? He was in your camp expedition group.'

'Vaguely,' Gem muttered. 'Why?'

'He remembers you, that's why,' Jake led his friend by the hand into the spacious lounge. 'Sit down and I'll explain.' Gem realised that Jake was also very animated and excited. They sank into the sumptuous leather lounge together. Amber poured them both a port and joined them on the couch. They sat either side of Gem while the explanation continued.

'He's been coming to see me. I can't go into details because it's confidential, but I can tell you he was one of the kids who found you the night you were raped. He's had some problems since.'

'So, why tell me? Surely you can't blame me for his problems?'

'Gem, darling, you're jumping to conclusions,' Amber remarked in a soft warm voice. 'Just listen, will you? It's important to us all.'

'Gem, when your ads for the computer shops cropped up in magazines and newspapers, this guy saw them,' Jake began. 'He'll be okay, by the way.'

'That's a relief. I'd hate to think I directly screwed up his mind.'

'Well, darling, you do screw up...' Amber began with impish delight.

'Just pass the book, please Amber,' Jake instructed. She picked up a well-worn school magazine from the coffee table and handed it to Gem. Amber sat close to their guest entwining her arm in his while Gem turned the pages. 'He became a bit obsessed really, had nightmares.'

'So? Anyone would think you've solved the crime

of the century.'

'In a sense, we have,' Amber nodded with excitement.

'Not a crime,' Jake added, 'more like a long-term puzzle.'

Gem wondered just what they meant. While scanning the old photograph, the young faces of a large group of students and several teachers looked out at him. They were gathered in front of a decrepit old bus.

'This photo was taken the day we left for the camp,' Gem stated. 'We're all here in our daggy gear ready to head off, so what?'

'You're all there?' Jake prompted.

'Yes. There's Terry Ayres, Cliff Roberts, and Alex Jerkovic. The guys I used to hang around with.'

'And,' Jake taunted.

'And the whole class and teachers, even the parents who helped out are in this one.'

'The teachers,' Jake prompted again. Then it dawned on Gem what they meant. There he was, Gerard Blackmore, the one who raped and beat Gem brutally so many years earlier. The face, the hair, the eyes, even the twist of a smile was all so familiar.

'We've been putting two and two together, Gem. Over some years, we've got to know your family. You're all unique, aren't you? With rare blood and your own home clinic and an ever-expanding family, with no strong gender-inspired role models,' Jake grinned impishly and pointed to the photo again.

'The thing that got me thinking was your interest in your friend, Terry. You really wanted to get involved with him, and I'm sure you would have sent out strong vibes about it. That teacher must have picked up on your feelings and gone ballistic.' Gem looked dubious and started to get up. 'The point is you have a child bears a striking resemblance to the teacher who raped you.'

'Maya, my God. My child does look like him, fairer of course in skin tone and hair colour.'

'Yes,' Jake answered with tenderness in his voice. Gem looked directly into his eyes. 'You are not homosexual, or heterosexual, are you?'

'I am who I am, Jake, I've told you that before,' Gem replied without daring to let their eyes lose contact. 'I came tonight to invite you to a party at our home tomorrow. Everything is going to come out in the open then. Do you want me to spell it out now?'

'You don't have to say it, Gem,' Amber spoke while slowly stroking the arm she held. Jake put down the photo and took hold of Gem's hands tightly.

'Tell us now, Gem. Is Maya your child?' Jake asked intensely.

'You know Maya is my child.'

'Yours by birth,' Amber stressed the point. Gem nodded afraid the admission might destroy their friendship.

'Gem, let me tell you a secret Amber and I share.' Gem could feel Jake take in a sharp deep breath. 'For many years, I've thought I was crazy. I wanted to touch you and hold you. I'm not gay. I'm as straight as a dye, but you always tempted me, Gem. Right from the moment we first met.'

Jake moved so close their eyes almost touched as their mouths melted together with a long tender kiss. Then Amber turned Gem's face towards her and planted equally lingering lips on the mouth still quivering with excitement.

'We both love you, Gem. I've always thought you were the most attractive and exciting person I've known besides Jake,' Amber spoke in a raw whisper. 'Let's all sleep on it tonight. Tomorrow we can go and party.'

Memories of that electrifying moment, of the joint caress and exhilarating touch of the two people Gem

loved most in the world, still left a headiness of disbelief.

Tonight, with the world watching, Gem sang to the
stars with the family and friends he loved, adding a silent prayer the love now freely given and received
would continue forever. The hope Amber would conceive was very real. As real as the desire for Jake's child
to grow within his own body.

Now, all three sat together, holding hands, watching, and listening. Could they really accept Gem entirely
without prejudice, now they knew the real history of the
Davidson family? They seemed very calm and uncon-
cerned during the whole day's amazing dramas.

'It's okay, Gem,' Jake closed his hand tight around
Gem's, 'we love you.'

Amber nodded with serene pleasure and smiled
agreement.

*They almost read my mind!* Gem smiled with exhilara-
tion and drew them both closer, warmed by the
flickering gas lamps and the kindling flames of love rising to engulf him.

CHAPTER FORTY-THREE

# LIFE IN THE SPOTLIGHT

### Winter 2000

The next few months were far from normal for the Davidson family. Polarised views in the local and international communities forced many changes to their everyday existence. The strain of public pressure fell particularly heavily on Richard's shoulders. Davrew noticed Richard had lost a lot of weight over the few months since the party the mass media had dubbed 'The Gathering'. His eyes had grown darker and seemed to lose their sparkle. A sullen expression clouded his face causing wrinkles on his brow, which never seemed to leave. Concern for his family dogged his thoughts.

Davrew walked across the yard from the orchard towards the verandah. Richard was sitting listening to the crowd, which had gathered again around the house. Mostly they would go home at night to be relieved by other intrepid alien watchers.

'I've collected a bag full of apples ready for the crates,' Davrew tried deliberately to sound cheerful while delivering the large bag to the side of the house. 'They don't realise shooting at the trees is helping us collect our crop.'

'It's terrible the lengths they'll go to, Dav. I wouldn't have believed it. Have you seen today's newspapers? Just look at those headlines and the rubbish they are saying about us!' Scattered around the verandah in several crumpled heaps were the national and local newspapers, filled with headlines such as 'UFO Friends or Foes', 'Dual Aliens/Dual Visions', 'Aliens Go Home!' Richard sighed. 'I hope it will pass soon and we can get back to some sort of normal life.'

'Are your shoulders still aching?' Davrew asked, trying to change the subject while walking up the steps. Moving to stand behind Richard's rounded shoulders, he slowly ran long supple fingers down his partners back.

'That's better,' Richard sighed.

'From what I've seen of people here,' Davrew commented, 'once they are sick of looking and seeing nothing, they'll go away and look for something more interesting. So, Richard my love, try to relax. We simply have to get used to us being the centre of attention, for a while.'

'By the stars, Dav, I'm glad I've got you. I know I've been hard to get on with lately. I just hate all this. It puts my non-intervention arguments out the window. We were better off living secret lives!' Richard stretched and took hold of Dav's hands. Rising slowly, he turned towards his lover.

'I guess it's time for us to get ready. Today will be another big day,' Dav smiled as they linked arms and walked inside.

Less than one hour later Richard was driving their skip out through the property gates. Davrew sat at his side and adjusted the force field around the home to allow their departure.

'The children are all coping well with the situation, Richard. The younger ones are still hoping they'll be able to go back to regular school soon. Most of the others are happy to continue with our regular curriculum at home,' Davrew reassured.

'Damn it, Dav, I want our children, and grand-children and great-grand-children for that matter, to grow up safe and free, able to go where they want whenever they want!' Richard pounded the steering wheel in exasperation. 'Cripes, the times they could miss, Dav. Remember when we wandered with our backpacks around Europe? It was a blast! Then coming home, setting up, making a new life here at our orchard was even better. Gee, Dav, I've always thought this is the place to be, at least until now.'

'It is the place to be, love. We had a lot to learn back then. You didn't always think the orchard was the bees' knees.'

Richard nodded and turned the skip onto the major highway exit leading to their destination. 'I know we made our mistakes, but Hell, Dav! That's life!'

'Making mistakes in the city?' Davrew couldn't help getting a little dig in but regretted it immediately. Richard was in no mood for teasing. The look he gave was severe. A wall of silence followed as they drove along the winding country road to town.

'I mean,' Richard finally spoke. 'It's all very well for Rakal to take Tam and Kat on worldwide 'Save-the-Planet' environmental campaign. It's well needed, and we can do heaps to change the world, help to clean it all up and make the planet weapon-free, eliminate hunger, wars, and the works. But what good is all that if our children are afraid to go out our front door? Mica is still revelling in the limelight. But what about the computer business we'd built up? Gem has had to go to each Manager and offer ownership at ridiculously nominal figures, just so they can stay open without having windows smashed or premises picketed. People have gone crazy.'

'Richard, darling, maybe you have too. We could have been there by now if we'd used the skip mode in this vehicle,' Davrew chided gently.

Richard grunted. 'I want to take my time in getting there. I'm a bit nervous about all this publicity Bon will be getting. This telling everyone about the differences between us could backfire, you know.'

'I don't think Bon's presentation this afternoon to the best physicians, psychologists, neurosurgeons, and even many politicians from all over the continent and the world will be bad for us. It can only be beneficial to clearly outline our anatomical differences.'

'You always see people accepting changes Dav. I only hope the everyday person on the street can get used to us being around. Otherwise...'

Richard left the statement dangling.

Flipping back the now greying locks from his eyes he turned the car into the expansive gates of the plush resort complex where the presentation was being held.

'Otherwise what,' Davrew snapped with irritation, Richard was being too tiresome. 'Otherwise we pack up and leave? Where to, and for how long?' They drove into the car park in silence, both dwelling on the possibilities.

Richard and Davrew had been shown to a side entrance to avoid an avalanche of media attention. They walked into the ballroom where hundreds of people were already sitting. The room was fully booked with a huge contingent of media expected to attend along with the dignitaries. Many better-dressed people milled around at the entrance. Their seats were in the front row nearest the platform erected on a small stage. Large pictures hung either side of the stage. Each depicted the two space-scape's most familiar to them; the one to which the Earth belonged and the other surrounding a half-dead planet on the other extremity of the universe.

## CHAPTER FORTY-FOUR

# CONSEQUENCES

### Winter 2000

The audience was arranged with the left side reserved for the various quarters of the media. The politicians were favoured with the right side, with the medical fraternity making up the seats behind. There was a notable absence of fanfare. Media representatives had a sea of cameras trained on the stage. There was a view screen centre stage to show the whole audience the day's ceremony.

A tall wavy-haired blonde wearing jeans and a polo shirt walked up to the podium. The murmur throughout the room was instantly hushed.

'Hi everyone, I'm Ash, sixth born to Richard and Davrew,' a murmur greeted the announcement. 'I'm a mechanic - not a doctor. Bon has asked me to come out first and tell you a bit about us. Just quickly, we're not monsters. The press has really had a field day, don't you think? Here we are not doing anything to anyone, and they've been saying all kinds of crazy things. With due respect to the media representatives here, I hope you all realise it's all hype,' he paused and scanned the faces looking at him.

'Like I said, I'm just a mechanic. I can fix your car, your toaster, your computer and just about anything. Antiques are a real speciality of mine. Bring me a car, even a Model-T and I'll bring it back to life for you. I designed and made our skips. They are basically cars that fly. By the way, if you've had trouble with your Mercedes, BMW or good old Ford or Holden, just bring it to the garage in the main street, I'm still working!' A wave of chortles greeted Ash's banter.

'One thing we all felt you should know about us is this,' the laughter dwindled, and the crowd waited expectantly. 'We consciously decided after lengthy and continued debates not to interfere with the natural progressions human-kind would make. We call this our Non-intervention Policy. We are pacifists, and most of all, we don't want to cause any conflict. Bon will now join me on the podium and tell you all the gory details you want to hear. I'll just sit down then, because I get a bit squeamish, and let you hear it all. We'd be grateful if you could leave any questions till the end of Bon's presentation. Especially from you guys on the left. Remember Bon is a doctor and the notes of the speech are virtually indecipherable.'

More tittering laughter cascaded throughout the assembly as Bon, dressed in a smart grey suit, white shirt and star design grey-and-white tie stepped onto the platform. Every bit the distinguished physician, his blonde locks were tied neatly back in a short ponytail, and crisp blue eyes were illuminated with intellect.

'Thanks Ash. Good afternoon ladies and gentlemen. Seated before me are eminent politicians, solicitors, and physicians from all fields of medicine. I welcome you all. My name is Bon Davidson, I am third born to Richard and Davrew, who I should mention are also here.'

Bon swept a long arm with extended palm towards the couple sitting in the front row. Cameras flashed and the media rose to their feet to get a better view. The whole audience saw their two faces on the view screen simultaneously and soon returned to their seats. Bon's torso quickly replaced the image of his parents as he began his speech.

'I will begin with explanatory diagrams appearing on the view screen to accompany my dialogue. However rudimentary, I hope this will be enlightening to you all. Briefly, our blood is quite different; it's mainly comprised of white corpuscles rather than red. We have dual reproductive organs, our lung structure, and heart capacity, physical strength, tolerances, and intolerances to certain conditions are different to full humans. Now I will cover each point in detail using diagrams of the various anatomical features which I hope will be enlightening to you all.'

An hour later, the speech concluded, and the questions began. This became tedious and unpleasant, with several obtuse media insinuations. Ash cut these proceedings short. He raised a champagne glass and announced, 'ladies and gentlemen and distinguished guests, both human and dual, we will continue with a more informal part of the evening. Hors d'oeuvres will be served, with refreshing drinks, while we are joined by our siblings, Miri and Sal, to answer any more questions.'

'Let's not stay long, Richard,' Davrew urged.

'Not long, love, we'll just have one drink and see Bon quickly before we leave.'

'This room is huge, but I feel stifled by this crowd.'

'I know what you mean, Dav, dear.'

'There's Bon,' Davrew nodded towards their offspring. They made their way through the milling guests to where Bon was standing bailed up by three people wearing press badges.

'Excuse me a moment,' Bon quickly sidestepped the media representatives and hugged both Richard and Davrew.

'How'd it go?'

'You certainly did a fine job, Bon,' Richard answered.

'You're glad you've done this, aren't you?' Davrew asked.

'Of course, with so many of our former friends deserting us recently and the vicious undercurrent of public response to our presence, these important physical differences had to be addressed.'

'It'll take a long time before things get back to normal,' Davrew remarked.

'If they ever do,' Richard suggested.

'Well, I hope this meeting today will go towards bringing sanity back into our lives.'

'We can hope,' Richard uttered, unconvinced.

After deciding to take a slow drive home, Richard and Davrew slipped out into the car park then continued with little fuss out of the grounds, thanks to the security guards planning their secretive exit.

'I can't believe some of the rubbish the press comes up with!' Richard spat in indignation.

'Some of the questions did seem a bit silly,' Davrew agreed. 'Especially after the clear and concise explanation Bon had already given. I thought it was obvious we can both conceive and give life.'

'Bonk and be bonked is the way that gorilla put it,' Richard growled. 'Some people only hear what they want to. This is the problem for us all now.'

Soon they had left the regional city behind them. Gentle rolling hills dotted with paddocks surrounded the long two-lane highway. The sky was clear except for a smudge of dark smoke rising unevenly in the distance.

'It's a bit early for burning off, don't you think?'

'Yes, Richard, it is. It's past our place, past Pat, and Bill's.'

Davrew nodded. The skip sped quickly on past their driveway as Richard decided to investigate. Sirens whirled in the distance and sounded as though they were quickly closing the gap.

'Fire trucks on their way,' Richard stated the obvious, 'seems to be not too far ahead.' Suddenly his stomach began to tighten. 'It's pretty near to Aunt Nance's old place, Dav.'

The fire engines were passing as they drove towards the old property's gate. Davrew watched as Richard's face drained of colour and he stamped his foot hard on the floor. Within moments they had pulled up behind two fire trucks already in action trying to douse the flames.

'Oh no, can't be, oh no.'

Bill was there with Pat and Sal's twins trying vainly to hose the fire into submission. The heat was intense even from several hundred meters. Firemen took over from the family but to no avail. Sal was above them in a large skip dumping sacks full of water. Rapidly, however, the old timber building was gutted before their eyes.

An intrepid reporter and cameraman had followed Richard and Davrew from the presentation. They had caught the frenzied activity, which soon died down to merely a mopping up operation. The black haze cleared to show the early moonrise as nightfall drew near. Davrew watched, feeling helpless. Richard walked over to Bill and stood beside his cousin who was slumped in his wheelchair. He put his hand on Bill's shoulder. They stayed silently watching the remains of their childhood home become ashes. Davrew felt his heart would break, watching the two cousins' in unified despair.

'This was our home, Richard. Who would do this to us?'

'I can't believe it, Bill,' Richard couldn't say any more, the smoke was getting into his eyes, and the lump in his throat wouldn't go away. They were both oblivious to the people around them, the firemen, their families and even the neighbours who came to lend a helping hand. The cameras rolled and captured their grief.

Davrew spoke to the fire chief about the cause of the fire.

'Looks like, when no-one was about, the perpetrators stacked a lot of rubbish behind the house and set it alight. The fire caught hold in no time and burned from back to front very quickly. No one was inside the home, I believe, so all's well. Of course, there'll be an inquiry.'

'Of course,' Davrew replied. 'You believe it was deliberate?' Pat and Sal had joined Davrew to hear the fire chief's explanation.

'Looks that way,' the fire chief remarked blandly. 'You may not be so lucky next time.'

'Next time,' Davrew repeated, and stared after the man as he walked away, startled by the comment. Pat gave both Sal and Davrew a reassuring hug and turned them towards their nearby car.

'You're both shivering like leaves. Hop in and I'll get you some hot tea to warm you up.'

The intrepid reporter caught it all on film as well. A little later in the evening, by the light of several car lamps, with an impromptu force field protecting the property, something else caught the camera's keen eye. Sal returned with all three children who knew the old weatherboard building as home. They were all visibly upset, especially the youngest, Raz, who at seven, clung to Sal and sobbed hunkered into his side. The eleven-year-old twins attempted to put on a brave face. The reporter caught their distress and asked the obvious blunt question.

'This has been our home for several years. How do you think we feel? We've lost everything,' Sal spluttered in exasperation barely containing the tears. Raz continued to weep. Richard came to comfort them. They sat together silently.

Strangely, Richard couldn't shed a single tear, although he felt he should. Sitting next to his child and grandchildren was somehow supportive. It was all he could do. The helplessness of the situation really hit home.

The world watched their anguish and was touched by it.

## CHAPTER FORTY-FIVE

# VENDETTA

### August 2000

Two weeks after the fire, things had certainly not cooled down for the Davidson's. Meanwhile, Nick had agreed to help his medical colleagues perform some basic medical tests on Bon. In anticipation he dialled Bon's mobile number.

'Hi Bon. It's Nick.'

'Hi Nick,' Bon didn't disguise his surprise or delight.

'I'm at the hospital. Can you come and meet me? I think we have to talk.'

'Sure. It's a bit late. Most of the family are home. We've eaten, so there's nothing much doing. I can get away okay. If I go by skip. It's safe enough. I can't be long though.'

'Good, I'll see you soon.'

'Nick, before you go, I think you should know. Our family have been having a lot of discussions about leaving,' Bon breathed heavily into the phone. 'I mean, travelling away from Earth.'

'That's a bit drastic, isn't it?' Nick was impatient to hang up. 'Still I can see where you're coming from.'

'Oh no, I don't want to leave, but the regular debates are becoming more heated.'

A gaping chasm had developed between Bon, Sandy, and Nick. They had been so close previously, and he knew this left Bon feeling bewildered. He might think this was a first step in reconciling their differences. Sandy had appeared calm but asked Nick to get her and the girls away as soon as possible from 'The Gathering' as the media had dubbed it. It had become a pivotal day in their relationship. Naturally, the shock of finding such a close friend was dual had been hard enough to accept. Nick told Bon the final straw for Sandy was the realisation Nick was Shea's actual father.

Nick had agreed to help his colleagues. What a reward? He hadn't expected to be tied up in a chair in an old operating theatre, in a disused part of the hospital. He was beginning to feel very cold and scared. Beside him on a sterile tray lay an assortment of vile looking operating tools. Adjacent to this was an ominous looking operating table covered with thick restraining straps.

'What do you think you're doing?' Nick struggled against the restraints. 'Let me go! This is crazy!'

'I would have thought it was obvious, Nick O'Donahue,' Alana Derwent stated blandly, 'you're a surgeon after all.'

'But why do this? Bon has already given us details of their anatomy. You told me you only wanted to do a few tests. I assumed you meant a general physical, nothing more. So why do you need the three gorillas over there, and why would you need a full table restraint?'

'The 'gorillas' are nursing colleagues from St Augustine's, and they are accustomed to strapping down people who are insane. Bon Davidson should be easy to handle, even allowing for the fact they have more body strength. It's no match for handling.'

'For Christ's sake! I've led Bon into a trap!'

'A trap. That's one way of looking at it,' Alana grunted. She was a short and slightly plump middle-aged woman, dressed in a white surgical gown and gloves, humming happily. 'I've been playing second fiddle to the both of you for years. Well, it's my turn to make a mark in history. We've no proof any of the anatomical information he gave us is real. Today we will discover the whole truth.'

'You can't be serious,' Nick spluttered.

'We are totally serious, Doctor O'Donahue. I'm only sorry you don't share our enthusiasm for this project,' a sultry voiced woman addressed Nick from behind a camera. She was wearing a business suit and looked immaculate.

'You're that reporter, Madeline something!'

'Madeline Trethowan-Sympkins since I married. My maiden name was Trethowan. I knew the Davidson's some time back and they thwarted my chances of early success. This is my big scoop. That bimbo Wendy Ashton stole the limelight with the fire at the old farmhouse. But that was nothing compared to this. I'll have the best news coverage of all. What really makes the dual person tick? That's my angle.'

'That's murder,' Nick argued.

Moments later the double swinging doors to the old operating theatre swung open. Bon could see the pallid expression on Nick's face. This should have been enough to warn of the danger. He reacted too slowly to retreat as the burly interns blocked his exit. Nick watched as Bon tried to barge through to escape, ducking the first interns grasp, but the second caught his arm painfully up behind his back. The other intern who appeared to be a direct descendant of an ape joined his colleague and gripped Bon like a vice.

'Bon, oh God, I'm sorry,' Nick spluttered helplessly. Bon saw the thick straps on the operating table, together with the instruments, which made his struggle more desperate.

'They said they just needed to confirm a few tests!'

Nick squealed, 'I was stupid enough to lure you into a trap. Please, believe me. I didn't know they meant to hurt you. For Christ's sake, let him go!'

Bon stammered while trying to free himself from the painful hold. 'You can't be serious, this is madness!'

'We most certainly are.'

The strong interns moved in unison, edging their victim towards the table with sheer body weight. Nick shuddered involuntarily. The muscle-bound brutes were obviously accustomed to the task.

'Let me go,' Bon pleaded. The cold pitiless stares made him shiver even more. As the straps were fastened tightly around his body, legs, arms and finally his neck, he tried to reason with the women and their assistants.

'This is murder! You will destroy both your careers as well as my life, all needlessly,' Bon pleaded.

'Listen to him, Alana,' Nick begged. 'There's no need to go over the top. Just do a physical and take some blood and tissue samples. That'll be enough. Let him go then and no harm will come to anyone, Bon or you.'

'Don't be feeble, Doctor O'Donahue. We need comprehensive details and we'll get them now,' Alana Derwent concluded. 'Is this creature secure, gentlemen? We have a lot to accomplish in a short time. Come along now.'

Expertly the interns began cutting away Bon's clothes.

Bon looked desperately to Alana. 'I am an intelligent being, not a laboratory rat. Stop this now before you regret your actions!'

'We have thought about this and planned it carefully. This whole thing is being recorded for future reference. I believe the world will thank us for our efforts today,' Alana replied. Her smug smile revealed her gloating at Bon's helplessness.

'Vivisection,' Bon mouthed, and the plump woman nodded her reply.

'Oh no, God no, Alana, you can't do that! It's inhuman and disgusting,' Nick pleaded. 'A few simple tests would confirm what you have been told!'

Bon swallowed hard. 'Are you going to use anaesthesia?'

'Say your goodbyes now, if you please, we have a tight schedule,' Alana snapped and nodded to the intern beside Nick to pull the chair over to the operating table. 'We'll sedate you, Doctor O'Donahue, so we can get on with the task at hand without interruptions.'

Nick was roughly hauled to his feet and pushed into the now naked and incapacitated Bon's chest. The head strap was yet to be put in place along with a mean looking biting piece. Nick raised his head and into the two pool blue eyes he knew so well.

'Bon, Christ knows I'm sorry I got you into this mess.'

'By the stars, Nick, no one could guess these jealous people could be so dumb!' He looked at Alana who was rearranging the tools on the tray. 'Alana, you are a good surgeon, can't you see how stupid this is? Just let me go now before anything happens.'

'Forget it, Davidson. We've got a job to do. This is no time for speeches, so say your goodbyes quickly.'

'Jesus, Bon, every-thing's been so mixed up lately. Sandy didn't know what to think when she found out about Shea. We've kept away, and now it's too late to change. I can't believe this is happening! I'm so sorry, mate. Can you forgive us for giving you the cold shoulder?'

'Nick, I'm sorry I deceived you back then. It was so wrong of me to trick you into believing you were dreaming when we made love. I wanted you so badly,' Bon gulped a few deep breaths. 'I don't want to die, and Nick, I don't want anyone else to suffer this way, none of my family, especially not Shea. Promise me, that won't happen, Nick. Please promise me.'

'This is crazy, Bon, I promise nothing like this will ever happen again.'

'You hope, Doctor,' Madeline scoffed. 'The world could just benefit from the knowledge we gain today and want to repeat it.'

'Nick, take my watch, wear it and remember me.'

The intern emptied the loaded syringe expertly into Nick Donahue's arm.

'Everything's spinning,' Nick mumbled, 'going dark.'

'I love you, Nick O'Donahue, and I love Sandy and the girls too. Don't forget that,' Bon croaked as the restraint gagged him.

## CHAPTER FORTY-SIX

# DARK DAYS

August 2000

Several hours had passed since Bon had left to go to the hospital. Gem was in their city computer-shop, the last remaining bastion of the chain of stores the family had previously owned. The day's takings were tallied and locked away, the bookwork for the previous month reviewed. The only task left was checking the showroom area to make sure all the computers were in order. Many needed to be switched off as they were left running during hours for the customers to try out. The doors were locked, the security system in place. The main computer diagnosis was running and back up would soon follow. Gem hummed happily in anticipation of returning to Amber and Jake at their home. The feeling of suffocation was less evident there, a privilege few Davidson's felt these days. Hiding in a secretive way seemed to be the go. Gem hated that and was glad to enjoy more freedom than many close relatives.

'That's funny,' Gem spoke to the empty office. An anomaly in the health records sounded an alert on the main computer screen. Quickly Gem dialled the orchard to locate Bon and get the watch physical read out repaired.

'What do you mean, Bon isn't there? Well, it's

strange his vital signs aren't registering. Bon is usually very particular about keeping body and soul together,' Ash heard Gem's concern and ran a quick check on the computer diagnostic at the property.

'Hang on a bit, Gem, there is a very faint reading. I'll just adjust the signals and it'll show there with you.'

Moments later a series of figures lit up the screen. 'By the stars, Ash,' Gem cried. 'Those are human heart-beats, not Bon's! What the Hell is going on?'

'I don't bloody well know, but I'm sure going to find out. We can pinpoint the location of the signal. Bon was going to meet Nick at the hospital. Looks like that's where it's coming from.'

Gem could hear the muffled voices of concern in the background. 'I'm on my way there.'

'So are we Gem. All of us in as many different ve-hicles as we can muster,' Ash replied.

Safety in numbers, Gem thought while dashing from the shop and leaping into the 'skip' car parked outside. Without checking the sky for clouds or to even think about who might be about to see Gem touched the illuminated control panel and took to the sky.

Nick awoke to the noxious stench of preserving fluids, chloroform and disinfectant mixed with the scent of death. Once his drugged eyes cleared enough to see, he screamed and shut them tightly again. He remained slouched in the dimly lit corner of the room. A huge bright light above the operating table illuminated the theatre. Madeline was taking a wide-angle shot of Bon's remains. He heard every word as she turned the camera around on the tripod.

'So, there is a conclusion to proceedings. All that remains is the laboratory tests on the vital organs as outlined earlier during operation.'

Alana was humming happily as she catalogued her prizes in the lap top computer beside the corpse.

Nick dared to open his eyes again. The image of bone and layers of skin peeled back on Bon's formerly perfect face was horrific. It revealed gaping eye sockets and nasal cavities and the agony of the last moments of life were still clearly visible. He bent forward as far as the ropes would allow and vomited.

Elsewhere in the city, a local television studio was alerted to the mass movement from the Davidson household. This was all bigger than Harry and Meghan's split with the Monarchy. Many spaceships were converging on the nearby hospital. Naturally, the media followed in droves.

Two reporters who were doing a mundane assignment in a nearby demolition site rushed to the hospital as the first few vehicles landed. They were quick to reach the rooftop and follow the now gathering crowd.

'What's happening? Why have you come here tonight?' the reporter asked the wan faces that offered no response. 'Keep rolling the camera, Brian, we're onto something big, I can feel it.'

'This way,' someone in the group shouted and they all headed downstairs.

'Get a good shot of this rooftop Brian. They all look like cars when they're stopped but remember we're fifteen stories up!' The reporter shouted over his shoulder.

'The life signs are more active. The human is regaining consciousness,' the voice at the head of the crowd yelled. They were approaching an old wing of the hospital in a lower level.

'The human is awake and active. Through here! Don't let anything stop us!'

'Why?' the reporter asked the nearest person in the crowd.

'We must find Bon, that's why,' the slender younger person answered absently. They crashed en mass through several barricaded doors. 'My bearer Bon has been gone for five hours. Now there are no life readings on our scanning devices,' Tris answered with a quivering voice.

'This is it! Through these doors!' a booming voice rang out from the front of the group. The group slammed through the doors to be greeted by burly stone-faced interns, who simply stepped forward to block their path. These men, with arms crossed and menace in their eyes, were unable to stop them.

'You're too late!' Nick screamed. 'They're murderers, murderers!'

With sheer weight of numbers, the Davidson's pushed past the brutes and surged into the room.

'No, it can't be! Bon, my wonderful child,' with an agonised groan Richard ran to the bed then turned on Nick. 'Why did this happen?'

Davrew joined Richard but turned towards the corpse. One side of Bon's face still had skin on it.

'How did this happen, Richard, how could this happen?' Davrew wailed and began to weep openly.

'I've got no answers,' Richard stammered as he watched as his partner begin to stroke the remaining skin on Bon's cheek. Davrew began to sing, soft and rhythmic tunes, songs to the stars, songs Bon had loved.

Shea stepped forward to untie Nick's bindings. They cradled each other in their sorrow and wept. Stunned, the rest of the group noticed the jars lined up and a woman with a lap top computer cataloguing their contents. Lar stood in front of the short plump woman who still sat with lap computer at the ready, looking surprised at the interruption.

'You had everything you needed. Why did you want more? Why take the life of someone so dignified, intelligent and gifted in healing?'

'Murderers,' Nick groaned again.

'Bon,' Richard murmured. He staggered then slumped to the floor. 'Dav,' he called in agony.

Nick realised he was watching the man having a cardiac arrest. The doctor in him rallied and went into action.

'Quickly, he's having a heart attack!' Nick pushed Shea aside gently and moved to the older man's side. All too quickly Richard stopped breathing and his pulse disappeared. Nick snapped out orders for assistance, before he applied life-saving resuscitation. The blue face and still body were pummelled with life giving determination.

'You've got to live, Richard Davidson, your family need you, now, more than ever!' Nick had started shouting while frantically applying CPR. 'I won't let you die on me! Not now, not after what they've done.'

The door burst open and four police officers joined the crowd. Two immediately cuffed the women. The interns, cornered, held their arms in the air in surrender.

'We saw all this on TV, buddy,' the Sargent said. 'Jay get around here quick.'

'I'm a fully trained paramedic,' the tall dark-skinned policeman knelt beside Richard's still form and took hold of his wrist. 'Keep it up. There's a faint pulse.'

In the new wing of the hospital several hours later, Richard lay attached to life support and monitoring machinery in the Intensive Care Unit. Davrew lay sleeping in a bed beside him with Bon's fourth born Tris keeping a close eye on them both. A distinguished middle-aged man with grey hair and dark bushy eyebrows cast experienced eyes over Richard's monitors.

'You are caring for Davrew? I believe you administered the correct sedative?'

'Yes, Doctor McFarlin,' Tris answered slowly. 'I'm competent in the matters of my own kind, but I'll admit we all relied on Bon for attendance to Richard's needs. I've still so much to learn,' Tris sighed heavily. 'Of course, I'm not the only member of the family in this field of study. Bon was the expert. He had trained right through the human medical school system.'

'It's a terrible situation losing someone so important to you all. So, it would seem, we can learn from each other, young Doctor Davidson,' the older man spoke slowly with kindness. 'I only hope we can do so for many years to come.'

Tris tried to remain composed and failed. The older man put his hand on the shoulder of the slouched younger medic. Tris felt comforted and grateful when after a few moments, the senior doctor left him to grieve. The fact his grandparents were now sleeping and relatively comfortable, was reassuring. Their nearness was precious. The memories of times with his loving parent crowded his thoughts. He knew he would be comforted by his siblings. But now all he could do was cry till the tears would no longer flow and slumber overtook the desire to fill a gaping hole in his heart.

## CHAPTER FORTY-SEVEN

# RECOVERY

### August 2000

Davrew kept vigil at Richard's side, for more than a week, speaking rarely, eating, and sleeping little after the initial sedative wore off, solely focused on his recovery.

Miri had carefully arranged for the removal of Bon's remains from the hospital. Tam, Rakal, Kat and Mica's team of linguists returned, astonished at the tide of hostility towards the Davidson family. Rakal became the self-appointed security guard for the homestead and grounds.

Richard sat propped up with several pillows in a small well-equipped private room. The large windows faced the west and the afternoon sun was streaming in.

'Dav,' Richard smiled and took hold of the slender strong hand he loved to touch. 'What are you thinking?' He didn't wait for a reply, 'let me guess. Will we leave here soon? Where will we be going? What direction in the Grid? After all the Ancient ones made a huge network for us to choose from and we've only used the one corridor till now. Perhaps it's time we all did some travelling. Is that what you're thinking?'

'You must be well first,' Davrew replied flatly. 'Is that what you're thinking?'

'I guess so,' was the vague reply. Richard shook his

head slowly.

'Or are you thinking, this is our home. This is where we built our lives. Here we bore our children, made friends and learnt more about loving each other than anyone else could ever know?'

Davrew fidgeted with the glass on the bedside table, turning it slowly around. 'This is our home, Richard. I don't want to be driven away by blind prejudice.'

Richard lifted Dav's free hand and gently kissed it. A petite dark-haired girl with hourglass figure and white starched uniform entered the room. 'Hi, I hope I'm not interrupting, but the postie has been and there's heaps of mail. Do you feel like going through it all?'

'Mail? More mail?' Davrew asked incredulous.

'Look,' Richard opened a cupboard beside the bed. 'The television report certainly got people thinking. Ever since that day, cards, and letters, wishing us well have been arriving.'

'Could there be ill-wishers too?'

'Could be, but I doubt it,' he smiled warmly at Davrew's concerned expression. 'Rakal has had security guards and sniffer dogs on alert. Nothing harmful will get through to me. I'm being treated with bags of tender loving care. Why, anyone would think I'd gone and done something stupid like have a heart attack!'

The young nurse deposited a sack of letters on the bed. 'I'll leave them then, but don't go over doing it. You mustn't tire yourself out.'

'Thanks Crystal,' Richard winked. 'Does that mean Dav and I can't get a little physical? I don't know how much longer I can hold out.'

'Now, now Mr Davidson, I don't know what you could mean,' the nurse smiled and rolled her large eyes in exaggerated innocence. 'Is there anything else you want?'

'Please close the blind a bit Crystal, I'm getting hot

and sweaty for no good reason,' Richard smiled happily as the nurse quickly lowered the curtain and then stepped out of the room. 'Most of the cards are the 'get well soon' variety, and the letters supportive and kind. People from all over the world are appalled at the barbaric behaviour of Doctor Alana whatever her name is.'

'She's been arrested and charged with murder, along, with Madeline Sympkins-Trethowan as accomplice to murder. It's all in the news, darling, and a huge story of the day. I've been watching it all on the box while you were asleep.'

'I've seen the papers, so I've not buried my head entirely in the sand,' Richard grinned. Davrew moved closer.

'You'll have to keep a hold on your desires, my love. Your body isn't quite ready for such exertion,' Richard took the opportunity to kiss the soft supple lips Davrew offered firmly.

'That's it! I'd better go now, so you can watch the box and wait for the time, soon my love, when you are ready for it,' Davrew flicked the remote-control switch on and pushed it into Richards hand, then hurriedly made for the door.

'Wait, Dav, look at this!'

'Oh, come on Richard, you can do better than that.'

'No, really, look who it is!' Richard turned up the volume on the remote control. 'Hey, Dav, it's good ol' Cal!' Davrew returned to see the screen. A petite woman wearing a stylish navy suit was speaking in a heavy Texan drawl.

'...Multi-millionaire Mister Callum Bennett, who made his fortune in the stock market on computer software and hardware, spoke today to a select media contingent.'

'Ladies and gentlemen, the reason I asked you here today is simple. I don't like what's been happening, and

I want y'all to know it. I'm a businessman and rarely does anything really make my blood boil unless it's a stock market crash.'

The man stood with his arms crossed like a bull ready to charge.

'This has really got my insides squirmin'! We all saw it, what the dim-witted doctor did in the name of science. Well I say pullin' a person apart just to see how they tick is as low as you can go. These-folk seemed to be straight with us, and what happened?' He paused to glare sternly into the camera. 'The long and the short of it, ladies and gentlemen, is this. If those dual people leave Earth, I think the loss is ours. It could be the worst Goddamn thing that could happen. I want to pledge my support for this dual family livin' in Australia. I also support their need for the same rights as any other citizen in our society. This world could learn from them. From what Rakal and Tam have been sayin' they can help us clean up our pollution, help us all live longer, and get us travelling to the stars and back. Hell, who knows what we'd lose if they go? So, right here and right now I want to say, don't go, we want you here!'

Cal Bennett then started pointed his finger at the camera.

'Good onya Cal,' Richard grinned.

'Do you know how that Richard guy pulled through from his heart attack? Well, I'll tell y'all, I rang his specialist surgeon over there in Australia and he told me. They've replaced his heart with a spare they grew for him. No rejection, that's for sure. Why would his body reject his own heart? No drugs either because of this miracle to medicine, cloning technique. Why, this could save lives all over the world! I'm flying out today to meet up with those people and ask them to stay put! We should be proud they choose to live on our little planet.'

'Cal's jumped the gun a bit, hasn't he?' Richard

shrugged, 'the media announcement about my cloned heart operation isn't till next week.'

'So, it'll give the press time to think up more silly questions,' Davrew smiled.

Richard laughed. 'Of course, Cal doesn't want to mention he was with us there, out in space, does he?'

'Or, for that matter, how many baby Cal's were born there,' Dav added with a giggle.

'He sure was a pro-duc-tive sperm producer.'

'Just like you, Richard darling,' Davrew chortled happily. 'Perhaps we do have a home after all.'

'Perhaps. I'm still worried about those nut cases out there,' Richard rubbed his forehead and slumped back into the pillows.

Davrew helped him settle and turned to leave. 'You don't want to over-do it yet, my love. I've plans for our future and it's a long-term strategy.'

'They still don't know about the others. Andre and Rimi, came back with us and Yosi in Japan who took a partner after a couple trips back to Orthama, so did that cockney twat Nev. Three other families from different parts of the globe. Unless they want to be known we'll let and them to carry on their anonymous lives.'

'I think we should keep it that way.'

After another tender kiss Davrew left the room.

## CHAPTER FORTY-EIGHT

# YEARS LATER

### September 2003

Davrew sat at the control panel of a new-generation skip. Richard was sitting comfortably enjoying the ride. They were on the way to Europe and delighted in skimming across the planet low enough to see people's faces.

'It's good to see people wave, and not shake their fists.'

Davrew smiled at Richard's observation. He always had the knack of putting everything into perspective. 'I still like to fly on clear days rather than rainy nights. Everything really has turned out for the best.'

'I love the sun in my face too,' Richard agreed while flipping his fringe back from his face. Just the way he'd done when Davrew first met him. The sky seemed cleaner and the planet greener. 'I guess people can learn to change.'

'I guess so,' Davrew nodded, 'even our workaholic friend Tod has finally settled down. You know...'

'What?'

'It's ironic really, Tod taking our grandchild Tris as partner.'

'Why? Tod has been a firm friend from our early days at the orchard. He's worked on most of our detailed interior decor and designs. He also stuck by us when other formerly close friends deserted us. He just rocked up at our party the media dubbed 'The Gathering' and fitted in naturally.'

'He always seemed to know, didn't he?'

'Maybe, but you still haven't answered my question.'

'Well, it's ironic because when you were playing up with that woman in the city, Tod and I were working on the house and…'

'You didn't!'

Davrew laughed openly at the horrified expression of his partner.

'No, I didn't, but I sure did fancy him.'

'Jeez, Dav, what a revelation after all these years?'

'Well, we are secure now. Those whims are in the past. There are other more pressing concerns now. You know what I mean?'

'Yes, I only hope Rakal's fears don't become reality,' Richard sighed.

'So, do I, my love, so do I.'

They landed the skip in a field beside a cottage in the Lakes district of England. The lush green meadows and wildflowers on the hillsides were breathtaking in their beauty. They entered the quaint cottage and stepped quickly up the stairs. Richard and Davrew watched a child being born. It didn't scream or kick as it drew in a first harsh gulp of air. Instead it swam happily beside the pale body it had emerged from. The liquid nurtured the life that explored the birthing tub.

Painstakingly the child's father had removed enamel and re-painted the intricate designs on the tub. Tod Longmire had been commissioned many times to create the masterpieces that formed the first source of information for the dual children. This one was his crowning glory.

Tris smiled and watched the child with delight. 'Aur is learning already. Tod, see how the stars glow in our tub. You're a wonderful craftsman.'

'No, you're the wonder Tris, taking on an old man like me,' Tod smiled. The broad grin on the bearded man's face had become a permanent fixture since they partnered.

'Aur, your great-grandparents want to say hello,' Tris cooed.

'You've a fine child there, our Tris. No doubt about it,' Richard glowed with pride.

Tod beamed ecstatically back at his family. 'True and our baby will live to a ripe old age. Speaking of which, Richard, you look very well. How is your replacement heart going?'

Richard chuckled. 'I've been living sixty-four years now and I'm told by reliable sources this heart could last as long again.'

'So, everything is well?' Tod grinned.

'Our Earth is a beautiful place to be right now Tod. We're well, our family is growing, you two have a beautiful new baby. I must be the happiest great-grandpa alive.'

'We must hope things remain that way, Tod,' Davrew spoke softly while rising from kneeling beside the tub. Gently Dav touched Tris on the cheek. 'Aur should grow up in an exciting world of exploration, to travel through the Grid in all directions, as we develop new trade links while meeting new civilisations.'

'So, the rumours of Rakal's former cohorts causing trouble are just rumblings from the stars?' Tris interrupted hopefully.

'We hope so, Tris love,' Richard replied, 'but let's not talk about it now. I want a cigar and a drink to celebrate another dual birth.'

'Good idea,' Tod beamed.

Davrew took hold of Richard's hand and squeezed it affectionately. The future held promise and dread in one breath. The nightmares - horrible images of a few survivors on a space station above a lifeless globe, just as his originators had done above their dead planet - had ruined his pleasant dreams. Would Rakal's prediction of war with former compatriots come to fruition? Space Pirates destroying their precious home world and the new colony they had so carefully struggled to protect? Richard lifted Dav's hand to his lips and gently kissed the fingers he loved to hold.

'Dav, we can learn by past mistakes,' Richard reassured. 'No one wants another Orthama.' Gently tugging Dav towards the window, he grinned. 'Look at our beautiful world, Dav. It's such a special day, don't you think?'

Davrew nodded. It was a brilliant day. He accepted the glass to sip the warm port, hoping it would relieve the knot building in his stomach.

# POSTSCRIPT

Dear Reader,

Now as I approach my 80th birthday, in January 2021, I reflect on my life, the struggles I endured, and so much more.

Davrew is still gorgeous, and I'm a frail old man, who is loved. My children have not all been able to see me live to this age. Bon, as I've recorded in these pages, was brutally butchered in those last innocent years before the 'War of the Worlds.'

After 'The Gathering' Rakal was true to his world and protected our little Earth. His greatest loss, and ours, was seeing Tam killed. But that's another story for a younger soul to relate.

In an alternate world, we could have faced a global pandemic, many deaths, and economic ruin for many governments. Instead, our world is now part of an interplanetary alliance which offers peace and prosperity for us all.

For now, I close my eyes on another beautiful day with my beloved Davrew at my side. If I see no more joy or sorrow, I am complete.

Richard Davidson

# ABOUT THE AUTHOR

Jill, born in Victoria, has always loved reading, writing, and creating wonderful worlds.

After her marriage and birth of their son they moved to Queensland.

As a member of many writing groups she honed her writing skills by producing book reviews, articles, and interviews for various online magazines.

Her published achievements include contributions to anthologies for children with 'The Ten Penners', six short stories in 'Fan-tas-tic-al Tales' 2009, nine stories in 'Mystery, Mayhem & Magic', 2019.

Further success with Michelle Worthington's 'Share Your Story' Group, one story in 'Spooktacular Stories' Thrilling Tales for Brave Kids, October 2019. Jill has a new story 'Larrikin Lyle' accepted for this groups 2020 anthology 'Tell 'em Your Dreaming'.

'Dual Visions' is the first book in 'The Ancient Alien Series' with 'Vashla's World' book two, and the third in the trilogy 'Travellers' to be released shortly.

Jill is also working on a young-adults Science Fiction called 'Microworld'. She lives with her husband and one cat in Kirra, Queensland.